T0316076

THE
BOY
WITH THE HAUNTED
HEART

Morgan Owen has always been a writer. One of her earliest memories is of sitting at her grandmother's dining table, folding pieces of paper to create makeshift books. Inside were illustrated stories of formless spirits and Sylvanian Families, which they read aloud together. A former bookseller and PR executive, Morgan likes worldbuilding in video games and buying knick-knacks to put in her curiosity cabinet. She has two black cats named Salem and Binx. *The Boy With the Haunted Heart* is her second novel. She is represented by Hannah Sheppard at HSLA.

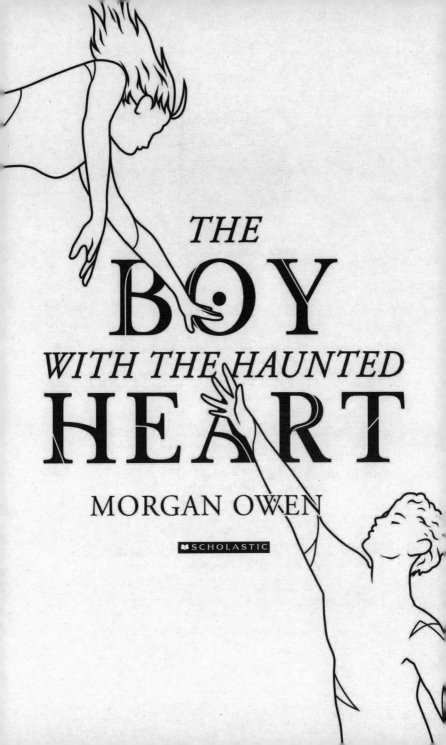

THE BOY

WITH THE HAUNTED
HEART

MORGAN OWEN

■SCHOLASTIC

Published in the UK by Scholastic, 2024
1 London Bridge, London, SE1 9BG
Scholastic Ireland, 89E Lagan Road, Dublin Industrial Estate,
Glasnevin, Dublin, D11 HP5F

Text © Morgan Owen, 2024
Cover and chapter illustrations by Jamie Gregory © Scholastic, 2024

ISBN 978 0702 31462 9

A CIP catalogue record for this book is available from the British Library.

Printed and bound in Great Britain by Clays Ltd, Elcograf S.p.A.
Paper made from wood grown in sustainable forests and other controlled sources.

1 3 5 7 9 10 8 6 4 2

www.scholastic.co.uk

To anyone who has ever been afraid of tomorrow

PROLOGUE

OLIVER

Last year, I died for six minutes.

I was lying on the floor of the Basilica of All Souls as a beautiful girl bent over me, her pale, freckled face blank with shock – Ruby, I thought her name was. No, Iris – no, *Lily*. She was mouthing something; I couldn't hear what.

I looked past her, looked through her, focusing in on the details of the underside of the cupola: a mural that showed cute chubby cherubs indulging in a feast of the five senses.

My eyes slipped out of focus. Past, present and future all bled together, dragging me under, dragging me inward, falling deeper inside myself as if tumbling down a steep incline.

My breath thinned and ceased. My heartbeat slowed and halted. I was cold and still.

This was it.

From the outside, I appeared convincingly deceased.

In those six minutes, Lily-Iris-Ruby raged and wept. My friends gathered around me, clutching at each other helplessly. The battle for the soul of a nation continued

1

to unfurl around us, ebbing and flowing as two factions grappled for the last dregs of power.

All of this I missed.

In those six minutes, I was not present in my body. I was somewhere else entirely, though I couldn't say where.

I was … dead.

Yet there was no staircase to heaven, no tunnel of light. My life didn't flash before my eyes, nor were my deeds weighed in the court of good and evil as I feared. None of my relatives were waiting to greet me. There were no winged beings or ornate pearly gates, no horned demons stoking brimstones … and all of this was a great relief, but also a terrible disappointment.

There was only utter nothingness. A complete and total void. It was the worst thing I could possibly imagine, just me and myself alone for an eternity.

I cared about nothing. I *was* nothing.

I became one with the darkness of the universe.

When a person dies, their soul dies with them. The Heart is first to go, its plump fruit shrivelling to an emaciated raisin, mossing and furring as it decays. The Song is next, its instrumental tunings fading away to the whisper of the audience, like the end of a concert. As its final act, the Shadow throws over a protective cloak of primordial darkness that snuffs out the fiery Spark, like a candle in a gust of wind. Only the pungent smoke of the Spirit is left. Finally, with its last gasp of sentience, the soul implodes, casting out a wave of energy.

Psyche. It imprints a person's most powerful memories upon their most beloved places and objects, like a living memoir. Their existence is written upon the fabric of reality.

This is the legacy of a soul.

After an unknowably long period of time, a crack of light poured in, shining through the void like a ray of sun. It caught me in its beam, a spotlight from above. I became aware that I was rising, slowly floating upwards.

I was … undying.

By the time the painted ceiling reappeared, by the time the sound of a roaring post-revolutionary rabble bled in, by the time I smelled smoke and tasted blood, by the time I felt Ruby's warm hand in mine, I had lived and died a thousand times, all in the space of six minutes.

I locked eyes with her, gasping, feeling my heartbeat synchronize with hers as reality filled in around us.

Her warmth was my anchor. Her soul was my home.

But in those six minutes, something in me had changed. Something was missing. Something was wrong.

My soul had been resurrected, but part of me was still dead.

1.

RUBY

Alone in my room, illuminated by a single candle, I unfurled the roll of parchment to read it again, its heart-shaped wax seal already broken.

> *Dear Lady Renato,*
>
> *I urgently seek your counsel at a secret meeting at midnight tonight to discuss the future of Providence and the empire beyond. The other heads of House have also been invited.*
>
> *Please, tell no one of this plan. The fewer who know, the fewer who can use their senses to spy on us.*
>
> *From the fruit of the heart,*
> *Lord Clements Cordata*

I had been summoned to Cordata House by my late father's former ally – a secret gathering of the five Houses to discuss how we could restore order to Providence. Three of the five had supported the rebellion: all but the Chancellor's own House Obscura, which was now headed by Oliver, and House Harmonia. All five were key to a new era, a new world.

I ignited it by mind. The letter burned and turned to ash in my fingertips, leaving me to dust the remains off my skirts.

Sitting at the dressing table that night, before a three-way mirror, I saw myself threefold, a triptych. I brushed my hair and applied blush, wondering which face was the best one, the real one. Each day, I told myself my own story, so that I'd never forget it again. It was the tale of Lily Duffy, Ruby Renato, and Iris Cavendish.

Somehow I was all of them ... and none of them.

I was born as Lily to my mother Mara in a small village in Green Valley, I reminded myself, both of us red-haired and small. I was named Ruby by my estranged father, who tracked me down and made me his weapon, using my tactile gifts to infiltrate the court of the Order. I became Iris after my soul was shattered, until I found my lost past hidden in a ring. Now, I had recovered my true name. Well, my names. Now, I was whole again. My father was dead, the Order had fallen and I ... I was free.

Or so I was meant to be.

Iris. Ruby. Lily.

Who did I *want* to be?

Iris the soulless thief? Lily the kidnapped innocent? Ruby the spy and rebel?

For now, I must only be Ruby. Ruby Renato. Revolutionary. Daughter of a dead hero. Ruler of the fifth House at sixteen years old.

Once dressed, I stood at the window, where a collection of

trinkets was lined up along the sill. Each one was a remnant, an object containing a memory, to remind me of who I was. My mother's tear-catcher necklace. An empty heart-shaped chocolate box. A wind-up music box. A cracked mirror. The ruby Renato ring I had worn when I was shattered, recovered from the river.

I slipped it on, letting the horrible vision pulse through me. A white-masked figure in black robes wielding an eye-topped staff stepped through the door.

The mask lifted – to reveal the boy I loved.

Gasping, I tugged it off, the heat inside me rising.

Technically, my boyfriend Oliver *had* tried to kill me, though he had been bodily controlled by the Chancellor at the time, and while he had fought against his father's power, only shattering my soul temporarily instead of killing me, the memory lurked insidiously beneath the surface, like a serpentine monster ready to strike. I shivered and pulled on the thin, red velvet gloves that protected me from psyche, allowing me to touch things without being drawn into their preternatural histories. Such was my gift, inherited through my father's side, while from my mother I'd been gifted a talent for remembrance.

A little before midnight, I climbed into the carriage that waited for me outside, cherry-red and embossed with the flame insignia of House Renato, the House of Spark. Within it, I was nestled by red velvet and lit by torches, swaddled by the nostalgia of days long gone.

We set off, rolling through the streets. I gazed out at the

gloomy remains of Providence, heart heavy. Six months after the spark of revolution had been extinguished, after the ousting of Oliver's father Chancellor Obscura, after the Eye network that spied on its citizens had been dismantled, the signs of an uprising still littered the streets. Toppled statues, vandalized monuments, broken glass and burned-out carriages.

The carriage headlamps lit up the vignetted roads and squares, illuminating small tableaux of city life *in situ*: here a dirty child pushing a dog in a pram, over there three elderly women begging under a bridge, in this square a hollow-eyed youth carving misspelled obscenities into the wall of an abandoned Inspectors' station, in the next one a group of unshaven men rolling dice outside an alehouse.

I told myself all was not yet lost. I refused to let the uprising have been in vain. Yes, the city was in chaos, but it was ours now, flawed as it was.

Renato House was in the Fifth Borough, the seat of touch and the Spark, where children had once been ferried in boats and wagons to the Reformatory to have their souls cleansed. Today, the Reformatory housed only the most dangerous prisoners, including the former Chancellor, who was being held there ahead of his trial for soul crimes.

We drove over a bridge and down a broad, tree-lined boulevard into the Fourth Borough. Across a cobbled courtyard stood a sandstone mansion. Cordata House. The caryatid pillars of its grand foyer held fruit baskets and ears of corn, visible tokens of the House's connection with the sense of taste and the Heart of the soul. Bronze statues frolicked in fountains with grapes and decanters of wine. Somewhere in the acres beyond was a small farm, with milk cows and chickens in coops.

I sat in the carriage, by turns wringing my gloved hands in restless impatience and clasping them in my lap, and stared at my reflection in the darkness of the window, watching as my face shifted between excitement and fear. My round freckled face was framed by a scarlet waterfall of curls, my wide-set hazel eyes world-weary. Beneath my black peacoat trimmed with fake fur, I wore a simple red dress. I toyed with the hem, picking at a stitch that was already unravelling.

A carriage pulled up behind mine, black with eye-shaped windows and a flock of dark Shadow birds circling above. My heart beat faster as a tall youth emerged from within. He ran one hand nervously through his untamed mop of black hair. His eyes filled with darkness as he inspected the perimeter of the courtyard.

Oliver Obscura. Also known as Evander Mountebank. The Chancellor's son, who had overthrown his own father – Tristan Obscura, a man responsible for so much suffering not just in Providence but around the world. If anyone was struggling with the weight of his new responsibility, it was Oliver. When I'd first met him, he was just a gangly bespectacled youth in a waistcoat, working in an underworld curiosity shop. He'd been secretive, guarded, yet helpful despite himself. We thought we were strangers to each other.

We didn't realize we had history. We had both found our way back to our forgotten past.

Now that I was whole again everything felt fresh and brand new. There was something bright and alive within me, and I was dancing with it. I was so full of life that I was swollen, bursting, hungry for something I couldn't even describe in words.

Eagerly, I exited the cab, my chunky shin-kicking boots slapping powerfully on the ground as I sashayed over to him.

"Lady Renato," he said, crossing to meet me.

"Lord Obscura," I replied, bowing regally.

These were our new names, our reclaimed names. We were the nobles turned rebels turned nobles again.

I drank him in, all gothic angles – a brooding portrait. That dark overgrown mop. That proud nose. He wore the elegant, high-collared black tunic of the House Obscura, subtly embroidered with eyes sewn in iridescent black thread. You wouldn't notice them unless you were looking closely, which of course I was.

The white streak in his hair was growing too, I noticed. He'd had it ever since the Night That Never Was, after his father shattered me while inhabiting his body...

No. No, I didn't like to think about that. He was alive now; we were together and that was all that mattered. The past couldn't hurt us any more. I wouldn't let it. History be damned.

Oliver drew me into a sweeping kiss, stooping slightly to reach my lips as I stretched on to tiptoes. I clutched at the fabric of his coat, like he'd just returned from a thousand-year war, every part of me yearning. Now that I was whole again, I found that I couldn't get enough of anything, especially him.

"Lily," he murmured into my hair.

Everyone else called me Ruby. Only Oliver and my mother used my real name. It sent a delicious shiver down my spine.

"It's been far too long," I said, raising the back of my hand to my forehead as if I were about to swoon. "The Heart grows fonder in your absence."

"I saw you just this morning," he teased, kissing my neck.

"That was in our minds. This is in the flesh. It's different." Heat flushed through me as we entwined closer.

"Oh, really?" he said, brushing a curl of hair out of my face and tucking it behind my ear. "Different how?"

"It's ... warmer," I said. "You know us fire souls ... always burning on the inside. Touch is our love language."

"I did rather get that impression, yes," he said.

I kissed him again, my lips lingering on his before we broke apart with a sigh.

"Are you ready to do this?" I asked, nodding at Cordata House.

"Must we?" he said, not sounding ready at all.

"I guess I'll have to be for the both of us then. Come on – let's find out what Lord Cordata wants."

Before he could answer, two more carriages pulled up behind ours, symbols for another two parts of the soul emblazoned on their coachwork. The first carriage was silver with musical instruments etched into its sides, the sounds of an exultant symphony resonating from within. A tall, sharp-featured gentleman in a grey suit stepped out and strode confidently towards the entrance with a rhythmic *clip-clop* of his buckled shoes. Lord Harmonia.

The second carriage was white and painted with flowers. A broad, elderly woman disembarked, her short salt-and-pepper hair carefully coiffed, a spray of fresh blooms pinned to her breast. She walked at an unhurried pace, her expression knowing yet wistful. Lady Memoria. She dabbed discreetly at her nose with memory-enhancing snuff.

We watched them climb the steps to the entrance.

"Can we trust them, do you think?" I asked in a low voice, when Lord Harmonia was safely out of direct earshot.

"Not as far as we can chuck them into the sea," Oliver replied, frowning.

"That's what I thought," I said. "Did you learn anything helpful from looking into their minds?" As a Shadow soul, Oliver had the ability to enter a person's subconscious unseen, to view their fears and dreams. It was a controversial tactic, but one we used sparingly, defensively, against those we might consider enemies.

Cordata, Harmonia and Memoria were technically our allies, but still…

It paid to be careful.

"Cordata's intentions are good but he is somewhat cowardly."

"I could've told you that," I said. "He kept his nose clean all the while my father was in prison, didn't he? He comes across as a simple, cheerful soul – but he knows how and when to play his hand. He is cunning, as well as charming."

"He wants all the glory with none of the effort," Oliver agreed. "He wants to be adored, ever the centre of attention. He and his wife have a very combustive relationship too, full of fighting and, uh, passionate making up."

I wiggled my eyebrows at him. "You don't say."

"But there is nothing particularly cruel about him. He has no real desire to cause suffering. That's an improvement on my father. A low bar, but we'll take it, as leaders go."

"What about the others?"

"Well, Lord Harmonia is a pragmatist. Being able to hear everyone's thoughts can do that to a person. He does what is best for him personally, because he knows the true depravity of human nature – the dark, unspoken thoughts that pollute all our minds. Other than that, he collects porcelain figures of cherubs and loves tragic operas where everyone dies at the end."

"And Lady Memoria?"

"Hmm. Lady Memoria is older, more learned, harder to read. She has an extensive catalogue of incriminating memories at her disposal, should she need to use them. She's a lot like your old friend the Countess, in that sense. No wonder the two of them are pals. She's also recently widowed. She's set in her ways, resistant to change, but she

13

has a taste for revolution now. A secret idealist, I suspect. Also, she has a lot of cats."

"So what do the three of them think about us?"

"They need us. That doesn't mean they like us, though."

In the weeks that followed the Battle of the Basilica, unrest had spread through the city. The resistance split into five disorganized gangs, divided by soul type, who each claimed vast swathes of the boroughs. Citizens weren't keen to be governed again after all they'd been through, but there were two names the people trusted, two figures widely considered to be the sweethearts of the revolution: mine and Oliver's.

Oliver Obscura and Ruby Renato. We were the ones who'd revealed the Order's evils. We were the ones who'd broken into the innermost chamber of the Basilica and battled the last armies of the old guard. Thanks to us, the surveillance network known as the Eye network had been blown to smithereens. To the people on the streets, we were the real heroes – the ones who broke the wheel. Now, somehow, we were responsible for fixing it.

"Well, at least we can count on each other," I said.

"Whatever trouble we're in, we're in it together now," he replied.

"There's no one else I'd rather be endangered with."

We drew together again, our lips like magnets, as time wasted away.

"Come on," I said, pulling back as he pouted slightly. "We're already running late."

Oliver gave a half-hearted groan before taking my hand.

Determined, united, we crossed the courtyard and disappeared into the gilded entryway beyond. We hurried down a long hall lined with paintings of seasonal banquets, decorated with spring flowers and gourds and paper snowflakes. House Cordata represented the Heart of the soul (just as House Renato represented the Spark and House Obscura the Shadow). Food was their thing, House Cordata being the guardians of the sense of taste.

We reached a well-appointed function room full of sweeping drapes, white columns and glinting gold accessories, including a bowl of inedible fruit. At the head of a pentagon-shaped table made of wood in five colours sat Lord Cordata, flanked by Lord Harmonia and Lady Memoria.

"Ah, finally," drawled Lord Harmonia. "The triumphant heroes arrive."

"Cutting it a little fine, aren't we?" sniffed Lady Memoria, checking her pocket watch with a sharp-tongued tut. "You know, it's always a good idea, when attending important arrangements, to be *on time*."

"We were just, uh…" My gaze drifted to Oliver, who flushed. "Um…"

"… Distracted," he said.

"Oh, to be young and in love," Lady Memoria said with a sigh. "Actually, scratch that – just the first one would do."

"Welcome, welcome!" Cordata boomed, jumping up and ushering us inside. "Come in, come in! Better late than never. I'm *so* glad you could make it." He wore a gold tunic with padded shoulders and a plunging neckline, a golden

15

medallion against his shaved chest, his bald head shining. He flashed a grin, enhancing the deep expression lines in his well-moisturized skin. His was a face that was used to smiling, and hard.

"Lady Renato … Ruby," he said, "the last time I saw you, you barely remembered your own name. Now you're the head of your House. Your father would be proud." (I wasn't sure about that – my father saw me as a weapon and nothing more – but I was even less sure that I cared.) "My deepest commiserations on the loss of dear Rubella, too." He fixed on a face of gravest sympathy. "She too will be remembered as a hero."

My grandmother, Lady Rubella Renato, had passed away not long after the revolution. Having her mind wiped by the Chancellor had left her vulnerable to dementia. Sometimes, when people forgot themselves, it was permanent. Fatal. In my grandmother's case, her memory wasted away before she died, until there was nothing left of her.

"I apologize for missing the funeral…" Lord Cordata added.

"I don't suppose she noticed."

"Rubella was a real firecracker, you know, back in her day," he said, as if he hadn't heard me. "The Bloody Battle-Axe, they called her. She taught your father how to fight – and, let me tell you, that man fought *dirty*."

"Oh, I know," I said. "She taught me too."

Smiling, Lord Cordata turned to Oliver and gave him a respectful bow.

16

"Lord Obscura the Younger," he said. "As I live and breathe, it's a pleasure to have you with us."

"Is it?" said Oliver, sceptically.

"Well, you're an improvement on your father, at least. Although that's not too difficult, is it?" He laughed and slapped him on the back as Oliver widened his eyes at me. "Never mind, this can be a fresh start for all of us, a chance to leave the past behind. Please, sit."

Cordata resumed his seat at the head of the table, Lord Harmonia and Lady Memoria settled themselves back down, and Oliver and I took our places next to them. The heads of the five Houses were assembled.

"Let's cut to the chase, shall we?" said Lady Memoria. "I have to get back to feed my cats – they're very particular about their schedule. If I'm late by even five minutes, they tend to take their revenge by urinating in my shoes."

Cordata, pulling a face that suggested he was perhaps more of a dog man, said, "I think saving the nation is a shade more important than your cats, don't you?"

"Saving the nation?" she echoed. "That's big talk, Cordata."

"The Shadow era is over," he said, grandiosely. "Now it's time to usher in the epoch of the Heart."

He'd definitely practised that line in the mirror a few times.

"Our country is in a state of chaos," he went on. "The people are tiring of the power outages, the food shortages, the roaming gangs of hoodlums stealing memories. We must take action, before it's too late."

"What are you suggesting?" asked Lord Harmonia.

"We must present a strong and unified front," Cordata replied. "We must act decisively and show strength. We cannot expect the people to obey a corrupt regime. But the people need governing nonetheless. That is why we must present ourselves as the *New* Order."

"The 'New Order'?" I repeated.

"Yes. A new government for a new era."

"Is it really new though," I asked, "if three of its rulers are the exact same rulers of the regime the people just violently overthrew?"

"That's why I need you and Oliver by my side," said Lord Cordata, getting to his feet and coming to stand behind us. The smell of his spicy aftershave filled my nostrils. "You are the 'sweethearts of the revolution', the 'star-crossed lovers caught in an ugly political struggle'. The daughter of a rebel and the son of a dictator, fighting side by side, falling in love despite so many obstacles." He sighed and touched his chest. "Who could resist such an enchanting tale?"

"But I'm the fruit of a rotten tree," said Oliver. "Everyone knows who my father was, and what he did."

"No. Chancellor Obscura was the rot at the heart of the Order, but we have rooted it out. You, my boy – and you, dear Ruby – represent a fresh start."

I chewed my bottom lip. This felt dangerously naïve, and apparently Lord Harmonia agreed:

"You really think these wide-eyed teenagers are fit to

rule a country?" Harmonia snorted. "Rulers are made, not born."

"Ah, but that's precisely why *you*'ll be there, Lord Harmonia," said Cordata, slithering over to him and patting his shoulder. "You and Lady Memoria will be the wise and steady hands to steer the ship. The people will have already forgotten your ... involvement in the old regime."

The Harmonias had run the old listening posts, eavesdropping on the passing thoughts of the public. They'd been pardoned now, but what would they do with the fresh slate they'd been given, I wondered?

"No more dictatorship!" insisted Cordata. "We shall create a council and vote on movements democratically. Of course, the people will need a figurehead for this new era of diplomacy..."

Here we go, I thought.

Sure enough, Cordata puffed out his chest. "Since *I* am already established as an opponent of the former Chancellor, *I* am naturally best positioned to rally the public. I won't call myself Chancellor, however," he added. "I shall be the Premier of the New Order."

"Why you?" said Lady Memoria.

"Yes, why not one of us?" asked Lord Harmonia.

"Cordata is the only House left that's relatively untainted by recent revelations. We didn't invade citizens' privacy, torture children or extract memories illegally. We simply hosted all the good parties." He laughed, bearing his palms. "Come, now, we don't have time to quibble – we need to tackle the recent crime wave. We need to subdue the gangs of the five boroughs, before the discord reaches our door."

"Subdue them?" I said, sitting up straighter.

"What's the problem, Lady Renato?" asked Cordata.

"We're all here today *because* of those gangs of rebels. They helped us overthrow the Chancellor." Among them were some of my good friends – Ash, Perpetua, Gus, Octavia and Rani. I wouldn't throw them to the wolves.

"Without their numbers we might not have succeeded in infiltrating the Basilica," added Oliver, nodding supportively. "We need to work *with* them, not against them."

"They're criminals!" scoffed Lord Harmonia. "Hooligans! Probably plotting to blow us up as we speak!"

"I see you're still as paranoid as ever, Harold," sneered Lady Memoria.

"And I see *you*'re still ready to turn the other cheek at the drop of a hat, Millicent," retorted Lord Harmonia.

The table erupted into a five-way conversation.

"Aren't we criminals too?" I said, raising my voice. "Every single person sitting at this table has broken the law to get here. Let's not be hypocrites."

Harmonia looked indignant, Memoria ashamed and Cordata nonchalant.

"The gangs aren't planning anything, anyway," Oliver said. When everyone turned to look at him, he added: "I may have used my Shadow to keep an eye on things … once or twice."

"What do they actually want, these gangs?" asked Lady Memoria.

"They all want slightly different things, hence the five factions, but they share one core aim: an end to psychometry as a tool of state oppression," said Oliver. "No Observers spying on their dreams, no one recording their thoughts, no memory extractions."

"The Eye network is already destroyed," said Lady Memoria.

"Yes, and we must rebuild it with haste!" snapped Lord Harmonia. "How else will we protect ourselves?"

"Hmm. I won't make the same mistake as the last man," said Lord Cordata. "I shall rule not with a fist of iron, but with a velvet glove."

"'*I*'?" said Lady Memoria. "What is all this '*I*'? I thought you were just a figurehead."

"*We*, of course I meant 'we'. How about this?" Cordata continued. "*We* will not clamp down on the gangs – but we will restore the Eye to watch over them: for their own good, you understand. It will be a Providence for the people."

Ugh. He even had a slogan ready.

"We can't resurrect the same system of surveillance that we destroyed when we overthrew the Chancellor," I said. "It's become a symbol of the revolution. We must find a way to protect ourselves while keeping the privacy of citizens intact."

"And you truly think the people will obey?" asked Lady Memoria. A rhododendron was pinned to her suit jacket.

The ribbon was tied to the right. In the language of flowers, it was a message to the aspiring Premier, a message that said: *Be warned.*

Be warned of what?

"In time," said Cordata. "In time they will be ruled by us willingly."

I wondered if he was smart enough to have noticed Memoria's warning.

"We don't have long to debate this," he went on. "While we were busy having an uprising, other countries moved into position. They're already there, ready to take advantage of us. The Empress of Arctica invaded two of our territories overseas," said Cordata. "The Governor of Constitution is blockading our trade ships in the Atlas Ocean. We have much to fear, not just in our streets but beyond the oceans. Order, so to speak, must be restored."

Lord Cordata was somewhat shrewder than I'd given him credit for. There was much of my father in him after all. I gave him a long, considered look. Cordata had remained in Ruben's shadow for years and now all eyes were on him. This was his moment and he was ready to shine. And yet, I thought, he had done nothing while my father had rotted in jail. He had merely shown up in time to take a cut of the glory. Could he truly be trusted? I wasn't yet sure.

"As stated, I propose that we form the New Order, with myself as figurehead," he declared. "The gangs will not be prosecuted for their part in the uprising that elevated us to power, but we will not ignore their ongoing criminal activities. We shall seek to repair the Eye network eventually – for emergencies only, you understand – but for now it shall remain inactive so we might earn the public's trust. What do you say? Let the five Houses vote."

Lord Cordata looked to Lady Memoria, who took another pinch of snuff as she ruminated, murmuring to herself.

"I say aye," she said eventually, nodding her head. "I have my misgivings about you, Clements, plenty of them. But the people need Order."

Lord Cordata turned to Lord Harmonia. "What say you, my Lord?"

"You are loyal to no one but yourself," harrumphed Lord Harmonia. "But I need to keep an ear on you. So I'll say aye."

Lord Cordata turned then to me. "Lady Renato?"

My eyes aligned with Oliver's. Mine, hazel and wide-spaced, with a keyhole pupil; his like two black holes for me to fall into.

The edges of the room melted, my vision tunnelling…

Before I realized it, I was tumbling backwards inside myself, falling down the psychometric rabbit hole until I was cocooned in the privacy of the space between Oliver's mind and mine. From an outside view, we were merely making intense eye contact for a few seconds, but, in private, we were in a world of our own making where time flowed differently, as in dreams. Part him, part me, it was a world

23

of fire and shadows, of low lighting and burning hearths – a cosy getaway from reality. We pressed our foreheads together, our fingers intertwining.

"What should we do?" I asked.

"Let's think this through," he said. "One of them will seize control. I'd rather have Premier Cordata than Chancellor Harmonia. Unless you fancy another rebellion?"

"Maybe next year," I said. "I'm still a little tired from the last one."

He smiled at me, his brown eyes softening. But doubt gnawed on my bones, like rows of small sharp teeth.

"My head and my heart are at war," I said. "I feel like a traitor, standing there next to Lord Harmonia. What about our friends? Octavia, Rani, Perpetua, Ash… How can we ally with the enemy, after all they've done? What if they hate us for it?"

"We can do more from within than from outside," he said. "Keep people safe. Stop the Order from sliding back into tyranny."

"I suppose so."

"If we don't take our place at the table, someone else will take our seats."

"You're right. We have little choice."

"I'm with you, always," he said, taking my hand.

Returning to the room, I took a deep breath.

"It's a yes from House Renato," I said, as the emboldening fire of power coursed through me, "but on one condition: we involve the gangs. We rose to power with the people and we must remain their voice. We will work with the rebels, not against them. Is that clear?"

"As a mirror," said Cordata. "And what say you, Lord Obscura?"

"I'm with Lady Ruby, of course," he supplied. "We shouldn't let the horror of the past prevent us from making a better tomorrow – for ourselves, for everyone."

A moment of poignant silence followed.

"Tremendous! House Cordata wholeheartedly agrees, of course," said the new Premier Cordata, clapping his hands. "Then that's settled. As of today, we are the New Order of Providence. We shall publish an official announcement in the press tomorrow. Then we shall sign an Accord in public, agreeing to govern justly."

Premier Cordata snapped his fingers and a stream of servants filed in.

"A toast," he said, when each of us had a full, bubbling glass in hand. I caught Oliver's eye as he gave a tiny shrug. "To the New Order!"

"To the New Order," we repeated, hesitantly.

2.

OLIVER

On the morning of the Accord, I had a strange and sinister dream.

No, not a dream – a nightmare.

This in itself was not unusual. I'd been having vivid nightmares for as long as I could remember – dark dreams about world-ending floods, loose teeth, and the people I loved turning to dust in my hands – but they'd intensified since the time I died for six minutes.

Maybe near-death did that to a person.

So, no, there was nothing unusual about me having a nightmare. But what followed this one was strange.

In my dream I was lost in a series of dark rooms. I drifted through a building that was crooked and crumbling. It was vaguely familiar but at the same time I'd never seen it before in my life. Everything – absolutely everything – was black, from the windows to the portraits on the walls. Every chair, every plant, every statue was black, as if painted by hand.

One corridor led to another, and that one to another, in

an endless nest of murky gloom. I was looking for something but I didn't know what it was. I couldn't remember how I came to be there in the first place.

An arch of distant light caught my eye, drawing me to it. To my surprise, an open door led out to a balcony. As I stepped on to it, curious, an endless crowd roared below, warm bodies packed into the square like fish in a net. They were blowing whistles and waving flags, clapping and stamping their feet.

The Accord.

I was witnessing the signing of the Accord, before it happened.

The sound was joyful and celebratory at first, but soon it morphed into a raw, howling sound. The National Anthem played, blasting out of the broadcast towers with the scream of feedback. Premier Cordata stepped out. He wore five gold medallions and waved mechanically at the angry mob. He was wearing a blank white mask.

I blinked, and the others were standing there too: Lady Memoria, Lord Harmonia and … Ruby Renato.

Ruby in a red dress with a phoenix embroidered on it.

All of us waving, signing our names in a golden book.

A drum sounded a beat. A trumpet blared. A cannon fired.

I scanned the sea of faces, settling on one in particular. His features twisted in cold hatred as his fingers squeezed the trigger of a strange weapon.

BANG!

Looking through the smoke, I turned to my left to

27

see Ruby, her mouth open in surprise. Blood dribbled from her lips.

"Ruby?" I mouthed, unable to hear myself for the ringing in my ears. "Lily?"

Her eyes rolled back in her head, her hands parting to reveal a heart-shaped hole in her chest. I caught her in my arms as she collapsed.

I watched as she took her last, rattling breath.

"No, no, NO!" I shook her, touched her face. She was cold, gone.

Pure white-hot rage filled my mind, blocking everything else out. Staggering, I gently laid her down and launched myself over the balcony towards the assassin. I floated towards him as the crowd cleared, leaving just the two of us.

"I'll kill you!" I raged at him.

He fired at me as I approached – dark, feathery projectiles that created black holes in the fabric of reality.

I manifested a portal of my own: a dark swirling void that hung in mid-air. Lurching sideways, I jumped into it as the assassin hurtled towards me; I narrowly avoided a bullet in the back. I teleported to the other side of the courtyard, catching my breath as the assassin advanced. I swerved left, and the projectile hit a pillar instead.

For the first time, I got a good look at him, this young blonde man in a black hood, a teardrop tattooed under one green eye, but as soon as I'd registered his appearance it shifted, transforming into the features of another.

The man became a young girl with pigtails, holding a

doll, giggling chillingly. It was an illusion, to mask their true identity.

"Who sent you?" I demanded.

"The monster with a thousand faces," she said, but her voice sounded like a dozen people speaking at once, different accents and intonations all blending together to create the sound of a crowd in unison.

Each time the assassin fired, their face changed again, becoming an Inspector, a pregnant woman, a mourner in black, a guard in armour.

"I'm not playing your games," I said.

"We're not playing." The muscular guard transformed into a masked ballerina performing a pirouette.

Roaring, I took my most terrifying form, becoming a devilish creature, like something from an ancient bestiary.

"Who sent you?" I thundered, my voice deep enough to shake the ground.

The assassin laughed, a hollow, unstable sound, reverting back to the green-eyed, tear-tattooed man I'd first seen.

"Beware the monster with a thousand faces," he said.

Knock, knock.

Huh? I fell back into reality like a stone dropped by a bird, landing back in my bed in Obscura House.

"Lord Obscura?"

It took me a moment to realize they were talking to me, that I was Lord Obscura now. Oliver Obscura. Heir to House Obscura. Son of a monster. Ruler of the First Borough at seventeen years old.

The knocking intensified.

I grunted, squinting at the clock on the wall. It was five minutes past seven.

"I'm coming, I'm coming."

God, what a wretched dream. I was damp with cold sweat, my heart thumping, but relief flooded through me as I acclimatized with reality.

I lurched out of the black four-poster bed, stumbling through the cold and gloom towards the door. I slid open the lock but kept it on the chain, creating a thin crack to peer through.

My guardian stood on the other side: Gabriel Reagan. A tall, lean man of a certain age with a quiff of silvery hair, his right eyebrow bisected by a thin scar. A flame symbol was embroidered on his black tunic, signifying both his employer (Obscura) and his gift (a fire soul who channelled the Spark in combat). A former employee of my father's, he'd been imprisoned by the old Chancellor for disloyalty: selling secrets to a foreign nation, supposedly. If my father had thought him a traitor, then I could surely trust him.

"My apologies, my Lord, but it's time to get up."

I sighed. "Another day, another pointless meeting…"

"Yes, that does tend to be how government works, my Lord," he said, lightly, "but today is no ordinary meeting, remember. You will sign the Accord and cement the foundations of a new institution."

The Accord…

The man in the crowd—

Fear trickled down the back of my neck like melting ice cubes, making me shudder. *Just a bad dream*, I told myself. Nothing to worry about.

"Shall I ask the kitchen to prepare your breakfast, Lord Obscura?"

But I wasn't hungry. In fact, I felt quite sick.

"No, thank you. And you don't have to call me that."

"Whatever you wish, Master Obscura."

"Or … *that*."

A smile tugged at the corner of his mouth. "What would you like me to call you, sir? How about 'my Liege'?"

"Just Oliver is fine."

Ideally, I would have remained Evander Mountebank, curiosity shop employee, resident of the World's End. But those days were gone.

Gabriel gave me a thoughtful look. "Very well, Oliver. Do try to make time for a little breakfast. It's the most important meal of the day."

I watched him depart, moving down the long dark hall at a brisk, commanding pace. He took a seat at the bottom of the stairs before the front door, picking up a novel in Latin. He was always reading something, often in another language; I had lost count of how many tongues he could read and speak.

Echoes of the dream still haunted me as my thoughts turned to Ruby. Warm hands. Sweet lips. The freckles on her cheeks. The smell of her hair as she leaned into me. The heat in her body as she pulled me closer, one brow raised cockily…

But then I saw her as she'd been in my most recent nightmare, open-mouthed again, blood running from her lips.

BANG!

A breeze gusted in, causing the window shutter to clatter and making me jump right out of my skin.

Get a grip, Oliver.

Once washed and dressed, I headed out to the corridor. Servants in black stood along the walls, hands behind their backs, waiting for me to direct them to a task. It made me uncomfortable, though it was what I'd known all my life. I greeted them all, trying to seem cheerful.

"Good morning… Good to see you… Have a good day…"

I moved through the haunted shell of a house, past the locked room that had once belonged to my mother and which always made me shiver; past my father's gutted-out study, which made me nauseous; past an enormous oil painting depicting the ideal psychograph…

It had been here for as long as I could remember. I paused in front of it.

I stared at the dark, flickering silhouette of the Shadow; the pale, nebulous phantom of the Spirit; the humming beat of the Song; the plump golden fruit of the Heart; and the bright flame of the Spark. In balance, they represented the best of humanity.

In discord, the worst.

Once, I had the perfect soul, or so my father said. My psychograph was used as a shining example, the golden standard of souls. It used to appear illuminated on tablets and billboards across the city for all other souls to be compared to.

"The Spark should burn steady as a candle," he'd tell me, projecting the perfect proportions on the wall with a magic lantern. "The Spirit should smell fresh and sweet. The Heart should be rich and full. The Song should be melodious. The Shadow should be perfectly symmetrical."

Tristan Obscura's soul was none of those things. It was forbidden, in fact, to look upon his own soul with a magic lantern. Yet he expected mine to be all things at once. "The perfect ruler should have the perfect son," he used to say, "and the perfect son should have the perfect soul." He would tap his pointer on the wall, making a loud, sharp sound that caused me to shrink inside my skin. He would snap and scold. He would blame and bribe. He would make me perfect, no matter how guilty he made me feel, or how much it hurt. I learned young how to obscure the broken, misfit parts of myself. I learned how to project a flawless image.

But people see the truth eventually. The illusion only holds for so long. One day, they saw the Shadow within.

On the wall, my silhouette briefly ceased mirroring me. It waved at me gauchely, its mind having become its own for a moment. Setting my jaw and my shoulders, I took control again. I was in charge now. United, we moved as one.

Swallowing hard, I continued on down the black-carpeted stairs, beneath cornices carved with watchful gargoyles. Downstairs, the foyer was full of gifts – baskets of fruits set among flowers, cases of wine, all trussed up in ribbons in the other House colours, all of them having been inspected and approved, deemed safe to be imbibed.

Gabriel waited for me here, along with the rest of the senior House staff, each one gifted in the magic of one of the soul's five parts. Three were old friends: Octavia, Rani and Gus. I moved along the line as was traditional, greeting them in turn.

Fellow Shadow soul Rani Sharma wore a black saree, her long dark hair in braids. Her eyes briefly filled with darkness, as mine did, drowning out the whites.

"All clear," she said, saluting me comically. "The time is oh-eight-hundred hours and Operation Precious Cargo is running like a well-oiled machine."

"Operation Precious Cargo?"

"That's you, by the way."

Rani's uncle had been my mentor, the late Arjun Sharma. I saw him in her eyes, reflected back at me. Arjun, with his curly moustache and jewelled turban, had been like a father to me ... before my real father killed him, that is. That was something else I would never forgive the Chancellor for.

I moved on to my Listener, Song soul Octavia Belle. Her tunic was silver, teamed with a long swirling skirt, and her thick brown afro hair was styled with a shiny barrette. She wore the same empty birdcage necklace as always, but this time the birds were hanging from her ears: tiny swallows in silver.

"Try not to worry about today," she said, reading my thoughts as she leaned in to fix my collar.

"I thought you weren't going to do that," I said. Octavia had a habit of prying into other people's minds.

She bared her palms.

"I'm just skimming the surface. No deep-diving into your psyche. Pinkie promise." She gripped my little finger with hers, grinning. I wondered if she'd sensed the nightmare I'd had. If she had, she didn't say anything.

Once, Octavia had worked for my father, transcribing thoughts for the old regime. That was before we betrayed him and ran away together. Now she'd come full circle and was working to protect House Obscura once again. She wouldn't say it aloud but I knew she had mixed feelings about all of this.

"Deep breaths and clear your mind, just like I taught you. This is a happy day, remember?" she said, dusting off my shoulders with her fingers. "The end of the old and the dawn of the new. This is a fresh start, for all of us."

She and Rani exchanged a glance, so open and tender I couldn't look at it directly; it was like staring directly into the sun.

"I'm really glad you're here," I said. "Both of you."

"Where else would we be?"

I moved on to Heart soul Gus Han, a spiky-haired teen who served as my House gourmand. He'd donned an embroidered black-and-gold waistcoat, his colourful patchwork of tattoos visible beneath.

"*Look*," he said, waving a plate of sugar-dusted wares enticingly. "Freshly baked! Not only are they delicious but they're also full of confidence. Go on, take one. Take several."

"Thanks, but I'm not hungry," I told him.

"Breakfast is the most important meal of the day."

"So people keep telling me, but not right now. I'm too nervous."

"OK. Well, make sure you grab lunch," said Gus. "They'll have a decent spread at the Basilica. Gotta love Cordata for that, at least. We Heart souls always bring the snacks."

In the distance, bells rang. "Time to go," said Gabriel, materializing at my side.

"I'll be right with you," I replied.

I paused, watching them all file out, leaving me standing alone in front of the magic lantern that had been set there to examine the souls of visitors. Though the Eye network was inactive, the lanterns still worked. They were still connected to the invisible web of psychic energy that connected all living beings. The science of psychometry was as unchangeable as entropy. It existed before we did and it would exist long after we were gone.

During the revolution, we had discovered that Providence ran on human souls. Psyche had powered the network of surveillance that once kept watch over the city. Its energy was adaptable, a mystical fifth element with many iterations and functions.

My father had taken that power and used it for evil. He had sacrificed so many souls to stay in power. I would not make the same mistake.

The withered, hollow-eyed faces of those poor prisoners in the chamber flashed through my mind, screaming their dull, drone-like screams, prisoners including Ruby's own mother and countless others. How many more could we have saved if we had only realized sooner?

Ruby's face, blood on her lips…

I looked around. No one was here.

I could just take one quick look, to check all was still well.

Holding my breath, I twisted the small knob that illuminated the lantern's bulb, casting my psychograph upon the wall.

At first, my soul appeared perfectly proportioned, like the oil painting down the hall. I sighed in relief. I was OK. But when I caught my own eye in the mirror, I heard my father's voice echoing inside my mind.

You're doing it all wrong as usual, Oliver.

You're making a fool of me again.

Look at you, you're pathetic…

You'll never amount to anything.

The Shadow bled through in tendrils, like the tentacles of some dark and terrible beast, drowning out the light of the Spark and the sound of the Song. I watched the image morph and distort, revealing the truth.

Sometimes you become the thing you hate.

In the end, the darkness always shows itself.

I turned the lantern off quickly.

I must have ridden in our House carriage a thousand times, mostly in the company of my father. If I dredged through the oldest and murkiest of my memories, I could see my mother there too, solemn and beautiful, her dark eyes fixed firmly on the window as she escaped her body, tuning out my father as he ranted about all the ways in which we had disappointed him that day.

I used to escape too, using my Shadow to wander far away. I was doing the same thing now, letting my Shadow roam as I gazed out of the carriage window. I saw it leaping from wall to wall, cast by the light of the lanterns.

In the First Borough, the eyes that once watched over Providence were now closed, asleep. Thousands of empty holes peppered the city walls. Some of the eyes were still just about visible, on lamp posts, in glass orbs and in windows, but their ocular lenses were cracked, shattered by the force of a great explosion. My father's Observers were no longer watching.

In the Second Borough, the archives and libraries of stolen memories had been looted, creating a carpet of empty vials that gathered in gutters. In the Third Borough, the listening posts that once spied on the stream of consciousness scattered the landscape like giant iron ruins, silent and abandoned.

There were still neighbourhoods full of sewage and closed-down factories. There were still colonies under the empire's rule, bound by the laws my father had written. For many in Providence and beyond, nothing much had changed.

But for me, two people in particular were missing. I felt their absence in the quiet moments, wondering how Ash or Perpetua would break the silence.

"This feels weird, right?" said Octavia. "Or is that just me?"

"Travelling in the Chancellor's carriage? No, it's definitely weird," agreed Rani.

"I keep thinking we're going to get pulled over and arrested, carted off in wagons to the Reformatory to have our minds wiped," said Octavia.

"One day you're a criminal on the run from society, the next you're riding in a noble carriage on your way to rule over it," I said.

As we neared the city centre, the streets suddenly filled with people, blooming into well-packed crowds. Octavia whistled.

"Cordata said this would be low-key," I moaned.

I could hear drums. Bunting was strung overhead. There were kids sitting on their parents' shoulders, people blowing horns and waving flags...

A happy, picture-perfect scene on the surface but I could feel the darkness of my dream bleeding in like spilled ink.

Octavia squeezed my arm, silently projecting: *You're OK*.

Traffic snagged as the roads crowded with carriages. We pulled up in front of a large banner. OLIVER AND RUBY! it screamed, surrounded by cartoonish hearts. We continued past a stall selling commemorative merchandise.

"Hey, look! It's the man of the hour!" said Gus.

"Jeez. Do I really look like that?" I asked.

"It's … difficult to paint on porcelain, to be fair," said Rani.

"That's when you know you're a big deal," said Gus, "when they have a plate with your face on it."

"Before they cover it up with gravy and mashed potatoes?"

"The important thing is, the people love you," said Octavia.

"For now."

"Oh, cheer up, come on! I know it's not really your thing, but let's have a little fun today, yeah?"

I gaped at her. "I'm fun. I can be fun."

"Sure you are, buddy," said Gus, as if encouraging a small child.

We rolled past a lone protestor with a placard.

NEW ORDER, SAME OLD SHIT! it read.

Every sudden movement jangled my nerves. A flock of escaping birds. A group of musicians with instrument cases. A young boy wearing a sandwich board. A woman with a black umbrella, even though it wasn't raining…

I thought of the man in the crowd, the monster with a thousand faces. Any one of them could be an assassin.

Just a dream, I told myself. Nothing more. Still, the nagging sense that something bad was going to happen lingered. I saw movement in the corner of my eye, fluttering, flickering. I turned my head, but there was nothing there.

We pulled up at the Basilica, the same building we'd broken into on the night of the battle, with its golden cupolas and intricate arches. A monument to the rebellion, it served as a reminder of what had been won, and lost. People still left bunches of lilies, now wilted, in front of the building, propped against the exterior wall. Others had left letters to their dead or missing relatives. They were dog-eared, their inky words running together in the smoke-scented rain.

The part of the building that had been destroyed in the revolution had been replaced by a vast construction of glass, a giant atrium made of a thousand different panes that glinted and turned colours, coming together to form a great cathedral of windows.

The sound of the crowd grew gigantic, amorphous.

"Lord Obscura!"

"Oliver! Over here!"

Climbing out of the carriage, we moved smoothly through a crowd of vetted journalists and citizens, all holding out autograph books to be signed or peering through pinhole cameras. There was a hardness to their smiles, mockery in their eyes. Some of them were merely here for the spectacle. Gabriel nudged me on as the photographers continued to holler questions at me.

"How does it feel to be back in the Order, Lord Obscura?"

My mouth was sandpaper as I leaned into his silver mic. "It feels … it feels like it's time for change."

"The Governor of Constitution has described Providence as an 'unstable nation'. What do you say to that?"

"That time … that time is over." My gums stuck to the inside of my cheeks. "Change can be difficult, disruptive … but it is necessary."

"How will the New Order distinguish itself from the last?"

"In every possible way we can."

"What about the food shortages? What are you doing about those?"

I took a deep breath and channelled an idealized vision of myself, one who was competent and compassionate, wise and calm. Everything a good leader should be. I was Arjun Sharma, rest his soul.

"We're working night and day to get the supply chains moving," I said, my voice steadier, louder. "We are in negotiations with Constitution and we'll keep you updated on the progress of those talks. A compromise *will* be reached."

The reporter actually looked impressed. The Chancellor's dipshit son, speaking in complete sentences? He must've had low expectations of me, and I couldn't blame him.

Another member of the press pack shoved a recording device in my face, hollering in monotone.

"Lord Obscura! Where's Lady Renato tonight? Trouble in paradise already?"

"What? N-no, not at all," I said, startled.

"Is it true that the former Chancellor used you to shatter Ruby Renato's soul?" he asked.

"Uh, I—"

"And that she betrayed you by stealing your memory to blackmail your own father?"

"All in the past," I said, more confident than I felt. I moved on swiftly.

"Well handled, my Lord ... Oliver," said Gabriel, catching himself as we passed inside. "But some advice, if I may? Don't give those vultures a crumb, or they'll choke you with it."

The entrance of the Basilica was artistically draped with silk and framed by flower boughs. Armoured guards stood on either side of the door. Sunlight cast prismatic rays as I stepped through the open archway.

I was hustled into the official area, lined with security, as everyone turned to stare at me. I scanned the crowd, palms clammy. No one looked like an assassin. But how could I be sure? If they were a Shadow soul, they might have the ability to disguise their appearance, like I did.

"Not that I'm listening or anything, but your mind is racing at a thousand miles an hour," said Octavia. "I can't keep up. Everything all right?"

"Can you see Ruby?" I asked. "She should be here by now."

The roar of the crowd.

The squeal of feedback.

BANG!

A high-pitched buzz filled my head.

A green-eyed man lifting his hand…

Ruby, her mouth open in surprise…

"Oliver?"

Turning my head, I stared into the cracked lens of another broken eye, this one embedded in the wall of the Basilica.

And I swear – this time, it blinked right back at me.

Somewhere, someone was still watching.

3.

RUBY

The funny thing about rediscovering my soul was that I was continuously learning new things about myself, things I'd forgotten, such as that I liked naps under heavy blankets, the bitter taste of coffee and the smell of freshly laundered sheets. I always stopped to pet a friendly dog or cat. I laced my shoes tightly. I liked the smell of the ocean, mystery novels and falling asleep in front of the burning hearth. I was fast to love and quick to bridle in irritation. I liked hugging people hello and painting dream scenes. I learned that I slept on the right side of the bed, that I could swim, that I made ridiculous noises when I ate something I liked. I learned that I despised waiting for things and that exercise made me feel better.

On the morning of the Accord, I woke at dawn to work out in the gymnasium at Renato House. Wearing a short red robe and sandals, I warmed up first, stretching my limbs. I practised channelling the life force of the Spark, battling the holographic enemies projected by the Shadow box on the wall: silhouette soldiers who attacked from all directions, employing different moves and tactics. I dealt with them fluidly, taking them down with ease.

Everyone had a Spark but not everyone could take the innate energy inside their soul and manifest it externally, physically, as I could. This knowledge had been passed down through generations of Renatos, connecting us to the Founders who discovered psychometry, the science of the soul.

Sparks flying from my fingertips, I wielded lightning in my hands. If I concentrated, I could paint with fire, forming shapes from this red, burning light in my mind. I made arrows and fireballs, slamming them into my Shadowy enemies. It energized me, filling my entire body with the fuel of Spark.

My father's face flashed behind my eyes again … the look he gave me as I watched him die. I saw his soul split apart, turn to dust.

The fire inside me bloomed, growing too hot. I lost control, showering the room with little flames. The sprinkler system turned on, extinguishing both me and the fire.

"What did I tell you about concentration?" came my father's voice in my head. *"If you let your mind wander, so will your centre of power. One day you will be the ruler of a powerful noble House; naturally you will inherit many enemies. It is crucial that you know how to protect yourself."*

"Everything OK in here?"

I turned to see my mother, Mara, at the doorway. She was wearing a red dress with a white flower embroidered on it. From her I inherited my freckles, my hazel eyes and my naturally curly red hair, my sweet tooth, my cleft chin, my lack of musical talent and my intense hatred of coriander.

Mara had returned to her role as the Renato House Memorialist, encapsulating memories for posterity. That was how she had met my father, how I was made, and how she figured out that I was best raised away from his influence, knowing he wanted a child for all the wrong reasons. As a common woman, she had not been safe under the Order's rule. They had captured her and used her soul to power their empire. She had been brought to the brink of death before we had freed her. All my life, she'd taught me that the Order was wicked, that it would destroy us all eventually, yet here she was standing by my side anyway.

I knew that if not for me she'd never set foot in this place again. She would've taken me far away from here. We would be living in a little cottage somewhere in Green Valley, like we used to. We would ride bikes with baskets through the lanes and hang our washing out to dry on windy lines. We would take Sunday lunch at the local inn, where a fiddle band played in the corner. She would sing along badly and I would hide my spluttering laughter behind my hand.

We would be happy.

But I refused to walk away from the revolution my father had started. I would not be a coward when it counted most. I would not abandon the people we'd liberated.

"What in the name of tarnation are you doing?" asked Mara, in her lilting Valley accent.

47

"Nothing to see here," I said, walking smoothly through the cloud of steam I'd just made. "Just got a little hot during my workout."

She raised one eyebrow. "Please be careful, my love. You don't want to burn the house down before brunch now, do you?"

I rolled my eyes but I was smiling. We'd spent years without each other. It was nice to be nagged again. Damp and defeated, I retreated to my dressing room to prepare.

I'd been too confident, got carried away. That was usually when you got knocked right off your feet. My father thought he was winning on the night of the Battle at the Basilica. He thought he had all the luck in the world, destiny on his side. Seconds later, he'd been killed by the Chancellor, dying before he'd even had a chance to understand his own hubris.

I didn't want to end up the same way.

Am I doing the right thing? Even now, I wasn't sure.

Telling our friends had been terrible. Just a few weeks ago, we had been living in the ruin of the Sanctuary, the residence of Birdie, murdered rebel and former voice of the Order. A grey marble, bird-infested mansion house in the countryside beyond the capital, the Sanctuary had been ransacked during the revolt and stripped of all its precious treasures. Yet the shell of the building had been enough to establish a base in, reinforced with the psyche of its many gifted members. It was still the heart of the resistance movement, though the rebellion had already begun to disagree, splitting into rival factions.

Straight after we'd agreed to form the New Order, Oliver and I had driven there at dawn in our House carriages. They must have suspected what we were coming to say. We were met with stony faces and porridge-thick tension.

We filed into the dining room where we'd once enjoyed a last supper, staring at the makeshift shrine to Birdie and Arjun Sharma atop the mantelpiece.

"Go on, then," Ash had said. "Spit it out." A Spark soul like me, Ash's head was shaved on both sides, leaving a dark strip, their hands covered by half-gloves.

"We already know you met with the enemy," Perpetua said. "I hope you left a trail of blood behind you." A Spirit soul, pale and ghostly, her eyes heavily lined with kohl, she wore a ragged fur coat that smelled strongly of incense smoke.

"Let me guess," said Ash. "They want you to bail them out and prop up their dying empire. They make me sick, snivelling dogs. I hope you told them where to shove it."

"Not ... exactly," I said.

Breathlessly, Oliver and I relayed to them what had been said, and to what we had agreed. When we finished, the room was silent.

"Well?" I asked, tentatively. "What do you think?"

"You're serious?" said Perpetua, her gaze ice cold. "You will really stand next to those people, after everything they did?"

"It wasn't an easy decision ... but we think it's for the best," I said.

Perpetua scoffed loudly. "What best? Who says it's best? Clements Cordata? That low-hanging fruit?"

49

"If you join us, you can join our Houses," said Oliver. "You can have a room of your own, all the free time you desire and enough food to eat."

"I'm sold," joked Gus. "We're probably going to die either way, so why not go out with full bellies? Haven't we all suffered enough?"

"It's not funny, mate," said Ash. They shook their head, crimson in the face. I could feel them burning from across the room.

"Just trying to lighten the mood," said Gus.

"You told me we would never return to the Order," said Perpetua. "You said we would never betray each other."

"No one is betraying anyone," said Oliver. "This is our chance to gain power, perhaps our only chance."

"Convenient for you," said Perpetua.

Rani was quiet, staring at the picture of her late uncle.

"Please, everyone, can we just listen to each other?" begged Octavia.

"Change can't happen overnight," I said. "At least we'll be on the inside this way."

"You have burned your bridges with me now," said Perpetua. "Never again will I trust you." She made a dramatic hacking noise. "People didn't die so we could replace one Order with another. You are making a grave mistake."

"Please. We're all friends. Can't we just—"

"You betrayed me!" Perpetua shouted. "You betrayed all of us. We are no longer friends now."

Oliver put out a hand to her. "You have to understand—"

"I understand one thing only, and that is you are dead to me, both of you," said Perpetua, stalking out with a flamboyant swirl.

Ash didn't utter a word, but they stormed out after her.

Oliver sighed and rubbed his forehead. "Well, that went well," he said miserably.

"For what it's worth, I think Uncle Arjun would have agreed with you," said Rani. "It's a tough choice, but I understand your reasoning."

Octavia swallowed audibly. "I swore not to go back there," she said, "but I can't bear to be apart from you either."

"Same. I just want us to all stick together," said Gus. "I guess that's not an option any more, huh?" He groaned. "All right. I'm with you. I'm in this. But Perpetua doesn't mess around. In her eyes, we're either with her or against her – so we should probably leave. Now. Right now."

On cue, we had all piled into the carriages and driven away.

We hadn't spoken to Perpetua or Ash since.

I stood at the dressing room window gazing out at the courtyard. A gilded statue of Ruben Renato stood in the yard surrounded by red votive candles: offerings to the martyr from fellow fire souls. Beyond the hedge wall, the eternal flame of House Renato burned high on the hill. I pulled out the heart-shaped locket I wore round my neck, opening it like a book to reveal two small memorial portraits: my grandmother Rubella, and my father Ruben.

As far as the people knew, my father was a hero, but they

didn't know the whole story. So far, I'd held my tongue. Better that the people had something to believe in than another reminder of the Order's vast corruption; better they think there might be something salvageable from the ashes. Yet in moments like this when I was alone, I wondered… Had my father been good or bad? Or a bit of both perhaps? Now that he was gone, I might never know the truth about him.

I reminded myself again why I was here, and why I was wearing this stupid dress: a red quilted gown embroidered with a phoenix in gold thread, the whole thing so heavy it felt like wearing a diving suit.

Knock, knock.

"Let's see you, then," came my mother's voice on the other side of the door. "Seriously, c'mon – I can't wait any longer."

I shuffled out of the dressing room, resigned to my fate.

My mother smiled, clasping her hands together. "Oh … beautiful … you look beautiful," she said, but I noticed the hesitation.

"What?"

"Nothing," she said.

"Go on, I know there's something."

"The dress is perfect," she said, "but the face…"

"What's wrong with my face?" I asked.

"Well, you don't look very happy, my love," said my mother, rubbing my upper arms, "and I want you to be happy."

"Today isn't about being happy," I said defensively. "It's about showing up and doing the right thing."

"It's not your job to fix this mess," she said. "Just know that you don't have to do anything you don't want to do. You're just a kid."

"I'm sixteen, Mum, and I'm not changing my mind," I told her. "This is just the way things are now, the way they have to be."

She enveloped me in a bear hug. "Oh, my love, I wish more than anything that I could spirit you away," she said, "take you back to the Valley where I know you'd be safe. But I also know your mind is already made up. Stubborn as an ox stuck in the mud, you are. Must've gotten that from your father."

"The people need us," I said, weakly.

"*I* need you," she said. "I need you alive and well. Remember that."

As we drew closer to the Basilica in our carriage, the streets filled with people: crowds of spectators who'd waited for hours to see our procession roll by for a second. They were cheering and blowing whistles, waving the five-coloured flag; some having claimed their spot by camping out in chairs overnight, goggling through binoculars, dressed up in House colours or wearing masks, waving pipes and bottles.

"This is really happening," I said in disbelief.

It was a peculiar thing to get used to. As Ruby Renato, I was Ruben's child but also a servant's daughter. A pesky bloodstain on the pure-white sheets of the noble Order. People didn't respect me. They didn't view me as an equal. When I was written out of history, my memory obliterated, there were few who truly remembered me. But now, suddenly, I was Someone. I was the one who brought my father's revolutionary dream to pass. People craned their necks and reached out their hands as we rolled by.

The carriage pulled up as staff in red tunics bustled around us. We headed towards the entrance of the Basilica, past the sweaty crowds held behind red velvet ropes, past the flocks of reporters who gathered in every nook and cranny, hiding behind every potted plant and pillar.

"Lady Renato!" one called out. "When should we expect an official notice of engagement?"

A what? "Are you kidding me?" I said, the Valley in my voice coming out.

"Don't listen to them," my mother said. "Marriage is the sort of thing you want to put off for as long as possible."

Unprompted, an image popped into my head. White doves. People in sharp suits and flowing dresses. Little children tossing petals from baskets. Ambrosia flowing and a band playing swoony torch songs. When I imagined the person waiting at the end of the aisle, there was no question. It was him.

It had always been him.

Still, I was hardly ready for marriage.

In a large room with net curtains and gold pillars, the rest of the Order waited, ready to sign the Accord before a gathered flock of journalists, photographers, councillors and donors. The press cameras erupted into a storm of bright flashes, causing me to screw up my face. Their static psychometric images hung briefly in the air, like bubbles. I blinked, squinted, and Oliver emerged from the glare, pulling me close to him. His face was tense and set.

"You're late. I was worried."

I took his hand, but I couldn't tell what he was feeling. Which was strange. He was keeping me out somehow.

"I'm always late... Something wrong?" I pressed.

"Just be careful, OK?" he said. "Be vigilant."

"Be vigilant? What does *that* mean?"

A bell tolled as the clock in the tower reached midday.

"It's time to make history!" said Cordata grandly. "Let us greet the people."

He stepped boldly out on to the balcony, making a sweeping gesture that drew a noisy cheer. The band below quickly began playing the National Anthem, the sound screeching horribly through the broadcast towers. It sounded sinister; a relic of the past come back to haunt us. That brassy dirge so often heard reverberating through the streets, like a warning.

I watched Oliver pale. He gripped my hand, too tight.

Most of the people were cheering, but there was something else underneath. A low sound. Booing. Jeering...

The anthem had stirred up some bad memories, it seemed.

"Citizens of Providence," came a voice over loudspeaker, "welcome your new Premier, Clements Cordata!"

Premier Cordata clasped his hands together, bowing in gratitude. He was dressed demurely for the occasion, in a plain tweed tunic. He had originally planned on wearing a fur-trimmed cloak embroidered with gold hearts and five gold medallions, one for each part of the soul, but I had convinced him that this might not be the best way to endear ourselves to the people, nor to distinguish ourselves from our predecessors. The others were similarly dressed, swapping their usual lace and silks for cotton and wool, their House colours reduced to a single splash: Harmonia's silver pocket square, Memoria's white-flower brocade, Cordata's gold neckerchief, and Oliver's gothic black tie. The only exception was me, in the red phoenix dress at Cordata's insistence. As the people's princess, I had to cut a striking and fashionable figure for the papers, he said.

"Welcome, Lady Memoria!" came the voice again.

She fluttered her lacy handkerchief as the applause remained steady. Word had spread that she was instrumental in the rebellion.

"Lord Harmonia!"

The cheers were *definitely* more muted for him. Lord Harmonia had been absent during the Battle of the Basilica. His allegiances were not yet clear, though some remembered his previous misdeeds as the Chancellor's loyal follower.

"Lady Renato!"

At my name the crowd exploded into a celebratory

roar. It was surreal. Thousands of people were cheering, waving, staring at me. I felt like a deity, or perhaps a human sacrifice. I wasn't really there, floating above the scene like a loosed balloon.

"And Lord Obscura!"

The cheers only grew. Oliver stared out at the crowd blankly. Alone, he would have been feared – the son of the old Chancellor. With me, though, he was revered. Locking eyes, we had the exact same idea at the same time, leaning in for a dignified kiss, chaste enough to be appropriate but tender enough to be romantic.

The cheers increased, mixed with whistles and whoops.

"Enough!" Premier Cordata said. I caught the irritation in his tone. He didn't like being upstaged. "Ah, *enough applause*, please." He smiled out at the crowd, waiting for them to fall silent before he began his speech.

"The history of Providence is a long and complicated one," he said. "The discovery of psyche – the dark matter of the soul – has transformed our society since the Enlightenment. Through knowledge, innovation and most of all truth, the Order rose to prominence. But slowly, humankind lost sight of its ideals, culminating in the reign of terror conducted by Tristan Obscura."

A chorus of acidic hatred, the sound filling the square.

"Six months ago, my associates and I removed the Chancellor from power. We destroyed the Eye network that, fueled by the souls of our own people, denied citizens privacy even within their own minds. Many lives were lost, including Lord Ruben Renato, to whom we owe our freedom. If not for him, the Chancellor's evil may never have been fully revealed."

And you did nothing, I thought, smiling falsely at him.

"That day, we swore we would never again live in fear of our own thoughts, our own memories, our own dreams. We vowed that our minds would be our own again, and so too the mind of every citizen would be free. Now Tristan Obscura sits in a prison cell awaiting trial. His ring of extremists has been dismantled. We have reclaimed our republic. The dark days are over!"

This triggered another roar from the crowd, five-colour flags waving, whistles sounding, stretching as far back as I could see.

Cordata was a good speaker, I had to give him that. He knew what people wanted to hear and he was willing to say it, regardless of whether it was true or not.

"We are here today to sign an Accord, our mutual agreement to govern as a union," he said. "The five Houses are the foundation of our society. We vow to govern fairly. You are all our witness."

When I looked to Oliver again, there was a gathering darkness in his eyes, dimming the light inside.

"Providence is no longer governed by one, but by five," Cordata continued. "We, the heads of the five Houses, shall each sign the Accord in turn, promising to govern to the best of our ability."

A marble podium was brought out, its flat pentagon-shaped

top divided into the five colours. Black for House Obscura. White for House Memoria. Silver for House Harmonia. Gold for House Cordata. Red for House Renato.

A book sat in the middle, waiting to be signed.

One by one, we wrote our names in black ink. Lady Memoria followed by Lord Harmonia, then Oliver, his hand shaking. I signed next with my scrawl. Finally, Premier Cordata wrote his signature, a large, looping scrawl with a heart wearing a crown on top of it.

"To the end of dictatorship and to the beginning of freedom!" he boomed, raising one fist in the air. "To the New Order!"

A smile was painted on my face. I waved endlessly, my arm aching. The crowd cheered back, the sound raw with sharp edges.

A drum sounded a beat. A trumpet blared. A cannon fired. The crowd began to ripple, as some unseen movement parted the people below, like a shark through the waves.

Oliver's face was a pinched mask, dark eyes darting back and forth. He gripped my arm, whispering urgently: "We need to—"

BANG!

I felt myself thrown across the balcony, collapsing into a pillar as a small dark projectile slammed into the wall, missing me by an inch.

"What the—" I began.

BANG!

I scrambled to my feet. The second projectile burned up

mid-air as I met it with fire. Oliver wrapped us in a blanket of Shadow, his eyes black.

In seconds, chaos erupted.

Another shock wave moved through the crowd as people started pushing and shoving, trying to run from an unidentified threat. A barricade was knocked down. A speaker tower toppled like timber. The writhing melee solidified. A tide of human bodies surged towards the Basilica as soldiers pushed them back, their weapons raised.

Lord Cordata stood frozen in position, smiling without his eyes.

"Everyone inside, now!" shouted Oliver, dragging me with him.

Something whistled over my head, missing me by a hair. People were screaming in every possible octave. We ran inside as another projectile bounced off a pillar. The Premier's guardian closed the doors, barricading them with a heavy wooden desk as we gasped and panted.

"Good grief," said Lady Memoria, falling on to a well-placed fainting couch. "I'm far too old for this."

The press snapped pictures of our distress, capturing our reactions. The dim room resounded with silence as a riot unfolded below.

"Is anyone hurt?" asked Oliver, as medics from House Cordata spilled into the room, laden with herbal remedies. One of them used a lantern to look for fresh wounds on our souls, while another talked in a calm voice about breathing exercises and safe places.

"A premeditated attack! That was an outright disaster!" said Lord Harmonia. "What in hell's name did you have us walking into, Clements? They could've killed us."

But the shooter hadn't been firing at him.

It looked like they had been shooting at *me*.

"Not the best start, granted, but a little resistance was to be expected," said Cordata, wiping his forehead. He was recovering quickly.

"A 'little resistance'?" echoed Lord Harmonia.

"It will all have blown over by the morning, I'm sure."

"The news will be halfway across the world by this afternoon," said Lady Memoria. "What do you think our allies will make of this? Or our enemies – the Empress and the Governor?"

"You need to take a firm hand like I suggested, crack down on the gangs," said Lord Harmonia. "Put the curfew back in place, restore the Eye network. It's time to get tough."

"That didn't work out so well for the Chancellor, did it?"

A squabble broke out, everyone talking over each other. My eyes drifted to Oliver, whose attention was already fixed on me, staring at me so intensely I felt self-conscious. He reached out to grip my shoulders, pulling me closer and kissing the top of my head.

"I need to talk to you, outside," he murmured.

No one noticed us leave. Out in the corridor, he produced a portal: a swirling Shadow that hung in the air like a mirror. We stepped through it, passing between the planes of waking and dreams. In half an instant, we were on top of the building, looking out over the discord now spilling out into the square. Guards on horses chased the people who were throwing flaming bottles. Oliver pulled us into a covered position as his Shadow paced back and forth patrolling the wall.

"Do you think it was the rebels?" I asked. It didn't seem possible that our former allies could turn against us. But lines had been drawn. Sides had been chosen. "We should talk to Ash and Perpetua. Find out what they know, if anything."

We watched the groups of people below, darting back and forth, tossing firecrackers as black wagons rolled in.

"You knew the attack was coming, didn't you?" I said. "How?"

He turned to me, taking a deep breath as if readying himself. "This is going to sound crazy," he replied, cautiously.

"I'm familiar with crazy," I said.

"It sounds silly to even say it out loud but … I had this weird dream," he said. "A vision, really. I … I saw the attack before it happened. I knew someone was going to shoot at us. At you. But in the dream, I was too late to stop it. They killed you."

My arms broke out into goosepimples, skin prickling.

"I chased after the assassin," he explained. "In the dream, I mean. He said something about a monster, a monster 'with a thousand faces'."

Silence stretched between us.

"It's probably just a coincidence," I said. "Your Shadow

62

is very attuned to danger." I inclined my head towards his silhouette, still marching up and down like a soldier on patrol. "You were worried about the Accord, about unrest, so you created a vision of it happening in your mind."

"Just because I'm paranoid it doesn't mean they're not out to get me," he said, half serious, half joking. "You don't think it might … mean something?"

"Like what? If someone wanted to kill us, why would they warn us – you – in advance?" I asked. "That doesn't seem very efficient."

"That … that's a point," he admitted.

"Did you actually see this assassin in the crowd? The one you saw in your dream?"

"Well, no."

"See? A coincidence. Because I didn't die, did I? Someone took a shot at us, but they missed. The vision you had was wrong. You know what the Shadow of the subconscious is like. It can be … dramatic."

His Shadow crossed its hands over its chest as if to say, *Me? Dramatic?*

"Maybe…" he admitted. "But everything happened almost exactly as it did in the dream. If I hadn't known what was going to happen, then I wouldn't have pushed you out of the way in time and you would have been—"

"Well, I'm glad you did," I said, interrupting the thought before it could spiral. "I guess your Shadow is always looking out for me, huh? Your subconscious has saved me more than once."

"It tries its best," he said.

Cast upon a parapet, his Shadow bowed to me.

I placed one hand on Oliver's chest, feeling his thrashing heartbeat.

"Please take it easy, Oliver. Remember what happened last time you put yourself under too much strain? You almost died."

"Only for a couple of minutes," he said, shrugging one shoulder.

"Six minutes, actually," I said.

"That was a close call today. Too close. I should have done something to stop it," he said, almost to himself.

"You can't protect us from every bad thing in the world. There are far too many of those. Besides, I'm pretty tough. I can look after myself." I raised one hand, summoning a small but feisty-looking flame.

"You're adorable," he said, his worried expression melting.

"No, I am fearsome."

"That too."

I imagined for a moment that we had turned down Cordata's offer to form a government. That we were living in the Sanctuary or underground in the burned husk of the World's End, that we were still part of the rebel gangs. I imagined that Ash and Perpetua remained our friends and that we were still committing crimes instead of trying to prevent them.

We would be down there fighting, instead of up here putting out the fires we'd started.

The fires that now threatened to consume us.

History was repeating itself but this time, we were on the other side.

4.

OLIVER

A hand on my arm, Ruby's voice in my ear. I spun round, confused.

"What did Cordata want?" she repeated.

"Huh?" We were at some kind of gathering at Cordata House, in the ballroom, with a feast painted on every wall, stone pillars carved with vines and grapes, chandeliers like cornucopias. There was an ice sculpture shaped like a giant heart on the table. A small string quartet played "Ode to an Old Soul".

"I saw him pull you aside. What did he say?"

I looked around. Lady Cordata and the Premier were arguing. Throwing up her hands, she stormed out of the ballroom, bumping into a server carrying a punchbowl and making him spill its contents. Lord Harmonia stepped aside to miss the flying liquid and spare his suit. In avoiding being splashed with punch, Lord Harmonia rammed into the table, toppling the heart-shaped ice sculpture. It wobbled dangerously.

"Are you listening to me?" asked Ruby. Her voice

dropped an octave, distorting as time slowed. The scene before me seemed to melt, stretching out and tilting.

At an unnaturally drawn-out pace, the sculpture toppled and crashed to the ground. It shattered, though excruciatingly slowly, spraying shards of ice across the floor. Frozen fragments hung in the air like suspended snowflakes, before time sped up again and ice pieces spewed in every direction. Reality resumed at a frantic pace, the room filling with shocked squeals and screams.

"Oopsie," said Lord Harmonia. "Butterfingers."

Servers rushed in to sweep up the ice.

"Pardon me," said Lady Memoria. "Coming through…"

Behind her, I spied a figure in a black-hooded robe, approaching Ruby at speed. Time tunnelled as I focused in on the tattooed teardrop.

The green-eyed assassin.

He was *here*.

I shouted to Ruby, but the words stuck in my throat. She couldn't hear me or see me as the crowd seemed to swell around us.

BANG!

Ruby turned to me, eyes wide, blood on her lips, a hole in her heart…

"No, no, NO!"

Crying out, I bolted awake again, my heart pounding.

Another dream. That was a new one.

It had been three weeks since the Accord and I'd dreamed of Ruby's death every night since, over and over again. The infinite possibilities of it terrorized me. She died in every place and time, the circumstances and scenery ever differing, offering a great range of settings – yet her death remained unchanged.

It haunted me.

God, it haunted me.

Sometimes we were walking in the gardens of the Basilica when it happened; at other times, we were combing through the burned wreckage of the World's End together. We were at a ball, or at the circus, or by the sea... Nowhere was safe. Her death could happen at any moment, it seemed. And no matter how different the details were each time, the final moments were always the same. Ruby was always shot by the green-eyed, tear-tattooed assassin who fired before vanishing into a curl of smoke.

In each nightmare, she expired in the same way, gaping at me open-mouthed as blood trickled from her lips, her hands clasped at her breast. When she pulled them apart, there was always a hole in her chest, and with each nightmare that hole grew bigger and bigger.

In the present, still very much alive, Ruby sat up beside me, rubbing my back as I grasped for her hand.

"Bad dream again?" she said softly.

"Mmm-hmm," I murmured into her hair as she held me.

"What was it this time?"

I cloaked my mind in Shadow, making it harder for her to probe my subconscious. After that first vision, I had kept them from her.

"I don't remember it now," I lied. "Something about …

68

birds. Lots of birds, all looking at me funny. I don't know. It's fading already."

I didn't want to lie to her, but I didn't want to scare her either. No one wanted to hear that the person who loved them was dreaming non-stop of their death. I didn't want my darkness to spread to her like soul rot.

The assassin who disturbed the Accord had yet to be caught, despite my many hours of combing the streets in Shadow form. The guardians of the five Houses had been sent out in search of him, including Gabriel, and although they had rooted out many criminals in the process, none were connected to this crime. The culprit was a ghost, invisible and uncatchable.

"Let's go back to sleep," said Ruby, pulling me back against the pillows with her. "Meet me in our safe place. I'll be waiting for you there."

"I'll try my best," I said.

"You can do it," she said. "I believe in you."

Ruby drifted off to sleep quickly, leaving me behind. Her breathing was rhythmic, her lashes twitching as I watched her dreaming without me, jealous and curious of whatever she was imagining that made her look so peaceful. Eventually I relaxed enough to let my psyche blend with hers, falling into her mind like a landslide. Her mind was warmer than mine, softer, safer. It enveloped me like a tartan blanket tucked round us as we sat in a cosy cottage before a crackling fire, snow falling through the darkness outside. In my head, everything was creepy and crooked behind the daydream scenes I'd built like theatre sets, but her head was snug and welcoming. It was safe and stable, like a real home. Combined, they were in harmony.

"Finally," she said, as I materialized next to her. "You know how impatient I am."

"Sorry to keep you waiting, my Lady," I said, kissing her hand. "Forgive me?"

A Shadow forest grew up around us, protecting us like a cocoon, its branches forming decorative curlicues as bright flowers bloomed around us, glowing softly and emitting a sweet scent.

"Scenery. Always the scenery with you," she said, smiling.

"What else do I have going for me?" I replied.

"Don't sell yourself short. You're pretty easy on the eye too."

"Oh, cheers. Is that it?"

"Pretty much." She winked at me.

I reached out to pluck a ripe fruit from a Shadow branch. A plump shiny pomegranate. I broke it open to reveal the jewelled seeds inside. When I scooped one out, it grew a vine to form a ruby ring. I slipped it on her middle finger, thinking about the future.

"It's beautiful," she said, gazing into its glittering facets.

"Like you," I said.

She rolled her eyes, smiling. "You're so cheesy, but I love it."

"Guilty," I said, kissing her hand again, my lips lingering on her soft skin. "Where shall we go tonight?" I asked.

In our shared dreams, we went on many impossible dates. We could cuddle in the curve of a crescent moon, or roll around on a bed of clouds. We could walk through fields of sunflowers tall as trees or take a stroll at the bottom of the ocean. But it was rather like standing in an enormous library, trying to choose just one book to read. The limitless options left us in imaginative paralysis.

"Wherever you like."

I shrugged, dropping her hand.

"No, you decide," she insisted. "I chose last time, remember? We had a picnic while boating on a lake of fire."

I was too tired to think properly, but I wanted to please her. "What about the city of love and light?" I tried.

The Shadowy forest shifted and swirled, transforming into a portal, its tangled, mossy vines forming the ring of the circle. The dark hole dragged us through it, spitting us out into the flowery streets of a cosmopolitan continental city lit up by a thousand lights. A latticed iron tower loomed on the horizon: the famous landmark of Florentine.

Ruby gasped. "It's so realistic!"

"I memorized it from a painting," I said. "It's not quite as good as the real thing, but it's a lot cheaper."

"Bit busy though," she said, stepping aside to let a family of five walk past. "Maybe something a little more secluded?"

"What about Ankh?" I said.

The imagined city disintegrated and wasted away, becoming a sandy desert settlement instead. The sky was now sunset pink. The streets were lined with palms. Three great pyramids stood solemn, dignified and mystical in the distance, while a bustling market made up of stalls and stone passages was illuminated by lanterns.

"I've always wanted to see the Valley of the Queens," she said. "But…" She tugged at her collar, pulling it away from the skin of her neck. "It's quite hot, isn't it? What about somewhere more chill?"

The sun plunged beyond the horizon, to be replaced by a dark sky full of stars and neon ribbons that kissed the snowy tops of the evergreen trees.

"The Eastern Lights of Arctica," I said, gesturing at the coloured streamers that tangled overhead, creating a shimmering aurora.

"This," she said, "this is perfect. Let's stay here for a while."

"Fine by me."

She manifested a fire while I made a tent out of Shadow, settling in to watch the sky, but that same fearful feeling kept catching in the corner of my eye, prickling the back of my neck.

"What's up?" she asked.

"Thought I heard something. Probably just a bear."

"You know, you could imagine it *without* bears if you wanted."

"What would be the fun in that?"

I tried to be aware only of the lights above, but the sound of small twigs and stones being scattered kept sounding nearby. I almost snapped my neck trying to see what it was but every time I fixed on it, that sense of being watched disappeared instantaneously.

It was just paranoia, I told myself.

Wasn't it always?

Leaning into Ruby, I focused on the patterns in the sky as the aurora formed a flower, a heart, an eye…

An eye?

BANG!

Before I'd had chance to regard his presence, the green-eyed assassin had invaded our camp, shooting his dark weapon, but this time he aimed it at me.

"Beware the monster with a thousand faces," he cried.

Laughing, he disintegrated to ash.

Stirring awake again, I found Ruby sleeping beside me, her brow furrowed. She was still in the dream, enjoying the light show. All she would know is that I'd gone again, her mind separated from mine once more.

I kissed her shoulder, her forehead, her ear, her hand … every part of her that I could access. I listened to her heart beating through her chest: the beautiful, powerful sound of her still being alive.

I tried not to imagine her lying cold in a coffin.

Enough, I thought. Enough dreaming and waiting, enough running in fear. Ruby would *not* die, not while I was here. I wouldn't let her.

Let's say, for argument's sake, that she *was* destined to be murdered by the assassin. Fortunately, I'd been given a gift – a vision of the future. I could prevent her death using the information I'd seen in these strange prophecies I'd been having.

This time, instead of recoiling in fear, I purposely recalled the assassin's face from my dream – that snarling, hateful, murderous face. His features were burned permanently into my memory now, yet I was sure I'd never met him before. He was a stranger to me, both in the waking world and in my mind. *Who was he…?*

I could discern three key pieces of information about him.

The first clue – his shapeshifting. That told me he was probably a Shadow soul, like me.

The second clue – the tear tattoo, a symbol that he'd lost someone close to him. It was a fashion that was popular among prisoners and members of the criminal underworld. So, was grief his motive? Did he blame the Order for the death of a loved one? Was that why he wanted us dead too?

The third clue – the weapon: an expensive-looking experimental contraption, the likes of which I'd never seen within the Order or outside of it. In my dreams it fired dark matter. And yet the gun used in the attack at the Accord had fired real bullets.

Perhaps the green-eyed man was just a hired goon. That meant he had an employer, someone more powerful who had trained and equipped him. This person would likely have plenty of resources at their disposal, and a strong motive. They would surely have something to gain from killing Ruby, but what?

I thought back to the day of the Accord. There had been some small differences between my vision and the reality. For one thing, the Premier had been wearing different clothes. The book we signed wasn't made of gold, as it had been in my dream. Ruby wasn't struck. But the drum beat, the cannon, the feedback screech … all that was the same.

Had I truly glimpsed the future?

There *had* to be a logical explanation for it.

I crawled out of bed, sloping out into the dark hall. Obscura House was a grim place at the best of times, all black furniture and dark mahogany, stone walls and black marble floors with reddish streaks. At the worst of times, it was a tomb: a cold, inhibiting place with small eye-shaped windows and claustrophobic corridors that made me feel like a rat in a maze.

I knew I could escape my body if I liked, wander the city as a Shadow, search for the assassin house by house. I could comb Providence for further clues. Yet something inside me told me that the answers I sought were closer to home, that they were right under my nose.

My mother popped into my head, unbidden. I paced back and forth in front of the room I always dreaded to pass, the room which contained her shrine. I'd lived without her for a long time, she'd been gone for more years than I'd had with her alive, but this was one of those moments where I wished I could turn to her for advice. She had been kind and wise,

I remembered that much, with a musical laugh and warm eyes and a soft voice. She gave good hugs and cooked tasty food. She read a lot of books and knew the names of all the constellations.

Eventually I built up the courage to crack open the door. I stared at the darkness inside for a moment before stepping in. When I turned on the light, clouds of dust motes churned in the air. On the far wall was an alcove that hosted, surrounded by spectral flowers, a minimalist statue of my mother in black onyx, her head shrouded. Her ashes had been forged into the black diamonds of her eyes. She looked like a sorrowful saint. NADIA MANDALA was engraved on a shiny silver plaque, along with the dates of her birth and death: just thirty-six short years.

"What am I meant to do?" I asked the statue. "I can't lose her again." My voice cracked. "I can't lose anyone else."

The stony figure of my mother didn't answer.

I collapsed on to my knees at her feet. "Why am I seeing such dark things?"

The clicking, slide-projector sound of a magic lantern startled me, coming on by itself. A sprig of dried flowers pressed between glass was caught in the lantern's beam, reflected on the wall. The memory trapped inside it began to play: the image of my mother bent down to pluck jasmine from a bush; she tucked some behind my ear, touching my nose.

"Boop," she said playfully, as I laughed.

The scene began again, playing in a never-ending cycle.

It was one of those short, perfect moments, a glimpse of unspoiled happiness that stood out starkly in the tangled tapestry of a complicated life cut short.

Four other objects were laid out on a dark counter next to the lantern, all of them remnants: sentimental treasures. Chosen by my father, the memories inside them were happy ones that flattered him. They did not reveal the fact that my mother planned to leave him before she died. That he had been the one to take her life, his Shadow acting as reaper as it pushed her from a balcony. My memory of that – stolen by Ruby at her father's behest – had been enough to condemn my father all by itself.

I picked through the remnants on display, playing them in turn. My mother's jet wedding ring contained the memory of my parents exchanging their marital vows in a gothic cathedral. A black wooden rattle captured the moment she first held me in her arms. A silver goblet engraved with an eye contained the memory of a lavish birthday banquet. A small framed portrait of an elderly woman in a black cowl encapsulated the memory of my maternal grandmother's funeral.

My grandmother, Aurora Mandala…

I didn't remember her well but I did recall that her dislike of my father was palpable, even when I was little. She communicated without words – the tone of her voice, her body language, her open gaze always telling the story of her feelings. Cursing him with her eyes.

Like both my parents, Aurora was a Shadow soul.

She came from Jardine, another conquered colony of the ancient Order. The Mandalas were an old-money family forced to kiss the ring of the imperial Chancellor. My grandparents hadn't approved of my father, nor of my mother moving to Providence. They were fearful of the match and with good reason – but the Chancellor was too powerful to resist.

All this I was too young to understand at the time, but with age, that history had coloured itself in, filled out, showing me reflections of the unseen.

In a rush, I recalled the letters my mother received from overseas, warning of a darkness yet to come. I recalled the snatches of conversation I overheard when Aurora called through the switchboard, her voice amplified through the silver intercom on the wall…

"Mama, stop, please!"

"I cannot. You must believe me – I have foreseen a great tragedy. You cannot trust him. That man will kill you."

"That's enough!"

"You must leave him, no matter what the cost. Please, come home. Think of Oliver. If you stay in Providence, terrible things will happen…"

I picked up the framed photo of Aurora, placing it into the lantern's light and casting a new memory to appear on the wall…

My grandmother lies in a silk-lined coffin in the centre of the room, wearing a black hooded dress, her hands crossed over her chest. Eyes are painted on her closed lids and she is surrounded by a vanitas

*of curios depicting the brevity of life: an hourglass, irises, sheet music,
a fruit basket, a candle.*

"Better is the day of death than the day of birth," drones the
priest in his towering black hat, his voice ringing through a hushed
cacophony of coughing and sniffling. "Such is the emptiness of all
mortal goods and pursuits, perishable and transient compared to the
everlasting nature of the soul. We must not fear the end of this life,
for that which awaits us is our true destiny."

Why had my father chosen *this* memory? Maybe he once
came in here to gloat, relishing in the death of the woman
who never liked him. I could imagine as much.

Unprompted, another memory bubbled up in my mind,
not frozen inside an object this time but stirred up from that
same inner seabed where the recollection of my mother's
death had been hidden for so long.

The recollection pulled me into it…

*My mother, my grandmother and I are walking through the
eye-shaped gardens of Obscura House in summer, crossing over the
covered bridge at the pupil pond. The many towers of Providence
loom beyond the trees.*

"I can't stand the weather here," Aurora says in her native
tongue, looking up at the sky. "First, it's sunny, now it looks like
it's going to rain."

"You get used to it," my mother replies brightly.

"How do you get dressed in the morning with such uncertainty?"
Aurora grumbles.

"I don't mind it. It makes me feel alive, never knowing what
the day will be like. Jardine is so hot all the time. It's nice to have

seasons. You should see it when it snows! It's so beautiful. Tristan made us an ice rink to skate on last year, didn't he, Oliver?"

I nod dutifully, as I've been taught to do.

In the present, I recalled that horrible day on the ice, skating on eggshells more like, with a forced smile. My father's kind gestures were always cudgels to beat us with. He didn't create the rink for us; not really. He did it so that next time he asked something of us, he could use it as leverage. How dare we defy him after he'd done something so considerate? We were the bad ones, the ungrateful ones, the disobedient ones. He was the good father and the good husband. He just had a terrible wife and son. That was the problem.

"Look happy," my mother would tell me nervously.

"Why?" I'd ask.

"Your father will be angry if he thinks we're not enjoying ourselves…"

"Well, I don't like it," says Aurora, back in my memory. "Such a dirty place, all moss and chimney soot."

"Oh, come on, Mama," my mother begs. "This is my home now. I've been blessed with two lands, instead of just one. You should be happy for me."

"I wish I could be," she says, "but you've not seen what I have seen."

"Not this again."

"Yes, this. One day I won't be here to protect you from that terrible man. You will be alone in the world."

They exchange a long look laden with hidden meaning.

"Why? Where are you going, Nana?" I ask.

She stoops down to meet my eye, gripping my shoulders. "Someday soon I will die and my soul will fly away like a bird," she says, matter-of-factly. "This is the circle of life."

Behind her, my mother makes a disapproving face.

"Can I still visit you?" I ask.

"Sadly not, but perhaps I can visit you," Aurora says.

"I don't want you to fly away, Nana."

She pats me on the head, watching as my silhouette curls up in a ball, crying the tears that won't come to me.

"Me neither, little Shadow, but it's not up to me. When the darkness comes for you, there is no resisting it. It's my time."

"Mama, stop. There's nothing wrong with you," my mother scolds. "The doctor says you're as healthy as an Olympian."

"Pah. What do doctors know?"

"Don't listen, Oliver," my mother says. "Your grandmother is very dramatic. She likes to think she knows everything about everything, too."

Aurora turns to me and winks, her smile crooked.

"It will happen soon, so you must be prepared," she says. "You must be a big boy and be strong for your mother. Can you promise me that?"

I squeeze her hand, my eyes stinging. "Yes, Nana."

"That's enough now. You're upsetting him," says my mother.

"I'll be watching over you, always," says Aurora…

The recollection faded out. Six weeks later, Aurora was dead. How had she known the end was coming for her?

That wasn't the only thing she'd predicted. Aurora had

been certain that marriage would lead to my mother's undoing, and she'd been right. She had begged my mother to flee, to divorce my father from overseas, to do whatever it took to escape from Providence with her life.

"Trust me, I have a sixth sense for these things," she'd said.

A sixth sense...

The words twigged in my mind, pulling like a fishing line. It was a common phrase, used casually to refer to a feeling of precognition, though some said there really *was* a sixth sense of the soul: one that gave a person the ability to predict the future. It was an old idea, medieval; a myth, really. Experts in psychometry only recognized five extra senses.

Still... I wondered.

I left the shrine room and made my way to the House library, searching rows of dark, leather-bound books, my fingers becoming grubby with dust, though I was careful to put each tome back in its right place. Regular textbooks were no use to me. I needed something a little more esoteric.

Finally, I located it: *A Compendium of Preternatural Psychometry.*

I vaguely remembered flicking through it once as a boy, long ago. I turned to the index at the back, located what I was looking for, and turned to the right page.

... The much-debated sixth sense is a legendary psychometric phenomenon associated with prophecy and soothsaying. The idea remains popular in certain communities but there is no

scientific evidence to support its existence. Supposed visions of
future events are commonly reported by individuals who have
had near-death experiences.

I paused.

Visions of future events ... reported by individuals who have
had near-death experiences. I had died for six minutes, hadn't I?

As a child, Aurora had almost died of influenza. An orthodox priest had read Aurora her last rites before her heart began beating again. I'd forgotten all about it until now, but she used to tell this story often, sometimes over dinner, always laughing, to reaffirm that she was supernaturally wise, claiming she had gained sight beyond the grave. I recalled my mother joking that Aurora had eyes in the back of her head. Maybe she did.

More memories flooded in now: of Aurora pulling me back from the road seconds before a stolen carriage raced past; of my grandmother putting up an umbrella even though the sky was blue, minutes before clouds rolled in and the heavens opened unexpectedly. I recalled her and my mother taking bets about what would happen in novels or plays, and how Aurora would always be right, no matter how improbable her theories sounded. "In the end, it will all be a dream," she'd say, or, "It was the butler who did it," sparking a chorus of groans.

Maybe Aurora had truly seen beyond the veil of reality.

I read on.

… Prophecies have been recorded since the ancient civilizations of Grecia, Ankh and Roma. It is theorized by fringe psychometrists that the process of reanimation creates anomalies in the soul's anatomy.

Maybe the sixth sense was real, a gift I'd inherited from my grandmother, unlocked by dying. If it was real … that meant the assassin was real too.

Stranger things had happened, especially to me. I wasn't imagining it after all.

Blood in her mouth…

A hole in her chest…

Ruby truly was in mortal peril. But first, I had to prove it.

5.

RUBY

"Oliver?"

His name echoed through the endless dark.

There we were, blissfully watching the light show together in the imagined woodland of our dreams but when I turned to smile at him and make some cute remark to amuse him, he'd faded out. He was gone.

He must've woken up, I thought. He'd be back soon, I was sure.

He always came back eventually.

I roasted a marshmallow over the fire, hummed a little ditty to myself for comfort and company, and waited for him to reappear. But he didn't return. The longer he stayed away, the more the scene began to deteriorate in my mind. The tent, the aurora, the woodland, it all wasted away, until I was alone in the dark place with empty hands and a growing feeling of ill-ease.

That was the last night Oliver and I spent together in our minds.

The following evening, I lay lonely beside his empty

body while his Shadow roamed the streets in search of something he wouldn't share with me.

"It's nothing you need to worry about," he said when I asked, but I could tell that he was lying. I could always tell.

It was the same the next night, and the next. Oliver was changing in front of my eyes, disconnecting from reality. I talked to him but he wasn't really listening. His Shadow on the wall appeared depressed, always slumped or hunched or pacing anxiously.

Then there were his strange new reading habits. When we were not gathered around the pentagon table at the meetings we attended as part of the New Order, when we were not discussing strategies and summaries, attending ribbon cuttings and dedications, Oliver was always surrounded by books. Old, dusty books full of myths and silly stories, with dubious covers featuring demonic beasts, skulls and snakes and crystals. Those were the most unnerving kind.

Weeks passed. I barely saw him. I wasn't sure when he'd last slept. The food I brought for him sat cold, untouched. The curtains were drawn, though it was the middle of the afternoon, and he had the pale, slightly greasy look of someone who needed to take a shower and go for a walk. The white streak in his hair was more noticeable than ever.

"Don't you think you should take a break?" I said, after weeks of this, leaning against the doorway of the library. "It's not good for you to sit in that chair for hours."

He didn't answer, he was somewhere far away. The room felt cold, as if a window had been left open. I crept over, lightly kissed his neck.

"Am I a phantom?" I whispered. "Can I no longer be seen or heard?"

The darkness in his eyes dissipated, revealing the brown irises.

"Sorry, sorry," he said, smiling crookedly.

I kissed him again, my lips lingering too long on his. He was back. We were back. Everything was fine and perfectly normal.

"Learn anything interesting?" I asked.

"Lots of things, actually," he said, more animated than I'd seen him in a while. "Get this: in the medieval period, in certain parts of the world, it was believed that *eating* the soul of a recently deceased person could give the diner visions of the future."

I pulled a face. "Please tell me you're not going to put that theory into practice," I said.

"I might," he said, spinning round in the chair, knocking me off my feet and causing me to fall into his lap. "I bet yours would taste delicious." He moved to bite my neck, like a vampire.

"Stop!" I squealed, but I really meant *Don't stop*. This was the most attention he'd paid me in days. Weeks. I looped my arms round him, my legs propped over the arm of the chair, giggling in delight. "I miss you," I said.

"I'm right here."

"Are you, though? Come play with me," I said, pouting. "I'm bored. I'm practically wasting away with loneliness."

"What about Octavia and Rani? What are they up to?"

"Octavia and Rani have their own lives. They work. They go on dates. They *do* things. Fun things."

"You want to go on a date?"

"Don't you?" I tugged eagerly at the lapel of the waistcoat he was wearing over an untucked shirt, collar unbuttoned, sleeves rolled up. "Everything is politics now. Every night and day. Can't we have a little fun too?"

His expression softened, melting at the edges.

"It's not a good idea for us to be gallivanting around town right now with an assassin on the loose," he said, shaking his head. "They missed us the first time but they might try again. It's too risky. We should keep a low profile."

I sighed. "That's sensible, I suppose. Boring, but sensible."

"We'll do something soon, I promise," he said, kissing me tenderly. "I just need to finish what I'm working on."

"Which is what, exactly?" I asked.

He bit down on his lip, dropping his gaze. He was definitely hiding something from me.

"I'm … not sure yet. I'm trying to protect us, just in case there's another attempt. I'll tell you if I learn anything useful. Soon we'll go out to dinner … or something," and with that, he went back to his work.

We did not, in fact, go out to dinner "or something".

I returned to Renato House in a foul temper. The drive seemed to take twice as long as it should've done. A mysterious messenger in a white woollen hat was waiting for me there. Without a word, he handed me a parcel and scampered off before I could thank him (not that I would've thanked him, in the mood I was in).

I unwrapped it, revealing a pearl-handled dagger, which reflected my tense expression in its shining blade.

Who would send me a knife?

Ominous, it thrummed and throbbed with the power of a remnant, so I pulled off the thin red gloves that served as a layer of protection, preventing me from being overwhelmed by all the psyche I could touch. When the bare skin of my fingers wrapped round the dagger, I was pulled into a vivid, recently recorded memory. Perpetua glared at me icily, from where she sat on a stool before a dull concrete backdrop.

"*Meet me at midnight,*" she said, "*at the Necropolis. Come alone. Tell no one. You should use this for protection … or not.*" She folded her arms tightly. "*I don't care either way.*"

The vision paled, returning me to the present.

"Perpetua," I said, mournfully.

After the incident at the Accord, I'd asked Octavia to try and make contact with our former friends, using her gift of Song to speak directly into their minds, but her communications were blocked. Through the whisper network, the psychic grapevine of sound that Octavia was able to access, we learned that Perpetua was now leading the Wallflower gang, which specialized in stolen memories. Ash was the ruler of the Firehands, who… Well, they mostly just liked to set things on fire, but they also liberated supplies from factories and warehouses.

This strange, sinister message was the first I'd heard from them since we'd told them we had accepted Lord Cordata's offer to form a government. And she wanted me to tell *no one*? Surely she didn't mean I couldn't even tell Oliver?

Whatever trouble we're in, we're in it together…

But were we? He was keeping secrets from me, I could tell. If I told him I planned to meet Perpetua, would he come up with a reason for us not to attend? He'd probably say it was too dangerous.

So I decided to go alone.

That night, when my mother and the servants were asleep, I pulled on a hooded cloak and a necklace that obscured my identity: a dark, eye-shaped pendant on a chain, a trinket stolen from Oliver's nightstand. It used light and Shadow to fool the observer, superimposing a false impression over my face. He'd been too absorbed in his candlelit studies to notice its absence.

I rode on the crowded omnibus rather than taking a Renato-branded carriage. Several pairs of eyes landed on me curiously, but no one identified me. The pendant was doing its job. I was invisible once more, just like when I'd been a soulless hollow.

It gave me a little thrill, to be up to my old tricks again.

The Necropolis was the main cemetery in the city of Providence, where all the bodies were buried, regardless of class. It was bigger than the largest palace or park, a long grassy rectangle that cut into the suburban neighbourhoods of the Second Borough. As I watched, a coffin train steamed into the station nearby, letting out a whistle as porters filled the platform to unload their morbid cargo. A small crowd of mourners flocked out in front, their veils and coat-tails flapping like bird wings in the growing wind, their hoarse cries cutting through the silence of the night. Head down, I pushed past them and slipped through the great wrought-iron gates.

The graves here were grouped by soul type, the fanciest ones embedded with gemstones in their House colours. Spark. Shadow. Song. Spirit. Heart. Even members of the same family were kept apart, divided by psyche.

The headstones at the front of the cemetery were clean and new with fresh flowers but the further back I went, the older the memorials became. Ancient tombstones fought their way through the ground, with gnarly trees and long grass giving way here and there to weathered statues, rain-stained cherubs and weeping angels, their souls burning in their chests.

Through the clouds of fog ahead, a shimmering spectre emerged, causing my breath to catch in my throat. A pale, almost translucent figure with cobweb hair and cold eyes fixed me with a deathly glare. Her clothes were slightly old-fashioned, like a relic of an era long passed, and she seemed to exist in spite of the world around her, as if occupying another plane of existence.

"Oh, hi, Perpetua," I said.

When I pulled off the pendant, she recognized me. She nodded, her expression stony as the graves around her.

"Come," she said. "Unless you want to rest in peace like the bodies you walk over." She looked pointedly at the grass beneath my feet as I gingerly moved back on to the path.

We had never been close friends, not exactly. I wasn't sure Perpetua was close to anyone. But we had been on the same team. Now, though, we were distinctly estranged. On the bright side, she didn't attack me at first sight. It was something.

I trailed her to a moss-furred mausoleum at the very rear of the cemetery, its padlock broken open. The pearl-handled dagger was stashed in my skirts, just in case, though I doubted Perpetua would have given it to me if she thought I might use it against her. That meant she probably wasn't planning on fighting me. Probably.

In the dark, damp-smelling tomb, Ash leaned against the cracked wall. Androgynous, with a shaved head and a scowl, they briefly met my eyes before cracking their knuckles and looking away, as if they didn't trust themself to gaze upon me without falling for my lies.

"Well, this is nice," I said, eyeing a preposterously large spider.

"I'm surprised you came," they said.

"All a bit cloak and dagger, isn't it?" I said, dropping my hood and looking around at the assembled urns and coffins. "We could've just met up at a grimy alehouse on the outskirts of town or something."

"It wouldn't be good for us to be witnessed with you, now you are lapdog for the New Order," said Perpetua. Illuminated by a single lantern, I could see how tired she looked, her white-blonde flyaway hair frazzled, dark crescents under her eyes.

"Ruin your street credibility, would it?" I said.

"It might. But also someone might try to kill you and I don't want to get blood on my coat," she said.

"It's good to see you too, Petra."

"Don't make nice with me, Iris, Ruby, Lily … whoever you are, I don't know any more." When I smirked, she scowled and pointed a finger at me. "I am serious. This is a warning. You are in danger. If you weren't, I would gladly never look at your face again."

"Me? Or me and Oliver?"

"If you are in danger, then he is a dead man walking," said Perpetua, miming a slit to the throat. "The people will tolerate you, for a while. They make excuses for you, at least. They will say you're young and naïve. So long as they think of you as a victim, stolen from your servant mother in hiding, you will not get a knife in the back. But Oliver was the devil's heir. If the people turn against you, they will tear him apart. He should not walk the streets without protection. Better, he should travel in disguise."

"So that's why you wanted to meet at midnight in the graveyard? To warn me?"

"It suits us both," said Ash. "We wouldn't want to ask a *lady* such as yourself to slop around with us plebian scum in public, would we?" They mimed clutching at pearls. They too looked thinner and harsher in the dim light, their shaved head growing out patchily.

"I'm plebian scum too, remember."

"Pfft. Your father was a lord," they combatted.

"A *rebel* lord," I said, "and my mother was a servant of the House. When we first met, I was stealing to survive, living on the streets, a fugitive on the run. Come on, give me some credit here, please! It was my idea to destroy the Eye network. I'm not exactly the bourgeoisie."

"What do you want, a trophy? A cookie?" said Perpetua. "Aren't you getting enough praise and attention from the press? What, you need *our* approval too?"

Ouch. "I just want you to know I'm with you, not against you. Whatever privilege I had, it was lost when my soul was shattered."

"It doesn't matter. You're one of *them* now." Perpetua spat at the ground. "The papers might fawn over you, trying to paint you as the people's princess, but you're a blue blood. You walked away from everything we fought for. Now you stand there on the balcony, waving, as that slimy eel Cordata makes a speech — and you think we can still be friends?"

"You … you were there?" I said.

"We were there. We wanted to see the traitors for ourselves, with our own eyes."

For a second, I envisioned the gun-toting assassin wearing their faces, shuddering as the dark vision gripped me.

"You too?" I asked Ash.

"Against my better judgement," they said.

"Did you see who shot at us?"

"We saw nothing of note," snapped Perpetua. "Especially not your new government."

I wanted to believe them.

"We can't fix all of Providence's problems overnight, not when the Order left us with so many. We have enemies outside our gates—"

"Which enemies?" asked Ash.

"The Governor of Constitution, for one."

"Is that what Cordata told you?" they scoffed. "He's full of it. The Governor is a bleeding-heart Heart, just like the Premier."

"What about the Empress of Arctica? Because she's sweeping up Order colonies like ashes from the fire. We need to stand firm against her."

Perpetua flinched. "You think you could stop the Empress if she wanted to take your land? She rules the frozen lands through ice-cold terror. She stalks like a Shadow in the night. Every soul alive trembles in terror of her. It ... is actually quite impressive, or it would be if she were not such a vampire. She is always twelve moves ahead, no matter what you do. If she wanted it, Providence would be hers before you even knew it was gone."

It felt like there was something lodged in my throat.

"I never pretended to be an expert," I said.

"Well, you should be, if you're going to rule a country," said Ash.

"Sometimes the right thing to do is complicated," I insisted. "It doesn't exactly stand out and scream at you, 'I'm the right thing! Pick me!'"

"Aw, it must be so difficult, living in a fancy villa, sleeping safe and sound in silk sheets, being waited on, eating pineapples…" said Perpetua.

"*You* could eat pineapples and sleep between silk sheets too, both of you, if you'd come with us and let us protect you. You could be safe."

"There is no safe. Never. Octavia, Rani and Gus should know better." Perpetua clucked her tongue. "The Order destroyed their lives the first time and now they're back for seconds? They think the snow leopards won't eat their faces but, believe me, they *will* eat their faces!"

"What snow leopards?" I said, after a beat.

"It is an old saying, back home. Only fools watch snow leopards eat people's faces then try to make them pets. They think it won't happen to them, but it will. The Order is the reason why my Papa is dead. Why Birdie and Mr Sharma are dead. They imprisoned your own mother. I will never forgive or forget, and neither will the people."

"Is that a threat?"

"Not from me." She was scowling, her thin lips twisted, her sharply lined face drawn.

"What does that mean?" I asked. "From someone else then?"

Silence. Ash gave an unconvincing shrug.

I took a deep breath and asked the question I dreaded

hearing the answer to most of all: "Do you know who did it? Who shot at us?"

"Hell, no," said Ash, firmly, meeting my eye this time. "As angry as I am, I wouldn't stand for that shit. No way."

"None of the gangs have claimed the attack," said Perpetua. "The word is, it was someone within the Order itself."

My heart began to beat faster. "Is that a theory, or do you actually know something?"

"Just a rumour. But people are talking."

"Do you really trust all those aristocrats you're cosying up to?" asked Ash. "Harmonia, Memoria … Cordata himself? One of them could still be loyal to the Chancellor. Or they could be trying to frame the resistance. The more unstable they make us appear, the better the case for them remaining in power."

I recalled Cordata's panic … Lady Memoria's fear … Lord Harmonia's horror. Unless they were all acting to dupe us, their reactions had been genuine.

"I doubt it. We looked like idiots, standing up there waving as a riot started below."

"Well, it wasn't the Wallflowers of the Second Borough," said Perpetua. "Some of our members may have joined in in the spirit of things, but it was a, how you say, *carpe diem*?"

"It wasn't the Firehands of the Fifth Borough either," said Ash. "You can trust me on that, fire soul to fire soul." They tapped their chest. "It's not the Hosts of the Fourth Borough either. They're pacifists."

"The Whisperers specialize in misinformation. They spread vicious rumours and snoop, selling secrets to the press," said Perpetua. "Assassinations aren't really their style."

"If it was any of the gangs, it would be the Shades of the First Borough," said Ash. "They want to see House Obscura dismantled. But they swore they didn't do it."

"Well they would, wouldn't they?"

"The leader of the Shades said, and I quote: 'If we did it, we would boast of it with great honour.'"

"Then who was it?" I asked.

Silence.

I took a deep breath. I hadn't wanted to tell them about Oliver's vision — it felt like a betrayal — but perhaps they could help.

"There's something I need to tell you," I said. "Oliver saw something, through the Shadow. A vision. He saw the assassin before we were shot at. He warned him about a 'thousand-faced monster'. I was the target in his dream and in real life. He won't admit as much but I suspect that he's driving himself mad trying to work out who it was and what it means."

They exchanged another terse look.

"If you know anything, please, just tell me."

They *did* know something. I could see it in the way they avoided my gaze; I could hear it in their silence.

"There is a reason we asked you to come here," said Perpetua.

She pulled out a folded sheet of paper and handed it to me.

I opened it up, revealing a cartoonish propaganda poster. Six people were depicted on it, drawn in unflattering caricature: Chancellor Obscura, Premier Cordata, Lady Memoria, Lord Harmonia, Oliver, and me. Oliver's nose was inaccurately large, while my face was unnaturally round.

SIX SHOTS TO FREEDOM! was printed beneath.

"A shot for each of you," Ash spelled out, rather unnecessarily.

"I got that. Why the old Chancellor, though?"

"He's still alive, I guess?" they replied. "If all of you are removed, the Order will be dismantled. Anarchy will prevail. I could probably get down with that, now I think about it."

"Who made this?" I asked.

"Someone with great artistic ability," said Perpetua. I cut eyes at her. "What? You cannot deny that. Their talent is wasted in this vocation."

I looked at the poster again, my hands shaking slightly. I tried to soak up the document's psyche, looking for a memory hidden within its print, but there was nothing. It was clean, like the reliquaries that once contained a lost piece of my soul.

That only made it even more suspicious, in my opinion.

"Where did you find this?" I asked.

"Nailed to a fence," said Perpetua. "They're everywhere. I saw a group of girls handing them out. Gen addicts, probably, promised drugs in exchange for easy work. Someone is clearly pulling strings behind scenes."

"If you were out in the streets a bit more instead of hiding away in your *villa*, you'd have noticed them too," said Ash,

"There are more rumours," said Perpetua, before I could respond. "Which might or might not be connected to this poster. Someone is recruiting members of the five gangs."

"One of the Firehands dropped off the face of the earth," said Ash. "We thought he'd been arrested but I bumped into him yesterday, walking free and fine as day. He said he was part of an exciting new movement, like he was trying to sell me something. He didn't want to say too much about it, but he used that phrase: *Six shots to freedom*."

"That … oh, that is not good."

"He invited me to a meeting. Tomorrow night, ten p.m. At the old Visage factory," said Ash. "The one with five chimneys. What you do with this information is up to you."

"We could infiltrate it together?" I tried. "It could be fun, all of us up to our necks in it again, together, like the old days."

"Not 'we'," said Perpetua. "No '*we*'. You. *Your* problem."

"You won't help?"

"No. You are with us, or against us," she said. "We did you a favour by telling you already."

I looked to Ash, my eyes appealing. "You too?"

"The public will turn on you," they said. "They always do, in the end. So you should probably watch your back."

Ash turned to depart, but I called out: "Wait!"

"What?" said Perpetua, stonily.

"If you learn any more about whoever's behind this, will you contact me?" I asked.

Perpetua shrugged. "If I'm not too busy, maybe. But, like I said, this is your problem now, Ruby Renato."

They disappeared as quickly as they'd emerged from the dark, leaving me alone in the cold mausoleum.

Back in my room at Renato House, I pulled the paper out again: SIX SHOTS TO FREEDOM!

In my head, I heard the *crack crack* of bullets being fired.

Someone wanted rid of us, possibly multiple people. Even a multitude of people.

I needed to go to this meeting tomorrow night. It would be dangerous to go alone, but it would be even more dangerous not to go at all. I couldn't rely on Oliver – he was consumed by his studies. Perpetua and Ash wouldn't help me. But I knew who I could count on. The same person I could always turn to for help.

My mind called out to Octavia, the sound travelling across the city in half a second.

What's up, babe? came her voice in reply.

"How do you and Rani fancy getting in a little trouble?"

She squealed so loudly I winced.

Ooh, I thought you'd never ask, she said.

6.

OLIVER

My mind had wandered without me knowing it again, and I had no idea where it had wandered to. I watched Ruby in the phoenix-embellished red dress running up a flight of stairs from behind, her long red curls tumbling. At the top, she turned into a room, along the corridor to the left, but as soon as she passed through the doorway, a loud gunshot resounded, throwing her backwards.

"Oliver?"

My name returned me to the present. I turned and saw Ruby, the real, living Ruby, come into view. She gently placed her hand on my arm. The room filled in around her.

Real, this was real. It was hard to be sure these days, but it had the sharp, rough, slightly jarring feel of reality.

We were at Cordata House, seated at a long banqueting table draped in golden cloth and laden with all the most delectable delicacies the House of Heart had to offer. Golden bread rolls dusted with herbs. Glistening wings of spiced chicken. Platters of silver fish in a thick creamy sauce. Arrays of cured meats and all manner of cheeses. It was the sort of spread that kept people loyal and we all filled our plates with it.

Our weekly peace dinner at Cordata House. Every Friday, we came to stuff our faces while avoiding difficult questions.

Ruby narrowed her eyes as I suppressed a yawn behind one hand.

"Tired already?" she said. "And among such scintillating company?" She inclined her head in Lord Harmonia's direction, catching him mid-stream in a monologue about audio production quality. The corners of her lips tugged with a smile.

"I was up late last night," I explained, rubbing the back of my neck.

"You were investigating again?"

While I was learning a lot of occult info about the sixth sense, I wasn't discerning much of practical use. But I wasn't giving up yet. How could I, when her life was on the line?

"All this because of a single dream?" she pressed.

"Not … exactly."

No, not one single dream. Night after night, the same vision.

Servers swooped in with ornate silver domed serving trays, distracting her.

Along with the representatives of the five Houses, I recognized some of the other guests, including Countess Cavendish, Ruby's former employer, who once directed Ruby to steal part of her own lost soul. She gave me a dainty wave, her golden gloves matching her golden dress, which she wore as a member of the House of Heart.

Another familiar face was Amelia Millefleur, whom I'd once mistaken for Ruby. When my father attempted to have Ruby wiped from my mind, my memories became corrupted, allowing Amelia's face to randomly fill the vacuum the procedure left behind. I'd thought I was in love with her for almost a year, when it was Ruby I was pining for all along.

We caught each other's eye, then awkwardly looked away. I could feel Ruby simmering quietly in embarrassment beside me, though she tried her best to look unbothered.

When offered, I accepted a second glass of ambrosia.

The *clink-clink-clink* of cutlery on glass called our attention to Premier Cordata, on his feet.

"I have a small announcement to make," he said, holding a gold fork. "One that I hope will please you all. It shows that all our hard work over the last few weeks has paid off and that people are beginning to trust us."

The hubbub died down.

"As you may recall, I had dinner with the Constitutional ambassador last night and I'm glad to say it was a success. It was such a success, in fact, that Ambrose Fairchild, the Governor of Constitution himself, will be visiting us next week to discuss our future trading partnership."

A surprised murmur ran round the room, like an excited child.

"Our relationship with Constitution has always been

difficult, to a degree. They had … concerns about the former Chancellor's authoritarian tendencies, shall we say? Under the New Order, I hope we can put the past firmly behind us and start anew. If we are successful, we will already have achieved something the previous regime could not, improving the lives of all our citizens here at home and in the colonies. No child shall starve, if we are in step with Constitution."

We had never received a great deal of global news in Providence under the Chancellor, but we knew that Constitution was wealthy with an abundance of resources, a formidable superpower. Governor Fairchild was known as a beacon in the world of international politics. An alliance with him would be a win for Cordata and a sign that the New Order could restore prosperity to our fractured country. In fact, I was surprised that Cordata had managed to persuade him to visit our unstable shores in the first place. The Governor was meant to be a cautious man.

All the same…

"This isn't really the best time for a state visit," I said. "We just escaped an assassination attempt."

"Well, I didn't exactly have much say in the matter, to be frank," said Cordata. "The Governor was quite insistent about coming."

Ah. So the Governor was calling the shots.

"Are you implying that he invited himself?" asked Lady Memoria.

"He's muscling in, obviously," said Lord Harmonia,

dabbing at his mouth with a napkin. "He can smell blood, like a shark."

Cordata smiled toothily but beads of sweat peppered his forehead, his eyebrows sloping upwards in concern.

"We need him as an ally, to protect us against the Empress," he said. "We need him for trade. If the embargo continues, it will be disastrous. He wants to see for himself that Providence is recovering before he'll allow imports to cross the border. It's extremely important that this visit goes smoothly. We cannot afford another … mishap."

"'*Mishap*'," Lord Harmonia muttered. "Is that what you call the attack at the Accord? That was a bloody big 'mishap', if you ask me."

"No one did ask you, actually," Ruby murmured beside me.

Lord Harmonia's head snapped up, drawn to the sound of whispering, his face curdled unpleasantly. People said he never missed a thing, that he could hear gossip from the opposite side of town. If he did, then he already knew what we thought of him.

"*Hmpf.*" He tightened his necktie, as if imagining it a noose. "Kids these days … think they know everything."

"I thought we were meant to be voting on things," I said.

"What is there to vote on?" said Lord Cordata, amiably. "Surely none of you will object? It will be our great honour to host the Governor."

"Never trust someone who invites themselves to a party," tutted Lord Harmonia. "We should not be pressured into making an alliance with a nation that could crush us like bugs."

"Is that not *exactly* the kind of alliance we ought to be making?" said Lady Memoria. Today, the flower pinned to her chest was an iris. It meant *I have a message for you*.

"Enough!" shouted Cordata, as everyone began talking at once. "The Governor is coming and that is that. We shall make sure he receives a historic welcome, with each House putting their best foot forward. For now, please, let us enjoy the rest of our evening."

I sat grimly in silence, brooding over what this might mean – another assassination attempt, perhaps. And soon.

Premier Cordata appeared behind me, scattering my thoughts. "Lord Obscura," he said. "May I have a word? In private."

He steered me away into the shadows in the corner. Ruby narrowed her eyes, watching suspiciously over her shoulder. He kept his arm round me.

"You know, out of everyone here, I think I value your opinion most of all," he said.

Flattery, but it wouldn't work on me.

"As the man who destroyed the Eye network—"

"That was really Ruby more than me," I said.

"Nonsense, dear boy. Your contribution was crucial. A creation of the Shadow can only be destroyed by the Shadow, and you are the most powerful Shadow soul of all."

OK, maybe the flattery was working on me a little bit...

"It wasn't what Ruben and I intended," Cordata went

on, "nor the most elegant solution to the problem – and yet you saw your opportunity and you took it." He made a fist. "I admire your go-getting spirit. Reminds me of myself when I was younger."

I waited for the *but* I knew was coming.

"However, the absence of the Eye network has left us somewhat … vulnerable." He was getting to his point, via the scenic route. "Given what happened at the Accord and the somewhat fragile situation, I wondered if you might be open to keeping an eye on things?" He said this in a low, conspiratorial tone. "It's vital that the gangs don't disrupt the Governor's imminent visit. We can't scare him off or have him think that we're easy pickings. I need you to keep tabs on the situation, *discreetly* of course."

I stared at him, into him, trying to interpret his expression. It seemed sincere enough. He had one of those warm, open faces with a broad smile and soft brows, though his forehead was slightly sweaty.

"It feels like a betrayal for me to spy on the gangs," I said. "What about the Observers?"

"Ah, well, you see, that's the tricky bit. We could, technically, use them, of course, but it won't make us look too strong or honourable after we promised not to in the Accord we all signed. It would be a lot of paperwork to get it up and running again. Red tape; miles of it. The Governor's visit presents us with a ticking clock. Things take time in a democracy, as it turns out."

"Have you consulted the other Council members?" I asked.

"No. No one." We looked over at the other heads of House, whispering furtively as they debated the pros and cons of aligning ourselves with Constitution and its friends.

"I suppose I can take a cursory look," I said.

"Wonderful! It might be wise for us to observe the Governor too," he added quickly, and in a quieter voice than before. "He may be a fellow Heart soul, but not all of us are as sweet as sugar, as they say."

Spying on the gangs was one thing but spying on another world leader sounded like the sort of crime I could be executed for.

"What are you expecting me to observe?" I asked.

"Hopefully, nothing. But in the name of national security, it would be prudent," he said, before leaning in and lowering his voice again. 'Between you and me, he may well have ulterior motives for stopping by."

"Go on," I urged.

"The armies of Constitution are commanding and vast. They visit countries with an offer they cannot refuse. They use no violence, they take no slaves, but they strip a land of its independence, its culture. They take it and make it their own. Constitution certainly has the power to take Providence in its weakness, should they want to."

I swallowed. The old Order had spied on its subjects as a means of mass population control. Now I was about to do the same.

And yet ... the gangs might have plotted the assassination

attempt. The Governor might be our enemy. Maybe he was even implicated in Ruby's death, somehow.

I had to be certain.

"I'll do it. But only this once."

"Of course! Fantastic. Good chap." Cordata slapped me on the back again as if we were old friends before disappearing into the crowd. There was another warning here but I couldn't quite discern it yet. Something about morality being a slippery slope. Wicked rulers often did not begin that way. Power corrupted the good. Very few could withstand its influence.

I caught myself in the mirror as I moved round the edge of the room, staying close to the wall. I looked sallow, sunken, sour. For a second, my father's face flashed before me, superimposed over mine.

A small band started up, playing the dreary dirge known as "Ode to an Old Soul". There were, I noticed, six musicians, including the bassoonist. Something tickled my memory, giving me a prickly, hypervigilant feeling, but it didn't connect in my mind yet. Six pillars. Six chandeliers. Six soldiers on the door ... and I swore there had only been five moments ago.

Everywhere I looked, I saw sixes. Six birds in the tree outside. Six carriages in the courtyard. Six cups. Six olives. Six cherubs on the light fixtures...

I blinked, then rubbed my eyes, but they were still there.

I grabbed another glass of ambrosia from a server passing with a tray, downing it to wash away the bitter taste of something I couldn't name.

Before I could catch my breath, Lady Memoria caught my arm. A statuesque older woman, she had a commanding profile and an authoritative presence, the effect spoiled only slightly by the cat hair on her skirts.

"We should talk, in confidence, about the future," she said.

The future. Ruby with her mouth open, blood on her chest.

"What about it?" I sighed.

"When will you and Lady Renato make a commitment?"

"We signed the Accord, didn't we?"

"No, not that. I mean to each other!"

Heat flushed my face, rising up my neck. "Is that any of your business?" I asked.

"The people need security. The union of two Houses would go a long way towards that. If you hesitate, you might find yourself too late."

I followed her eyeline across the room, where Ruby was conversing with Lady Memoria's grandson Henry, a shovel-jawed youth with sculpted muscles who had a penchant for rugby and flower arranging.

I bristled defensively. Memoria was wrong – Ruby loved *me*. There was no way she'd be interested in this ridiculously handsome, surprisingly sensitive, devastatingly attractive hunk … Oh no. Oh god…

With an enigmatic, arch-browed look, Lady Memoria moved away again, leaving me alone with my thoughts.

Always a dangerous thing.

Anxious, I drained yet another flute of sparkling ambrosia.

Ruby and I had history, carriages full of baggage. Her father had trained her as a spy and sent her to infiltrate my mind. In return, my father had shattered her soul while possessing my body. We had forgotten each other. I had thought I was in love with someone else…

Like I said, baggage. A train station full of it.

But we were past all that. We had told each other everything.

Well, almost everything. There were, admittedly, still secrets I was keeping from her, like the fact that it was my fault she'd been returned to the Order in the first place. Her father, Ruben Renato, had wanted to track down his missing, perhaps powerfully talented, child. He had begged my father, and my father employed me to locate her. In the form of dark birds, my Shadow had roamed the countryside in flocks, flying from cottage to cottage until I found the red-haired woman whose picture I'd been given, and the young girl who had Ruben's charm. When the Inspectors came for them in black wagons, it was because of me. When Mara was imprisoned and Lily made into Ruby Renato, it was because of me. Had my father known Ruben's true loyalties, he would not have assisted, and yet I had done his bidding without question.

I was too afraid of losing her to tell her the truth. I feared her judgement, her disappointment, or how she might cool on me. Ruby and I had promised there would be no more secrets between us, but here I was hoarding them again like a greedy dragon.

And yet Ruby was keeping secrets from me too, I thought, as I argued silently with myself. I had seen her travel to meet Perpetua. I knew about the secret rebel meeting at the factory she planned to attend. But I had no real grounds to be angry with her. Not when I was hiding so much from her. That was the thing that kept us bound in silence.

Perhaps she would be better off with someone forthright and flawless, like Henry. I glanced again at him. There he was, nodding earnestly as Ruby spoke. By leaning in and reading their lips, I could follow along with their conversation.

"I've never actually had a pet," she was saying. "Can you believe that? My mother had a favourite sheep we always said hello to on our way into the village but whenever I begged her for a dog, she said they were too much like a second child, and one was enough."

She'd never told *me* that.

I shook my head at myself. Stop it, Oliver. You're being jealous again.

But she was standing so close to him, and smiling so easily.

"Perhaps you could adopt a new familiar for House Renato," said Henry. "If only phoenixes were real, that would be ideal. Or perhaps Lady Memoria will let you take in one of her new kittens. There's a ginger one you might like. He's very feisty."

"How many cats does your grandmother have now?"

"At the last count, twelve. She says you can never have

too many, but the odour of her abode gives me pause for thought."

Ruby's laugh rang out. Was there a part of her that could be happier with someone less complicated? Less ... broken?

People floated in and out. Snatches of conversation. The sound of clinking glasses and burbling conversation faded away, paling along with the room.

"Lord Obscura, we must discuss your father's upcoming trial." (That was the Premier's aide, a pompous man in a powdered wig.)

"How good to see you again, Lord Obscura! I thought you were your father there for a moment." (That was Countess Cavendish, her plate laden with macarons.)

"Would you like a palate cleanser, Lord Obscura?" (An unknown server handing me yet another glass...)

"Go easy on the ambrosia, OK?" (Ruby, knowing me too well.)

"Lord Obscura, you really must come to my gentleman's club some time. All the rising stars of the jazz scene have played there, so if ever you're looking to sow some wild oats, you know where to find us." (Lord Harmonia, passing me another glass...)

I ducked behind a pillar and crashed right into Amelia Millefleur, flushing as the memory of her-as-Lily waltzed through my head. Holding her light in my arms, tall and graceful, her blue eyes sparkling, her blonde hair tumbling over her shoulders as I spun her around... I'd spent so much time dreaming of her face, unaware that it was actually the *wrong* face. Memories implanted by my father. What a mess.

"Oh, hello, Oliver," she said, showing the whites of her eyes.

"Hi, Amelia," I said, cringing violently on the inside.

"So, uh, how are you?" she said.

"Right now? Slightly mortified, to be honest. You?"

"Same. Perhaps I shouldn't have come," she said, playing with one of the bangles on her wrist. "I hardly know anyone here. I don't have many friends any more, to be honest. It's funny, how quickly people drop you when your mother is arrested for torturing children. They all think I must be rotten like her. You know what they say, about the fruit of the tree… I thought maybe you were one of the few people here who could understand that."

"I do, as it happens," I said.

"She wasn't always such a terrible person, I'm sure. There was one time I remember, when I was ten, when I fell off a horse. I was in a coma for a week. Doctors didn't think I'd make it. Broke my spine. They had to put a metal plate in, just so I could stand. She cared for me so sweetly and gently all that time. She was a bad person, but a good mother. You know what I mean?"

"Not really," I said. "I think mine was an even worse father than he was a leader."

We fell quiet.

"I'm sorry I got you confused with Ruby," I said. "That was … weird. And awkward."

115

Amelia looked away, pulling an inscrutable face.

"Consider it already forgotten," she said, though clearly it was not. "Take care, Oliver."

She walked away.

Could this night possibly get any more uncomfortable?

As if in answer to my question, the lights flickered, off, on, off. The room began to spin. My vision darkened, vignetting around the edges. *What now?* With a sinking feeling, I turned to face the band, who were playing "Ode to an Old Soul" again. My eyes jumped quickly to the large ice sculpture on the table, shaped like a heart.

I had seen this before.

I had seen it in my dream.

"Hello?" said Ruby, waving at me. "Are you still in there?"

The assassin was coming, yet the punch was not yet spilled. The ice sculpture was not yet shattered. The attack hadn't yet happened.

What I had seen in my vision had been a warning. Now it was happening for real.

But I could still stop it. There was still time to stop it.

In panic, I grabbed Ruby's wrist, pulling us towards the door.

"Hey! Wait! You're squeezing a little hard there," she said.

"Something bad is about to happen."

"Oliver, you're scaring me."

"Just listen. Watch," I said, forcibly. I turned her to face the Premier and his wife. "Any second now, the Premier and Lady Cordata will start arguing."

We stared at them, waiting.

"Is this some sort of prank?" Ruby said. "Because you know I hate pranks. I still haven't forgiven Gus for egging the windows on your birthday."

On the other side of the room Lady Cordata drew back, her face spoiling.

"Don't you talk to me like that, Clements," she snapped. She turned on her heel, her long braids swinging.

"See?" I said. "I told you. Now Lady Cordata is about to bump into that server carrying punch." I turned Ruby towards the door to watch. On cue, the collision occurred.

"Lord Harmonia will try to dodge it," I narrated, seconds ahead of the action, "but he'll hit the table. The ice sculpture will fall and shatter." And so it played out, the shards of ice causing the server to scream in shock as they sprayed the room.

"OK, OK, I believe you," said Ruby. She sounded more curious than frightened. "What the hell is going on, Oliver?"

"The assassin will arrive any second," I said, pushing us through the crowd. "We have to get out of here."

"Assassin?" she shrilled. "You didn't think to mention that first?"

But her hand slipped from mine as Lady Memoria cut between us. "Pardon me. Coming through."

A blur caught in the corner of my eye. A fast-moving figure crossed the room with fierce determination.

Hooded and cloaked, they raised an arm...

Ruby, blood in her mouth...

Ruby, falling to the ground.

I reacted instinctively, closing the space between us and slamming the stranger against the wall, cracking the plaster slightly and attracting the attention of the other guests.

"What do you want?" I demanded, in a low, thundering voice.

On the wall, my Shadow metamorphosed, becoming giant, monstrous. The assassin's hood slipped…

A total stranger stared back at me, a gold envelope in his trembling hands. It wasn't the green-eyed assassin, but a helpless boy.

"I-I'm just here to d-deliver a m-message," he stammered. "From the Governor of Constitution." A wave of camera flashes followed.

Falling back, I released my hold as my Shadow stood down. A teenage messenger with a baby face. It was so obvious that he was from Constitution. The accent, the distinctive ship motif on his tunic, the apple seal and the fear in his eyes…

The silence of the room filled with whispering and muttering.

"Have you lost your mind, Oliver Obscura?" snapped Lady Memoria, clipping over briskly. "What are you doing to him, the poor boy?"

"I'm sorry," I told the messenger, my heart still hammering. I dusted him off. "I apologize. I … I overreacted. I thought you were an intruder. I'm sorry, everyone – I thought he was reaching for a weapon."

"A weapon?" cried Lady Harmonia. "It's an envelope,

dear. There are five guards on the door. You sound more paranoid than Lord Harmonia."

Five guards. My gaze shot to the door. Only five? Weren't there six before?

Premier Cordata forced a laugh to lighten the mood. He turned to the messenger. "Apologies, my dear boy – we're all a trifle nervy after that business at the Accord. Can I get you a glass of champagne? Or a canape?"

Trembling, the messenger handed the envelope to Premier Cordata and fled before I could terrorize him again. Cordata opened it, still eyeing me uneasily.

Everyone was staring at me.

"The Governor has embarked on his journey across the ocean," announced the Premier, reading the letter. "He will be arriving in Providence in three days."

A chorus of murmurs. As the others talked, my guardian Gabriel appeared, passing me a flask of water.

"How are you feeling, my Lord?"

"Pretty stupid."

"Understandable."

I clutched at the water flask, glugging it thirstily. I was hot and cold at the same time, and I couldn't stop shaking.

"Let's go outside," Ruby said. "Get some fresh air."

We drifted out into the garden of the Basilica, the location of our first and last dances, past the regrown topiaries and the lake, no longer frozen but rippling under the moon. We sat on the steps of the bandstand, our old haunt, staring out into the endless starry night.

The silence between us stretched, unbearably taut.

"I'm sorry, I don't know what's wrong with me," I said at last. "I'm seeing things, things that don't make sense."

"No offence, but that's not exactly new, is it?" Ruby said.

"Not like this. I saw the assassination, before it all played out for real. Only…"

"The assassin never came," finished Ruby. "Oliver, how many of these dreams have you had?"

"I've lost count how many times I've seen you die," I blurted out, no longer able to hold it in. "Over and over again. I can't stop it, no matter what I do. I … can't save you, Ruby."

I watched the colour drain from her face.

"How and where exactly do I die?" she asked, mouth hanging agape.

"The location changes. But you're always shot by the assassin. A green-eyed assassin with a teardrop tattoo, the same man I saw in my dream before the Accord, the same man I saw interrupting the party tonight." I took a deep breath. "I know how this will sound, but I think I'm experiencing the sixth sense."

"Sixth sense?" she repeated. I didn't like how she was looking at me. The same nervous expression as the others had displayed when I'd thrown the messenger against the wall.

"That's what I've been studying. Those who experience death or near-death and return to life, they can return with extra perceptions. Having passed into the unknown, beyond the veil of reality, they come back with an extra sense that others don't have. A sixth sense."

Ruby stared at me as if I were ringing a bell and wearing a sandwich board announcing that the end of the world was nigh.

"Isn't that just superstition?" she said eventually, carefully. "An old wives' tale?"

"Maybe those old wives were on to something, and no one believed them because they weren't wealthy men of academia. When I died for those six minutes last year, something happened to my soul. I felt it, in the moment. A void. Like a part of me *had* died. I think I unlocked a secret sense. It's given me the ability to see the future. That's how I knew what would happen, with the sculpture and everything."

"OK," she said, and I swear she took a step back. "OK, let's just take a second here and think about this logically."

"Logic can't explain this," I said. "This is something else … something more. My grandmother Aurora, she predicted things too. I remember now. She knew she was going to die. She knew my parents' marriage would end in tragedy. She even knew when it would rain. Maybe it's not just a legend, or an old wives' tale. Maybe the sixth sense is real."

"But if you do have this sixth sense, why did you think that poor innocent messenger was coming to kill me?" she said.

"I … I'm not sure. Maybe what I'm seeing are possibilities. Future possibilities, like the threads of destiny."

"So there *might* have been an assassin tonight?"

"Yes! Only their plot went wrong. Maybe the assassin planned to kidnap the messenger and come in their place. Or maybe they got lost or – oh, I don't know. All I know is, the next time, they might really do it. They might succeed."

Ruby nodded. "I suppose anything is possible," she said slowly.

"Do you believe me?" I asked, trying to read her face.

"I … I believe that *you* believe it," she said. "I believe that what you're experiencing feels extremely real, but…"

"But what?"

"What if someone is messing with you, Oliver?" she said.

I shifted, dropping my gaze. "How so?"

"I don't want to rub it in, but tonight wasn't exactly your best moment. Attacking Constitution's messenger, letting your Shadow go full baddie in front of everyone…"

I felt myself flushing, turning away slightly as shame coursed through me.

"What if someone is trying to discredit you?" suggested Ruby. "What if someone is … feeding you these visions somehow and trying to make you seem paranoid? We have enough enemies to choose from already."

I swallowed. "So you *don't* believe me?"

"I…"

"I thought you were on my side."

"I am! I'm always on your side. That's why I want to protect you."

I stood up, angrily. "You made your point. Let's just drop it now."

We were standing by the bandstand. I recalled the Night That Never Was and the argument we'd had right here, in this same spot.

Snow. Drops of blood.

Ruby must have recalled it at the same time for her face softened.

"Look," she said, "let's not fight. I agree there's something going on here – something we need to investigate. We need someone who understands psychometry, the mysteries of the Shadow. There must be someone who can help."

We both thought of Mr Sharma. His easy smile, his musical voice, his hand on my back. What would he advise? His memory grew ever fainter.

Ruby was frowning deeply now.

"Go on," I told her. "I sense that you're thinking something unpalatable."

"Do you think … this might have something to do with your father?" asked Ruby, in a small voice.

"My father?" I repeated. "Why do you say that?"

"Whoever's doing this, it's someone manipulative, insidious and powerful… He's just the first person who comes to mind."

"That's fair."

"Maybe he wants his House back. He might have

followers still. I mean, his trial hasn't even started yet. He could be planning something and using you. It wouldn't be the first time."

I ran my hands through my tangled hair, which was growing ever whiter.

"The cell he's in at the Reformatory is supposed to keep his psyche locked in," I said.

"*Supposed* to."

"The only way I can find out for sure is if I enter his psyche myself – and there's no way in hell that I'm risking that," I said.

"That's probably for the best. Especially if you're already … you know … a bit…"

"Unhinged?"

"I was going to say 'vulnerable'."

But I didn't want to be vulnerable either. I wanted to be strong, a protector. *Her* protector. I was so tired of feeling weak, powerless despite my power.

"There are others who might want to mess with you, too," she continued. "There are the rebel gangs, for one. Memoria or Harmonia might want you to seem unreliable so they can take greater control of the new government. The Premier – he seems friendly enough, but maybe he wants absolute power… The list is long."

We settled into silence, but it wasn't comfortable.

"Maybe someone wants to drive a wedge between us," Ruby added. "Maybe they're succeeding?"

"I'm sorry," I said again.

"What for?"

"I don't know, everything? Not making more time for us. Not telling you sooner. I know things have been a bit difficult lately, but I want this to work more than anything. Us, I mean."

"Me too," she said, eventually, but I sensed a growing distance.

Desperate to close it, I took her in my arms. I held on to her a little tighter than I needed to, trying to claw back whatever it was that I'd already lost.

"I'm sure you're right," I told her. "I just … got carried away, that's all."

She sighed heavily against my chest, clutching at my shirt, apparently relieved that I had come to my five senses again.

"We're going to figure out who's messing with you," she said, "and then I'm going to kick their arse. Repeatedly."

As Ruby pulled back, smiling, I saw my Shadow on the wall, shaking its head and turning away.

7.

RUBY

As Octavia, Rani and I made our way to the rebel meeting, travelling undercover through the city to the Visage factory on the riverside, I filled them in on my meeting with Ash and Perpetua, and on the incident with Oliver at Cordata House. Since I was already betraying Oliver by being there, I decided to go all-out and tell our friends the whole story.

"So, in summary, Oliver thinks he's prophesying my death," I finished. "I don't know what to think, about anything – except that we need to be careful tonight."

"You shouldn't have kept all this to yourselves," said Rani, slightly offended. "I'm supposed to be his House Observer."

"No wonder Oliver has been acting so strange lately," said Octavia, more sympathetically. "Stranger than normal I mean."

Ahead, the factory loomed. One of many such workhouses that once belched dark-matter smoke into the skies of Providence, servants of House Obscura had once turned mind to matter here, creating rare and unusual objects to be sold at high cost. The New Order had managed to reopen several such factories to ease the trade blockade, but this one – a blackened, hollowed-out husk like an empty wasp hive – remained eerily deserted, for now.

Octavia whistled. "Well, here we are. Girls' trip."

Gus was supposed to accompany us but, at the last minute, he'd cancelled, blaming a headache, though we later spied him sneaking out dressed as if for a party.

"It's been a while since we had a proper edge-of-your-seat adventure," said Octavia. "Not since we broke into the Basilica and blew up the Eye network. Boy, that was a riot."

Octavia Belle loved and loathed danger, being both anxious and adrenaline-seeking.

"Yeah, I've missed this," Rani filled in.

Rani Sharma was more sensible, yet she had a grief-born streak for radical justice that belied her practical, dependable persona.

Around my neck, I wore the stolen pendant that obscured my identity, making me appear as someone different to each person who observed me. Oliver still hadn't noticed it was gone.

Oliver… Guilt grew a tree inside me, its branches scratching at my soft insides. I should have told him where I was going tonight. After all, he had been honest with me – even if his theories were far-fetched.

And yet … *were* they so far-fetched? What if he was right, as impossible as it seemed? What if I *was* being pursued by an assassin, with my future changing as fast as his plans and my luck? I could have died last night, or at the Accord...

"Do you think... Do you think Oliver could be right?" I asked. "About him having a mysterious sixth sense?"

"People *do* sometimes say they have a sixth sense for things," said Rani. "When they get a gut feeling about something, or an intuition that something is going to happen. It's not completely unheard of."

"Have you ever heard of anyone predicting the future, an event before it happens, though? In real life, I mean?"

"Nostradamus?"

"I had an aunt who liked to think she was psychic," said Octavia, "but she was only right about half the time."

"Would it be possible for someone to manufacture the visions instead?" I asked. "To merely make Oliver *think* he was seeing the future?"

"With what motive?" asked Rani.

"I don't know... Maybe they want to get rid of Oliver, or dismantle the New Order, or make Providence look unstable in front of the other nations. There are a great number of reasons, when you think about it, and just as many suspects who might be capable of it."

"Who do *you* think it could be?" asked Octavia.

"It could be the Shades of the First Borough," I mused. "They have the right gifts and a grudge against Oliver. They get to discredit the new regime while taking revenge against him."

"That makes sense."

"It could be Lord Harmonia: he's a hardliner; he might be loyal to the old regime. Memoria is a wild card. It could be the former Chancellor, trying to get back in power. Or even the Governor of Constitution attempting a takeover. So, what if someone … implanted a vision and then acted it out for real?"

"Think of the difficulty of staging that, though," said Rani. "A cast of actors to make Oliver think what he had predicted was true. The servants, the messenger … a whole conspiracy."

Put like that, it *did* sound far-fetched.

"Good point."

Down a gravel path, we approached the disused building now surrounded by overgrown lavender fields. A retired titan of industry, the enormous skeletal silhouette of the factory loomed over a wasteland of rusted machinery that once channelled the power of human souls for capitalist gain. It was a hulking beast of pylons and silos, cable rolls and felled poles.

"We'll be safe, right?" said Octavia. She wore no make-up, her hair scraped back messily. "Infiltrating a meeting arranged by people who probably want to kill you? That's a totally ordinary, low-risk activity."

"I thought you were hankering for a little danger," I said, elbowing her gently. "You said you've been having withdrawal symptoms from not breaking into any buildings lately."

"I did say that, but I'm feeling chicken now," she said. "I

want to experience thrilling things again … just at a non-threatening distance."

"We lived through the Battle of the Basilica. We can handle this."

"What if they figure out who you are?"

"Then we'll just run away really fast."

As we neared the factory entrance, we passed a train carriage on abandoned tracks, a rusted black behemoth, its ornate gold lettering faded and peeling. The door was guarded by people in balaclavas carrying repurposed lanterns and orbs.

"Can you see anything inside?" I asked Rani.

Her long hair squashed under a bowler hat, Rani's eyes flittered black. "Just a bunch of people standing around bin fires."

"Octavia, hear anything?" I asked.

"Only small talk," she said. "The weather, dinner, the time."

"We're safe to proceed with Operation Break Skulls," said Rani.

"No one is breaking any skulls," I said, sharply. "We're just here to listen and learn."

"Aw," pouted Octavia.

"Boo," joked Rani.

"Maybe next time."

We advanced. The first thing I saw, tacked to a wall, was a SIX SHOTS TO FREEDOM! poster. *Great. Super…* I pushed on. When the guards in balaclavas scanned me, they saw only what I wanted them to see: a forgettable stranger with vague features and mousy hair. Someone they wouldn't be able to recall later if questioned. They patted us down, looking for hidden weapons. When they found none, they nodded us on, and we shuffled further into the room, joining the other masses who'd walked in off the street.

They could be anyone.

We could be anyone.

Inside, the old factory was adorned with bioluminescent graffiti. *KILL THE PIGS* read one, and I didn't think it meant farm animals. *EAT THE RICH* read another. The floor was littered with chains and oil stains, and what might've been vomit or blood. Or both. A group of people gathered round a circle of large bin fires, as foreseen, burning what looked like bloodied clothes for fuel. There were a dozen other side rooms, some doorways covered with sackcloth curtains beyond which unknowable activities were taking places. The windows were pasted over with posters proclaiming anti-establishment propaganda.

We inched nervously towards the rear of the factory, where most people were gathered; we tried our best to look nonchalant.

"OK, here's the plan: we're looking for information on the shooter at the Accord and to find out if anyone here wants to harm us. Rani, you use your Shadow to look for signs of violence. Octavia, you listen out for radical thoughts. I'll examine all the objects in the room to search their memories for clues."

"Roger," said Rani, saluting.

"And remember: don't do anything to draw attention to yourselves," I whispered, out of the side of my mouth.

My fingertips tingled as I sensed the room, a network of warm, humming energies that were interconnected in many more ways than could be seen. The crowd was apprehensive, anticipating the arrival of someone important.

Their leader, I assumed.

I noted their clothes, and the array of gang colours on display. White. Black. Red. Whoever was in charge here, they were recruiting from across the five boroughs, despite the differences that had split them up. I watched Shades shake hands with Hosts, and Whisperers talking to Wallflowers. Here too were servants and beggars and the unemployed. Anyone who had felt the sting of the Order.

Someone had managed to unite these people – and it wasn't the New Order. Someone had achieved in practice what we had merely promised to do on paper. I would've laid down and given them my seat at the table, were it not for the fact that they were trying to kill me.

We threaded through the throng of people, eavesdropping on their conversations.

"First time?" said one man to another.

"Yeah, can you tell?"

"You'll soon be right at home. I've been to a few of these now. I always walk away feeling like I'm part of something bigger than myself, you know? Like I have a purpose in this life."

We continued on, warming our hands next to a group of youths all dressed in black.

"My parents are always moaning about society being rubbish, but do they actually do anything? No!" said one girl.

"I only came because I heard they might have booze," replied her friend. A splutter of laughter broke out.

Deeper into the crowd, the people got scrappier and surlier, their faces bruised and hollow, an unwashed stench clinging to them.

"The New Order ain't done shit for me," said one man.

"They're running scared already."

"All they do is have parties and talk."

That's not true, I thought. Or was it? Premier Cordata did seem to be rather fond of entertaining, to be fair.

Someone had left a newspaper on a table, next to a spread of leaflets. I picked it up. CHANCELLOR'S SON SPARKS DIPLOMATIC DISASTER, read the headline. It accompanied a photograph of Oliver pinning the Governor's messenger to the wall.

"Boy's finally lost his last marble," said a woman, nodding to it.

"I always knew he would. He's cracked, that lad," said one of the others crowding around to read.

"What else can you expect with a father like that?"

"And that girl. I thought she was all right but she's just a little grifter."

"We don't even have to do anything to destroy the New Order," chuckled an old man. "Just sit back and let it burn."

"Six shots to freedom, am I right?" Another fellow mimed a gun with his hand. But they were all talk, I decided. No one here was actually homicidal, as far as I could tell.

Papers were thrown into the bin fire, causing a roaring blaze.

I added mine to it, cheering in pretend agreement for my own removal.

CLANG!

Someone had pulled shut the factory's double doors. The crowd had swelled further, all of us packing in as greater numbers huddled round the steel beams. I could sense the energy of the room changing, growing teeth.

The lights plunged but for a single spotlight, hoisted in the industrial rigging overhead. A group of burly-looking brutes shepherded a trio of women on to a raised, stage-like platform before a backdrop of defunct machinery: a young girl, maybe eight years old, who cried for her mother; a pregnant lady who begged for mercy; and an elderly woman, her face haggard with fear. All three of them wore the fine tailoring of members of the upper class.

Kidnapped nobles.

My senses burned, immediately alert, as my hands formed fists at my sides.

The factory fell pin-drop silent.

As I watched in horror, the little girl stopped weeping, falling quiet as her face went blank. She twitched, jittering back and forth as if avoiding a wasp, before she seemed to grow calmer, slowly raising her head and gazing placidly at the crowd.

"Welcome, children," she said, in a mechanical voice. "It is my great honour to host you at this gathering tonight." Despite her young age, she spoke with the parlance of a much older person, wise beyond her years.

She'd been taken over, her body used as a puppet, as another soul inhabited her by force. The unseen leader.

"There are some new faces in the crowd," she observed, and I shrank back. "It's a pleasure to have you join us. You are always welcome here, in the Sixth House."

The *Sixth* House? But there were only five Houses: Obscura, Memoria, Harmonia, Cordata and Renato...

Something inside me clicked into place.

A sixth house. A sixth sense.

The girl collapsed like a sack of potatoes as the pregnant woman suddenly jerked up her head, as if switched on.

I looked at Rani, who gulped.

"We know why you are here," the woman began. "Because your children are hungry, because you're cold and homeless, because you have no employment. Bored, restless, frustrated, you are here because you have nowhere else to turn. The old Order hurt you. The New Order ignores you. The gangs drove you apart. Let the Sixth House open our arms to you and shelter you, when the rest of the world has failed you. You are at home here, with us."

There was something peculiar about her pupils.

"The New Order claim there is no food, but they lie," said the older woman, in the same strange tone. "They may have turned their backs on you, but we never shall.

Whatever you need, we shall deliver it to you in abundance. We will be the family the world denied you. We will be the safety you have never known."

A squeaking sound heralded a large wooden cart being wheeled out, overflowing with barrels and sacks.

"The Sixth House nourishes and provides. Please," said the little girl, "help yourselves!"

The crowd rushed to the cart, tearing sacks open to reveal coal, flour, medicines, water.

"No wonder these meetings are so popular," I whispered.

"Who has the money to fund handouts like this?" Rani whispered back.

"The New Order told you they would protect you," said the pregnant woman on the stage, "but where are your revolutionary heroes now?"

The hubbub died down, as people clutched their aid parcels.

"Only the Sixth House is here giving you what you need to survive. Come now, repeat after me: only the Sixth House."

"Only the Sixth House," murmured the crowd.

"The Sixth House has friends in high places," said the older woman. "We are led by a power much greater than the New Order. Soon, our numbers will grow so large that no army in the world will be able to defeat us. Our time will come, and then there will be only one."

"Only one," said the girl.

"Only one," repeated the pregnant woman.

I noticed it then. The pupils of all three of them were crescent-shaped instead of round.

What in the…

"In the name of the Sixth House, we shall rise!"

"In the name of the Sixth House," chanted the crowd.

I shoved my way to the front, trying to get a better look. The people standing around me barely seemed to notice the intrusion, frozen on the spot.

"In the name of the Sixth House, we shall triumph!"

When I looked out across the crowd, I could see those same crescents shining in everyone's eyes. The people now seemed to move as one, swaying in time with each other, like rows of trees in a breeze.

I knew what this reminded me of. Chancellor Obscura and his army. But I'd looked into the eyes of the people he'd controlled like puppets, including Oliver, and I'd never seen those strange crescents before. No, this was something even more wicked and powerful than him.

"Six shots to freedom!"

"Six shots to freedom!" roared the crowd.

"We need to get out of here," I muttered to my friends, but no answer came. The silence rankled. I turned back to Rani and Octavia as my heart lurched sickeningly.

A half-moon shone in place of their pupils.

"Oh no."

"Death to the New Order," they chanted, vigorously. "In the name of the Sixth House!"

Everyone had been affected except me … and, I noticed,

137

one other. A man standing on the other side of the factory floor, who was looking at me curiously, his pupils still round and full. Did I know him? He didn't look much like a rebel, with that conservative moustache and combover hair, but you could never be sure. A spy maybe?

"Death to the New Order!" chanted the trio on stage.

"Death to the New Order!" the audience chanted back in perfect unison, the sound as sharp and regimented as an army's.

I grabbed Octavia and Rani by the hand and tried to drag them to the exit.

"Silence!" cried the child, causing me to halt in my tracks.

I froze, dread surging. The crowd stopped chanting.

"It seems we have a guest tonight," she said, cloyingly. "A special visitor from the New Order." She raised a hand slowly and pointed right at me.

The crowd swivelled as one. A thousand pairs of eyes watched me.

"We have a message for you and your Premier," the child said. "Tell him that we are coming for you. We will level you, House by House, until we are all that stands. Death to the New Order, in the name of the Sixth House!"

The room erupted into riotous cheering.

Chest tight, I made a run for the doors, blasting them open with a fireball and dragging Rani and Octavia behind me. Even as I ran, I could hear that chanting. *Death to the New Order, in the name of the Sixth House.*

I pulled us under a bridge, watching as the rest of the

Sixth House filed out, dispersing through the city to spread the word. Folding at the middle, I tried to catch my breath, every muscle aching with the effort. Rani and Octavia's chants gradually trailed off, until they looked at each other in confusion.

"Death to the New... Wait, what?" said Rani.

"What just happened?" asked Octavia, touching her face as if for confirmation that she still existed.

"You were ready to level me and topple the New Order," I said. "They had you both in thrall, just like that."

Rani shook her head, looking at me blankly. "All I remember is this euphoric sense of peace and togetherness that came upon me," she said.

"I felt that too!" said Octavia. "Like everything was falling into place and I was just one of millions of little pieces." She sighed wistfully.

"Why didn't it work on me?" I said. "And what are they playing at?"

"They're amassing an army," came a voice behind us.

I yelped in surprise, spinning round to face the stranger with the conservative moustache.

"Who the hell are you?" I cried, summoning fire in my palms.

His face melted away, revealing the true image underneath.

Oliver.

"I should've guessed."

He tossed away the stolen identity card he'd used to create

the photorealistic illusion. "Why didn't you tell me you were coming here?" he asked.

"Why did you spy on me instead of making your presence known?" I said.

"Guys," Rani said. "Let's focus."

"I wasn't *spying*," Oliver said. "I – I just wanted to say goodnight, so I came looking for you in your mind. I sent out my Shadow to discern your location. When I saw you here in this strange place, I got worried, so I hopped through a portal."

"Their control didn't work on you either?"

"No, actually. It didn't."

"Why not you? Why not me?"

"Not sure. The question is: who is controlling those people? It wasn't the three on stage. They were merely conduits."

"You couldn't sense who was behind it?"

"No. The minds of the three speakers were curiously empty."

"So they were just acting as mouthpieces," I said.

"Do you think this has something to do with the visions I'm having?" he asked. "Sixth House, sixth sense, six shots to freedom?"

"Maybe. Or maybe whoever is behind this is manipulating you too."

He nodded slowly, unconvinced.

"Can we go home now?" said Octavia. "I have a headache."

"Me too," said Rani. "Feels like whoever broke into my head really stomped around and made a mess."

Back at Obscura House, armed with cups of tea, we ran through what we knew.

"The leader of the Sixth House is surely rich," Oliver said. "They must be, to afford all those supplies and print all those posters."

"Maybe it's not just one person," I said. "Maybe there's a whole collective of people conspiring against us."

We sat together in near-silence, heavy and contemplative from the day, watching as dawn slowly lightened the sky. When Octavia and Rani had departed at last for their quarters, Oliver and I were left alone, with all of the unspoken between us.

I collected up the dirty mugs, putting them in the sink and running some hot water. After a moment, he came up behind me, looping his arms round my waist.

"Hey," he said softly, his lips brushing my ear.

"Hey."

We swayed back and forth to the sound of our song, the Haunted Heart. It was the song that had been playing when I first fell in love with him, the song that had helped me recover part of my lost soul. When he touched me, it played in my mind, echoing through his.

"I'm sorry I've been so absent lately," he said. "I just …

I'm so scared that something is going to happen to you. It's killing me."

I leaned back against his chest. "That's just what it feels like sometimes, loving someone," I said. "I'm scared of losing you too. But we can't waste all our time worrying about the what ifs, can we?"

"You're right," he said. "You usually are."

"I'm sorry I didn't tell you we were infiltrating the meeting," I said. "I didn't want to worry you even more. It was a bad call."

"It doesn't matter now."

"If we're going to figure out who's behind the Sixth House, we need to work together. Stick together. We need you more than ever." I turned to face him. "*I* need you more than ever."

His arms tightened around me. "I need you too, more than you know."

"Whatever we're in, we're in it together, remember?" I said, and this time I meant it – with all my soul.

8.

OLIVER

"Let me see if I understand this correctly," said Lady Memoria, taking a generous pinch of snuff from a small white box made of bone. "Lady Renato, yourself, and two servants from Obscura House infiltrated a meeting arranged by a secret rebel faction who are plotting to overthrow us and are potentially connected to the assassination attempt we survived; and at this meeting an unknown individual took control of almost everyone in attendance, using a small girl and two women as a mouthpiece to issue us with a warning?"

"Yep, that's about the shape of it," said Ruby.

Memoria took another sniff of snuff, tutting and shaking her head.

"Too old for this," she muttered.

Ruby and I had agreed to keep quiet about the visions I'd had. I didn't trust them, not completely. But we passed round the SIX SHOTS TO FREEDOM! poster.

"This caricature is a hate crime alone," said Lady Memoria.

"Find the artist and arrest them immediately!" ranted Lord Harmonia.

"We should've seen this coming. You know the old saying?" said Memoria. "'What follows a coup but *another* coup'?"

"The timing could not be worse," lamented Premier Cordata. "The Governor is due to arrive on the thirteenth. It would be quite the disaster for him to turn up just in time to see us overthrown only a month into our rule."

"That is why we must act now," said Lord Harmonia. "We must crack down fast and firm. We will send our people to this rebel warehouse and have every single one of them charged with treason."

"Just as the Chancellor would have wanted," said Lady Memoria drily.

"No, we must be careful, strategic," said Cordata. "What can you tell us about this supposed Sixth House, Oliver?"

"Not a lot," I said, rubbing my forehead. "We know their leader has the ability to control many souls at once. We know they have money and influence. Their numbers are growing. We need to take them very seriously."

"We need to reach out to the gangs, if they'll still talk to us," said Ruby. "They won't be happy about losing members to the Sixth House. Someone might be willing to talk."

"And we need to step up and provide for the public," I warned. "If people are desperate, they'll follow whoever feeds them."

Lord Harmonia slammed his hand down on the pentagon table, making all our cups and saucers shudder.

"What we need to do is what *I* suggested," he said. "We

need to make public gatherings illegal. Impose martial law. Pass a decree that makes attending their meetings a criminal activity."

"That will surely backfire," said Ruby. "People are already gunning for us; a crackdown won't help convince them we're the good guys. It'll send more people running to the Sixth House – who will welcome them with open arms."

"We need to think carefully about our next move," I said. "We need to win over public confidence. We need—"

"A ball!" said Cordata. His hands sketched a rainbow in the air. "A grand, fantastical ball. A ball … for the people. For peace."

Silence.

"A what?" said Lady Memoria.

"I'm sorry, I must be hallucinating," said Lord Harmonia acidly. "I thought you said you wanted to throw a ball for the people who are currently trying to kill us."

"We can invite members of the public to wear their finest gowns and join us in a celebration," said Cordata. "We will feed the nation and entertain them at the same time. Show the people that we're all in this together."

"And what about the rebels?" said Lord Harmonia. "What about these people you encountered last night, chanting 'Death to the Order' and such? Are we to invite them too?"

"A ball," repeated Premier Cordata firmly, as if he weren't listening. "Yes, it's just the thing. We shall arrange it as the finale to the Governor's visit. We'll invite the leaders of the five gangs too, to show that we are still on the side of the resistance.

A symbolic moment as they return to the former seat of power – not as outlaws, but as equals! What do you think?"

Ordinarily, I might approve of such bold diplomacy but the assassin's face flashed behind my eyes. His features seemed to sharpen, becoming more defined. I could see the pores of his skin, the stubble on his chin, and the tattooed teardrop, suspended in a permanent state of falling.

He was becoming more real, I thought.

A surge of panic gripped me. A public ball would be the perfect opportunity for another attempt on Ruby's life.

"No. We can't do that. It's too dangerous," I said.

"Finally, someone with a lick of sense!" said Harmonia.

"I wouldn't say 'dangerous' so much as 'misguided'," said Lady Memoria. "I appreciate the sentiment, but Lord Obscura does have a point."

Ruby met my eye, reading me.

"Rather than throw a ball, maybe we should employ what's left of the army to hand out supplies until the blockade is over," she suggested.

"Unfortunately, our soldiers are currently holding the line against the advances of the Empress," said Premier Cordata. "The situation there is unsettled, to say the least."

"Then we can do it ourselves."

"Ourselves?" he repeated, as if struggling to understand.

"You would see the leaders of the great and noble Houses handing out food packages like missionaries?" said Lord Harmonia.

"Why not?" said Lady Memoria. "We're perfectly capable

of getting our hands dirty, aren't we? Let's show the people what we're good for. Remind them of why we're here and maybe they won't wish to remove us forcibly."

If hosting a ball was a bit risky, then going out into the boroughs to rub shoulders with the people was downright perilous.

"Sorry to put a dampener on a good idea, but we're forgetting our recent security concerns," I jumped in. "Representatives can hand out supplies for us."

Ruby appeared hesitant. "It wouldn't be good for the people to think we are afraid of them," she said. "That might embolden the Sixth House."

"Governments should always fear their people," I said, recalling the sudden ease with which my tyrannical father had been overthrown.

"Fine. We'll put a pin in the ball idea for now," sighed Cordata. "But let us agree on this: until the trade blockade is over, we'll give out supplies each week on Sundays. We shall arrange a meeting point in each of the five boroughs, and find a representative of the gangs to liaise with. This can be our olive branch, so to speak. Are we agreed?"

"Fine," I relented, "as long as we use a go-between."

"Splendid," said the Premier. "Then it shall be done. The Governor of Constitution will be impressed by our charity. As for the logistics, I shall leave ... those ... to all of you."

He gestured vaguely and swept out.

"By 'logistics'," muttered Ruby, "I assume he means 'all the hard work'."

I smiled back at her, squeezing her hand, but inside I felt sick with dread. The assassin's face was clearer than I had ever seen it.

Back in my room, I surrounded myself with dusty books and scrolls, trying to create a protective wall of knowledge. *An Encyclopaedia of the Occult. The Secrets of the Soul. An Alchemist's Guide to the Elemental Foundations...* They were the sort of books the masters at the Academy would've turned their noses up at. The sort of books my father would've banned from the house. But I would go to any lengths to find the truth.

Slowly, I was piecing fragments together.

The sixth sense came to those who had experienced near-death, causing a crack in the soul between the Shadow and the Spirit, allowing the gift of foresight to worm its way in and enabling the owner to see the future.

But the future, it seemed, was also shattered, in pieces. The visionary had no control over it. They were helpless to prevent what had been foretold because the future was too complex to be controlled. The more of it that could be seen, the more divided the future became. Even an attempt to predict something simple such as what you were going to have for lunch was fraught with thousands of possibilities when you took into account everything from the freshness of the vegetables in your pantry to whether the sandwich shop owner down the road fell ill that day, to whether a suggestion from a friend meant you fancied stew instead ... even whether the heating pipes would be frozen or an unexpected visitor would disrupt your meal preparations.

Anything could happen.

Well, that wasn't good enough – not with Ruby's life in the balance.

What I needed was another vision. Something to work with. Ever since I'd learned about the Sixth House, my visions of Ruby's murder had slowly begun to settle, like sediment forming patterns at the bottom of a glass. They were clarifying and crystallizing, transforming from shifting kaleidoscopic patterns to something more solid.

I was close now; I could feel it.

I lay down on a black chaise longue, closed my eyes and attempted to trigger another vision. Falling deep into the darkness inside, I walked through those pitch-black rooms again, as the building around me took form, assembling itself brick by brick. A grand staircase with golden rails rose up, meeting a heart-shaped stained-glass window.

It smelled musty, with the grand stature of a cathedral. It was decked out for an event – I had the impression of flags and banners. I tried to focus in on the details but my vision was blurred. I was unsteady, too, on my feet, as if drunk.

That tracked.

Here was the painted cupola I'd lain beneath.

Here was the place where I died.

For the first time, I knew exactly where I was – and it felt all too real.

I was in the Basilica of All Souls.

Ghostly figures in formal dress passed through me. They weren't really here, but then neither was I. I saw Lady Memoria and the Governor, both dressed in their finery — but no sign of Lord Harmonia, or the Premier himself. I could hear distant music, a familiar sweeping symphony, but also … explosions. Soft, scattered booms ricocheted off surfaces.

Something was happening.

Something momentous.

The ground shook. The chandeliers rattled. A sudden sharp scream startled me, drawing me down a red-carpeted hall.

In the room at the end of the corridor stood Ruby before a round window that looked out on to a thin crescent moon. She wore the same red dress with the embroidered phoenix she'd worn at the Accord. The city was burning behind her, the high eye-topped tower of the Observatory bursting into flames as dark ships filled the skies.

This was it.

As she turned to face me, the green-eyed assassin emerged through the door behind me, moving so fast that his edges were blurred. He shot past me, striking Ruby in the heart.

BANG!

Shouting out loud, I gasped awake, finding myself slumped on the chaise longue where I'd drifted off.

If some of the visions had seemed hazy, one aspect had felt as solid as the wood beneath my fingers: Ruby was going to die at the Basilica.

That same place we'd ransacked on the night of the revolution was the location of her future assassination.

There was a sinister kind of symmetry to it, as if we were being punished perhaps, for betraying the people.

Fear and relief gripped me simultaneously as I rocked back and forth, hands in my hair. The horrifying vision I'd had of Ruby's death was real, but I had clues to work with at last.

I saw the flowers, the curtains, the faces of the guests. There had been a moon hanging in the window, I realized, thin as a scythe or a fingernail cutting.

A cursory look at the lunar calendar told me that the next crescent moon would occur in two weeks.

That bought me some time, at least.

On the thirteenth of the month, the day the Governor arrived in Providence, a dense smog settled on the city, blanketing everything in a gloomy shroud that blocked out the sun. Rain came with it, hard and relentless. There was flooding in the streets. Sirens seemed to sound all day long too, as if heralding an emergency that never fully emerged, while a small crowd of protestors had gathered in front of Cordata House. The fellow with his NEW ORDER, SAME OLD SHIT! placard was still there, but now he had thirty friends, all of them ranting as we drove past.

It was safe to say that the city of Providence was not looking its best for the arrival of our VIP guest.

The morning papers blazed with incriminating headlines: NEW ORDER ON THE BRINK, NEW ORDER IN FLAMES, NEW ORDER CLINGS TO POWER. One asked CAN NEW ORDER PERSUADE GOVERNOR TO LIFT TRADE BLOCKADE?

The Governor arrived on a titanic steel ship that was said to be unsinkable, with sails bearing the country's nautical flag. We were told to expect a motorcade that would stretch from South Harbour, all bells and whistles and girls twirling batons, but the Governor arrived humbly in a single carriage, with an old hunting dog at his side and wearing a simple tan suit.

He was tall, with leathery, wrinkled skin, a deep baritone voice and a drooping silvery moustache like a broom handle. He wouldn't have looked out of place behind the wheel of a ship, or riding a horse through the mountains.

The servants inside Cordata House lingered at the windows, desperate to get a look at the world's most powerful man.

"Greetings, Providence!" he said, stepping out of the carriage and removing his wide-brimmed hat in a sweeping gesture.

"Welcome, Governor Fairchild," said Cordata.

I'd done as Premier Cordata requested and attempted to penetrate the Governor's mind, but either Ambrose Fairchild was extremely deceptive or he was exactly what he appeared to be.

With most people, soul-searching was like free-diving through murky waters full of potentially hazardous mysteries. It was like traversing an ever-changing landscape without a map. My soul was like a dark forest, Ruby's like a fertile valley, Cordata's like a festival. There was always so much going on, it was hard to focus on any one thing. You might wander into a random childhood memory, a recurring nightmare, a nameless floating feeling. The country of a soul was disorganized and chaotic. Even the most psychically advanced minds were comprised of a shifting web of disconnected scenes, vignettes connected together by tunnels like rabbit holes. Yet the Governor's head was an endless orchard. Sun-lit and blissful, birds singing near and far. It stretched out in every direction for miles, those neat rows of fruit-bearing trees.

There was nothing sinister – or, if there was, it was very well hidden.

The Governor moved down the red-carpeted line we'd formed in the courtyard, shaking hands with everyone. He said something different to each of us. He started with Premier and Lady Cordata, before greeting the rest of us in turn. I noticed how easily he charmed everyone, making Lady Memoria blush and Lord Harmonia chuckle.

"It's a pleasure to be here, in your fine land. It's a shame about the weather, but maybe we can bring the sunshine with us."

Even Ruby was charmed by him. He made her laugh, throwing her head back in amusement as she batted her hand, embarrassed but flattered.

Finally, he reached me.

"Lord Obscura, it's a pleasure to make your acquaintance."

People said his gift was that he put people at ease; he made them feel at home wherever they were.

"Governor Fairchild," I said, bowing respectfully. "I really must apologize for the dreadful misunderstanding the other day, with your messenger."

"Got a little hot under the collar there, didn't you?" he said, in a gentle, fatherly tone.

"Not the greatest of first impressions, I know."

"Don't worry. I've never made a habit of judging folks in their weakest moments. I'm not about to start with you."

"That's … very gracious of you."

"How are you finding the fast-paced world of politics?" he asked.

I tried again to read his energy, dipping unseen into the edges of his mind where all the thin, floaty bits of the subconscious could be spied and pried, but all I could see was that endless orchard of fruit.

"It's a learning curve," I answered, carefully.

He chuckled. "I'll bet. Must be tough, to be catapulted into the ruling seat after witnessing your father overthrown."

"I didn't just witness it, I helped," I said.

"I heard all about it. How is the old man now, by the by?"

"Rotting in prison."

"Hmm… Families can be tricky," he conceded. "I have three daughters, so I know a thing or two. They don't listen to me, no matter what I tell them." He pulled a strip of photos out of his inside pocket, three miniature portraits of three young women who unmistakably took after him, minus the handlebar moustache. In the bottom picture, all three of them were hugging him at once, their smiles wide and goofy, unselfconscious.

"You all look … very happy," I said, awkwardly. A loving father was as alien a concept to me as the atmosphere on Mars, or the characteristics of classical Sanskrit.

"We are for the most part, but some days our hearts are heavy with grief… We still feel the loss of my wife, you see. Appearances can be deceiving. That's why it does no good to judge the covers of things."

I considered him. The Governor could certainly be behind the Sixth House, causing our people to turn against us. He was powerful enough. It would be possible to direct operations from afar, for a man like him. And yet he seemed so … serene. Maybe it was a ruse?

"I never was much of a fan of the old Chancellor, as it happens," he said, lowering his voice. "We in Constitution pride ourselves on our freedoms and he didn't have much time for liberty." He gave me a disarming smile. "Let's go inside. This rain isn't good for my old bones."

House Cordata had put on another extravagant dinner, this one themed around our guest of honour. Green beans and pulled pork, fish soup and garlic bread, buttery potatoes and beef cutlets, with three different pies for dessert.

"Well, isn't this nice?" said the Governor. "Enjoy the peach pie. That's my mother's old home recipe. I *heartily* recommend it."

Conversation was cautiously good-natured at first, everybody being careful not to offend. But Premier Cordata never could resist the allure of a fine bottle of wine. It was the most relatable thing about him. He soon started talking more than the rest of us. He began to tell a long, dull story about a safari he and Lady Cordata had been on for their anniversary ten years ago.

"In the middle of the night, there was a wildebeest stampede," he said. "My first thought was to grab my shotgun. I'm a lover of all the kingdom of earth's creatures of course, but in that moment I was just a humble man, facing down a horde of angry beasts."

A titter of forced laughter filled the pause he left for us to fill.

"My guide told me to hold my horses. He said, 'If you shoot one, the others will trample you, and you don't have enough bullets to kill them all.' I couldn't help but think it was a metaphor for being in government."

He was getting loose-lipped, his eyes shining with false confidence as the liquid sloshed out of his glass.

"So, what did you do, my friend?" asked the Governor.

"I hunkered down in my shelter as the good lady here snored like a wildebeest herself. She slept through the whole thing!"

The fake laughter intensified as Lady Cordata glugged

furiously from her glass, glaring at her husband. The Governor smiled easily, chuckling.

"Good sir," he said, speaking clearly, "you've clearly not learned how to stay out of trouble, if you insist on disrespecting your good wife in public."

Cordata's face froze.

The First Lady laughed, placing one hand on her husband's shoulder and saying, "You tell him, sir."

Cordata smiled nervously. It was clear who wielded power here, even by a gentle touch.

When our plates were empty, the Governor patted his belly and made time to thank every server personally, sliding coins into their palms.

"Thank you all for a heart-warming evening," he said. "It has been my honour and my pleasure. Perhaps we can raise a toast together?"

"Of course. Yes, I – I was just getting to that," said Cordata, briskly clapping to signal the waiting staff.

When everyone had a drink in hand, Ambrose Fairchild stood up and raised his glass. He seemed to command the room without even trying, which clearly irked the Premier.

"To fresh starts and new friends," he said.

"Hear, hear!" we cheered.

I took a prim sip and put the glass back on the table. I hadn't touched a drink since the night I'd attacked the messenger boy. I wanted a clear head for this.

"Governor Fairchild," said Premier Cordata, lowering his voice, "I hate to bring the mood down when we're all having such a good time, but perhaps we can discuss the trade blockade now? The issue is becoming increasingly urgent."

"There'll be plenty of time for that later," said the Governor dismissively "First, I'm afraid there's a rather more pressing reason for my visit."

"Oh?" said Cordata, paling.

"The Empress. She is causing quite a stir in your colonies, isn't she? I sense that she's planning something. It makes us in Constitution uneasy."

"It's all under control," said the Premier.

"You sure about that? The Empress will not engage in diplomacy, no matter how nicely you ask, nor how many gifts you shower her with. We have learned that ourselves, the hard way."

I caught Ruby's eye, exchanging a brief flutter of fear.

"From Heart to Heart, she is steadily gaining in power as her influence moves this way. She thinks no one stands between her and global dominion. Her armies are manned by creatures made of Shadow. They feel no fear, no remorse. This is why I came here so urgently."

The room had fallen silent, all eyes and ears on him.

"At times like these, it's important that we're on the same page, don't you agree?" said the Governor. "We must stand together."

"Ah … absolutely," said Premier Cordata.

"You have endured a revolution and your armies are exhausted."

Ruby widened her eyes at me again.

"Will you allow our military to visit your bases and resecure the borders out there? Just a squadron or two? We and our friends are counting on you holding the fort, as it were."

Something about the exchange felt wrong. The Governor was sending his armies into our territories. Perhaps he was just the other side of the same terrible coin as the Empress. In this moment, I felt the future fracturing. I saw no visions, but I felt it breaking all the same.

"Providence would appreciate the aid," said Cordata, before any of us could object. "You can rely on us to stand with you. We will form a united front."

"I thought as much, good man. Now, let's talk trade. I'm sure we can resolve our differences with a few sweet words over a whiskey and a cigar, so long as you can assure me that your days of kidnapping children are done."

"Indeed, those days are long gone, Governor Fairchild!" said Cordata. "There is no doubt about that. This is the *New* Order now."

"Tremendous! Let's get that in writing, shall we?"

The two men drifted off to the parlour together as conversation resumed, though Cordata turned back to us to flash a triumphant thumbs up.

"What do you make of him?" asked Ruby, turning to me and gently touching my arm. "Governor Fairchild?"

"He seems like a perfectly lovely man, so naturally I'm suspicious as hell. I think he's hiding something. I'm just not sure what."

"He *is* a little syrupy."

"Let's not dismiss him too quickly," I said. "He's keen to get his armies stationed here."

"I told you he was muscling in," said Lord Harmonia, popping up at my elbow. "He has a plan, coming over here, but Cordata is too dim to notice."

"Go on," prompted Ruby.

"Once, the Order was an empire on which the sun never set. Wherever day was dawning, it touched our colonies. But this a New World now. Our power is waning as new powers grow stronger. Now we're stuck between a rock and a hard place. The Empress and the Governor. We could find ourselves in the middle of a war."

War…

The horrible image I'd seen tore through me, the Observatory exploding, the sky red as blood. Could it be? Would it be?

With every vision I had, the future seemed to get worse.

Later that night, after the Governor had retired to his guest suite and everyone else had gone home, the prophecy washed over me again as Ruby slept beside me. The assassin crept into the space between wake and sleep, drawing me into a prophetic scene.

I was still in the Basilica but the décor was clearer now, with anchor flags hanging from the walls to symbolize

Constitution. The room filled with people dressed in blue, holding drinks and talking over the sound of a brass band onstage.

I watched Ruby move upstairs, walking along the mezzanine corridor that connected the imperial staircase to the upper floor. I trailed after her, following her to the room with the round window, the crescent moon resting atop her head like a crown as the assassin manifested behind me, his lean face contorted with rage in the pale light—

BANG!

No, no, no.

I lay awake for hours, afraid to dream again. The room felt claustrophobic. My limbs were restless. I needed to do something, even if I wasn't quite sure what. I could go to the study to resume my investigation, but if I did, I knew I wouldn't sleep until dawn permeated the windows. I would search and search for answers that weren't forthcoming.

Before I could stop it, I felt my Shadow splitting from my body to roam the city. My silhouette drifted through the empty streets, flitting from alley to alley, scouring every corner and crevice for signs.

Most of the civilians I encountered were innocently minding their own business, commuting home from a night shift or reading in bed next to a warm, snoring dog. I could sense no involvement with the Sixth House.

I floated through the five boroughs, from the eye-topped watchtowers of the First, to the fire-lit villas of the Fifth, inspecting everyone from the drunkards being thrown out of alehouses to the sex workers waiting for customers.

Among the late-night crowds at the Grand Bazaar and down at the docks, I spied them – several crescent-eyed individuals shuffling around as if being piloted. Their minds were blank, foggy, obscuring my vision of what dwelled in their souls. Many more such individuals flocked around clock towers and fountains, in front of the Necropolis and the Auditorium. They spoke to passers-by, eagerly clasping their hands.

"Are you hungry? Come with me, I know a place that has food."

"Have you heard of the Sixth House? They can help you."

Some people just pushed past them, but some stopped, intrigued. The physical contact seemed to lure them in, as they convinced another group of youths to join them.

The Sixth's influence was growing, spreading like a weed. It reminded me of my father's army, though I couldn't recall his soldiers ever having crescent-shaped pupils. Besides, my father was, as I had told Governor Fairchild, rotting in jail. He couldn't be behind this… Or could he? I knew I wouldn't be able to relax until I was certain.

In my Shadow form, I floated through the walls of the Reformatory as if they were nothing. I risked only the briefest glimpse of him: awake and pacing furiously, rattling an empty bowl across the bars of his cell. As I watched, holding my breath, he suddenly pulled up, jerking his head as if he'd sensed me.

Panic spiked in my blood, making me cold. He was a kind of Medusa, and his gaze would turn me to stone.

Just as he turned, I retreated rapidly, frightened that he would sense me spying on him, though I let my gaze linger just long enough to confirm that his pupils appeared ordinary. With that, I fled, my heart hammering unnaturally fast and hard.

If my father wasn't the mastermind, then who was? I ran through the other suspects in my mind. There were the leaders of the gangs, of course. I checked on Ash and Perpetua first, finding them downing pints in a pub together, despite their different gang colours. The Wallflowers and the Firehands had made a pact; their assembled members were celebrating raucously.

I knew less about the other gangs, the Whisperers and the Hosts, but when I dipped in, they too appeared to be working in unison, running a soup kitchen and selling rumours about us to the press. I saw them brainstorming new ways to damage our credibility with false exposés.

That left the Shades. Its leader was a charismatic figure known only as Blade: a dark-skinned man with dreads, his leather coat falling open to reveal his scarred chest, a web of wounded skin. The Reformatory had tortured him, by my father's command – which might make him a prime suspect. But when I tracked him down, he was busy enjoying the company of an unseen partner, who called out to him from a bath in the next room, "Come on, lover … I'm waiting."

The voice sounded familiar, but I didn't pry. I moved on

quickly. Enemy or not, Blade deserved some privacy. The bedroom and the bathroom were firmly out of bounds.

Defeated, I made my way back to Cordata House, where the Premier and his wife were sound asleep, the latter snoring at vibrational decibels. No wonder she'd looked so embarrassed when Cordata had shared his story earlier.

I sought out the Governor, but he was safe in his suite, writing a saccharine letter home to his daughters about how much he missed their mother.

Over at Memoria House, her Ladyship tended to the night-blooming flowers in her greenhouse as her cats flocked around her curiously, while over at Harmonia House, his Lordship listened to a recording of his favourite operetta.

All was well.

I lingered a moment, watching Lord Harmonia sipping his whiskey and humming along in perfect pitch, but as I moved to leave, something caught my eye—

A silhouette ascending the stairs, something concealed in their hand.

Lord Harmonia, singing along to the finale in a reedy falsetto, was oblivious to the imminent presence. The door swung open with a creak, revealing a hooded figure, their face half hidden in shadow.

As they stepped into the light, I saw him clearly – the green-eyed, tear-tattooed stranger; lightly stubbled, with pale hair that shone.

His pupils, round and full, reflected the moonlight.

I tried to signal to Lord Harmonia, urgently waving on the wall, but I was just a Shadow. Unaware of the danger he was in, he sensed some movement behind him and turned.

"Who in the name of—"

Before he could finish his question, the assassin fired his weapon, its projectile striking his Lordship in the chest. It drove into him, tunnelling, creating a black hole, like a portal.

It wasn't a vision this time. It was all too real.

Lord Harmonia gave a rattling gasp, his humming now a tuneless wheeze.

As I was not physically present, and my body still lay asleep at home, I was too late to save him, I already knew that. I could only watch in frozen horror as a glowing orb rose out of his body. It should have split apart, decaying to dust before my eyes like Mr Sharma's had, but instead it remained strangely intact, allowing the assassin to capture it, sucking it back into the dark, five-chambered pistol.

The orb, still glowing, was trapped in one of its glass chambers.

The assassin was *stealing* Lord Harmonia's soul.

With a dramatic thud, his Lordship toppled, crashing to the floor just as the aria's crescendo climaxed.

Blood splattered the wall around my silhouette.

The assassin lifted his head, appearing only now to notice me, a disembodied Shadow on the wall, my hands raised in fear.

"In the name of the Sixth House, death to the New

Order!" He lifted his gun to the wall, aiming at the place where my head would be.

BANG!

Abruptly returned to my body in my room, I stared into the dark.

A few minutes later, my door was wrenched open. Octavia, holding a lantern and dressed in her favourite frilly nightie. She stood in the crack, a haunted expression on her face.

"I just received an urgent message, from Harmonia House," she said, breathlessly.

"I already know," I said, as she blinked at me fearfully, reading my mind. "He's dead."

9

RUBY

Food was piled high on the table at Harmonia House, spoiling quickly. It looked like one of those still-life paintings meant to remind people of the brevity of life and the inevitability of death. Sweating meat. Greasy cheese. Stale bread. Gravy with a skin.

Nothing lasted for ever.

The house was full of sympathy flowers, vases of lilies and white roses, hyacinths and chrysanthemums, arranged in cut-glass vases against the patterned silver walls. Their sweet perfume masked the stink of the rotting spread. A buzzing bluebottle danced in through the window, landing on a bruising peach in a fruit bowl.

Behind a closed door, the newly widowed Lady Harmonia wailed and sobbed, the sound ripping and tearing.

A string quartet played softly, bringing out the emotions I was trying to push down.

In the adjoining room, a queue of mourners lined up to pay their last respects, leaving offerings around Lord Harmonia's coffin. I'd visited him briefly and seen the eyes painted creepily on his lids, but I didn't last longer than a minute before retreating.

Everyone in the sphere of the New Order was present. Flanked by guards in golden armour, Premier Cordata stood at the door, thanking everyone for coming. He looked as if he'd aged ten years since coming to power, his face lined. The Governor, too, was here, hat in hand, moving around the room and saying comforting things in a soft voice. He seemed to have a way of putting people at ease, even in these most dire of circumstances.

There were more guards, in fact, than there were guests; some of them were armed. Security across the capital had increased fivefold since Lord Harmonia's murder. Throughout Providence, the illuminated billboards that once displayed state propaganda now bore the face of the green-eyed assassin, calling on citizens to identify him. The picture was faded and hazy, captured through remote viewing from Oliver's memory, but surely *someone* would recognize him? The Inspectors had been recalled too, to patrol the streets in search of the culprit. Following a vote, we had reopened the listening posts to broadcast details about the new city-wide curfew. We were falling back into old patterns, in the name of fear.

The papers were split, some deploring the terror that gripped the capital, while others celebrated the death of a dictator's enabler. The protestors gathered outside Harmonia House continued to grow in number, some of them playing instruments or singing rally songs.

Lady Memoria dabbed her face with her lacy

handkerchief. "Poor Harold," she sniffed. "I never liked him much – *deeply* unpleasant man – but he didn't deserve to go out like this."

"What will happen to House Harmonia now?" I asked.

"There was a daughter, but she died years ago. Lady Harmonia hasn't the birthright to rule alone. Perhaps a distant nephew...?"

Without an heir, the House would be dissolved. I pictured again the posters I'd seen: SIX SHOTS TO FREEDOM! Now it was only five, and one of those was already in prison, where the assassin could not reach him.

"Who of us will be next?" Lady Memoria said. "It's merely a matter of time. Unless we can locate that assassin, our days are already numbered."

She wandered off to greet the Countess.

Oliver looked haunted, even more white in his hair than yesterday. "I should've tried to get there in time. I knew that something was about to happen. I could feel it."

"Stop beating yourself up," I said, rubbing his back absently. "If you hadn't witnessed it, we wouldn't know what happened."

"It confirms that the assassin I've been seeing is real, but it doesn't give us much more to go on," said Oliver. "It's pretty clear they've been sent by the Sixth House. But we're no closer to unmasking who's behind all this."

We watched Ambrose Fairchild moving through the crowd. Premier Cordata, shaking hands. Lady Memoria, absently re-arranging flowers.

"You still think their leader is someone powerful?" I asked.

"I'm certain," said Oliver. "Someone with money, with a great gift. The green-eyed man is just a pawn."

"All the same," I said, "he offers us a way in. Someone is bound to recognize that face — it's distinctive enough."

"I have my guardian Gabriel on the case. He's an expert tracker, using his Spark to trail a person's life force. Hopefully he can find something," said Oliver.

"Rani and Octavia are monitoring the situation too," I said. "Octavia put a tag on certain key words so that whenever they're uttered, she's alerted. With the audio device Lady Harmonia gave us, it amplifies those thoughts with the strength of an entire listening post."

"Lady Harmonia, huh?"

"Yes. She wants to find the assassin most of all."

"Until he's found, we should avoid being in public." His eyes darted round the room. "It isn't safe. My last vision of your death took place in the Basilica. There were Constitution flags waving. I think it's a warning about the Governor. He could be behind this… If only the visions didn't change so much. Whenever I think I've figured out what's going to happen, they shift again."

"You weren't led to Harmonia's murder by a vision," I said gently. "It was only by accident that you were there at all."

He frowned. "True. But I wonder if it was the sixth sense that led me there at the right time to witness the murder. It probably works in subtle ways. If I could control it, I would truly be able to protect us, like a real leader should." He was talking mostly to himself now. "I've exhausted the archives. I've read every book I can find on the topic. But it's not enough. I need to know more."

We stood at the window, staring out at the dark clouds. The smog that had arrived with the Governor seemed to be getting denser and more persistent, filling the wide grey sky.

"Let's think about what we know for certain," I said. "We know the Sixth House is indoctrinating people and sending an assassin to pick us all off. We need to find the Sixth House's base and infiltrate it. They must have some kind of headquarters where their leader is sheltered. If we can find them, we can bring down the whole network—"

I turned back to face him, but Oliver was already gone.

Annoyed, I scanned the room in search of him. Instead, I saw a familiar figure dressed all in black standing in front of the fireplace: a small but strangely intimidating older woman with soul-piercing eyes. It was my one-time employer, the Countess. She and her butler, Graves, next to her, were both staring at me.

She wiggled her fingers, inviting me over.

Now that Tristan Obscura was languishing in prison, Countess Agatha Cavendish had been welcomed back into the New Order by her old friend Premier Cordata. Both Heart souls, they had been associated with the fringe group of nobles who secretly plotted against the Chancellor. The Countess was back in favour and fashion. Though she no longer had a motive for thievery and blackmail, I didn't doubt that her house was still full of stolen treasures.

"Iris, or should I say Ruby Renato now?" she said.

"Ruby is fine," I said. "I have too many names already."

"All the best people do," the Countess replied. "I myself was born Agatha Cramp, before becoming Agatha Landry, Agatha Patterson and Agatha Cavendish. Perhaps one day soon, I might take another new name." She gave a coy little smile across the room to the Governor who smiled back, bewildered.

"I thought you said love was a crock and a sham," I said.

"It is, dear, but money and power... Now, those are things you *can* rely on."

I couldn't help but scoff at her shamelessness.

"When I first met you, you were a mere urchin thieving trinkets for coins," she said. "Now you're ruling over an entire country. I hope you won't forget your dear old friend the Countess now that you're on top of the world. Don't you recall how I helped you recover your soul and remember yourself, hmmm?"

"How could I ever forget?" I said, tartly. "But nor will I forget how you blackmailed me and sent me on a fool's errand that almost got me killed."

"You're still here though, aren't you, dear?" she said. "That's the important thing. We can help each other now. Speaking of which..." She rummaged in her black-fringed handbag. "I thought you might take an interest in this."

The Countess held out an object that glittered with the power of psyche, temporarily dazzling me. When my vision cleared, I could see that it was a playing card. The King of Hearts.

"When I saw the papers this morning and recognized the man on the billboards, I knew I had to bring it to you."

"The assassin?"

"Who else, dear? He is captured in this anonymous remnant."

I took the card gently from her, feeling the vibrations of psyche beneath my fingertips. It was pulsing with a memory, something vivid and bloody, stirring just beneath the surface. I peeled off my gloves, allowing myself to be sucked bodily into the moment of the remnant's creation, as if I were present at the scene, squatting in the body of the memory's maker…

I sit at a table with a green cloth, looking at my hand of cards and recognizing a royal flush. My opponent is a man in military uniform: the tan-coloured fatigues of the Constitutional army, with embroidered patches on the sleeves, medals and ribbons on the breast.

"I'm all in," he says, holding my gaze.

What looks like a casino fills in behind him, with marble pillars, purple carpets and an extravagant glass ceiling.

By looking into the man's eyes, I can see his hand, reflected in the mirror of his pupils. He has four aces. He thinks he has me beaten, but I'm about to ruin his night. I raise the cards to my lips to kiss them, then splay them out on the table with a flourish.

"Read them and weep," I say, my voice unnaturally distorted.

He groans good-naturedly.

"The House wins again," he says. "The Sixth House, I mean."

I chuckle, the sound low and rumbly.

Another round of drinks is delivered to the table by a waitress. I gather up my winnings and deposit them on her empty tray.

"For your services."

She tucks the coins into the pocket of her apron, her gaze lingering.

"Thank you, sir."

A pale young man appears in the doorway and is waved through by the guards. He moves through the crowd towards me with a gloating look of pride.

"Would you mind excusing me?" *I say to my opponent.* "My ten o'clock has just arrived and I'm hoping he brings good news."

The soldier departs, moving on to the roulette table.

Now the stranger sits down opposite me and removes his hood, revealing himself further. His eyes are green, and he has a narrow, slightly gaunt appearance. He has white, slicked-back hair, and a tattooed teardrop beneath his right eye.

"Is it done?" *I ask.*

He smirks, pulling a metal box from his bag and placing it in the centre of the table. It's wrapped in sackcloth.

The assassin lifts up one corner surreptitiously, uncovering a little grilled partition.

"Oh, it's done, sir," *he says.* "He's done."

Something inside the box is glowing, pulsating, changing colour.

A live soul.

It emits a strange, garbled noise, replaying the final crescendo of an aria.

I stash the cloth-wrapped box beneath the table and slide a black case across to my companion.

"Here, as agreed. Your reward."

The assassin opens it briefly, his expression impassive, before closing it again. He stands up, taking the case with him.

"What now, sir?" he says.

"Wait for my instructions. Watch with both eyes."

The assassin salutes.

"One down, five to go."

"In the name of the Sixth House."

The scene ended abruptly, returning me to the wake.

The memory's creator was still no clearer to me. A man – a powerful man – in league with the army of Constitution. A gambler who stole souls to order.

The moment must've taken place on the night of the murder. The killer had gone straight from Harmonia House to this casino, to deliver the soul he'd been hired to "liberate". The assassin's pupils, I remembered, appeared normal, too.

I hadn't been able to see much of the boss with the royal flush, apart from the coat they were wearing (high-collared, grey) and their hands, which were clad in black leather gloves. Their voice had been distorted beyond recognition but they were addressed as "sir". They commanded a certain authority.

It wasn't looking good for the Governor.

"Where did you get it?" I asked the Countess.

"Is that all you have to say?" she replied.

"Oh, I have plenty to say. I just thought I'd start there."

"I have many little spies. Some of them are pickpockets, some of them are burglars, some of them are grave robbers. I can't be expected to keep track of which is which, or who delivered what. Too many of them, and too many trinkets. Life is too short to keep such meticulous records. But it's curious, isn't it? Here we were thinking destroying a soul was the epitome of depravity, but it seems there are worse things."

"For what purpose would someone require a whole, *live* soul?"

"A soul can be a powerful weapon," she said. "You know that. Yours sparked a revolution, after all. The greater the power, the bigger the sacrifice."

"Any idea as to who might be behind this?"

"The former Chancellor comes to mind."

"But he's locked away. Oliver made sure of that."

"There must be people who'd be glad to do his dirty work for him, though. Perhaps his Shadowy allies are working to seize power again, contacting him somehow through the subconscious. I've heard rumours, about the Shades of the First Borough."

The Shades – the Shadow House gang led by Blade, whose chest was a cobweb of scars.

"Thank you, that's … actually useful."

"Don't sound so surprised, dear. We all have something to fear, should the country fall into chaos. Let us hope you can stop it."

I considered her, my head tilted to one side. "You know, in all the time I've known you, I don't think I've ever fully understood what your gift is," I said.

"Who says I have a gift?" she said. "Some of us only have grift," and, with that, the Countess glided over to the Governor.

Later, Oliver and I returned to Obscura House, where Rani, Octavia and Gus were waiting, along with my mother. They had not been invited to the intimate inner-circle wake, a largely nobles-only affair. The mood was sombre. Lord Harmonia had not been well liked, but the implications of his murder were dark.

"You're just in time for dinner," said Gus. "I think everyone could do with a bit of Heart food right now."

"Thanks Gus. You're the best."

Gus baked feelings into food but he was also what was known as an empath – a person who soaked up the emotions of those around them, both good and bad. Somehow, despite this, he always seemed cheerful.

Over a feast of turkey, potatoes and stuffing, we discussed what we'd learned so far.

"I've been investigating the gangs," said Rani. "Their numbers have been decimated by the emergence of the Sixth House. Their meeting houses were half empty. The only gang that still appears to be holding up the resistance front is the Shades and their leader, Blade. He's certainly an interesting character…"

"More food, anyone?" said Gus brightly.

"He keeps the company of many lovers, men and women alike. He has a taste for fine arts and urban culture. He's an orphan, a prisoner, a thief, an activist, perhaps even a killer, but he is also a charitable figure known for supporting vulnerable people and local communities."

"Do you think this Blade fellow could be the leader of the Sixth?" asked Octavia, pushing food around with her fork.

Almost mechanically, Gus began heaping more potatoes on to Oliver's plate, spooning out a carbohydrate mountain so intimidating that Oliver had to hold out his hand and beg him to stop.

"Sorry," said Gus. "I'm a bit nervy right now. On edge."

"We all are," said Octavia, her fingers drumming the table.

"If Blade *is* the leader of the Sixth," said Rani, "then how did he amass so much power? No one knows much about him – not even his own people – yet he has access to a vast fortune?"

"He must be working with someone else," I said. I pulled out the playing card. "The Countess gave me this, at the wake. It might give us a clue as to who we're looking for."

I held the card in front of the lantern produced by Oliver and we all watched as the scene in the casino replayed.

"That can't be Blade," said Octavia. "Blade is Black.

178

That man's hands are white. You can just make out the skin between his shirt and his gloves, see?"

"Well that's that then," said Gus. "Blade is off the hook."

"We should still talk to him, though. What about the casino? Does anyone recognize that?" I asked.

The assembled group shrugged or shook their heads.

"Sorry, I'm not much of a gambler," said Rani. "I'm not very lucky, except, you know, with the ladies." She winked at Octavia, who giggled and twirled a curl.

"There's a casino in the First Borough," said my mother. "It has pillars just like that on the outside. The Lucky something."

"Oh, the Lucky Hand!" said Gus, watching the memory's projection again. "I have a friend who works there. I can ask if they've seen this teardrop fella hanging around the place. They might be more inclined to talk to me than the Inspectors who are investigating."

In all this time, Oliver had said nothing; he just stared broodingly at the playing card, turning it over in his hands.

"Poor Lord Harmonia," sighed Octavia, resting her head in the cradle of her arms on the table. "Wherever he is, I hope he's not still conscious."

"He probably is," said Rani, with an apologetic look. "They must want him alive for something, at least … for a while."

Octavia pulled a face and buried her face in her hands.

I shuddered too, imagining being trapped in a box, with no way to get back to my body.

"A fate worse than death," my mother said. "The Chancellor kept me in a cage ready to use my soul for fuel. I wouldn't wish it on anyone, not even the Chancellor himself."

"What do you think they'll do with it … with *him*?" asked Octavia.

We fell quiet, reluctant to imagine.

"These catatonic people in the Sixth House remind me of my father's army," said Oliver, suddenly. "He took over their souls, puppeteering numerous bodies at once. He used the soul's power for control. He used the loyalty and adoration of his followers against them. That's what made him so formidable. Maybe … maybe history is repeating itself."

"If the leader of the Sixth House is using the same kind of soul power to manipulate people," I said, "they'd require vast amounts of it. I mean, you inherited your father's gift so you could probably control a handful of people at once by yourself."

"If I desired," he replied. "But we're talking a few at most. My father could command a troop but not an entire population. Whoever this is, they have a vast power at their disposal."

"So our many-faced monster might actually be a secret Shadow army?" said my mother.

"Run by someone who wants to assassinate the New Order and then use them to seize control?" said Rani.

"Are we truly safe here, do you think?" asked Octavia.

"The House is surrounded by a dozen soldiers," I said.

"Besides, the assassin should be more scared of us than we are of them. We're quite a team."

"That you are," said my mother with a smile. She looked round admiringly at the gifted group, but concern remained in her eyes.

A knock on the door caused us all to startle.

"Assassins don't usually knock," said Gus. "We're probably good."

"Oh, it's just Gabriel," said Oliver. "My guardian."

Gabriel was something of a silver fox, with grey eyes and a scar through his left eyebrow that made him look distinctively dashing. My mother had clearly noticed too – I saw her eyes widen, her cheeks flush, as she hastily fixed her hair.

"Evening, all," he said in his gruff voice. His keen eyes scanned the room, resting a second longer on my mother, a slow smile spreading over his face.

"Oh, hello. I'm not sure we've met yet," he said.

"Gabriel, this is my mother, Mara," I said, "so watch yourself, mister." I was just teasing, playing the part of the parent with her as the amorous teenager, but her face burned bright red.

"Oh, ha ha!" she said, in a voice that was higher than usual. She gave me a side-eye death glare. "Don't listen to Ruby, Gabriel. She's such a joker. It's a pleasure to meet you. Oliver has told me so much about you."

"The pleasure is mine, Mara, all mine," said Gabriel, eyes twinkling invitingly, before he turned to Oliver. "The

Inspectors have found something curious, my Lord. I wanted to bring it to you right away."

Crossing the room, he placed a small object into Oliver's hand.

"It was discovered at Harmonia House," he explained. "We don't yet know if it was left by the assassin, but his Lordship's servants don't recognize it. So it stands to reason that it was."

Oliver turned it over in his hands.

"What is it?" I said, leaning over to get a better look.

"It's a dice."

"As in dice, like you might use in a casino?"

"Not just any dice," said Oliver, holding it up, "but a dice *with a six on every face*."

The Sixth House.

"Where would be the fun in that?" said Gus. "That's not much of a game, is it? 'Ooh will I roll a six, or a six? I can't wait to find out!'"

It was just a simple, harmless thing, a toy really, but even so I shivered, sensing a dark presence about it. Oliver handed it to me gingerly. I ran my fingers over the six little pits in each of its faces, trying to draw out its psyche, but it gave off no vibes.

"First the playing card, now this?" I said.

"It must've been left behind deliberately," said Oliver.

"What if they're trying to lead us to this casino on purpose? What if it's a trap?" I said.

"I think it's more like a warning," he said. "It's saying

the Sixth House is coming for all of us, our downfall is inescapable."

To lighten the mood, I stood and rolled the dice carefully on the floor. We watched as it landed on an edge, suspended between faces as if defying gravity.

"How did you do that?" said Oliver, chuckling in surprise. It was good to see him laugh, even if it was just for a moment.

"Just a little trick I learned on the streets," I said. "See? Not everything is inescapable, even if it feels like it."

"I hope you're right," he said. "But the odds—"

"We're going to find the assassin and his boss, and put an end to this Sixth House," I said. "Screw the odds."

"That's right!" said Rani.

"I'm with you," said Octavia.

"We all are," said Mum.

I sparked a fireball in my hand, then contained it in my upheld fist. Holding my gaze, Oliver drew out his Shadow, which formed a monstrous figure on the wall, a horned demonic beast. Rani smiled and projected a serpentine creature with wings. Octavia closed her eyes, putting one finger to her right ear as she sang a shrill note, the sound throbbing as it pulsed mid-air, ready to temporarily discombobulate her victim. Gus surprised us all by casting a wave of fearsome ass-kicking energy, like a general giving a rousing battle-cry speech without words, causing us all to whoop and cheer. My mother joined in too, her eyes turning white as she projected public remembrances of the old Order's misdeeds on to the wall. Even Gabriel got into the spirit, finishing off the display with a plume of fire that shot through the open window and burst into embers in the sky, creating a bright, stellar waterfall that reflected in my mother's pupils.

Later, I walked my mother to the door.

"He's quite the charmer, isn't he?" she mused.

"Who?" I said, pretending not to understand.

"Oliver's guardian. Gabriel." She toyed with her sleeve. "Does he have kids? Has he a wife or a partner or…?" She trailed off.

"You know, I think he might be on the market," I said. "Oliver says his wife died, but it was a long time ago now."

"Oh no. Poor Gabriel, and here's me thinking only with my Spark."

"Maybe he's lonely and would like some company."

"You think?"

"You deserve to be happy," I said. "Even in dark times. *Especially* in dark times."

"You're right," she said. "Life is short. We might as well get what pleasure we can out of it, at the end of the day."

"I don't want to hear about that!" I said. "But … you should stay here tonight. It's safer if we're all together, and there are enough spare rooms."

"If you want me to stay, I'll stay," she said, hugging me.

"Plus, Gabriel can protect you here," I teased.

She thwacked me lightly before kissing my forehead.

"Listen, sometimes you have to take love where you find it," she said softly. "Before it's gone. Before we're all gone."

I joined Oliver upstairs in bed, drawn under the comforting cloak of his Shadow, falling into him as he embraced me.

But if I dreamed that night, I didn't remember it.

10.

OLIVER

I waited until Ruby fell asleep before I slipped out into the night, not in the form of my Shadow as promised, but in my own body. That put me in greater danger but it meant I was more dangerous in turn. I wouldn't lose another soul to the assassin. I had watched my mother being killed before my eyes. I had watched Mr Sharma die. I had let my father use me to shatter Ruby. Each time, I had been too weak to stop it.

I would not be powerless again.

I would not lose the person who mattered to me most.

I'd swiped Gabriel's identity card from his jacket on my way, using it as a blueprint to assume his form. If I used my own face, I wouldn't get too far. Sorry, Gabriel. I hoped I'd be back before he noticed it was gone.

There was something we were missing, I knew it. But what?

I would start with the clue of the dice and the playing card. I would locate the casino. I found the Lucky Hand in the First Borough, showing Gabriel's pass to gain entry on the door, but as soon as I entered, it was obvious that it wasn't the right place. The tables were blue, the carpets were patterned, and there was no glass ceiling above the bar.

I moved on, criss-crossing the city maze in search of the right casino, but none of them matched the vision we'd seen in the playing card I carried in my pocket for reference. I followed the criminal trail of the Shades instead. I let it take me, like the tide, ebbing and flowing in different directions. Quickly, I located their base, a dimly lit nest of rooms above a bookshop, where a small group of hooded youths looked through stolen records and photographs, but no Blade.

"Still no sign of him?" said one, their voice catching my ear.

"Maybe he's gone underground," another muttered.

"In hiding, you mean. He's pissed off, left us… What a coward."

So Blade was missing. That was interesting.

When one of them turned my way, appearing to glimpse my Shadow on the wall, I pushed deeper into the web of rooms, watching gang members drinking, smoking, making love… For a second, I forgot what I was doing there, becoming an observer. I was strangely envious of these people, who lived without the burden of ruling a country, but also without the privilege.

I slid back into the corridor as a woman with an unusual tattoo wheeled past. The Eye of Obscura was crossed out like a stop sign. A former loyalist of the House who had now turned against it. Her mind was full of crimes, her pockets full of stolen remnants, like Ruby's used to be. Something prickled – my sixth sense perhaps, telling me that she was worth following.

I trailed the woman at a distance, through a series of courtyards and into a crooked building with a shimmering psychometric sign above the door that read: PLEASURE HOUSE. Not the sort of establishment I'd usually frequent, but I was on a mission tonight.

Inside, the venue was packed. A rowdy group of Constitutional soldiers were gathered near the lobby, making bets on who would be successful in their sexual endeavours. Punters sat at a series of curtained booths, drinking from glowing chalices and watching the projections of the orbs on the table. Chorus girls. Monster fighters. A football match. Some of them glared at me fearfully, suspiciously, even lustfully, but none of them seemed to recognize me behind the disguise.

Looking down, I saw the carpet was purple.

The woman in the wheelchair had vanished already, melting into the throng of a moving crowd. I pushed on to the centre of the building instead, where card tables were arranged beneath a glass ceiling. Green tables.

I was in the right place.

My sixth sense had led me here, somehow. It was more than just visions. It was a part of me now. It worked with my Shade, giving me glimpses of the future, and this was it: something important was here, waiting to be found.

If I concentrated my Shadow, I could see the souls of

every person present, as if projected by a lantern. I could sense the edges of their minds, their raw, naked impulses. If someone had a desire to hurt others, it was like a red flag, a bright bloody smear. The room was full of bad intentions, but those stains were faded, old blood, not the fresh, raw feel of a recent act of violence.

No one had murder in mind right now.

"You looking for company tonight?" A woman in a red dress materialized at my side. Curvaceous. Long-lashed. Shiny lips.

Wherever he went, Gabriel seemed to draw eyes. Perhaps he was not the best choice for a disguise. I hadn't realized how handsome he was until this moment. He had the kind of bone structure that made him look vulpine and dignified, with the aura of someone who had grown wise through experience. He moved in a quietly confident way, assured of his own power.

I played up to it, touching the woman's arm softly as I said, "I'm on a mission tonight. Maybe some other time. You're beautiful though."

"Too bad," she pouted.

To escape her hungry gaze, I joined a group of furtive-looking men being escorted to the barely lit backrooms. They didn't notice me lingering nor did they talk to each other, but their pockets were fat with cash. A sign saying LIVE SOULS flashed on the wall in psychometric neon.

We walked down a dark corridor lined with peepholes for customers to look in on, revealing a series of seedy private suites where spectral forms of otherworldly beauty danced and glittered incandescently. At the end of the hall, a group of people with pure black eyes were attached by thin shining threads to the dancing visions they projected for the audience in the room beyond the red curtain. They were escorts, mostly Shadow souls, who used psyche to assume whatever form the client desired. One weedy girl took the form of a muscular Amazonian, while a skinny young man projected the image of a buxom woman in a bikini. A brief dip into their minds told me they performed for days on end without pay, slept in crowded dormitories and lived off crumbs.

"Take your pick, gentlemen," said a greasy man who seemed to be in charge. He wore a badge that said MANAGER. "Forty crowns for thirty minutes, sixty for the full hour. Any special requests? Come talk to me."

Toppling my father had done much good for Providence, but without the Eye network, organized crime was now thriving. Inflation was rising. People were hungrier and angrier and more hopeless. Kill one bad guy and another popped up to take his place…

I surreptitiously sent a signal to the leader of the squadrons of Inspectors, calling them to my location, then I let the monster of my Shadow take over from me. Smiling serenely, I erupted into a creature of horns and claws, like a sleep-paralysis demon.

"You're a sick piece of shit," I growled.

The greasy manager was swept up in dark tentacles,

which pinned him to the wall like a fly in a web. The other punters fled, pouring out through the fire exit into an alley. The escorts gawked at me glassily, in fascination and fear.

"Go!" I said. "You're free now."

Their faces were blank with shock and confusion.

"GO!"

Slowly they gathered themselves, disappearing into the night. I turned back to face the manager, his face bright red.

"Where do you think they'll end up now, with no money?" he said.

"Tell me what you know about the Sixth House," I growled.

He spat at me, a putrid glob of phlegm. "Piss off."

I growled again, manifesting an even more menacing appearance, mimicking the skeletal goat-like monster I'd seen illustrated in one of those pseudoscientific soul tomes.

The man paled and swallowed.

"Start talking, or I'll make you regret it," I demanded.

"Who the hell are you?" he said, struggling uselessly against me. "I know people. People with connections."

I laughed in his face. "Really?"

"You're gonna regret coming in here and swinging your Shadow around, pal. You don't know who you're messing with."

Smiling crookedly, my eyes open slightly too wide, I let my true identity shine through the illusory disguise.

I watched as he recognized me, the colour draining from his face.

"Oh, I think I know a few more people than you do," I said.

"Oliver Obscura," he gasped.

The dark restraints squeezed tighter.

"Come on, speak up. Cat got your tongue?"

"I don't know nothing, I swear," he rasped. "I'm a bottom feeder."

"You work for Blade?"

"Blade? You must be out of the loop. He's been missing for weeks. Someone else is calling the shots now."

"If you don't have anything else useful to tell me, I can find another use for *you*, I'm sure," I said, lifting him into the air and dangling him there. "My father taught me plenty of wicked tricks. Maybe whoever's selling stolen souls through your establishment will have need for another one. You know how they acquire a soul, do you? They rip it right out of your chest."

I created a large arm of Shadow, winding it back as if to punch him as he squirmed.

"The Sixth House, they want to dismantle the New Order," he said quickly, wincing in expectation of pain.

"Who leads the Sixth?" I demanded.

"No one knows," he said. "One person says it was a man, another says it was a woman, even a kid. They appear different to everyone."

The monster with many faces.

"The Sixth pay us to keep quiet and look the other way, OK?" he said. "They use this place to store the…"

He trailed off, fearful that someone might overhear.

"The what?"

He hesitated, reluctant to say the words out loud.

"Tell me!" I yelled, slamming him against the wall again.

"*Souls*," he blurted. "They're *collecting* souls."

So there it was. The Sixth House was amassing power, literally.

"What about *him*?" I said, broadcasting the memory of the assassin on to the wall. "Do you recognize him?"

"I … I might've seen him coming in, once or twice."

"I think you're still keeping secrets from me," I said, "and I don't like secrets."

"No, please, no," he begged, watching my pupils dilate.

I violated his mind, a filthy den, tearing through clouds of fantasy and memory like a winding arrow. I focused in on the assassin, watched him coming and going from the bar, but the manager had never seen him speaking to anyone. He was always too busy with his creepy customers. I saw the people who paid the manager in coin each week in exchange for his silence, a different face every time. I saw the pallets in the loading bay, stacked with glowing boxes.

I went deeper…

The manager has a sister named Verity. A thin, tragic little thing, dark under the eyes, lugging around the latest purse she's stolen. It's full of psychogens, the reality-escaping drugs she's addicted to. He goes to see her every Sunday, gives her money and bread, sharing some of the earnings he makes so she stays off the streets. I narrow in on a single memory, of her sitting in a beat-up armchair and talking about her new friends.

"*The Sixth House will make everything right,*" *she tells him. Her pupils are clear and full, not crescents. She's been converted in the traditional way, with sensational rhetoric and empty promises.*

"*They're just telling you what you want to hear,*" *he counters.*

"*Don't be like that, Frankie,*" *she says.* "*Ain't you sick of this? Always hungry, always poor, always wantin', no matter who's in charge? Wouldn't it be nice to be happy for once? Don't we deserve that?*"

"*The Sixth House won't do shit, Vez, just like the New Order and whoever comes after 'em,*" *said the manager, Frankie.*

"*You haven't seen what I've seen,*" *she said.* "*They're planning something big this time. There's going to be a war and you need to be on the right side…*"

The memory faded, falling into obscurity.

I paused, falling back.

There's going to be a war…

A war had been raging in my vision of Ruby's death, at the Basilica. Was the Sixth readying its followers to fight?

I glanced at the cowering manager. The memory I'd seen had made this monster human. Desperate times make for wicked people. Yes, he was a fleshmonger, but he was capable of love. It made him somewhat redeemable.

I released him, leaving him crumpled on the ground.

Sirens sounded in the distance, growing louder.

"You have about thirty seconds to disappear without a trace."

With that, he scrambled up, tripping over his own feet, while I departed into the night, drunk on my own power.

I could feel the Shadow coursing through my veins, making my blood dark. It was so much easier, so much more fun, to be a monster than to be myself.

The red-skied apocalypse I'd seen taunted me, haunted me.

With every piece of the puzzle, the vision grew stronger.

On the night of the crescent moon, Constitution's flags would fly in the Basilica, a war would break out, and Ruby would be shot by the assassin.

I decided to walk home to mull over what I'd learned, my disguise fading as I became consumed with my own thoughts. If the assassin wanted to confront me, so be it. I was ready to fight him.

I was so lost in contemplation, I forgot to check if I was being followed until a strange noise drew my attention, its din growing until it became a roar. I turned just in time to see a black speck of darkness stretching into a large void, its edges rippled and feathered. A portal swarmed into being, swirling outwards like water filling a bathtub. Its vibrations were so strong it trembled my bones and my skin, making me feel like a cocktail shaker.

I raised my hands, wrapping thick Shadows round them, ready for combat.

A petite figure stepped out, her high heels planting themselves delicately on the rain-slick cobbles. The portal broke apart to form three dark-matter soldiers, all of them holding devastating-looking scythes.

I blinked rapidly, unable to believe what I was seeing.

It was the Empress. The general currently holding Constitution at bay. The woman at war with our own fragile army. Providence's mortal enemy.

Empress Matrina Nox, ruler of the vast frozen lands of Arctica in the north. Her cloak was black and purple, rimmed with snow leopard fur.

Perpetua had spoken of her. Said she could identify a person's fears just by looking at them, that she could kill with a single side-eye…

And she was staring right at me.

"I've been watching you, Oliver Obscura," she said, in a sing-song voice that sent a chill down my spine.

She moved to stand in front of me, shadowy wisps of dark matter still curling around her like smoke. Her face resembled a mask, so perfectly smooth and even, her dark hair woven into an ornamental headpiece, with elaborate make-up that formed swirls around her eyes.

Yet I hadn't sensed her in my head. Her presence was feather-light.

She circled me, leaving a shadowy trail behind.

"Don't be so surprised," she said, as if reading my mind. "I'm the most powerful Shadow soul in the world." She blinked out of existence, reappearing on top of the nearby wall. "That's not a boast. Merely a fact." She vanished again, reappearing behind me. "I can find anyone. I can explore their soul just by thinking about them. But it is you I wished to find. Aren't you lucky?"

She had the same accent as Perpetua, both soft and deep, sharp and liquid, the vowels running into one another.

"Why?"

"Curiosity," she said. "I have watched you for a while, as I watch all my enemies. Recently, I have noticed a change in you. You have begun to explore the dark arts. The sixth sense. This intrigues me."

"What else have you seen?" I asked.

"Many things. That you are powerful. Not as powerful as me, but you could be, if only you could defeat your demons."

Up close, I could see how young she was beneath the make-up. Not quite as young as me, but still young to be ruling an entire empire.

"I have seen your monster of a thousand faces," she said. "I have seen the master turning people into puppets. I have seen the war that will soon begin, on the night of the Governor's farewell ball. I have seen things, as you have seen things."

I saw red skies in her eyes, and that thin crescent moon, sharp as the weapons her soldiers held.

A crescent like the pupils of those controlled by the Sixth House.

"You mean, the sixth sense?"

She held up her hand and her dark-matter guards dispersed again, their bodies breaking apart to create a tunnel that burrowed through reality.

"Come," she said. "Follow me. Quickly."

Could I say no to the Empress? Perhaps, but it wouldn't be wise.

I trailed her into the dark, emerging in a lavish hotel room with black marble furnishings and black rose petals scattered on the bed.

"I want to understand," I said.

"First, we play."

She gestured towards two chairs and a table, set with a black-and-white chess set.

"Sit," she said. It was not a question but an order.

Dutifully, I took my seat as we launched into a game. I sacrificed a pawn, while she boldly put forward her queen.

"You and I, we are the same," she said.

"Because we're both Shadow souls?"

"No, it is more than that. We both are capable of precognition. I died as a child and came back, like you came back."

That caught my attention, for sure.

"Ever since, I have the second sight. The sixth sense."

"It's true, then?" I said, though I'd known it all along. "It's real? Everyone told me it was just a story. A myth."

"People do not understand the mysteries of the world. They see only the first layer of reality and they are satisfied with that. But those who have seen beyond the veil cannot deny it. They cannot look away."

The Empress took the moment to seize one of my knights.

I stared at the chequered board, trying to work out my next move.

My father used to make me play chess with him. He would always win and then scold me for losing. I wasn't smart enough, he said. I didn't anticipate far enough ahead; I had no mind for strategy. *"You're no son of mine,"* he'd say. *"I didn't pay so much money to raise an idiot."*

"I have a proposition for you, if you're willing to hear it," she said, cutting through my thoughts. "I can teach you what I know about the sixth sense."

"What kind of proposition? Because I have absolutely nothing to offer you in return," I replied, taking her castle.

"Not nothing. You don't know what I want yet."

"Whatever it is, I can't help you," I said. "I'm part of the New Order. Last I heard, you were invading our colonies."

She shook her head. She wore extravagant earrings like spades of jet, which scratched at her bare neck.

"I took them only for my own protection," she said. "The people did not fight. No blood was shed. I am not the monster the world sees me as, but powerful forces are conspiring against me, just as they are conspiring against you." She moved her knight into position. "You must persuade Premier Cordata not to ally with the Governor of Constitution."

She seized my knight with nimble fingers.

"The alliance is crucial to our survival," I said.

"If you believe that, you're as foolish as Premier Cordata. The Governor has a plan. He will take Providence and then, with your armies combined, he will attempt to take me and my world. He is set on global domination."

"Isn't that what they say about you?"

She smirked, her black lips twitching.

"The history you have been taught is biased. Dig a little deeper, Oliver. History is written by those who win. My father and my grandfather both ruled before me. Both were executed by your father's spies, in favour of the puppet installed by the Order. The Chancellor thought me weak, a mere child, so he let me live in the shadows, hoping I would serve his purposes. He didn't know what he'd meddled with. He hadn't reckoned on me."

"That does seem to have been a grave mistake," I said.

"I killed that puppet emperor and I took back my country. I swore vengeance against your father, until you saved me the job and toppled him yourself. Now we both face a much greater evil, and a much graver danger."

"Fairchild doesn't seem dangerous," I said. "I've examined his psyche. There's nothing in his head but fruit."

"The reason you cannot penetrate his mind properly is because his identity is a façade," she said. "Some say he is not a Heart soul at all, but a Shadow soul like us."

"Why would he lie?"

"To hide his true nature, of course. Everyone likes Heart souls. They're warm, charitable; they have a way of drawing people to them. Shadow souls?" She shook her head. "People don't trust us." She gestured to me. "Your move."

I looked down at the board, contemplating. What now? She had me trapped. No matter what series of moves I planned out in my head, they all ended in me losing.

A faint vision shone in my mind. I could just anticipate the mistake she was about to make in two turns, losing her queen's bishop and the last of her pawns, leaving the monarch exposed. This was it; this was how I could win.

"People complain about bloody revolutions and public executions, but at least you know where you are with violence," she said. "A soul like me will tell you exactly how I'll kill you, and why, before I cut your throat. But a soul like Ambrose Fairchild will kill you slowly, in secret, asphyxiating you as he watches, like a serpent wrapped round your neck."

"I'm afraid it's too late. He's signed an agreement with Premier Cordata," I said.

"It cannot pass. I have seen this future. I know it will lead us to war. You must tear it up. Burn it down. Use your visions to guide you."

"But I can't control the sense," I admitted, reluctantly. "I see only flashes, fragments. I'm utterly lost with it."

"I was once lost too, but I learned to take hold of the visions and direct them to my desire. You must jettison a piece of the past in order to see the future. A memory works best. One of your own, relevant to whatever answer you seek."

"I have to forget the past to perceive the future?" I said. "That makes a twisted sort of sense, I suppose."

"I have sacrificed many memories. There are things I knew I would be better to forget... Perhaps you will feel the same."

They flashed through my mind, involuntarily, those things I wished most to banish to oblivion. My mother falling from the balcony. My father's Shadow on the wall, looming monstrously. The moment Ruby led me to that locked box inside her, in which I saw the truth of her deception... But most of all, the blood on her lips...

"Why should I believe anything you say?" I asked, moving my piece.

"Because I can show you how to save her."

My breath caught in my throat. She smiled like a tilted dagger and moved her queen into place, the movement smooth.

"Checkmate," she said.

The vision I'd seen was false. A trick.

"Do you see how easy you are to conquer?" she said. "The Governor will soon have you eating from the palm of his hand. He is not to be trusted. If Premier Cordata allies with him, the war will be unstoppable. You will not be able to spare your lover from the end she is destined to meet."

Her voice was lyrical, enchanting.

"Tell me," I said, already dreading the answer, "in the visions you've seen of the future, has Lady Ruby come to harm in some of them?"

"In all of them," she said.

I looked up from the black and white tiles, meeting her eyes, the batwings of her make-up sharp as knives.

"I will show you what I see," she said.

In her doll-like face, I read pity. Reaching forward, she touched my temples with her fingertips, pulling me forcibly into her mind. Her nails were painted black. Her dark lacy dress had finger-point sleeves. I flinched slightly, but I couldn't resist.

Her mind was like ancient catacombs, dank and cold, lined with skulls. In each alcove, I saw a vision…

A group of people in a darkened room, chanting, waving weapons. Here are Perpetua and Ash and the leader of the Shades – the man known as Blade… And standing next to them are Gus, Rani and…

"Octavia?"

They too had turned against me.

A blurry figure stands at the top of an imperial staircase, their face shadowed. Maps, barrels, caches of chemicals and weapons. People fighting in rings. A group of nobles trussed up and tied to chairs, held hostage by rebels wielding dark pistols.

Souls in crates, thousands upon thousands of souls.

"Death to the New Order," people chant. "In the name of the Sixth House!"

The man atop the stairs steps forward, revealing himself as Ambrose Fairchild. I see the green-eyed, tear-tattooed assassin moving through the darkness to the Basilica of All Souls, reaching Ruby in the room with the crescent moon in the window.

BANG!

Blood on her lips, a hole in her chest.

Ruby in a coffin, surrounded by vanitas, eyes painted on her lids, as I wail like Lady Harmonia.

Outside the sky is burning, falling. Dark airships flying the flag of Constitution. Soldiers riding on horses, psychometric energy rippling across a darkened battlefield like lightning…

Time skips, jumps forward. Now I'm the person commanding the troops, dressed in my father's robes. They beg me to listen to reason but I can't, I won't.

"But Chancellor Obscura, we—"

"Just do it. They took her from me, so now I'll take everything from them."

"Sir, they will destroy us all!"

"DO IT!"

I see the hunger in me, my desire for all the world to burn.

I see myself as I could be … a monster.

Back in reality, I bent over, sickened and winded.

"If that is all you see, then there is no hope," I said.

"You are wrong. There is still time to rewrite destiny."

The Empress handed me a slim black leather-bound book without a title. I flicked through it to see it was full of handwritten notes and illustrations, including a complex tree of neurology. "My research will show you how."

My heart pounded. Here were the answers I'd desperately longed for. The key to changing the future. But the solution came at a price. Didn't it always?

"Do not tell Ruby that we have met," she ordered. "Do not tell her what you are planning to do. This must be our secret."

"But why?"

"If you tell her, you risk altering the future in unknown

ways. You may create a dark path that you cannot deviate from. It is safer for her not to know," she said.

"I … I can do that. If I must."

"The union between Constitution and Providence must be sabotaged."

"But—"

"War must be prevented. Stop the war, save the girl," she said.

Those were her parting words, before she vanished into a pinpoint.

11.

RUBY

"Ruby, dear? Are you still with us?"

I looked up from the tea I was stirring hypnotically to see Lady Memoria and Countess Cavendish staring at me. The clink of silver spoons against porcelain cups. Two elderly women dressed in their fineries, meeting for their weekly shindig in a tea shop in the Second Borough where the décor was all florals and chintz.

They had invited me along, and for some foolish reason, I'd agreed.

"Sorry," I murmured.

The Countess clucked her tongue. "Daydreaming again?" she said. "You'll waste away to nothing if you carry on like that – just like that beau of yours."

"Agatha, really," shushed Lady Memoria. "Mind your tongue."

"You can't deny he's looking thin. He needs a good meal, if you ask me." The Countess slid another éclair on to her plate. "Most people do."

"You Heart souls think food is the answer to everything,"

tutted Lady Memoria, spritzing herself with some musty perfume.

"Isn't it?" said the Countess.

"What that boy needs is a bit of snuff, to bring him back to reality."

They made a somewhat peculiar duo: Lady Memoria in white, lilies pinned to her suit jacket, her short aristocratic hairdo decorated with silk flowers; the Countess slightly witch-like in black and gold lace, her white hair covered by a wide-brimmed black hat, and wearing a large gold necklace in the shape of a heart.

"Can we talk about something else?" I said. "Literally *anything* else?"

"Oh dear," said the Countess, knowingly. "Has love's young dream turned to dust already? Don't say I didn't warn you."

"Did I say anything about Oliver? No. He's fine. I'm fine. Everything is perfectly fine."

The Countess widened her eyes at Lady Memoria.

"You don't need to lie to us, dear. We read the papers."

"What's that supposed to mean?" I said, grumpily.

"You haven't seen?" said the Countess.

"They're speculating that it's all over between you," said Memoria. "I can't say I blame them for making such an assumption. You haven't been seen together in weeks."

"We don't go out at all," I said. "For our safety, he says. That has nothing to do with anything."

"Curious then, that the *Eye on Providence* is running

a story about him gadding about town last night," said the Countess.

She slapped today's edition on to the table, angling it so I could see.

The front page bore a blurry picture of Oliver in a pleasure house full of erotic dancers; he seemed to be terrorizing a terrified-looking man with tentacles of Shadow.

CHIP OFF THE OLD BLOCK: TYRANT'S SON GOES WILD! screamed the headline in large block letters.

"Paranoid and out of control," said Lady Memoria. "Just like the night he attacked that poor messenger boy."

"The press will turn anything into a scandal," I said, tossing the paper aside, but my mind was whirling.

What was Oliver *doing*?

The Countess leafed through a few more pages to the centrefold, revealing a double-page spread about the Empress's reign of terror, while an opinion column mocked the New Order's attempts at ending hunger, calling them 'naïve' and 'amateurish'.

I picked up my cup, intending to drink, but in seconds the tea was boiling, bubbling, heated by the fire in my hands. I dropped the cup with a clatter as several people rubbernecked.

Lady Memoria arched one brow before resuming the conversation.

"No wonder he has his issues, with a father like that. Ruby betrayed him, he destroyed her while possessed by the Chancellor… A lot of baggage there."

"Yes indeed. Spark and Shadow can be a difficult combination too," agreed the Countess, "one possessive and hot-tempered, the other avoidant and self-destructive. But where there's smoke, there's fire."

"I *am* still sitting here, you know," I said. "I can hear you."

"Well, speak up then," said the Countess, tapping the table. "Why hasn't Oliver asked for your hand yet?"

I prayed for a black hole to open up beneath my chair.

"I don't know, maybe because we're teenagers? Maybe because we're busy trying to prevent the collapse of civilization as we know it?"

"That's no excuse," said the Countess, shortly. "I was already wed at your age. The first time, I mean."

"You don't have to get married yet. You just have to be engaged," put in Lady Memoria. "It's merely a symbolic gesture."

"Yes, do it for the headlines. It would give the people something to look forward to. Everyone loves the fairy tale of a happy marriage."

"A happy alliance," corrected Lady Memoria.

"It's not 'an alliance'," I said.

"You're telling me."

"We're in love."

"Same thing, dear," said the Countess, signalling to the waiter to bring another round of tea. "Every marriage is a business arrangement at heart."

"We'll give the boy a few months," said Memoria. "Then we might have to meddle."

"Is that not what you're already doing?" I asked.

209

"Oh no, dear, this is just us gently enquiring," said the Countess. "When we're meddling, you'll know about it."

"Don't you have bigger problems to deal with?" I said. "Lord Harmonia is dead. The Sixth House is plotting to kill us as we speak. The people are rising up against us, the Empress is on the warpath, the Governor is sweet-talking us into letting his army in. Is my love life really so high on your list of priorities?"

"Without gossip, what else have we to look forward to, when everything else is so grim?" pouted the Countess. "I'm just saying, an engagement would—"

I stood up, abruptly. "OK, that's enough. I'm leaving."

Draining my cup, I hastily departed and went straight to Obscura House, using the key Oliver had given me to let myself in. Trouble in paradise? I'd show them. I'd prove them all wrong. Whatever darkness was storming in the world outside, Oliver and I were safe in each other's arms. Nothing else mattered.

But first, he owed me an explanation for last night.

I found him in his room, nose in a book again.

"Have fun at the pleasure house, did you?" I said.

I held up the newspaper I'd snatched from the table.

"Ah," he said. "That."

"Yes, *that*. What the hell is going on, Oliver? You never tell me anything any more. We promised to face this together." I looked away. "Or have your feelings towards me changed?"

At this, he actually put down his pen and came over, pulling me into his arms. "No, I swear. Never that."

"You're sure?"

210

"More than anything," he said firmly. "My love for you will never pale or fade away. I swore I would never lose you again, and I meant it, with every part of my soul, I meant it. Please believe me on that."

He kissed me again and again, covering my face with his kisses.

"We need a night away from all this, a night together," he murmured.

"In real life?" I said suspiciously. "Not in our dreams?"

"In real life."

"Now?"

"Well, uh … I was just on my way out actually."

"Whatever," I said, heading for the door. "Another time."

"How about this?" he said, catching my wrist and pulling me back. "There's an opera at the Auditorium tonight. *The Magic Mirror*. I saw it once as a child. We still have an Obscura family box. Let's use it."

The opera. I'd always wanted to go, to be one of those cultured, glamorous girls in silks and fake furs. I'd seen him take dates there in the past, back when my father was still training me in espionage. My stomach flipped.

"To the opera, really?" I asked, my bad mood forgotten. "Can we carry opera glasses? Shall I wear elbow-length gloves? Will you wear a monocle?"

"Yes, a resounding *yes* to all of the above," he said. "Well, maybe not the last one. But all the others, definitely."

"I've never been to the opera. I saw a ballet with Rubella once, but she fell asleep halfway through."

"I promise I'll be better company."

"We're really doing this?"

"Be ready for seven o' clock. We'll take a carriage."

"I'm so excited!" I said, clapping my hands together. "I have to prepare. Maybe Octavia has an opera-worthy dress I can steal."

Oliver laughed and shook his head, before vanishing into a black hole.

"Ruby Renato, you're going to the opera!" I announced to myself.

I hurried to Octavia's room, begging for her fashion assistance. I tried on various dresses as she played Birdie's records on the gramophone. After a lengthy debate, we settled on a purple dress of stiff silk with a tulle underskirt. I threw it on, twisting back and forth in the eye-shaped mirror, pulling faces and poses as Octavia whistled and clapped.

I will be mature, sophisticated, a woman in love, I told myself. *We will sip champagne and kiss during the interval. We will hold hands through the emotionally devastating scenes. I will look over during the finale and he'll have tears in his eyes, and I'll be reminded of his deep and infinite love for me.*

That was the plan, anyway.

Once dressed, I popped my head back into Oliver's room, but he wasn't there. The desk was a mess of papers, all of them covered in illegible scrawls and strange diagrams. His coat was hanging on the hook.

Guess he wasn't back yet from … wherever he'd gone.

Near the foot of the stairs, I found Gabriel reading what looked like a romance novel. On the cover, a woman in a frilly dress swooned into the arms of a sexy pirate.

"Have you seen Oliver?" I asked. At the sound of my voice, he hastily thrust his book behind him out of sight. "Did he tell you we're going to the opera?"

I was ready far too early, and already itching with anticipation.

"No, I haven't seen him since last night," Gabriel replied. "Though today I find myself missing an identity card," he mused, his tone light. "Oh and" – he cleared his throat – "tell your mother I tried that recipe she suggested. She was right. More garlic did the trick."

"I'll be sure to let her know," I said, fighting a smile. My mother wasn't generally known for her culinary skills, but maybe her cooking had suddenly improved.

I found Gus in the kitchen, staring into space as he chopped onions, a towel thrown over his shoulder. I had to say his name twice before he turned to me, blinking.

"Oh, hey, Ruby. Sorry, I was a million miles away. Wow, you look great! Going somewhere nice?"

"Hot date at the opera."

"Aw, I'm jealous. Right now I'd take a picnic in a cemetery." He gave a deep sigh. Gus had never been lucky in love. For as long as I'd known him, he'd been single.

"Have you seen Oliver?" I asked.

"Not since yesterday. You want something to eat?"

"No. Thanks, though."

"Well, OK. Holler if you change your mind."

Rani was in her study, nose-deep in a book, her hair frazzled. She waved at me distractedly as I came in.

"Have you seen Oliver?" I asked again.

"Only in the newspapers," she said. "Actually, I'd like to talk to him about that. Has he gone solo? Doing the lone wolf thing? Because the place in this picture looks like the one we saw in the remnant. We want to know what's going on. Sharing is caring, remember."

"We do need to talk. But first, he and I are going to the opera."

"Oh, well, that's your prerogative."

Octavia was in the conservatory, watching the birds at the feeder.

"I haven't seen him," she said, before I could ask.

I sat down beside her and stared at the smoggy city in the distance. Surely he would be back soon? I hoped he hadn't become distracted by one of his wild theories. The sixth sense seemed more important to him than anything now, even me.

"He's just trying to keep you safe," Octavia reassured, before adding: "in his own neurotic, rather annoying way, obviously. Gus says he hasn't been coming down for meals either, not even his favourite ones."

The bud of worry I'd started the day with was getting

larger and more tangled by the hour, like a thicket of brambles with sharp thorns, each of them poking me in the side.

"He loves you. I can tune into the frequency of his mind, remember?" said Octavia, reaching over to grip my hand. "I mean, I'm not supposed to, but I've heard enough to say for certain that he's obsessed with you."

"It doesn't really feel like it sometimes," I said.

Half six rolled around and still he wasn't home. I sat in the bay window in the uncomfortable wooden seat the Obscuras intended as a place for reading, trying to distract myself with novels, but they were all about love or murder and I couldn't think about either right now.

Quarter to seven. Now in a slightly slumped pose, I watched the window. I didn't know why. Oliver was more likely to portal into the hallway right in front of me than turn up in a carriage and come through the door, and yet I watched. I waited. In vain.

"Do you want a cup of tea, honey?"

Octavia, smiling at the door.

"Why not?" It would give me something to do, maybe it would even fill that hole of anxiety that gnawed on my stomach.

Seven arrived. He'd probably just lost track of time. He'd remember soon. He'd check his watch or catch sight of a clock…

Quarter past seven. I climbed up from the window seat, numb to the rear and holding an empty cold tea cup, stretching my arms and legs. I looked for him in my mind, closing my eyes and letting my soul slide, reaching out in search of his psyche. Normally my impulses carried me to him like a breeze, letting my psyche brush gently against his, bleeding into each other, mixing together, but I couldn't feel him now. I couldn't feel him at all. I paced back and forth a bit, trying to ignore the queasy dread in my stomach before giving up and going into the sitting room, watching Octavia and Rani finishing their game of chess.

"I hate this," said Octavia, as Rani took her queen.

"You just hate losing," said Rani, chuckling as she bested her.

Seven-thirty. Eight. Eight-thirty. Nine.

The bodice of the purple dress was digging into me. My feet were aching, now released from their tight, strappy shoes. I knew I ought to get changed but the petty part of me wanted him to see me like this. I wanted him to face the sight of me all dressed up with nowhere to go.

Octavia and Rani were looking at each other intensely, talking in their minds where I couldn't overhear.

"What the hell?" I blurted, out of nowhere. "Where is he?"

"I don't know, but I'm worried too," said Rani.

"He's probably absolutely fine," said Octavia, unconvincingly.

The terrible feeling was expanding rapidly inside me, burning, churning, yearning.

Just come back. Just be OK.

Nine thirty. The pit in my stomach grew. It felt like a cannonball now, dragging me down to the bottom of the sea. Octavia and Rani's faces were drawn and grave.

"I really don't want to say it out loud, but maybe something bad really *has* happened," said Rani.

"Not listening," said Octavia, shaking her head. "Not listening."

"He's got a target on his back," said Rani.

"If *you're* panicking then I'm positively terrified," I said. "You're the sensible one."

"We should look for him," said Rani. "I'll try the pleasure house he visited. I bet he found something there and has gone back to investigate it."

She searched the Shadow for signs, her eyes turning black, but when she returned to the room, she shrugged apologetically.

"OK, maybe not. Looks like the Inspectors closed it down last night."

I was starting to feel the flames of my Spark, roaring, growing, casting embers into the sky. I swung between anger and concern. I hated him for standing me up, but what if he was injured … or kidnapped … or dead? What if the assassin had attacked and he hadn't seen it coming, distracted by his pursuit of the sixth sense? Every dreadful possibility raced through my mind, grabbing at me with small hands, demanding I pay attention to them.

"What if the assassin caught up with him?" I said.

"The Sixth weren't exactly subtle when they killed Lord

Harmonia," said Rani. "If they've harmed him, I'm sure we'd know about it by now."

"That's … comforting, I guess."

"You should get an early night, honey," said Octavia, taking my hand. "Everything will seem better in the morning."

"But … the opera," I said, weakly.

"I think … uh, I think it already finished, love."

I looked at the clock. It was nearly midnight.

When Octavia and Rani went upstairs to their quarters, I returned to the bay window, where I sat facing the door. I could feel the pressure increasing, rising gradually inside me until my shoulders started to shake. I pulled up my knees, sniffling into the fabric of my skirts as I tried not to make any noise.

This wasn't the first time Oliver Obscura had let me down. On the Night That Never Was, I'd stood waiting for him, the clock ticking down in the courtyard outside. I'd finally told him the terrible truth about what my father had asked of me and what I'd stolen from his mind as he slept. If he could forgive me, as I'd hoped, then we could be free, unbound by the secrets that tried to make us enemies. We could run away together and start afresh. We were meant to flee the city together that night – but he came only to shatter me. I recalled the tightness I'd felt in my chest as I watched the seconds wasting away, each one more painful than the last. I remembered the howl in my throat, the stitch that pinched my middle. I remembered the feeling of helplessness. I recalled the insatiable, restless ache as I burned my own apology on the fire. The last thing I saw before my soul shattered, taking my memory with it.

Him, removing the mask. Him, holding the staff.

Oliver Obscura had broken me once, and now he was doing it again.

My last thought before I drifted asleep was that when I woke up, he would be back. He would be here. I would be angry and hurt and yell at him for being so inconsiderate, but at least he would be here, alive.

All night long, I dreamed that we were fighting and kissing, fighting and falling, fighting and making love.

But when the dawn light came pouring in through the window, bathing me in its golden rays, I was still alone in the hall and his room was still empty.

I cursed into the silence of a new day.

12.

OLIVER

From the Empress's little black book, I learned several things.

One was that Shadow souls were more likely to develop the sixth sense than other soul types, born first from the chaos of the universe's creation.

Another was that, while visions appeared unbidden, to conjure a prophecy at will you needed to sacrifice a memory related to it. Not a copy of a memory, as Ruby made when she stole from my mind, but the master.

That meant once the memory was gone, it was gone for ever.

Removing a memory wasn't simple, either. The soul had many neural pathways that connected it to the brain. It was a delicate, complicated business, like removing a tree complete with its root system. Only the most gifted Spirit souls could do such surgery.

That's where I was in luck.

The old Order had used various machines to remove memories, often operated by Amelia's mother, the imprisoned Doctor Millefleur. Ever since the revolution, they'd been sitting in storage in the Memoriam, the old museum of memories and institute of psychometric experimentation. I was certain no one would notice, should one of them mysteriously go missing.

Besides, I could do whatever I wanted now.

Portalling over to the Memoriam in the Second Borough, a whitewashed building with rose windows and a cold, malevolent vibe, I avoided the scant security that patrolled the largely disused building, concealing myself behind cabinets of glass vials before proceeding to the basement. Here, there were many locked rooms off a long maintenance corridor with flickering lights, everything clinical and white. I used the Shadow to slip inside, unlocking the door from within. The darkened room on the other side contained towers of equipment. I easily located a small, portable memory remover, one that came with its own carry case, then I smoothly fled the scene before anyone noticed me.

I needed to find a private place for this. I couldn't tell anyone – certainly not Ruby. The Empress had made me swear.

"If you tell her, you risk altering the future in unknown ways. You may create a dark path that you cannot deviate from," she'd said.

My research said the same. For example, if I told Ruby that she would die on the night of the crescent moon, she might decide to stay home or leave the city to avoid it, unknowingly making herself vulnerable to the advances of an attacker who would find her cornered and alone. The net would tighten round her more inexorably than if she was unaware, perhaps even leading her to a more terrible fate, a more wretched death. I had told her too much already. I would be helpless to protect her then, war would be inevitable, and all our struggles would be for nothing. That was what the Empress had meant by a "dark path".

Besides, I already knew what Ruby would say: *Don't trust her, Oliver.*

Perhaps she was right. The Empress was clearly dangerous. And yet, she was the only one I'd found who believed in the sixth sense. The only other person I knew who had it.

The only *living* person, anyway.

I needed to go somewhere where I could be safe. Somewhere no one would think to search for me. Somewhere I had been once and never returned to.

Creating a Shadow portal was one of the most complicated of all the psychometric arts. My father hadn't instructed me in it; afraid, perhaps, that I would use it to run away from him (which I eventually did). I had taught myself how to channel the dark matter of the Shadow and use it to create a tunnel. Portalling required a clear visualization of the destination, along with an awareness of its geographical position.

I saw the portal in my mind before it took form in the world. I saw the bright opening at the end of the tunnel, revealing a faraway place bathed in sunlight. I stepped into the swirling, oil-black passage and teleported further than I'd ever travelled through the Shadow, all the way across the sea to Jardine, where my mother and grandmother had come from. The hole was unstable, stretched to the limit of my abilities.

It purged me, violently expelling me from its void before exploding.

Thrown face down into the sand, I rolled on to my back and gasped, letting the waves dampen me as they lapped the beach. I listened to the hiss of the tide and the exotic calls of unknown birds, closing my eyes and enjoying a minute's blissful peace.

Jardine was an island of palms and ferns, a rocky outcrop surrounded by the glistening sea. It was surmounted by a dormant volcano which seemed to loom out of its core, with little villages stuck to its spiralling sides like barnacles on a ship. In Jardine, people rode bicycles or travelled up and down the many inclines by funicular, which stretched up to the summit. The harbour was lined with stalls and small hole-in-the-wall fish restaurants, while hungry cats prowled the boardwalks, past crab traps and piles of bones.

But soon the urgency of the situation rolled over me again. There was no time for sunbathing or sightseeing. Tired, hungry and hot, I climbed the ascending road to reach the tumble-down villa that once belonged to my mother's family, the Mandalas. My grandfather had died before I was born, and, with my mother and grandmother both gone, the ancestral home had been left to ruin. Despite this, it emanated a feeling of innate warmth and safety, calling out to me.

I'd been here just once as a child, for a summer. My father

hadn't been one to let my mother and me out of his sight, but there was a time, when I was young, when she still had the power to escape. She had brought me here. For a moment, I could feel my grandmother's embrace, plump and loving, her smell a mix of sweat and perfume. The heat was thick, the air sweet, lush palm forests stretching to the mountain range on the horizon.

The house itself had been partially reclaimed by the earth, its walls rough and crumby with salt spray and covered with gull shit, the spiky ferns in the garden growing wild. Anything of value had long been looted, leaving an empty shell. If I closed my eyes, I could remember Aurora leading me up this path, telling me stories about the gods and how they had created the five parts of the soul, one for each sense. In Jardinian history, it was not the Founders of Providence who'd uncovered the secrets of psychometry, but the ancient spirits who created humanity. This was a knowledge the people of Jardine had possessed for centuries before the Enlightenment.

The empire of the Order had stolen their souls, in so many ways, and used them to conquer the world.

I didn't even need to portal inside; the porch door hung open. I moved through a series of abandoned rooms. In the kitchen, a tree branch had broken through the window. In what was once the dining room, the chandeliers wore curtains of cobwebs. Half-open to the elements, the bathroom offered a panoramic view of the glittering sea.

I descended to the basement, lighting a candle to navigate

my way. It was flooded up to my shins, the detritus of a family life floating on the surface of the dark water: books, toys, shoes, tools. A faint glow caught my attention: a shining key, floating past me. Fishing it out and drying it off, I turned it over in my hands, marvelling at the intricate eye design of its handle.

Through trial and error, trying each door in turn, I learned that the key unlocked the attic. Its lock and hinges now stiff with rust, the door screeched horribly as it swung open. I poked my head inside, emerging into the dust-speckled gloom.

The atmosphere was skin-tingling. I felt that I was being watched, but there was no one there but me and the spiders. Shivering, I crept further inside, boards creaking beneath my feet. The candle illuminated a small dark desk, with a stylized eye painted on the wall above it. A single object sat atop the desk – what looked like a small, black, incense burner, caked in old ash.

It seemed as good a place as any to experiment with the darkest art of the psyche, so I set up the memory removal machine. Not having been used in some time, it shuddered and coughed up clouds of white smoke before it settled into a sedentary hum. I followed the instructions engraved on the side, attaching myself to the device using a finger clamp.

Sitting down in the broken desk chair, I exhaled nervously. Finally, I was ready. Now all I needed was a memory to jettison. As a test, I started by isolating irrelevant memories of mundane things: rained-off events, tedious plays, disappointing birthdays, mediocre meals. I needed to see how it worked first, before I sacrificed something relating to Ruby.

I had quite the surplus of shitty, useless memories, as it happened, locked away in the old trauma vault. Things I could barely remember. Things I'd never miss. Things I'd actually be glad to be rid of. When these memories appeared on the wall, I used the machine to excise them, drawing them from my mind and into one of the machine's glass vials. According to the Empress's research, once the memory had been removed and isolated, it could be burned, creating psyche vapours that would trigger the sixth sense when exhaled. Spirit, the sense of smell, defined memory on a soul-deep level.

My eyes fell on the incense burner on the desk. It fit the glass vial perfectly. Only then did I understand why I'd come here, *been drawn here* by my sixth sense.

This was where Aurora had come to experiment with her own memory, desperate to use it to save her daughter.

I was merely following in her footsteps.

Everything was falling into place again.

I next burned a memory of my father berating me on my eighth birthday. A hard prophecy appeared – one that showed me drunk and pissing on his grave, older than I was now. So it worked... It actually worked! But to find out what happened to Ruby in the future, I needed to lose a memory *of Ruby*, specifically. There was no way around it.

Yet my soul resisted it. I would have to be careful. Nothing too romantic. Those memories were what kept me warm, and human. I reminded myself it was the only way to make sure that she was safe. I had to look at this methodically. Like a scientist. I had to do what was necessary.

I searched my mind for something less valuable, less dear to me. After some internal debate, I chose the memory of our first meeting. Not the Renato ball where we had danced for the first time, but the formal debutante event where Ruby Renato was first introduced to society, as Ruben Renato's illegitimate but gifted daughter...

A string quartet is playing. She drifts down the stairs in a red silk dress, arm in arm with her father.

"Lord Ruben Renato and his daughter, Ruby Renato."

The low, imperceptible hum of scandal moves through the room. For many, this is the first they're hearing of Ruben's secret love child, but I was the one who'd found her hiding in the Valley and told my father about her. It's because of me that she's here. For some reason, and I don't yet know what, my father must be keen to keep Lord Renato on side. Perhaps he senses danger in him. He always fawns most over those he fears might destroy him.

Ruby's father greets mine, hers smarming as usual, mine perpetually displeased, forcing us to acknowledge each other.

"May I present my daughter, Ruby?" says Lord Renato.

She executes a smooth, well-practised curtsey, but there is a stiffness to her lip, a stubbornness in her forehead, a dancing light in her eyes that makes me think she takes all this for a circus. Perhaps it is.

My father nods, wary but showing little interest. "And this is my son and heir, Oliver."

I'm in a poor mood, having just listened to another edition of "Why You're Such a Failure", so I merely tip my head slightly in her direction, barely hiding my irritation.

"Say hello, Oliver," my father prods.

"Hello," I say dutifully. The greeting is blunt and flat, as cold a greeting as my father had given her.

"Your reputation precedes you, Master Obscura," she says.

I'm not sure what that means, but it sounds like an insult.

"Oh? What do people say?"

"I'm not sure you wish to know," she says, lowering her voice.

"Well, you should hear what they're saying about you."

"I don't care what they think," she says, but her face flushes pink. We fall into an awkward silence for a moment.

"If you say so," I say eventually, drifting away.

"He's even more insufferable than you said he'd be," I hear her say to my back, as her father shushes her fearfully.

So it appeared to be hate at first sight. I'd been rude to her for no good reason and she had been unimpressed by me, complaining about me as soon as she could to Ruben. I had little to lose by sacrificing this memory.

I homed in on it in my mind, visually separating and incising it, drawing it into the vial to be burned. It gave me a funny feeling, a dull inexplicable ache, like banging my funny bone, or stubbing my toe.

This time, five visions of the future appeared in the darkness behind my eyes, as if on five different planes. I could see all of them at once, and yet was able to process them individually, though they unfolded simultaneously.

In one, we got married, kissing beneath a floral bower on a beach. Ruby wore a white dress with a rose of red lace at the hip. Our friends were there; we were all older and it was so sunny I could feel the warmth on my face.

In another vision, we split up, screaming at each other in the hallway of Obscura House.

"*We bring out the worst in each other,*" said Ruby, aiming a fireball at me, before whirling out of my life for ever.

In another vision, we were enemies on opposite sides of a battlefield, my Shadow and her Spark forming giant manifest monsters that grappled in the space between us.

In one vision we had a child together; a toddler swaddled in winter clothes, swinging between us as we walked through the snowy gardens of Obscura House.

And one vision in which I lay on my deathbed, my lids painted with eyes as she cried over me again—

Shuddering, I was transported back to the moment. I found myself rocking back and forth with the visceral horror of the last scene.

One of these visions would become the future, but which one? The Empress had explained this, or tried to. At first, the visions would proliferate. Eventually the options would narrow, until the true prophecy was revealed. I had to sacrifice another memory of Ruby to get the answer I was seeking. There was no other way.

This time, I would lose a memory that related to my prophecy of her death. I chose the scene of me attacking the messenger, reliving the fear in the boy's eyes as I shook his shoulder, his head wobbling. I recalled, with horribly vivid clarity, the look in everyone's eyes as I turned back to the room – the look that said they saw me as a monster. Ruby had stared at me as if I was a stranger, her hands clasped protectively over her chest. Nausea rolled in my stomach.

It was even worse than I remembered.

As the memory burned to ether, I experienced a wave of dizziness. My mind felt pitted and fuzzy. My teeth itched. It was like drinking something incredibly cold and sour, causing me to screw up my face as needles probed all the softest crevices in my brain.

Panic set in. I had a nagging sense that this memory might be connected to something, something important – and if I forgot this, about the messenger, then I might forget other things I needed to remember. That the whole system might start to unravel … if I forgot the … the—

Wait. What had I forgotten?

Something about a boy… Constitution? No, it was gone.

The panic faded with the smoke.

My mind divided again, refracting into five new planes of reality. This time, it was Ruby in the Basilica, times five.

In one future, the building was decked with

Constitutional banners for a dance. The brassy swing of a celebratory song rang out, but it slowed down as my vision broke apart. The dance hall was full of people in costume, all smiling, drinks in hand.

In another vision, it was busy with frightened-looking citizens covered in dust, some bloodied, too.

In another, the Basilica was empty but for Ruby. I chased after her, calling her name, but she couldn't hear me, or didn't want to.

In another vision still, it was pitch dark. In the last of the five, the Basilica was on fire, fear written upon Ruby's face as she cut through the foyer. It popped and crackled as the building caved in on itself, consuming us both in the blaze.

The five visions all had something in common. In all five, Ruby walked up the imperial stairs, looking around as if in search of something. She trailed down the left-hand corridor towards the room with the round window. In all five, the crescent moon hung high in the sky, but the view from the window differed each time, ranging from Providence as it normally appeared to Providence as a burning wasteland. Each vision ended the same way, with the assassin emerging from the room on the right-hand side, although his outfit changed each time: in one he was dressed in the uniform of a server, in another he wore a fine tailored tuxedo; in one he had on the rough-and-tumble garments of a rebel, in another a hooded black cloak, and in one he even wore a suit of black armour.

But his face was always the same.

BANG!

Blood in her mouth. A hole in her chest. Every single time.

The image prickled and faded, deteriorating even as I tried to revive it, straining and breaking apart until it became corrupted.

I could try again, but I was exhausted now. It was dark outside the windows. There was somewhere else I was supposed to be, I realized.

With abrupt, all-consuming doom, I glanced at my watch.

Shit. The opera.

Back at Obscura House, I searched every room, looking for Ruby. The only sign that she'd been there at all was a note on a table in the hall by the door.

Thanks for keeping me informed about your activities, it said, in handwriting I could only describe as visibly sarcastic.

Crumpling it up in one hand, I attempted to locate her through the Shadow, but I quickly hit a wall in her head: a literal wall, with graffiti sprayed on it in dripping red paint: *GO TO HELL!*

Cursing, I faded back into my body. As if things could not be worse, Gabriel appeared, holding out his hand, his expression stern.

"I believe you have something of mine," he said.

His stolen identity card. I'd forgotten.

"About that," I said, passing it back sheepishly. "I was—"

"Don't waste your breath. I'll ask you kindly not to take

232

my property without asking again." I lowered my head, cheeks burning. "I don't know what you were up to tonight, but by the looks of you, I'd say" – he looked me up and down – "illegal psychotropics."

I held my tongue. Better he thought I was doing drugs than … well, whatever *this* was.

"You have responsibilities, my Lord. You're meant to be part of the government, for goodness' sake."

"You're not my father," I said, fully locked into self-destruct mode.

He chuckled. "No, thank god, I'm not."

"I'm the Lord here. This is my House now."

He looked at me thoughtfully. "Yes, and if you want to keep it, you'll do your duty to your people. Unless you want to lose some other things too, and I don't think you do."

"Whatever," I said, petulantly, though he was right.

"My Lord, may I offer another word of advice?"

"If you must."

"You've been given the chance to improve the lives of your citizens and the means by which to achieve real change. Instead, it appears that you're, well, 'pissing away' the opportunity to do anything at all. Be a better man, Oliver. Be the man your father could never have imagined. I know you're more than capable of it."

He handed me a slip of paper.

"You've been summoned to the Basilica for an important meeting. I suggest you attend – after you've cleaned yourself up, of course."

His disapproval lingered, long after he had stalked out of the room.

I washed and dressed and made myself semi-human again, travelling through the Shadow to the Basilica to meet with the others. I dreaded going there at all, knowing it was the planned location of Ruby's death, but the moon was not yet a crescent and she was not wearing the red phoenix dress. We were safe, for now.

I saw her standing at the foot of the stairs, about to ascend. Her face was rumpled, as if she hadn't slept well.

"Lily," I said, catching up to her. "I'm so sorry."

"Where have you *been*?" she snapped, looking me up and down. "Actually, don't answer that."

The flash of a camera alerted me to the presence of the press.

"I'm sorry," I said. "I was being completely selfish. There's no excuse for it. Whatever it takes to make it up to you, I'll do it."

"You can start by telling me the truth. Where were you last night?"

"I … uh, I trailed one of the Shades," I lied. "He became suspicious. I got carried away. You know how hard it is to control my Shadow. One thing led to another… we got into a fight… It all got a bit out of hand."

I watched her face, trying to work out if she believed me or not.

"I waited for you for hours, Oliver!" she said. "I didn't know where you'd gone or whether you were hurt. I kept thinking, 'Something bad must've happened to him, because he'd never leave me hanging like this. He'd never do that to me.' But you did. You *did* do that!"

I avoided her burning eyes.

"I tried to contact you but I couldn't," she went on. "It was like you were purposely keeping me out of your head."

"Only so the other guy couldn't get in there."

"You could've sent a message directly into my psyche if you really wanted to. The truth is, I didn't even cross your mind. You forgot all about me."

"That's not true," I insisted.

And it *wasn't* true. She was all I'd been thinking about the entire time. How to keep her safe, in particular. But I couldn't tell her that without reminding her of the apparent inescapability of her demise and the fact that I was still pursuing something she thought was madness.

A gong sounded, interrupting us. It was time for the meeting.

"We'll talk about this later," she said. "In case you hadn't noticed, we have a country to run. Trade negotiations to complete. People are depending on us, Oliver. If you don't care about me, surely you care about them."

"I care about you," I said, "I promise, I care more than anything."

Her eyes traced my face. She must've seen something authentic in my expression as I watched the hardness of her features melt slightly.

The Premier waited for us, sitting at the pentagon-shaped table. We took our places as servers brought us drinks. We all stared at the empty silver-coloured segment where Lord Harmonia used to sit, unsure how to address it.

"I'm pleased to say that, however deeply upsetting Lord Harmonia's death has been, the Governor's visit has been a success," said Premier Cordata. "We are putting the finishing touches to the trade agreement."

My mind raced. The agreement with Constitution was the alliance I was supposed to prevent if I was to save Ruby…

"That is fortunate indeed!" said Lady Memoria.

"Ambrose Fairchild has also kindly arranged for Constitutional soldiers to help defend the borders against the advance of the Empress, while a new army base will be established here in Providence to provide support during our transition period."

My mind spiked, my palms instantly clammy. The Governor and his army were taking positions of advantage, ready to take us over, just as the Empress had said. But I could still stop this. I *had* to stop this.

"Suffice it to say, I don't think the Sixth House will be troubling us for much longer," said the Premier. "The Governor's men will be working with us until we are able to identify and arrest the assassin. Current intelligence points to the leader of the Shades, a man known as Blade."

So missing Blade was the fall guy. It didn't make sense. How did a former Reformatory convict amass the resources necessary to launch such a campaign? No. Blade couldn't be behind this on his own. He needed a silent partner, someone with deep pockets to fund his campaign.

"We want to give the Governor one last taste of what Providence has to offer," Cordata was saying. "I suggest we revisit the idea of the People's Ball."

My mind ticked back to the event I'd foreseen at the Basilica. What had the Empress said? The Governor's "farewell ball"? I knew, on a cellular level. I *knew*: it was the People's Ball I'd seen in the prophecy.

Nautical flags, swirling dancers, a brass band...

BANG!

"Surely the Governor won't want—"

"It was the Governor who brought it up, actually."

Oh gods! He was setting us up.

"He said how delightful it would be, to have a proper send-off."

I bet he did.

"But Lord Harmonia has just been assassinated," I objected. "Should we be seen to be celebrating so soon?"

"It would be the alliance we are celebrating, not poor Harmonia's demise. So let his death not be in vain."

"The assassin will use the occasion to target us."

"Fear not, Lord Obscura. Security will be extremely tight. It'll be worth it, I assure you. Picture this: the Constitutional anthem played by a brass band, drinks in every hand, guests dressed in Constitutional colours, with the flag fluttering on banners and bunting..."

He was describing the exact same scene in my vision.

This was what the Empress had warned me about: the ball was what I was meant to prevent.

It would be the night Ruby was destined to die. *Stop the war, save the girl.*

"Yes, yes. See the vision. There will be a lavish dinner and a dance. I've selected the location. It will be held at the Basilica. A symbol of our achievements, following the fall of the Chancellor – to remind the people we are not the enemy."

The Basilica… That was where Ruby died.

It was all true. Everything I'd seen would come to pass.

"No, Lord Cordata. It's far too decadent. The people won't like it," I said desperately.

"But the people will attend also! On the last Saturday of the month we will invite one hundred citizens, randomly chosen by lot, to celebrate with us," gushed Cordata. "And we will also invite representatives of the five gangs, to show solidarity in the face of the Sixth House's advances. It's perfect, truly."

I turned to the lunar calendar on the wall. The last Saturday of the month… That put the ball during the phase of the crescent moon.

Something erupted inside the darkness of my mind as the worst possible future crystallized – a vision, gaining in clarity.

A single clear scene emerged. Ruby in the Basilica, wearing the red phoenix dress. A sign announcing THE PEOPLE'S BALL, banners flying on high, people gathering in

238

the foyer, some dressed in their finery, others more casually clad. Framed by the window upstairs, airships flocked like dark birds around the moon. The Observatory exploded. The assassin emerged, dressed as a server, reaching for his gun before...

BANG!

This was it. This was the future I'd dreaded. This was the very destiny the Empress had told me I must do everything in my power to prevent.

Sacrificing those memories had worked – the visions had coalesced into a single prophecy. Now I knew for sure. It was terrifying, but there was also a sense of completion, of understanding, and of relief. This was the moment. *The dark path*. The prophecy that would become reality. The pieces all fell into place, but they didn't form a pretty picture.

The Governor was manipulating us. It was clear to me now. We had signed the trade treaty and allowed his armies to join ours. Providence had nothing to defend itself with. At the People's Ball held in his honour, he would announce his intention to rule over Providence. He would reveal himself as the ruler of the Sixth House and launch an invasion. We would fight back, of course. And Ruby would be shot in the revolt. She would die in my arms.

I had to sabotage the ball. Destroy the alliance.

My chair screeched as I suddenly stood up.

"No."

Their faces turned to me, bewildered.

"This ball … it will be a disaster. It can't go ahead. You

want to open our doors to the rabble out there?" It sounded reasonable, in my head at least.

"The rabble?" mouthed Ruby.

"The gangs are largely reduced by this Sixth House," said the Premier.

"Which is still a threat!" I shot back. "They killed Lord Harmonia. Any one of us could be next, including yourself."

For a moment, the Premier hesitated, but when he saw two Constitution soldiers passing by the window, he shook his head.

"No, Lord Obscura. We will look weak if we cancel now. The show must go on."

I balled my hands into fists. "Premier Cordata, I really must insist—"

"Is it really such a radical idea that we might meet the Sixth House at the table and not on the battlefield?" said Lady Memoria. "We must not make them martyrs. We must not build them up to be fearsome monsters. We must show the people that we are not afraid of them."

"If the Governor wants a ball, then he shall have a ball," said Cordata.

"Is that what it comes down to, in the end?" I said. "What the Governor wants? Can we really trust him?"

"What are you implying?" asked Cordata.

Ruby widened her eyes at me. *What's with you?* she said, without words.

"Lord Obscura, won't you please calm down?" murmured Lady Memoria. "The Governor is a good man. He's sending in extra troops to cover the additional security needed on the night of the ball, or did you forget?"

The vision in my head developed rapidly. It expanded, filled itself in, the background taking shape and form, growing in detail and complexity.

A tower of champagne formed a pyramid. Pillars were wrapped with streamers. A net of balloons fell from the ceiling. Dancers spun slowly in time with the music as children looked curiously over the decorated balcony, waving sparklers.

The soldiers in tan fatigues would be right there, on hand to turn on the crowd immediately, firing their weapons. The Governor would be directing the battle from the top of the imperial staircase. The crowd would be held spellbound, their eyes turning to crescents as the Governor directed his men to slaughter them.

Fire. Blood. *BANG!*

With every passing moment, the future became more predetermined.

"No," I said. "I forbid it."

"You *forbid* it?" said Cordata, brows raised.

"I – I have information. The Governor is planning an invasion. He will reveal his true intentions at this ball. He has the ability to command many souls at once, and he is building an empire to rule us all."

A shocked and – I had to admit – disbelieving silence followed, as everyone gawked at me sceptically.

"Who gave you this information?" asked Premier Cordata.

"I can't reveal that," I said. "I have to protect my source."

"You cannot cast aspersions without offering any proof for what you say, particularly in regard to someone so important," said Lady Memoria uncertainly, but with a sniff from her snuffbox she seemed to gain a new perspective. "Hmm. Perhaps we should investigate further. I say let's delay this ball of yours, Cordata."

Premier Cordata stood tall, seeming to grow in stature. When he spoke, there was an unusual authority in his voice.

"Lord Obscura, you are underestimating the importance of us not offending the Governor. He has proved himself trustworthy. We will have a special relationship with Constitution, one that will stand the test of time."

For a brief second, a crescent flickered in his eyes.

I shrank back, winded in shock. The Sixth's influence ran even deeper than I thought. The conspiracy went all the way to the top.

"You're in on it," I said, pointing at him.

Cordata blinked, returning to himself. "What?"

"The Governor already has his hooks in you, doesn't he?"

Ruby gave me another warning glance.

"Look at his eyes," I accused, but his pupils were no longer crescents.

"I'm sorry, Oliver. I can't see anything," she said with a worried shrug.

"Let me remind you, Oliver," Cordata said, placing one hand on my shoulder, "you jumped to the wrong conclusion once before. We all saw you attack the Governor's messenger."

It was as if someone was setting me up to look foolish. Untrustworthy. Perhaps Ruby had been right, that I was being sabotaged.

"Not to mention you were also seen recently attacking the manager of a nightclub," said Lady Memoria. "Was he 'in on' this too?"

"This is different. We mustn't go ahead with this ball. Trust me."

"I'm afraid it's not just up to you, Lord Obscura," said Cordata. "We shall vote on it, of course. That's what democracy means."

"Then I vote nay," I said, a little louder than I needed to.

"Well, *I* vote aye," announced Cordata.

"I vote aye as well," said Lady Memoria, ignoring my accusing look. "The Governor is our best defence against the advance of the Empress. Unless, of course, you can present me with some actual evidence to back up your wild claims."

Ruby turned to me, gazing deep into my eyes.

"And I vote … nay," she said, trying to read me. "If Oliver thinks it's a bad idea, then I trust him. Give him a chance to prove it to you."

Thank you, I mouthed, gratefully.

"That means we have a tie," said Lady Memoria.

Strangely, I found myself missing Lord Harmonia. He would surely have said nay to the People's Ball.

"Not quite so," said Cordata, wagging one finger. "There

243

is a clause in the Accord you all signed which states that in the event of a tie, the Premier casts the deciding vote. That means the ayes have it. The ball goes ahead."

I gaped at him, fuming. "You can't do that," I said.

"Read the small print, Oliver. This is in our best interests, I assure you. Every measure will be taken to ensure our safety. You needn't worry."

I felt my voice deepening, my eyes darkening as I replied: "Remember that stampede you told us about over dinner, Premier Cordata, the night the Governor arrived? *'If you shoot one, the others will trample you, and you don't have enough bullets to kill them all'*. You said you thought it was a metaphor for being in government. And it is. Because it's you that will be trampled if you make the wrong choice here."

He flinched. "You can't intimidate me, Lord Obscura."

I sensed my Shadow morphing on the wall behind me, becoming larger, less human.

"Oh, I think I can, actually. It's something of a family gift."

Ruby shook her head minutely, as if to say *Stop!*

"I say," murmured Lady Memoria, scandalized.

I whipped round to her, searching her eyes for crescents. "What? Did he get to you too? Are you also under his spell?"

She shrank back, fearful. "Did *who* get to me?"

"The Governor!"

Cordata rose angrily. "Stop this, Oliver! You're behaving rather abominably. I don't want to have you removed from the council but so be it if you're incapable of civility."

"Don't do anything too hasty, Premier, or I will make you regret it. " I snarled. "I could break you. I could shatter you and…"

This sentence was too horrible to complete. When I met Ruby's eyes, she looked equally furious and frightened. A silence stretched out. I could see myself reflected in their pupils: a monster, just like my father.

"I think, perhaps, it's time for you to take a breather, to get your head straight, before you make a mistake you can't recover from," said Lady Memoria.

Huffing, whispering, the two of them marched out.

Ruby followed, but I caught up with her at the door.

"'I could shatter you?'" she said with a look of utmost disgust. "Why would you say such a thing? What are you thinking? You looked a fool! You made *me* look a fool."

"I … you're right. I'm sorry. I definitely shouldn't have said that. I didn't mean it. But please, Lily, you have to understand where I'm—"

"You're so obsessed with the sixth sense that you're not seeing what's right in front of your face!" she raged.

"What?" I said. "What am I missing?

"*Me*," she said, tapping her chest. "I'm right here, and I'm still alive."

But for how long? I thought, as I watched her storm away.

13.

RUBY

If I was frightened for Oliver before the meeting, it was nothing compared to what came after.

The real trouble began with the eyes. They appeared on the dark walls of Obscura House one by one, black blinking orbs, multiplying rapidly like some kind of virulent insect infestation. They were made by the same Shadow magic that had created the original Eye network, except this time they were in our home, spying on us in our private moments instead. Oliver had created them, like a one-man Observatory.

Gus watched the eyes nervously while drinking his mug of tea. Octavia muttered under her breath about the "difficulty of working in these conditions". Even Rani, a fellow soul of the Shadow, tried to avoid looking at them directly, shading her face with her hand or pulling her black hood up as she passed.

Despite our reticence, we took what Oliver said seriously at first. We combed the Governor's background for any evidence that he was working against us. We examined the minds of his men, scanned his troops. We followed him and searched his subconscious as he slept. Nothing.

We investigated Blade too, the missing leader of the Shades, and while we couldn't find the man himself, we also found nothing to connect him directly to the Sixth House, other than the notion that he was clearly being set up as a scapegoat by a much bigger, badder villain.

Besides, the eyes were not focused out there, but fixed on us. As if we were the ones Oliver suspected. At first, they were only in the corridors, then in the kitchen and the library. When more eyes appeared in the living room, Octavia exploded with an ear-splitting cry of: "I can't live like this any more!"

She stood up, throwing down her knitting. "I'm sorry, Ruby, but I was spied on my whole life. I said never again and I meant it. Now Oliver is doing the same as his father. This isn't good for me, or him, or anyone!"

"Octavia is right," sighed Rani.

"I'm sorry. I know. I'll talk to him," I said.

Gabriel watched us from the doorway, his expression grave.

"I know I can't exactly talk about invading people's privacy," said Octavia, wringing her hands. "But why doesn't he trust us? Why does he think he needs to keep tabs on our every move? We're supposed to be his friends."

"Tell me about it," groaned Gus. "A few weeks ago, I was having a … well, I was having a *moment* with someone. In the pantry."

Rani made a face. "Where the food is?"

Gus shrugged. "Sometimes, the moment is happening before you can think better of it. Anyway, I look up and there's another bloody eye on the wall. It didn't see us, luckily. I know it's only Oliver doing his security checks and that he's not really interested in my love life, but still."

"Wait… You have a new boyfriend?" I asked, elbowing him. "What did I miss?"

"Not exactly," he said. "It's more of a … a fling thing. Or it was. He's not been in touch since. But the Heart wants what it wants, right? I can't stop thinking about him. He's different to anyone I've ever met before. He's—"

"Can we focus?" said Rani. "Happy for you though, pal."

"Look, this is our home too, you know?" said Octavia. "We don't really have anywhere else to go. We need to feel comfortable here. And we need to trust each other if we're going to solve this." She looked at me appealingly. Octavia hated conflict: a throwback to her days as the Chancellor's personal Listener. "I get that Oliver is anxious, but this is too much," she said.

"Of course. I'm sorry," I said. "I'll sort it out. I promise."

"There's something else," said Rani with a second, even heavier sigh. "We haven't been able to get in touch with Ash or Perpetua."

"Oh… no."

They'd promised to keep us updated about any information regarding the assassin and, angry as they were, both had kept their word in the past.

"We did some digging," Rani went on. "Ash dropped

248

out of the Firehand gang a week ago and vanished off the map. Someone else is leading them now."

Just like Blade and the Shades.

"Perpetua is still working with the Wallflowers but she hasn't been seen all week. She's always been kind of flaky, I guess, but she's never completely vanished before."

"You don't think they've joined the Sixth, do you?" said Octavia.

"I hope not."

"Well, keep looking," I said. "We'll find them."

Later that night, I found Oliver hidden away in his room, hunched over his desk, squinting at another old manuscript in the dim light.

I watched his Shadow pacing angrily up and down the wall.

"You'll need real glasses if you carry on like that," I said, recalling the spectacles he wore in his Evander Mountebank disguise.

He didn't answer. He was vaguely aware of my existence, possibly, but the rest of his attention was somewhere else.

"Gripping read, is it? A real page-turner?" I asked.

I snuck a peek at his notebook, which was all prismatic diagrams and maps of lifelines, along with a sketch of a nightmarish behemoth with many eyes. His handwriting was illegible, in some kind of code.

"Hmm." He patted my arm without looking up from the page. I was far away from wherever he was in his mind.

I sat on his desk. "Oliver, where are you?"

He didn't seem to hear me. I leaned in, cupping his cheeks with my hands and kissing him gently on the lips, holding the position until his eyes cleared...

That seemed to do the trick.

"Hi."

"Hi," I replied.

"I'm here," he said.

"Are you, though? We need to talk about your DIY Eye network out there. It's creeping our friends out."

His brow wrinkled. "There's an assassin on the loose. I think I know now when they'll come for you but I can't be completely sure. I need to cover all bases. I'm not interested in anyone's private business, if that's what they're worried about. Unless it involves murdering you, of course."

"You think our friends might have homicide in mind?"

It was a joke, but Oliver didn't laugh.

"No one can be completely ruled out at this stage," he said.

"You're serious?"

"The Sixth House hypnotized Rani and Octavia, remember? There's always a chance that they are being directed, that they've been taken over by the leader, like Cordata was before. They might use them as pawns in the war against us."

"You're ... you mean that?" I said, watching his face.

"I didn't want to tell you this, but... Look, our friends

will betray us, OK? I've seen it," he said. "In the future. It's better to create distance now."

"That's ridiculous! They would never do that to us willingly. If they're in danger of being caught up in the Sixth's influence, we have to protect them. You should ask Rani for help," I said. "She's your Observer. Maybe she knows something you don't."

"Rani doesn't have any experience with the sixth sense," he said. "Hardly anyone does. Most people think it's nonsense, including you." I bit down on my lip, guiltily. "No, I need to do this alone. You'll just have to accept that."

"What choice do I have?" I said, grudgingly.

"When I'm done, we'll go out on the world's most amazing date, just you and me." He reached out and kissed my hand, clasping it between his.

"That didn't work out so well last time, did it?" I said.

"Huh?"

When he looked blank, I added, "You know, the opera?"

"The opera?"

"You don't remember?"

He slowly shook his head. "Am I meant to? Ooh, you know *The Magic Mirror* is on right now. I saw it when I was a kid. We should go. We have a House box that's just sitting empty right now. We could make a night of it."

I backed away from him, blood running cold.

He'd already forgotten about our fight, about our missed date. It hadn't registered as important – not as important as *this*. I swallowed down my fear, fighting back tears.

251

"I thought you might want to know that Ash and Perpetua are incommunicado," I managed. "I'm worried about them."

"OK, I'll keep an eye out," he said, but his tone was oddly casual.

"Our friends are missing, Oliver."

But he didn't respond, turning back to his books.

Still there was no word from Perpetua or Ash. Octavia and Rani spoke to people from each of the five gangs, but the two of them seemed to have dropped off the face of the earth. I tried to reassure myself. They were probably just lying low. Maybe they'd gone undercover. They would reappear when they had something important to tell us.

Meanwhile, Oliver seemed to be forgetting more and more – just little things, at first. He no longer remembered that my favourite flavour of ice cream was pistachio. He didn't recall details like my birthplace or Octavia's last name. It annoyed me at first, that we meant so little to him, but after a while I became more concerned than irritated. His Shadow had taken him over once before, with disastrous consequences. Could it be happening again? Whatever the reason, he did not dismantle the Eye network as promised.

One by one, the others moved out. There was no real bad blood between us but our closeness faded. We became civilly estranged. First Gus got a new job at an inn, saying he needed to step back from the New Order, then Octavia and Rani found their own place and gave the same reason. I hung on a few more days. Eventually, I moved back to Renato House to live with my mother, while Gabriel stood watch over Obscura House, but I returned frequently to check up on Oliver, becoming more and more worried each time.

One morning I found him standing in front of the locked door on the ground floor, trying the handle uselessly.

"What's in here?" he asked.

His expression was skin-crawlingly vacant, his eyes flat and empty.

"You know what's in there. That's the room with your mother's shrine in it."

He tried the handle again. "It's locked. Why is it locked?"

I fought down panic. "It's always locked now. The key is in the cabinet in the dining room." This forgetfulness reminded me of my grandmother, before she passed.

"Oh, right," he said, absent-mindedly. "Yes, of course."

"Oliver, are you … do you—"

"Where is my father?" he asked me suddenly, looking around him anxiously as if the former Chancellor might pop out of a closet or a decorative vase.

"Your father?" I repeated, in disbelief.

"Are we safe here? What if he comes for us?"

"Oliver, your father is imprisoned in the Reformatory."

He blinked. "Oh, right. I see."

"You don't remember?"

"I … no, I guess not." He smiled that distant smile of his and kissed me. "I need to go and work now."

Is that what he was calling this? Work?

I waited a moment, then followed him. I gently tried the handle of his room but it was locked. It was always locked now too, a sign that he was keeping me out. Keeping us all out.

I fetched a glass and pressed it to the wall. I heard voices, murmuring. Sometimes it sounded like more than one person, like an entire conference of people all talking at once.

I needed help and, unlike Oliver, I knew where to go to get it.

"Ruby!" Octavia said, waving at the door before I'd knocked. She was dressed comfortably and looked well, her thick hair wrapped in a colourful scarf. "I was expecting you."

"I figured you'd still be checking in."

"How is he?"

"Not great. Can you … do the thing people always ask you not to do and listen in to his mind?" I asked. "Please?"

"As if you have to ask." She grinned. "Come on in."

Rani and Octavia's new apartment was small and cluttered with boxes, but cosy – full of leafy plants and furry throws, framed prints and wall hangings. In the living room, we all took a seat on the sofa with its mismatched cushions. A bird in a large cage sat in one corner.

"OK, let's do this," said Octavia.

The room fell silent, before a steady bong sound echoed.

I turned to see Rani with a small drum between her thighs, cocking one eyebrow.

"The rhythm helps her concentrate," she whispered.

Octavia did some deep breathing, her eyes closed. She made weird noises with her throat and tongue. She tuned into the stream of consciousness, searching for the sound of Oliver's soul, which she said was like a sad, sad song played backwards.

"Something about a broken cross … a pale horse … a man whose hair is on fire," she interpreted. "Something in Slavic."

"Is that, uh, normal?"

"Definitely not."

We fell silent for a few moments.

"Even if he is right, and these visions really are prophecies of my future death, it's not OK," I said. "It's not helping. It's not … it's not healthy! Is it?"

Octavia slowly shook her head.

"No babe, it's not."

"I don't know what to do."

Octavia and Rani each took one of my hands.

"Try not to worry. We'll figure it out, together," said Octavia. "Like we always do."

Back at Renato House, I paced the hall until a knock at the door scattered my thoughts like spiders in bright light. My mother looked out through the peephole.

"It's Countess Cavendish," she stated, her voice high-pitched with surprise.

"Let her in," I said.

"Must I?" she moaned. "She's such a busybody."

"I can hear you, Mara," the Countess called through the door.

She bustled in past my mother, putting down her black rain-damp umbrella and pulling up the funereal veil that covered her face. Looking behind her, I saw Graves sitting in the cab of her carriage, parked on the street.

"I know it's late, but I had to come right away," she said breathlessly, her cheeks flushed with drama. "It simply couldn't wait."

"What is it?" I asked.

"Ready yourself, dear. This one is going to hurt."

She pulled something out of her handbag. A single black chess piece. A queen.

"Another remnant?" I said.

"I told you I had my uses."

"Where did you get it?" I asked.

"The Hotel Quintet. Third Borough. The Empress has a chess set in her suite." She watched my reaction. "That's right, she's here, in Providence."

I took the piece from her, dumbstruck.

"I thought the Empress was off invading the Order's flailing colonies?" my mother said.

256

The Countess shook her head. "The Empress can be in many places at once, it seems. But I didn't help overthrow the Order to let *her* sneak in unnoticed."

As my fingers closed around the queen, I was sucked into a memory; I opened my eyes to behold a specific moment in time.

I saw Oliver and the Empress standing close together in a dark alley. They were both visible, as if the memory had been captured by an unseen third person.

"I can find anyone," says the Empress. "I can explore their soul merely by thinking about them. But it is you I wished to find."

The scenery changes. Now they are in a luxurious hotel room with a panoramic view of the city, playing a game of chess.

"You and I, we are the same."

"Because we're both Shadow souls?"

"No, it is more than that."

She reached out to touch his temples. She was showing him something but I couldn't see what it was.

"I have a proposition for you."

"What kind of proposition?"

The image skipped, stuttered. I counted one, two, three. Then suddenly she was kissing him. He was kissing her. They were entwined, in raptures, stumbling backwards towards the bed as he tore at her clothes and she removed his with Shadowy arms, leaving her hands free to...

I dropped the queen to the ground with a clatter, abruptly severing the stream of images.

"I don't believe it!" I cried.

"I know," said the Countess. "Men are dogs, dear."

"No, I mean – I actually *don't believe it*," I said, shaking my head. "It's not real… Oliver wouldn't do that to me."

"You don't trust your own eyes?"

"It's a false memory."

"Is that what you're telling yourself, dear?"

"It's possible, isn't it?" my mother interjected, on my behalf. "The Order has been using false memories to manipulate people for centuries."

"If every woman who found a remnant containing evidence of her lover's infidelity thought it a fake, well, there would be fewer divorces," observed the Countess drily.

"But that's not the Oliver I know," I said. "Why would he be cavorting with the world's most wanted woman? He's cautious to the point of paranoia."

The Countess and my mother looked at me, pity and worry in equal measures.

"Well, of course … you *might* be right," said the Countess gently, at least for her. "You know Oliver best. Anything is possible isn't it, technically speaking?"

I looked away – the sceptical look on her face was too much.

"But he always did have a few girls on the go at once, back in the day," she added, unable to help herself. "I knew he'd stray. I just didn't predict that it would be with the Empress." My mother elbowed her sharply. "Oh… But yes, you might well be right. It *could* be a false memory of some sort, I suppose."

Something inside me was fracturing again, cracking like glass.

"I think that's enough," said my mother, watching my face. "You've passed on the information, Agatha. It's time for you to go now."

"Don't shoot the messenger," said the Countess, baring her palms. "Someone has to deliver the bad news as well as the good, you know. Remember how I protected you before, my dear. I'm on your side."

When she was gone, my mother put an arm round my shoulder. "Ruby," she began.

"I don't want to hear it."

"I can't lie, you know that. I don't know what to think. Maybe this sixth sense thing is rotting his brain. But…"

"Don't say it."

"I have to, I'm sorry, but I'm your mother … and I love him too, I do, but Oliver, he … he's troubled. And he betrayed you once before. Who's to say he won't do it again?"

"I need to talk to him," I said. "I have to ask him for myself."

"Please, in the name of the five parts of the soul, be careful," she said. "There's still a killer out there, remember?"

"How can I forget?" I replied, kissing her. I removed the pearl-handled dagger from my skirts and showed it to her. "I'm good, see? I'm covered."

I climbed into a carriage and travelled to Obscura House, using my own key to get in.

"Good evening, Lady Renato," said Gabriel.

"It's not such a good evening for me, to be honest," I said.

"I'm afraid his Lordship is busy."

"Too bad." I bustled past him but he caught my arm, forcing me to turn back to him. His grip was firm but his expression was surprisingly kind.

"I wouldn't advise that you go up there," he said. "You won't like what you'll see."

Was *she* up there with him?

I pushed past Gabriel, past the collage of blinking eyes that peppered the walls of the corridors, all of them following me.

When I couldn't get into Oliver's room, my furious knocks and shouts drawing no response, I melted the lock with fire of my Spark and kicked open the door, barging in.

"We need to talk about … oh … my god."

The furious speech I'd prepared escaped from my lips in the form of a shallow puff, until I couldn't remember a word of what I'd wanted to say.

Oliver was in a strange, catatonic state, sitting cross-legged on the floor, his eyes pitch black and empty, ringed with the same darkness he used to create portals. Shadow matter poured from his chest like plumes of smoke, as a black hole seemed to grow there.

He was chanting jumbled strings of words, never breaking for breath, their ends running on so they all blurred into a single, endless word, and as he chanted he was looking right through me.

"Oliver?"

"TherewasneveranyotherwayIamsorryithadtoendlike this—"

All around him thousands of tiny peepholes were scattered, each one black-rimmed, feathery and shimmering, reflecting visions of futures that might be, all of them playing at once.

"ItriedtosaveyoubutitwastoolateIhadtowatchyoudie again—"

In one of the peepholes I saw airships. The Basilica was burning again, like on the night of the revolt. I watched, wide-eyed, as a missile fell, as if in slow motion. It plunged through the glass of the Observatory, exploding into a fireball with a thick mushroom cloud.

"Whyareyoutellingmethiswhenit'salreadytoolateto stopit—"

Here was me, bleeding. Here was the Governor, laughing. Here was the Empress, embracing him.

I knew what the voices were now. They were the voices of thousands of possible-future versions of myself, of Oliver and others, all talking at the same time from their different tomorrows.

"*Something bad is already happening!*" I said in one.

"*Please don't go,*" he said in another.

"*Providence will soon be mine,*" drawled the Governor.

"*Lady Memoria is dead,*" announced the Premier.

Finally, I could see what he saw: all those fast, fragmented scenes, all broken and mixed up like shards of glass tumbling through the darkness of his mind in a chaotic, senseless stream. In among them, several moments stood out starkly, sharper than all the others.

Fire, dancing, champagne, blood.

In all the visions, I was dying. I watched myself die a thousand times, each time in the same room of the Basilica, as a crescent moon hung high in the dark window above me. There were only minute differences between the images: the flowers in a vase, the exact positions of the stars, the presence of a servant, the weather, the blackened burn marks that scarred the building.

On a notepad on his desk, the same words were written ad nauseam: *SIXTH HOUSE, SIXTH SENSE, SIXTH HOUSE, SIXTH SENSE…* I traced my fingers over the page, gravity tilting and surging, before I glanced over the other items on the desk—

With a gut-dropping shock, I recognized the memory removal machine that Doctor Millefleur had once used on me, and the cloudy orb inside one of its vials…

It was a living memory, not yet spent but extracted. *His* memory. I could sense his energy in it. I pressed my fingers to the glass, jolting as the singular remembrance pulsed, rippling through my entire body…

We are lying together in bed at Obscura House, kissing, whispering sweet nothings, wrapped in black silk sheets.

"Lily, I … I think I love you," he says, for the first time. "No, not think. I know. I know I do. I love you."

Reflected through his eyes, my mouth hangs open. For a

second, I don't say anything in response. From the outside, it might look as if I doubt my own feelings when I know the truth of them has merely taken me by surprise.

"I love you too," I say, yet there is a tinge of conflict in my face. He sees my hesitation. He doesn't know it's guilt, at knowing what I must do. "I love you, Oliver."

I must steal his memory, at my father's bidding. It's wrong, I know it is, but it will set him free. It will set us all free.

I steal from him, and yet I love him. The duality is jarring.

Hours later, he wakes to find I'm missing, half the bed empty. He senses that something else is gone, but he doesn't know what it is…

Back in the present, shame seized me. It was a terrible moment in time. I could see why he would want it removed. But … if he'd removed this core memory, what else had he sacrificed? What else had he forgotten about me? About us? Not wonder he was having memory problems.

There was another extracted memory in a bell jar beside the machine, waiting to be used up. A cold terror ran down my spine as I touched it, drawing me into the recollection.

"I have a special task for you," says the Chancellor. He's younger, sitting on a balcony overlooking the Obscura garden with its eye-shaped pond.

"What is it, father?" I ask.

I am young Oliver, sipping iced tea brought by servants in black uniform.

"There is a girl, Ruben Renato's daughter. Her mother ran away with her when she was just a baby."

263

I look to him, curious.

"People say that they're living in the Valley, hiding away from him," my father continues. "Ruben wants to find her and bring her home to the Order. He longs to find her. It is a tragedy, for a man to grow up without knowing his child."

I don't agree. Perhaps not knowing him would be a blessing for her. I know it would for me. But none of this I say to my father.

"I need you to find her for me."

He hands me a photograph of a red-haired woman. She's wearing the red robes of a servant at Renato House, with the flower symbol of a Spirit soul on her breast.

"Her mother is a commoner?" I ask.

"Ruben has a certain affection for women of a lower station. He liked grubbing around in the gutters, so to speak. This one is Mara Duffy," he says. "If you find her, you will find the girl. Will you do that for me?"

As much as I hate him, I am eager to please him too – so terribly eager to prove myself, to earn his love. I don't yet know that I never will – that such a feat is impossible.

"I can do it," I say. "I bet I can find her faster than an entire squadron of your army."

"Good. Then let me see it."

When my father stands up and moves away, I split my Shadow from my body, letting it soar away in the form of three birds. They fly for hundreds of miles, scouring the rolling green hills until one of them spies the curly red hair of Ruben's runaway lover; she's hanging clean sheets on a washing line, singing to herself off-key.

Rejoicing, rejoining, three becoming one, I land on the rooftop. A young girl sits on the stoop nearby drawing a picture, sketching the trees and the hills with a worn-down pencil.

Lily Duffy.

It's … me.

The memory rapidly disintegrated, bringing me back to Oliver's room.

I recalled the night Inspectors came for my mother, forcing me into a wagon and her into a gaol cell. Ruben Renato had found us, had found me, and I never knew how.

Until now.

Oliver Obscura had helped him.

I turned to look at him. His eyes snapped open, still black with the Shadow.

"Lily," he said monotonously, in the voice of a stranger. He reached for me, as if in fear, but I pushed him away. I stepped back unsteadily instead, creating more distance between us.

"*You* were the one who found me? You were the one who found me in Green Valley? You're the reason I was taken from my mother, and brought here to serve my father?"

He blinked, rubbed his face, and saw me, really saw me. He gazed around, taking in the scene I had just witnessed, looked to the excised memory waiting in its bell jar.

"I can explain—"

"First you're sneaking around with the Empress of Arctica and now you're sacrificing memories of me?" I said, the Valley coming out in my voice. If he could do that, then maybe he really did cheat on me. I took another step away from him. "Who even *are* you, Oliver?"

"I can't tell you anything – it would endanger you—"

"I saw you, Oliver. I saw you kissing her!"

His face blanked, youthful with shock. "Who?"

"The Empress! Of all the people you could've cheated on me with, you had to pick our most feared and most dangerous enemy? Why? *Why*, Oliver?"

"But I didn't—"

"I don't get it. You've been telling me that the Governor was the one we should be scared of, but all the while you were colluding with her – if that's what I should call it. Who knows what you've told her! Or what she saw in your mind when you kissed her."

"Kissed her? *No*, that didn't happen."

"Please don't lie. I saw you, Oliver. In this!"

I tossed the chess queen at him, my face twisted, but he didn't move to catch it. It bounced off his chest. He picked it up, staring at it in confusion for a moment before placing it in front of the lantern.

We watched as he and the Empress cavorted in silence. I forced myself not to look away, as much as it hurt.

He paled, steadying himself against the table. "That can't be," he said.

"Do you love her?" I asked.

"No! Of course not. There's *nothing* between us!"

"Then what is *that*?" I said, pointing at them kissing on loop.

"I don't know. I can't remember it," he said.

"Show me your version of the memory, then."

"I don't know if I can," he said, staring at his hands. "I've been removing so many memories. I can't even remember what I've lost."

"Then how do you know it didn't happen?"

He had no answer for that. I turned to go, but a long, Shadowy arm stretched out, shutting the door as I opened it.

"Wait. We can talk about this. You did what your father asked of you, too, didn't you?" he said. "You violated my memory and stole from me."

"Let me out!" Grunting in frustration, I threw an involuntary fireball his way. It missed but it burned a hole in the wall before vanishing.

Oliver gaped at me in hurt, his expression wounded.

"Look at us," I said, staring at my palms. "We're making each other worse... We're the worst version of ourselves right now."

"Please, Lily. Don't say that. I don't even know what's happening right now. I'm so confused, all of the time. What occurred, what didn't..." He was shaking. "What will be, what won't... I'm losing track of which future I'm in. I see everything, all of the time, and *I can't stop*. I can't stop because, if I do, something bad will happen."

"Something bad is already happening!"

He gasped and stepped forward, grasping my hands.

"Wait, what did you just say?"

Something bad is already happening... We'd both seen it on

267

the wall, before the sentence came out of my mouth. Was I just parroting what I'd already seen there? Subconsciously, perhaps? Or was it evidence, that the future could indeed by predicted?

"You see?" he said. "The prophecies are real."

"No."

I extricated myself, bursting out of the room into the hallway.

"Please don't go," he said, following me. "Lily, please. You're everything, my whole world. I'd never do that to you, I swear. I met her only once and there was definitely no kissing. Please, you have to believe me. You're the reason I'm doing all of this. I'm frightened you're going to die, and it will be my fault."

"I could die crossing the street! People die, Oliver, but first they live. That's the part you're missing. Maybe you're right. Maybe the sixth sense is real. Maybe my days are numbered. But what good is this doing you? You're no closer to the truth than I am! I'm going to die and you'll have wasted all this time when we could've just been happy together."

"I … I wish I could make you understand," he said.

"Tell me you'll stop sacrificing memories," I said. "Promise me that, and then I'll stay."

His expression hardened. "I can't do that," he said simply. "It's for your own good, Lily. I won't risk losing you. Even if it means…"

He didn't finish this sentence.

"Then it looks like you're losing me anyway," I said, finally making my exit. "I guess you should've seen this coming."

My mother was waiting for me back at Renato House with open arms, as always. One look at my face was all it took for her to read my feelings. Not because of her extrasensory perception, but because she was a parent.

"I'm so sorry, love," she said.

I could've run to her and sobbed like a baby, but if I did that, I wasn't sure I'd ever stop. Maybe I'd fall down and never get up again. It was much easier to be mad. I wanted to kick things, break rocks, smash plates.

"I don't want to talk about it," I said, running up the stairs. I threw myself face down on the bed. In the silence of my room, Octavia's voice drifted into my mind, quiet and gentle at first, then louder, more solid.

"*I sensed you needed a friend,*" she said.

"Sensed?"

"*OK, I heard you two arguing from a mile away.*"

"Great." I envisioned her sitting on the bed beside me, holding my hand.

"*Talk to me.*"

I opened my mind, letting her listen to my stream of consciousness. I was only faintly aware of it, letting it ebb and flow freely without intervention, but I was uncensored. I had nothing to hide from her.

"*I don't know what to say,*" she said.

"Yeah, no shit."

"*Maybe this is all part of the plot,*" Octavia was telling me. "*Someone is messing with Oliver and they want to drive you apart. You're the sweethearts of the revolution. Together, you're powerful. It makes sense, to try and split you up, and he's definitely not himself right now.*"

"I guess… Maybe."

"*Think about it. If the enemy was conspiring against Oliver, wouldn't this be exactly what they'd want? Him sacrificing his memories, losing himself like you did before, pushing everyone away so he's isolated, neglecting his duties, betraying even the person most dedicated to him? It's like a villain's wish list.*"

I sat up. "You're not wrong there."

I'd been stupid. Missed what was right in front of my face. My first hunch had been right all along.

Someone was doing this to Oliver. To us.

"We have to find out who's ruling the Sixth House and what it has to do with the Shades. Maybe Tristan Obscura is behind this after all."

"*I'll keep an eye on him.*"

"I think he's still hiding something. Oliver, I mean."

"*He loves you. I know he does. He loves you more than anything. I hear it in his mind. All the time.*"

"*We love you, Ruby,*" came Rani's voice in the background. "*We'll solve this thing. Tomorrow, we'll find out what's been going on.*"

I felt them drift away, allowing me to close my mind

again, but I left the smallest of cracks open for Oliver to get in if he so chose.

I waited in the place we shared in our minds, but he didn't come.

14.

OLIVER

When I was a child, my father discovered that I had a terrible gift. I could penetrate the minds of those around me.

It began on the elementary school playground, with the boy who bullied me relentlessly. Nathaniel Mannerson. After he'd tormented me for weeks about being a nerd, for being ugly or any number of reasons he took to despise me, I found myself tearing through his psyche in search of his worst moment, so I could broadcast it to the class, so I could humiliate him like he humiliated me.

I did it without knowing how. The secret was already within me. I'm not proud, but I was a child. A terribly unhappy child.

I found the memory of him wetting himself on a family day trip and projected the image in such excruciating detail, that he cried. The other kids pointed and laughed, flocking around me to relish in Nathaniel's misery, but also because they didn't want to get on the wrong side of me themselves. Nathaniel didn't fuck me with after that. No one did.

My father should have been concerned when he learned about this, should have lectured me perhaps about consent and tolerance and peace, but instead he laughed.

It was, perhaps, the first time he'd seen himself in me, and rather than being horrified, he was proud. For once, he was actually proud.

He trained me to use my Shadow, teaching me never to use the skill against him in return. He used me as a weapon to harm his enemies. With my mother gone, it was our only bond, the only time I ever felt close to him. He had set me loose on many a vulnerable psyche in search of a person's weaknesses – whatever my father could use to toy with them – and I had been glad to do it for him. He was skilled in the arts of sabotage and deception, and he taught me well in them.

I called upon those teachings now, as I attempted to derail destiny.

I'd sworn to myself that I'd never be that person again, that I would never use my Shadow for dark deeds, but it seemed I had no choice. This was a monstrous world, and sometimes the only way to survive it was to become a monster yourself.

I didn't feel good about it, but it was necessary.

I would do whatever it took.

First, I would stop the ball.

I started small. First, a collapsed pillar resulted in structural damage to the Basilica. But Cordata simply drafted in a team of engineers and builders to fix things.

The scheduled band and caterers were unfortunately booked by an anonymous client, with an offer they couldn't refuse. Cordata merely called upon Song souls to fill the vacancy.

"A people's choir for a People's Ball," he said, brightly.

Next, the Governor received a call from one of his daughters urging him home on a medical emergency, but he quickly determined that it was a hoax when she didn't remember his beloved dog's name.

That was foolish, on my part.

I gave the waiters mild food poisoning. I blocked the drains. I flooded the kitchens. No matter what obstacles I threw at him, the Premier gracefully avoided them, and the Governor was always at his side, eager to lend a hand. There was no problem so large that the mighty Constitution couldn't fix it. The future appeared unstoppable.

I fed stories to the press that set the remnants of the gangs against each other, ensuring there was trouble on the streets, petty fighting and rioting. I hoped that civil unrest might persuade the Governor to leave early, thus causing the ball to be cancelled, but the gangs called an unexpected truce. Now they were working together to distribute supplies. I was glad about that, and yet it frustrated my goal. I had to find another way to stop the ball.

The problem with the Premier was that he was optimistic

to the point of naivety. He believed in the best of things, for as long as it was possible to do so. There was little chance of him being convinced that his impressive new ally and Heart soul kin was conspiring against him.

I tried giving Premier Cordata nightmares, recurring ones, where he was the subject of a violent mob that took his head off. But every time Cordata awoke, he merely shrugged off the dream. He ate a fruit salad, talked to his House counsellor and lifted some weights. He journaled his feelings and made love to his wife. He wasn't haunted by the weight of his choices.

I envied him that.

I was stuck. The days and nights passed by far too quickly, like grains of sand in the hourglass. I could no longer lean on my friends – they had abandoned me, or I had abandoned them; I wasn't certain. Ruby was barely speaking to me. Only Gabriel remained and even he seemed distant, disappointed, despite the fact that I paid him to serve me.

The papers were having a field day. The Chancellor's unstable son had finally lost his mind, just as everyone always knew I would.

What they couldn't understand – what no one could apparently understand – was that I had no choice. Because every time I closed my eyes, I saw Ruby ascending the imperial staircase at the Basilica in her red phoenix dress, walking to her death in the room with the round window as the war exploded around her, missiles falling… The assassin appeared from the darkness and…

BANG!

She met her end in every future I could see now. Because of the ball. The ball was the common thread. A simple party, and yet I was unable to stop it. I became ever more convinced that the Governor had sensed my suspicions and worked to thwart me.

I had jettisoned many memories in search of the truth, so many that the chronology of my life had started to collapse. All the times and places and people of my life mixed together. Improbable things happened. My mother danced with Arjun Sharma. My father played chess with the Empress. Ruby waved from a balcony next to Ambrose Fairchild.

I startled when I bumped into a stranger in the hall, only for him to tell me, with a worried look, that he was my hired guardian, Gabriel. I became confused to discover that Gus had tattoos, that Octavia liked birds, that Rani and Octavia were dating. How had I forgotten so much, just by removing those key memories?

Nothing made sense any more.

Days passed and I didn't remember what happened in them.

Ruby tried to fix things; she really did. She came to meet me one morning in the Obscura House gardens. We sat by a black, brutalist fountain, watching the dark clouds above.

"Your eyes have changed," I told her. "They used to be green."

That was the wrong thing to say.

"My eyes have always been hazel," she said, stiffening.

"Are you sure?"

"I think I know the colour of my own eyes."

Fuck. I'd done it again.

"No wonder you're getting mixed up, though, with so many different women in your life," she said, shoving a newspaper at me angrily. I read the headline: LORD OBSCURA SEEN ON DATE WITH OLD FLAME AMELIA MILLEFLEUR.

"Is it true?" she asked.

When had I seen Amelia? I wouldn't do that, surely, not when I was so in love with Ruby? But if I was innocent, why could I recall us dancing? Why did I remember her face in such detail? If I closed my eyes, I could imagine myself kissing this girl who wasn't Ruby.

I must've done it. I must've cheated.

"I don't know," I said. "I don't remember."

It was real.

It was all terribly, horribly real.

When I looked up, Ruby was already gone.

In an instant, horrifyingly, it was three days before the ball. Tomorrow was coming and I didn't know how to stop it. Maybe I couldn't.

I no longer recognized my own house, or myself in the mirror. Surely I'd not been so gaunt-looking before, with so much silver in my hair? I didn't remember my face looking so weathered, or my eyes so sad. I wasn't me. This reality was no longer mine.

I knelt in front of my mother's statue.

"I don't know what to do," I said, clutching at the sculpted folds of her hard cloak. "I've fucked everything up as usual. She's going to die and I don't know how to stop it."

I had lost the battle with Cordata, I had lost to the Sixth House and, worst of all, I had lost Ruby. I'd lost everything. My mother's absence was an ache.

"Are you there?"

Outside, the wind howled.

"I need your help, Mama. I've never needed you more. Please, I beg you, send me a sign. Show me I'm not alone."

Silence resounded, the sound of no hope, before a single sentence cut through the void, Ruby's voice in my head, soft and tentative: *"Do you think … this might have something to do with your father?"*

I had nothing left and only one person left to turn to, which just so happened to be the one person I hated most in this world. Resigned to what I had to do, I held up my hand to create a portal. I travelled through the infinite dark to the Fifth Borough, where a long walkway lined with torches led to the prison where my father was being held.

Somewhat ironically, the former Chancellor was imprisoned in the Reformatory, the very same building where he once tortured children like laboratory rats, hoping to turn them into "model citizens". The Reformatory was no longer heaving with vulnerable souls primed for reprogramming, but the building was haunted by their left-behind psyche. It created a prickly atmosphere of unease, woven into the cracked, paint-peeling walls, smeared into the dirty floors, loitering in every operating suite, every doctor's office, every abandoned classroom, every cell. Filmy memories of those once imprisoned here now flitted between the walls and doors, replaying events that once were.

Spirit was my weakest sense – history and memory being my biggest vulnerability – so these sylphs were faint to me, barely perceptible. They passed right through me, unaware of my existence, unaware of themselves. They were not alive, just reanimated memories.

I didn't ask for permission from the skeleton staff who protected the Reformatory's last remaining prisoners. I didn't know who I could trust. Not any more. Instead, I portalled directly into the wing that contained his cell, easily incapacitating the guards stationed there, their eyes turning black before they fell asleep. I walked along a line of specially made cages, reinforced by the protective psyche of all five Houses.

Now the watcher was the one being watched. It seemed a fitting punishment.

My father was fed and kept alive. He had access to a spartan bed and basic bathing facilities. But beyond that, he sat in constant darkness, tormented by his own fractured Shadow. He was tortured by himself.

I pulled up in front of his lonely cell. The former Chancellor was sleeping, the dark projections of his sinister subconscious casting on the wall of the cell as he dreamed: a legion of soldiers, my mother falling to her death, me crying, the monster of his soul...

For as long as I could remember, Tristan Obscura had a clean-cut, pristine appearance, his dark hair slicked back, his goatee razor-sharp. Now he looked like an old man, his face withered, his hair straggly, a long preacher beard hanging from his chin, just like one of the vagrants he'd terrorized.

He cracked open one red-rimmed eye, clocking my presence. His Shadow assumed his technically human form as he sat up, rubbing his eyes.

"It's you," he said. "You came. I didn't think you would."

"Trust me, it's a last resort," I said.

He peered into the darkness as I stepped out from the shadows. When our pupils aligned it felt like a punch, a kick to the groin.

"Don't try to use your powers on me or I swear I will make you regret the day you ever made me," I said.

"I can't." He banged on the bars. "This cage prevents my Shadow from escaping beyond its bounds. All I have to go on is a father's intuition."

"Looks like you're screwed, then."

I'd never wanted to set eyes on him again but, now that I had, I felt a twisted kind of relief. He looked smaller, weaker. He was no longer the terrifying creature I'd built up in my mind since he'd been away, but he was still the godawful father I'd known all my life.

"I'm glad you came, Oliver," he said, struggling up on to

his knees and grasping at the black iron bars that separated us. "Whatever the reason for it."

"Wow, you must be bored," I drawled.

"There's not much to do in here, as you can see, but that's not the reason. I…" His voice was strangled. "I've missed you, son."

I couldn't help but laugh, though the sound was hollow. "You *missed* me? Really? Is that the best you could come up with?"

"You find this amusing?" he asked.

"I find it somewhat difficult to believe, that's all," I said.

"You don't think that I love you? You're wrong. Perhaps I was too harsh with you when you were growing up, but everything I did was for you. I wanted to make you strong, so you could survive this world. Now look at you. You are leading our House, as I always hoped you would."

"I don't do it for you." I stepped closer, snarling, my hands balling into fists. "Nothing I do is for you. Not any more."

"Then why are you here?" he asked calmly. "Why are you wearing my clothes, and bearing my name as Master of our House?"

I looked down at myself, realizing I was wearing the House Obscura tunic although I had no memory of getting dressed.

"I did it for the people, not for you."

"The *people*? The people are monsters who would tear you apart, mount your head on a spike and parade it about town."

I flinched.

281

"But you already know that, don't you?" he said, infuriatingly smug. "Everyone else has turned against you."

I swallowed down bile, sickened by myself. He was right. I'd lost them all. Ash and Perpetua. Cordata, Memoria. Gus, Octavia, Rani. Even Ruby.

"You don't know me as well as you think," I said defensively.

"It happens to the best of us. Power corrupts all it touches."

"I'm not corrupted."

"You can't lie to me, son. You feel it already, don't you? The rot in your soul. It is already in your blood, in your flesh. For here you are, every bit the scion of the aristocracy you claimed to hate. You're more like me than you think."

"Shut up. SHUT UP!"

"Look at you. You're so afraid. You fear the thousand-faced monster you created."

The "thousand-faced monster"... *The monster with a thousand faces*—

"Tell me it wasn't you who sent the assassin?" I said shakily. "Tell me it wasn't you who created the Sixth House?"

My father slowly shook his head. "Whatever are you babbling about now, Oliver?" he said. His tone was convincing, but I knew better than to believe him.

"You're puppeteering people to do your bidding, aren't you? You founded the Sixth House to seize back power. Sent an assassin to try and pick us all off, one by one. But you didn't realize I had the sixth sense. You didn't realize I could see visions of the future. What's next? Are you working with the Governor?"

He gawked at me, his mouth open, but the corners of his mouth twitched in some kind of glorious revulsion. "The sixth sense? That arcane nonsense?"

"You said 'the thousand-faced monster'," I said, scowling. "Why?"

"You've never heard that expression before?" He paused, drawing out his response, knowing it was torture to me. "The thousand-faced monster is the people, Oliver. There is nothing greater to be feared than the public. The monster of the mob. Individually, a person is weak, no match for the greatness of the state, but combined, they are undefeatable. The identity of the thousand-faced monster can never be pinned down, you see. It can't be stopped by killing one face, or ten, or a hundred. With every head you cut off, another head grows in its place."

In the silence that followed, my father watched me hawkishly.

"But now I'm curious," he said. "Someone is clearly trying to do you harm. What kind of trouble are you in, son? Tell me, let me help."

He was practically giddy at the idea of me having a problem. Two factions warred inside me, like territorial wolves. One was screaming at me not to trust him, but the other was desperate to hear what he had to say.

"OK, fine. I'll bite," I said. "Someone has founded a new house, the Sixth House. They're brainwashing citizens into their thraldom. Whoever it is, they can take over souls to puppet their bodies, like you did with me."

"Intriguing," he said.

"What do you know about the Governor of Constitution?" I asked.

In his dark eyes, I saw confusion. He was trying to stitch together the scant bits of information I'd given him.

"You think Fairchild is behind this? I doubt that," he said. "He may have the greatest armies, the biggest navies, but he is reluctant to use them unless he's certain the battle will be easily won. He has no stomach for bloodshed."

I thought of the eerie orchard in the Governor's mind and wondered.

"And what of the Empress?" I asked.

He laughed, a low, rumbling sound, like a single marble in a tin. "The Empress is as mad as your old Nana Mandala was. A catastrophe waiting to happen. She thinks herself a prophet. Is she the one who has planted this sixth sense nonsense in your mind?"

"Aurora knew what would happen. She knew my mother would die at your hands. She saw you for what you were and you hated her for it, didn't you?"

"Your grandmother was a raving lunatic. The sixth sense is truly madness. Chaos in its purest form. No single mind can comprehend the vastness of future possibilities." He watched me closely. "Tell me you haven't succumbed to this insanity, Oliver. Tell me you don't truly believe now in the sixth sense."

His words cut through all the smoke and mirrors that stood between us. In that instant, I could tell that he still saw me as a child, and that in my sheepish expression he read the truth.

"Oh, Oliver."

"I don't want to hear whatever it is you have to say," I said. "It never makes me feel better, anyway."

"You mustn't put stock in premonitions. They are mere illusions of the Shadow, reflecting your desires and fears. They cannot be relied upon. They cannot protect you. Look how it all ended for your grandmother. Who did she save? What did she prevent? No one. Nothing. She couldn't even save her own daughter."

It was the closest he'd ever come to any accountability, to admitting that he'd actually murdered my mother, but it was just breadcrumbs.

"You're disgusting. I'm done with this conversation. I'm done with you," I said, walking away. "For good this time. Remember my face, because you won't see it again."

"No, wait! Stop now, Oliver, before it's too late. Be warned. If you're mixed up with the Empress and her chaos, no good will come of it. You must heed my advice. You must swallow your pride and listen to me—"

"No! I hope you burn in the hell you made for yourself, because when you die, I'll be dancing on your grave," I said, spitting out the words. "I'll throw a goddam party, and I'll invite every person you ever hurt to come piss on it."

I drew the shadows of the room around me like a cloak, disappearing into the black hole I'd created. I fell into it, plunging into the darkest part of my soul, where I kept all my fantasies of brutally killing him. *Hate him. Hate him. Hate him.*

Going there had been a mistake. A distraction. He couldn't help me. I needed to stop the ball, whatever it cost.

Desperate times called for desperate measures, after all.

I portalled back to the Basilica, using my Shadow to deliver me directly into the ballroom. The decorations were already up for the event, the tables draped under cloths ready for a feast. Here was the tower of glasses, ready to be filled with champagne. Here were the flags and bunting, the pillars wrapped with streamers, the net of balloons ready to drop. Even the instruments of the brass band were laid out ready to play, with a drumkit and a microphone.

I needed to destroy it.

Destroy it all.

Hidden in darkness, I pulled an emergency lever that sounded every fire alarm in the building. The blaring sound triggered a mass evacuation, which proceeded in an orderly fashion as if fire drills at the Basilica were fairly routine.

"Not again!" I heard one warden wail.

I sent out my Shadow to scour the Basilica's many rooms, searching for left-behind souls. When I was sure the building was empty, I picked up a ceremonial torch, removing it from its metal wall mount, feeling the heat on my face as it crackled enticingly. Incitingly.

This was it. The singular moment when I took the future into my own hands. I looked to the wall, seeing the beastly silhouette I cast.

I had the power of a god, but the Shadow of a demon.

Touching the flame to one of the flags, I watched as the fire caught on, its sparks filling the room with a fiery glow.

It was done. It was over.

I watched as the celebratory banners burned, flames eating them up until there was nothing left of them. The glass overhead cracked and shattered, creating a roasting hot cacophony of little explosions.

I laughed into the fire, hysterical and numb. There would be no People's Ball now. I'd made sure of it. I'd stopped the future. I'd changed the world of tomorrow.

I was going to be in so much trouble when they caught onto me, but at least Lily wouldn't die such a terrible death. I had spared her from the worst fate.

The alliance would fail, Providence wouldn't fall.

Ruby Renato would live, despite the odds.

Out on the street, I joined the crowd of onlookers, watching the building burn. For a fleeting moment, I felt a sense of deep and resounding peace, until a flock of black-coated Inspectors filed out of a wagon. I readied myself to be arrested for arson. I hadn't exactly been subtle about it. They approached hesitantly, nervously, their faces grave.

"Your Lordship, we have some terrible news," said one, removing his top hat.

"Oh?"

"It's your father."

"Don't tell me the bastard has escaped," I said.

"No, he… He's dead, my Lord."

The gathered crowd awaited my reaction, but none came.

"I see," I said.

"His soul was ripped right out of his chest."

"You don't say."

They looked to each other, frowning in confusion at my nonchalant response.

"The former Chancellor has been murdered, my Lord."

"Right. I heard you the first time"

The street crowd exploded into whispers and mutters. My last words to him played in my head: *I hope you burn in the hell you made for yourself.*

One of the Inspectors cleared his throat. "Lord Obscura? We'd like you to come with us. We have a few questions we'd like to ask you if that's—"

Ignoring them, I vanished into a portal, leaving it all behind.

I could feel that crack inside me growing.

15.

RUBY

"I have news."

I opened my eyes, recognizing Octavia's voice in my ear.

"I'm listening," I said, heaving myself into an upright position.

"There are rumours all over the city about a gathering of the Sixth. They're meeting at Lavender Hill in the Second Borough, south of the river, tonight."

"I'll be there."

"We'll come too."

"No, I – I'm grateful for your help, but I don't want you to risk getting taken over again. If they have a big event planned, they could force you to do something bad."

"But—"

"I love you, but it's less risky this way, if I go alone. I don't want to have to fight any more of my favourite people."

"If you say so. You'll be safe, won't you?"

"Of course. I can disguise myself. I still have that pendant I stole from Oliver," I said.

"I'll be in your ear, and Rani will keep watch through the Shadow."

I put on the necklace, my favourite black hooded cloak and my shin-kicking boots, just in case. As I moved through the city, my heart and my head were at war once again. In the blue corner was my head. The simplest explanation to what I'd seen was that Oliver had succumbed to the advances of the Empress. She had seduced him. He was human, and she was beautiful. Maybe part of him enjoyed the danger, the juice of the forbidden fruit. Maybe the Countess was right about men being dogs, in the end.

But in the red corner was my heart, and it was putting up a damn good fight. It stubbornly told me that this wasn't all it appeared to be at first sight; that something was very wrong with Oliver and that what I saw could have been a false memory, implanted to cause utmost drama.

And behind the curtain was someone pulling the strings – but who? The former Chancellor? Blade? The Empress? The Governor? The conflicting thoughts I was having were so heavy they made my temples ache.

"Uh, maybe you should focus on the Sixth?" suggested Octavia gently, privy to my wandering mind. *"You're walking into a nest of vipers. It would be wise not to get too distracted."*

"Good call."

When I arrived at the location Rani identified, I saw a steady stream of people in bright, shabby outfits heading south, some holding anti-establishment placards denouncing the New Order: NOT IN MY NAME, NO ORDER ONLY CHAOS, SAY NO TO THE NO-BILITY. Across the river, I joined their pilgrimage: a long chain of souls walking alone or in small groups. No longer divided by class or anatomy, they banded together, no conflict between them. They shared bread and water, laughing and singing, decorating each other with face paint.

"Here on your own?"

I turned to see a tall girl with flowers daubed on her face and bruises on her shins, her curly hair held back by a headband.

"Thought I'd check it out," I said, faux-casually. "The Sixth has got everyone talking. I don't really know what to expect."

"You're lucky, getting to experience it for the first time. I'm jealous! You won't regret it, I promise," she said.

I had no idea what she saw when she looked at me. The necklace's charm worked by projecting a person's own subconscious biases on to me. They saw only what they expected to see.

"You should stick with us," she said, indicating a group of people who lingered a few paces ahead. "We'll look out for you."

"*Be careful*," Octavia whispered, though no one could hear her but me. "*They look friendly but they're loyal to the Sixth.*"

When they asked me who I was, I told them my name was Lily, which was true. Most people knew me as Ruby, and Lily was a common enough name that it drew no suspicion. I told them I was a maid and that I was bored of my life, which they seemed to find satisfactory, as backstories go.

"What brought you here?" I asked in return.

"New Order, old Order, nothing ever changes around here," said one.

"Maybe only chaos can truly bring order," said the girl with the flowers painted on her face. "Maybe the city needs to burn so something new and beautiful can grow from the ashes." She smiled sweetly, though her words were dark. Her pupils weren't crescents – none of theirs were. No washing of psyche was required to draw this crowd. The Sixth had genuine support among the young and the old, the rich and the poor.

We trailed all the way to Lavender Hill, where a stage had been assembled, complete with undoubtedly stolen speaker towers. Food trucks surrounded the lawns as stalls were set up. It had the lively atmosphere of a festival, as attendees played instruments and tossed balls around, setting up chairs and picnic blankets.

Over the course of the next hour, thousands of people gathered, stretching across the fields in every direction. The crowd thrummed with nervous energy.

The wait stretched on, the hazy sun dropping in the sky.

As twilight fell and the temperature dropped, a procession of carriages arrived, pulling up behind the stage.

The subdued crowd came to life in an instant, jumping to their feet and waving their placards and banners. To the sound of triumphant applause, the two women and the girl I'd seen taken over before stepped out, followed by a group of people wearing the five colours of the soul: black, white, silver, gold and red.

"Welcome, my children," said the youngest of the three conduits, the little girl. "You'll see we have some new friends with us today."

She was referring to the five leaders of the rebel factions, recognizable by their edgy haircuts, tattoos and weathered faces. Here at last was the dreadlocked Blade in his black leather jacket. Here was the robed, barefoot leader of the Heart soul Hosts, and the ruler of the Whisperers with a listening device in her studded ear. Their pupils were all crescents. They were clearly not in on the plot, but mere tools of it.

In the crowd on stage, I saw someone else I recognized. My stomach dropped.

"Perpetua," I whispered.

I felt Octavia's startled response in my mind, *No! What's she doing there?*

Perpetua's crescent pupils locked with mine. Neither of us blinked.

"The Sixth have converted her," I murmured.

Further back in the crowd, I saw Ash, also staring out at the sprawling audience with no expression.

"Ash, too." Ash and Perpetua were the first people to alert me to the cult's activities, and now they were a part of it.

"Who are you talking to?" asked the girl beside me, frowning.

"No one," I said quickly. "Just … narrating my own life. Doesn't everyone do that?"

She eyeballed me oddly.

I began pushing my way towards the front of the crowd, ducking under arms and swerving around cheering citizens.

"Where are you going?" the girl called after me, but I didn't answer. I kept my eyes on Perpetua and Ash.

"Today marks a special moment in the history of our movement," declared the pregnant woman. "The five gangs of Providence have chosen to ally with us."

The crowd erupted, exultant, some shooting psychometric flares into the air overhead: streaks of black and gold, silver, white and red. Many of them were gifted with innate abilities they could use as weapons.

"There is only one movement now," said the older woman. "One house."

"Only one!" chanted the crowd.

"With the gangs joining the Sixth, we are ready," intoned the little girl. "We finally have the numbers we need to take Providence. To destroy the New Order."

"The people are strong, united, as one," said the pregnant woman. "Soon it will be time for us to rise up and welcome our nation's new leader."

A new leader?

"The Sixth House shall create an everlasting empire, one that governs by looking to the future, not back to the past."

"One in which all souls will be equal."

"There will be no nobles, no Houses, no rich nor poor, no suffering!"

The crowd roused, ready to fight for this glittering vision. It reflected in their eyes, every face now rapt, their pupils becoming half-moons.

"In the name of the Sixth House!"

"In the name of the Sixth House!"

"*Might be time to get out of there?*" suggested Octavia.

But I couldn't leave, not now. Not when I might learn the identity of their leader.

"The hour is upon us. In two days, we move."

Two days? That's Saturday! The same day as the ball.

The people cheered, creating a tremendous din.

"But first, we must deal with the traitor in our midst."

The noise of the crowd dramatically depleted as the youngest of the trio pointed directly at me, her head cocked to one side.

As one, the crowd all turned to stare too, every pair of eyes reflecting those peculiar crescents. All of them except mine.

"I can see you, Ruby Renato," said the child. "Lily Duffy. Iris Cavendish. You can't fool me with that disguise."

The people parted, creating an aisle as the rebel converts advanced towards me. They walked in a shuddering, jolting, unnatural way, as if controlled with invisible strings from high above. But their controller remained unseen.

"*What's going on?*" came Octavia's voice.

"I'm in deep shit," I said.

"*Ruby—*"

Ash held a flame thrower. Perpetua was armed with a

metal thurible on a chain, incense smoke bleeding from the perforations in its orb.

"Death to the New Order," she said, advancing on me.

"This isn't" – I ducked deftly as she swung the weapon at me – "this isn't you, Perpetua! I know you're mad at me but" – I ducked again – "violence won't solve anything."

She ripped off my necklace, destroying my disguise. I channelled my Spark, creating a wall of fire that held her at bay. In the back of my mind, I could hear Octavia and Rani talking in high, frantic voices.

"Please, Perpetua," I cried, watching her through the curtain of flames. There must have been a Spark of her still in there, but I couldn't sense it. I couldn't reach her.

"No Perpetua," she said. "Not any more."

The wall of fire extinguished itself, wasting away to smoking embers.

"We were friends once," I said, backing away. "Don't you remember?"

She swung the thurible again, causing me to swoop and duck.

"No friends."

For a brief moment, a second face seemed to shine through her features, as if she was wearing a mask, but it happened too quickly for me to identify them … the One, possessing her.

Possessing them all.

Perpetua advanced closer, swinging the thurible. It glanced off the side of my head, causing me to yelp in pain. I brought my fingers to the wound and they came away bloodied.

"Does it hurt?" she said, delighted at having injured me.

"Not as much as it's going to hurt when I knock you the hell out of my friend's head!"

I manifested a lightning tree of soul fire, crackling and splitting into fractals. It surged through Perpetua's body, causing her veins to glow briefly. My intention was only to drive out the presence that was possessing her. But before I knew it, I'd gone too far. I'd pushed too hard. Her eyes rolled back in her head as she collapsed into a singed heap.

"No! Perpetua? Perpetua?" I shook her vigorously, calling her name. She still had a pulse, but she was out stone cold.

A flume of fire blasted just inches from my face. I spun round to see Ash looming over me menacingly.

"Wake up, Ash! I know you're still in there."

"Not Ash. I am everyone," they said. "I am everything, everywhere, always. I am the monster with a thousand faces."

My power spilled over, electrifying them as I'd done with Perpetua and rendering them unconscious. Ash's body slumped to the ground, my horror growing.

Now another figure was stepping forward: the burly, dreadlocked Blade, with skulls etched on his knuckles, his chest scarred.

I knew they would just keep coming, with the One possessing them all. I couldn't fight them – not alone.

"A little help here would be great," I said.

"*We're working on it!*" came Octavia's voice.

As Blade approached me, I lashed out at him, locking eyes for a second. But his pupils were not crescents.

"Run!" he said.

"Huh—"

I doubled over as a sudden pain pierced my head from behind. I could feel something moving inside me, winding through the labyrinth of my brain like a dark serpent.

The One was inside me.

It felt like a hand on my head, pushing me down, making me smaller and weaker. Inside my head, I could feel myself falling.

"Every soul is mine now," said the One, in a thousand voices.

"Not every soul. Not mine!" I said. "You can't take hold of me."

"Don't speak too soon," they said.

I tried to crawl my way back up, scratching and struggling, as if trying to escape the bottom of a well.

"Now, let's see how this works," came my voice, though it wasn't me who formed the words. It was someone else, speaking in my voice.

I–not–I flexed my hands, until fire burst forth. I–not–I felt it tingle, even from deep within this mental prison, as they tugged on the strings of my nerve endings.

No. "Get out! Get out of my body!"

It was intolerable, being possessed. It felt like being trapped in a small cupboard with a bug crawling in your ear. Making myself huge in my mind, I pushed up, up, up, exploding out of the mental prison my consciousness had been trapped in. The One was forced out of my mind and out of my body, hopping back to the vessel of another rebel – the barefoot man in golden robes, the gregarious leader of the Hosts who ran soup kitchens.

Blade had vanished.

"*Ruby? Ruby? Ruby?*" I heard Octavia calling.

"Fascinating," said the barefoot man, in the voice of the One. "You were able to expel me. Another with the sixth sense. There are many more who have survived death than I thought."

This caught me off-guard. Another with the sixth sense?

The One jumped bodies again, to occupy one of the rebel members, this one a youth wearing an eye-patch. I recognized him from the streets, along with his friends Bird's Nest and Shoeless. I'd once watched their souls bared by an Inspector with a magic lantern. They'd escaped the Reformatory along with us on the night of the revolution. So the Sixth House had swept all the lost urchins up too. Now they were just bodies for the One to use and discard.

"Your soul was shattered," said Eyepatch.

"For a split second, you were dead," said Bird's Nest.

"I don't remember that."

"Most people don't remember dying," said Shoeless.

"The gift is weak. But it's there," said Bird's Nest.

"It won't help you now, though," said Shoeless, in a sing-song voice. "You can't win against so many."

"And you … you can't possess an entire country," I said.

"Can't I?"

The One seized the whole crowd at once. All the hundreds of people present at the rally slowly marched towards me, surrounding me on all sides.

"No one dares challenge me. No one person can hold me," said the Sixth House, in unison, their voices carrying over the fields. "I am too powerful to be contained."

"Am I supposed to be frightened of someone who hides inside the bodies of others?" I yelled. "Step up and show your face. Your *real* face."

On the One's command, the crowd stood to attention, saluting sharply.

"Seize her!" they boomed. They closed in on me, eyes blank.

Just as I was drawing upon my Spark to form a shield, a loud screech emanated from the speaker tower by the stage, a noise like cat claws on a chalkboard amplified infinitely. Instinctively the masses clutched at their ears as they bled.

I recognized the sound of Octavia screaming. She'd somehow used her Song to hack into the stream of consciousness, broadcasting it through the listening posts. Around me, everyone's eyes changed, briefly freed of the One's control before they clawed their way back into the people's souls again. Under this cover, I ran, emerging on to a dark street.

"I'm safe!" I panted. "Thanks, guys. You really saved my neck."

"*Never mind that. We need you back here,*" Rani's voice answered.

"Where's here?"

"*Obscura House, now.*"

When my carriage pulled up in front of Obscura House, the courtyard was crowded with black wagons. I went around the back way, keeping my hood up, waiting for two Inspectors to pass before I slipped through the open door. Inside, there were even more detectives in uniform, some of them carrying out boxes, others dusting down furniture while wearing white gloves.

Octavia and Rani were waiting in the living room, their faces drawn.

But there was no sign of Oliver.

Dread clutched at my heart.

"What is it?" I asked, on the verge of hysteria.

"It's Chancellor Obscura," said Rani.

"He's been murdered in prison," said Octavia.

Something grabbed my guts in a tight fist, squeezing them.

"They're searching the house for evidence. They won't talk to us. They just say there will be an investigation," said Rani.

"The murderer took the Chancellor's soul," said Octavia. "They stole his soul, like they did with Lord Harmonia."

"Where's Oliver?" I asked.

"Upstairs, being interviewed."

Without a thought, I raced up to his room, pushing open the door just as two uniformed Inspectors came out, whispering to each other. Oliver was sitting on his bed, staring at the wall with an empty look in his eyes. Hearing me come in, he looked up.

"What's going on?" I gushed.

"What happened to your face?" he said, standing up and crossing the room to me, touching the injury gingerly.

"Perpetua beat me up … long story. I'm so sorry, Oliver."

I watched as all the hardness of his expression washed away, his features cracking as he buried his face in his hands.

We fell back on to the unmade bed together. I forgot about the Empress. I bundled him up in my arms, holding him so tight I made him a part of me again.

"I don't know why I'm crying," he said, laughing in embarrassment as he wiped his eyes. "I hated him. So fucking much." His voice cracked on the last word.

"It's OK," I said. "Whatever you're feeling right now, it's OK."

I pulled us backwards so that we were lying down, my body wrapped round his back. I held him as he cried silently, his shoulders shaking.

I watched his Shadow on the wall, this time sullen and sobbing in unison with him, curled up in a ball and rocking back and forth.

We stayed like that until he fell asleep, drifting away

in my arms, but I didn't sleep. I couldn't sleep even if I'd wanted to.

One thought tumbled through my mind, again and again. Oliver hadn't predicted his own father's death.

He hadn't had one single inkling.

Whatever the future held for us, we were still blind to it. The sixth sense couldn't save us.

16.

OLIVER

There would be no funeral for my father.

There was no one alive who wanted to mourn him and, if they did, they weren't willing to admit it in public.

Tyrants didn't get to rest in peace. The people on the streets celebrated openly, making stuffed guys in his image to burn on fires. They threw block parties and house parties. They had picnics and launched fireworks. Their drunken, triumphant cries echoed through the long dark night: *"Death to the Order! Freedom for the people!"*

I watched them from the eye-shaped window of Obscura House, where I'd barricaded myself in. I listened to their bouncing battle cries, remembering the night of the revolution. I watched from my ivory tower, but it was already burning in my mind.

The Sixth House seized the chaos on the streets as an opportunity for revolt. Days of riots had followed my father's death, while the soldiers of Constitution worked with the Inspectors to hold back the growing masses. The audio network had been taken over by the Whisperers. They

304

blasted out cheery big band tunes interspersed with audio clips of the former Chancellor's most terrifying speeches. Revolution was in the air again.

How had it happened? How had it all gone so wrong?

As far as the people were concerned, whoever killed my father was a hero. I was questioned – as the person who hated him most and the last to see him alive. The killer had left no trace, but to enter the Reformatory they must've been a Shadow soul, or so it was concluded. Many people had a motive, but none so great as mine. Inspectors followed me from place to place, recording my daily activities. Now it was I who was being watched by the eyes of the state.

I hadn't done it. I was sure of it. Though my memory was failing me more and more, I was certain I'd remember a thing like that.

Someone had removed my father's soul whole from his chest, just like they had done with Lord Harmonia. They could have killed him, but they didn't. They needed the power of his soul for some wretched purpose – controlling large swathes of the population, perhaps.

I knew who had killed him, at least. The same assassin who had killed Harmonia. The same assassin who haunted my visions. The Teardrop Assassin.

But why couldn't I find him? Where was he?

I'd searched every inch of the city and beyond and still there was no trace of the green-eyed man beyond my visions and what I'd witnessed at Harmonia House. No one knew his face. The assassin was a ghost.

My one ray of light was the fact that the ball had been cancelled due to the fire. I hadn't received official word but the Basilica was definitely out of action, and right at the last minute. Added to which, there was no way the event could go ahead after the former Chancellor had been murdered, in a guarded cell, no less.

It would be entirely unseemly.

And yet it hadn't stopped the nightmares. The visions still plagued me.

Tristan Obscura was hastily cremated. Only I attended the ceremony, such as it was. Ruby had offered to come with me despite everything, but I persuaded her not to. I wanted to do it alone. I didn't want anyone to see me cry for him again.

As I scattered my father's ashes on top of the hill behind Obscura House, I looked out at the city, full of little fires and shrouded in smoke as another firework exploded in the sky. I searched my mind for a happy memory involving him, but I couldn't settle on a single one. The bad in him had poisoned everything, making even the most innocent of recollections seem sinister. I recalled a particular birthday party at which he had given me a gleaming black bicycle, but he didn't have the time or the patience to teach me to ride it. After I fell off, he shouted at me for being clumsy and careless, for scratching the paint. The bike was no longer a gift, a thing of joy, but had been stashed away in a cupboard to gather dust for a decade.

"A happy day," came a voice.

I whirled round to see the Empress gliding towards me, her dark–matter soldiers trooping behind her: Shadowy figures equipped with scythes, not truly alive but animated through psyche. She was dressed for a funeral, veiled and in black.

"And yet … our problems are just beginning," she said.

"You shouldn't be here," I told her.

"None of us will be here soon. The war is upon us. You were meant to stop it."

"But … I burned down the Basilica. The ball is cancelled."

"Is it? Are you sure? Then why do I still see war in my visons? And why do you still see Ruby's death in yours?"

She was right. Since my father's murder, the visions had changed but not ceased. When Ruby walked through the Basilica, it was now blackened, damaged by the fire I'd started. But the dress, the moon and the assassin were all the same. The future remained strangely unchanged, though I couldn't say why. I saw Ruby turn, and BANG! There was the hole in her chest. I couldn't escape the image. It was engraved behind my eyelids.

"She … she's still going to die," I said, not a question but a fact. The words came out choked. I'd lost everything, and it still wasn't sacrifice enough.

"You still haven't figured it out," she said. "You still don't understand what must be done, to save her, to save everyone."

"Then tell me," I pleaded.

"No," she said. "I will show you."

She held up her hand, darkness swirling in her palm.

I felt something strike me with force, pushing me deep inside myself.

In the void of my mind, several images floated past, so fast I struggled to keep up with them… *Ambrose Fairchild, collapsing to the ground … a coffin draped in the flag of Constitution… his soldiers retreating in their trucks and ships. The Sixth House has disbanded. The leaders of the rebel gangs sign an armistice with the New Order. Ruby ascends the imperial staircase at the fire-burned Basilica… As she gazes out at the crescent moon, I appear behind her, wrapping my arms round her as fireworks explode in the sky.*

The end.

Fin.

Hope flickered, its flame reigniting. Returned to my body, I stared hard into the dark eyes of the Empress.

"You cannot mean…"

"If the Governor should come to harm, Constitution will withdraw," she said. "The alliance will be thwarted. There will be no war. Providence will be free. I will return to my lands. You will recover yours. Ruby will live. There will be peace. You can live happily ever after."

"What … what are you suggesting, exactly?" I asked.

"I think you already know."

"I need you to say it out loud, so we're both on the same page."

"You must kill the Governor of Constitution. It is the way. It is the *only* way."

I began vehemently shaking my head, before I was even aware of it.

"No. Hell no. I'm not doing that."

"Even if it means hundreds of thousands of deaths on your conscience, including your beloved's?" she said. "Somehow, some way, his death will give her life. This is what they call the butterfly effect. The flapping of tiny wings can create hurricanes."

Ruby, with blood in her mouth...

Ruby, a hole in her heart...

"Anything but that," I said, my voice soft, begging.

"His death is the one variable you never changed, in all those visions. She never lived because he still does. Take one life to save many," she said. "That is your choice."

With that, the Empress bled into the darkness.

The moon above was almost a scythe.

There was no wake for my father, but Premier Cordata had suggested we all gather at Obscura House, to "reflect on the Chancellor's dark legacy", as he put it. The Governor would be in attendance, along with the remaining rulers of the Houses.

Immediately upon my arrival, I downed half a bottle of ambrosia straight from the decanter, causing everyone to stare at me with pity and disgust. If I was going to commit murder, I needed a little courage. The ambrosia would have to do.

"Lord Obscura," said the Premier, taking my arm. "Such

dreadful news. If you need to make yourself scarce for a while, I understand."

"That would be convenient for you, wouldn't it?" I said.

We stared at each other in loathsome silence.

"Such a strange and terrible occurrence, that a mysterious fire should tear through the Basilica so close to such an important event, and with no suspect in sight," said Premier Cordata. "I wonder... But it all worked out in the end."

I shot him a quizzical look.

"Oh, didn't you know? We're still going ahead with the ball. Nothing can come in the way of destiny. It will be an event to remember."

The Empress was right. I hadn't stopped it. There was only one thing I could do now.

"An event to remember? Oh, I'm sure it will be."

The Premier slunk off. The room whirled around me. People swooped in to offer their sympathies before spiriting themselves away again, until I lost all sense of time's passage. The music was dreary, subdued.

"How are you holding up?" asked Ruby. Her mouth was a hard line. Bags under her eyes, her hair askew.

"Barely," I said, honestly.

"Then let's go. Let's get out of here. Just me and you."

I shook off her hand. "No. There is something I have to do, something I *must* do."

The Governor was there, right in front of me, nodding sympathetically as he listened to Lady Memoria. He took her hands in his.

"You have a home with us any time you want to visit Constitution," he said.

"What?" asked Ruby.

Somehow, some way, his death will give her life.

The Governor was not a wicked soul. He seemed gentle, considerate, on the surface at least. That was the difficulty. This would be a real sacrifice. But if I loved Lily, wouldn't I kill to save her? Wouldn't I do anything?

His guards looked over to me, as if they could hear my thoughts. Damn it all to hell. I was running out of time.

"Are you listening to me, Oliver?" said Ruby.

It was now or never.

I drained the rest of my glass, readying myself before walking over.

I would kill him with my Shadow, then flee the scene.

"I am sorry about your father, my Lord," he said, removing his hat when he saw me approaching. "A complicated man, but still your father. No matter how many mistakes our fathers made, they still gave us the gift of life."

"Talking of mistakes, I think you're about to make another one," I said. "Thought you could take us for fools here in Providence, did you?"

He frowned. "Excuse me?"

In my mind's eye, I pictured my Shadow reaching for the sword of a nearby guard and stabbing Fairchild in the back. It would take less than a second. But on the wall in front of me, my real Shadow shook his head and made an X with his arms, signalling that he wouldn't do it.

"I know what you're up to," I said, slurring my words. "I know your game … friend."

"I'm sorry?"

"You're a lying dog, is what you are. Are you even a Heart soul?"

He looked bewildered. "I'm here to negotiate a trade deal and to secure military support," he countered, his voice rising in irritation. "To support your new democracy. And" – he gripped my elbow – "right now, to support you, physically, from falling down on your ass."

As he held me upright, I leaned in, my voice a whisper.

"You're not fooling *me*. I see you, sir."

"Lord Obscura, I think you're confused," he said, "and drunk."

"I'm not confused," I said. "You want something from us. Why else would you stick around after two murders? You must have an ulterior motive."

Governor Fairchild looked at me for a long time, as if weighing me up. "You've got me there, son," he said eventually.

"I knew it!" I said.

"I never say no to making some profit."

I blinked at him.

"I want this trade agreement to go ahead just as much as Premier Cordata does," he said. "Importing native goods into the Providential market will help fund my new infrastructure campaign. Bridges and motorways across the country, connecting all the major cities. It will bring Constitution into the next generation."

"Bridges?" I echoed.

"That's right." He beamed. "That's my ulterior motive right there."

"Then why are so many of your soldiers here, huh? Why are your big ships gathering at the ports? We don't need that many soldiers. No one does."

"Again, you've got me there," he said. "It's important that Providence does not fall, for the rest of our allies will fall along with it. We have selfish motives for defending you, it's true, but also because that's what we do for our friends, as we hope they would stand beside us one day, in our hour of need."

"No, that's not friendship. Friends help each other because they can, because they want to. Not so they'll be owed a favour. I don't believe you, Governor. No, I don't think we're friends at all. I know you've been working with the Sixth House."

"Lord Obscura, you are looking in the wrong direction."

He nodded behind me and I turned.

Raised voices. The music halted abruptly.

Premier Cordata was walking towards me, backed by a dozen guards, with a dozen more Inspectors behind them.

"Lord Obscura, we must ask that you come with us at once."

"Why?" I asked. "What for?"

Premier Cordata stuck out his chest. "We have evidence that you are responsible for the murder of your father, Tristan Obscura," he said, loud enough that everyone could hear.

The crowd exploded into conversational chaos.

"You are also suspected of the murder of Lord Harmonia, and the arson attack at the Basilica. Finally, Lord Obscura, you are being investigated on a count of treason, accused of fraternizing with the enemy."

This, I did *not* predict.

"No, you're mistaken!" said Ruby, rushing to stand at my side in solidarity, looking gloriously furious. "Show us this so-called evidence."

The Premier nodded at the lead Inspector, who dutifully turned on his lantern. A clouded memory was projected on to the wall. It showed me entering the cell through a portal, engaging my father in conversation.

"I hope you burn in the hell you made for yourself, because when you die, I'll be dancing on your grave. I'll throw a goddam party, and I'll invite every person you ever hurt to come piss on it."

The shock in the room was palpable.

"So I visited him," I said. "So I cussed him out. I won't deny that."

"What did you wish to speak to him about, exactly?" asked Cordata.

I couldn't answer, or I could, but it wouldn't help my case.

"Lord Obscura's visit wasn't recorded by the entry system," said the lead Inspector. "He wasn't seen by any of the wardens. He didn't sign in. He used his Shadow to access the building."

"That does rather suggest he didn't want to be seen,"

314

said Lady Memoria. "Why wouldn't you declare yourself, Obscura, if it was an innocent visit?"

"My business is mine, and no one else's," I replied.

A sudden movement caught my attention. Just like everyone else, my eyes were drawn to the memory on the wall, watching as I morphed bodily into a monster, plunging one clawed hand into father's chest, pulling out a throbbing, pulsating orb of five colours.

"What? That … that's not … it's not real," I said. "That can't be real!"

But a voice in my head whispered, *Can't it? How do you know? You can't remember anything any more.*

My mind was soft, with holes in it. The drink had made me slow and slippery.

"This is … a miscarriage of justice," I slurred.

"Lord Obscura admits to being at the scene," said the Premier.

"He and his father were discussing forbidden psychometry," said the Inspector, playing the rest of the memory.

"The sixth sense is truly madness… Tell me you haven't succumbed to this insanity," my father says.

"I don't want to hear whatever it is you have to say."

"You mustn't put stock in premonitions… Stop now, Oliver, before it's too late… If you're mixed up with the Empress, no good will come of it."

The room fell deathly silent.

"The Empress?" whispered Lady Memoria.

"Yes," said the Inspector. "We have been observing Lord Obscura for some time, ever since suspicions were raised about his loyalty to the New Order. He has been meeting her in secret."

Ruby's nostrils flared. I swore I saw steam coming out of her ears.

The lantern flickered again, projecting us standing together behind Obscura House.

"What are you suggesting, exactly?"

"I think you already know."

"I need you to say it out loud, so we're both on the same page."

"You must kill the Governor of Constitution… It is the only way.

"I … I didn't do it," I said. "Look, he's standing right there, very much alive. I thought he was conspiring against us."

"But you planned to kill him? You and the Empress, conspiring to assassinate the Governor?" said Cordata, sweatier than I'd ever seen him.

"Son, I'm hurt," said Ambrose Fairchild.

"There is something else," the Inspector said heavily. "We searched Obscura House for evidence. We found Lord Harmonia's soul."

"No," murmured Ruby, and the whole room burst into a stirring shower of scandal.

Oh, I saw it now. I was muddled by drink and memory loss, but I saw it clear enough. I was being framed.

"Why did you want Harmonia's soul?" asked the Governor.

"Lord Obscura was embarking on dark psychometric work, in pursuit of his visions of the future," the Inspector answered for me. "It appears he was using human souls for this purpose. And colluding with our enemy to undermine the New Order."

"No," I said, and my voice deepened.

The room seemed to darken as the crowd shrank away from me.

"There's a real threat here and you don't even see it." I pointed at the Governor. "It's him! He wants war! It's obvious."

I sounded unhinged. I could hear it. It was hopeless.

"Being a ruler of a House does not mean you're above the law, Lord Obscura," said Premier Cordata. "Innocent until proven guilty, of course, and if you say you didn't do it – well, there will be a full investigation. But for now, you must accompany us. Please do come quietly. Let's not cause a scene."

"I'm not going anywhere," I said.

"Sorry, Lord Obscura. Such is the way of democracy," he said. "If you won't come quietly, then you leave us with no choice. Guards, seize him."

They advanced, backed by Inspectors, as Gabriel watched on in horror.

If I was imprisoned, I couldn't stop the ball. I couldn't save Ruby from the assassin. I couldn't prevent the war.

I *had* to get out of here.

My eyes met Ruby's.

"Oliver? Can … can you hear me?" she said.

317

Guards in three colours of armour advanced from all sides, nervously jostling their guns and spears.

"Back off," I growled, in an inhuman voice.

They formed a circle round me, their sparking batons ready to torch me to a crisp. When I shifted my weight, a Renato guard panicked and threw a fireball.

I raised my arm to draw a portal and accidentally smashed the red-armoured soldier against the wall.

"No! Stop!" cried Ruby.

Time slowed.

In the reflection of a black-shaded window, I saw myself.

I had metamorphosed into a monster – not just my Shadow, but my whole self. Horns. Wings. Fangs. Grey flesh, stringy with dark veins, forming the very same beast I'd seen in the false memory. The fabric of my physical being had been completely reformed. Wherever my true self was, it was deep within the body of this horrible creature.

The lead Inspector approached me, his face hard with determination. "Take him down, dead or alive," he said.

When he blinked, I watched his pupils waste away to crescents.

The guards fired streams of Spark fire, dragging me under, sending me tumbling to the floor. In my last moments, it occurred to me that I had become exactly the monster I always feared I was.

I was the monster with a thousand faces.

When I came to in the Reformatory, I was reassuringly human again, lying on the hard stone floor next to a grisly stain: a black, bloody, grimy splotch in the shape of a human being.

I was imprisoned in the very same cell where my father died. That ugly stain was all that was left of him now.

I tried to form a portal but it hurt my hand, which – "*Ouch!*" – a bone-breaking sound echoed as a wave of pain cramped my fingers. I shook it off and attempted it again but only a fine mist of dark matter spurted out anticlimactically.

"You're wasting your time, nepo boy," came a deep voice with a strong accent – someone from one of the islands to the west, I guessed, between Providence and Constitution.

"Huh?"

"Don't you remember? This cell was built to keep your father in. You won't be able to use your Shadow in here."

I peered through the darkness, making out a figure in the cell opposite.

Leather jacket. Dreads. A look of burning hatred.

"Never thought I'd end up in the nick with the Chancellor's prick son, but so it goes. Looks like we're stuck here together."

My vision cleared and I saw it was Blade, the leader of the Shades.

"What are you doing here?" I croaked.

"When the Sixth came to convert our gang, I realized the One's mind control didn't work on me. Probably after those guards in the Reformatory beat me half to death with fire batons a few years back. I got kidnapped and put in jail, when your daddy was Chancellor, but I refused to behave, so they tried to kill me. Guess I died and came back with the sixth sense, like you."

He pulled open his jacket, indicating the scars that glistened.

"I went undercover for a while, even let the Shades think I'd gone AWOL so it'd be convincing. I let the One take over me a couple of times just to learn more, even though I could've pushed them out. They didn't figure me out until I ended up at one of their 'community gatherings'. The One wanted me to fight your little girlfriend, but I refused."

I raised my eyebrows questioningly, realizing Ruby's explanation had only got as far as "*Perpetua beat me up … long story.*"

"The leader of the Sixth was trying to take over her mind but she got away. Maybe she has the sense too. Not sure what good it will do any of us now, though. Look at you – what sort of leader are you, man?"

I glanced around the cell. "You're not doing a much better job."

"Better than you. I swore I'd dismantle you with my own bare hands. I even infiltrated your House. But you did it all by yourself."

I knew it. The others said I was merely being paranoid, but I *knew* there was a spy. I could sense them. "How?"

His eyes slid away, a conflicted expression on his face. "By romancing your friend, Gus. I think he really fell for me.

Maybe I could fall for him too, if the world was different. But now I'm stuck here. Inspectors caught up with me after I fled the Sixth. Crescents in their eyes. Guess they're working for the One too. Stuck us in here so I can't use my abilities. You too, by the looks of things. Unless you have any good ideas for a change, we're screwed."

Blade shut his eyes and leaned back. He was right. I couldn't create a portal. I couldn't send out my Shadow. I couldn't reach Ruby or even escape into my own mind.

For the first time in a long time, longer than I could remember, I was a prisoner of reality. I couldn't disappear inside myself, even if I'd wanted to. I couldn't hide from my inner pain, nor the terrible truth of my own accountability. Perhaps if I hadn't pushed everyone away, I wouldn't be so alone right now.

Even my Shadow was missing and couldn't comfort me.

I gazed deep into my imagination but the images were faint and faded, hard to focus on. I couldn't visualize anything.

I kicked the bars of the cell repeatedly, hoping to exploit a flaw in the corroded black metal, but they stood firm. I cursed as loud as I could, but the guards didn't return. I threw myself at the door, hoping to budge it. I tried to break the lock, but it was impenetrable with my bare hands.

"I told you, dimwit," said Blade, cracking open one eye, "there's no use. I'm twice as heavy as you are and I can't shift it."

Struggling for breath, I tried to hone into my senses as

I'd once taught Ruby. Five things I could see: a spiderweb, a crack, mould, Blade, the body-shaped stain that used to be my father. Four things I could hear: screaming, shrieking, cursing, sirens. Three things I could smell: smoke, dank, the stench of death. Two things I could touch: my pounding chest and the cold hard floor. One thing I could taste: bile, in my throat.

Disgusting as this was, a degree of calm descended. I couldn't use my Shadow, but I still had the sixth sense. If I thought about it hard enough, physically straining to hold the picture in my mind, I could still see Ruby in the red phoenix dress, walking up the Basilica steps, towards the round window where she always met her death. But the image couldn't hold. It cracked, splitting into tiny pieces, until I could make out only glimmers.

A stream of memories tugged at me, pulling me into them forcibly. Ruby and me, dancing in the snow after the Battle of the Basilica. Us, eating chocolate from a heart-shaped box in front of a carousel. Us, hiding under the covers in bed as rain hammered the window, staring at each other with the deepest, wordless, brings-tears-to-your-eyes kind of love.

But after a moment, the memories paled and became crooked. The snow turned to ashes, and the fairground to a battlefield... I was forgetting her. My memories of Ruby were all fading, falling into oblivion. I had unpicked too many of them. The threads unspooled.

Oh god. What had I done?

"You know, you're right about me," I said to Blade, "I'm kind of … a piece of shit."

"No arguments here."

"If only I'd listened to her, I would've figured out that I was being set up. If only I hadn't been so singularly obsessed on the future, I would've seen what was happening and who I was becoming in the present."

"Would've, should've, could've," said Blade, settling down to sleep again. After a few minutes, his breathing evened, forming a steady rhythm,

I closed my eyes too and waited, embracing the nothingness I'd glimpsed when I'd died for six minutes. Once more, I floated on a sea of nothingness, an endless chasm of pitch black. I waited, hoping to forget myself too.

A faint ray shone through the dark. Against myself, I began drifting towards it. The beam of light became a jagged crack, a split in the fabric of space and time that stretched endlessly above and below.

Through the crack, I could see a bright, white, glowing place.

Squinting, I saw two figures – distant but recognizable, both hooded and dressed in white like angels. It was my mother Nadia and my grandmother Aurora, huddled together as they peered through the gap.

"Do you think he can see us?" asked my mother.

"Maybe, but he won't remember."

"He doesn't believe in the Beyond."

"It doesn't matter," said my grandmother. "It exists

whether he believes in it or not. We all come here, in the end."

"Do you think he'll be all right?"

"He'll join us one day, but not today, sadly."

"Sadly?" my mother said. "Don't you want him to live?"

"Of course I do," my grandmother said, "but the world can be cruel. It's nicer here. The weather is better too."

"He is so lost inside himself," my mother said, mournfully. "I'm frightened for him. Do you think he'll find his way out again?"

"Not everyone can be found in the darkness. But I believe in him. I believe he will find the strength to try."

They drifted away.

"Don't give up, Oliver," my mother called, fainter now. "I don't know if you can hear me, but you have to keep fighting."

"Give them hell, my darling boy," said Aurora. "Just listen for the sound of the soul that loves you. It will bring you home."

They faded away, leaving me alone in the infinite darkness.

17.

RUBY

An oil painting of an apocalyptic sunset hung on the wall of the conservatory at Renato House, its light making the Observatory look as if it were burning. It really framed my mood, with its growing sense of impending doom. I stared into it, my feelings plummeting further and further, until my Heart met the core of the Earth and burned up.

"Please don't go, Lily," my mother begged. "Please? This damn bloody ball is a terrible idea."

"She has to go," said Lady Memoria, sitting in my grandmother's old chair. "With Lord Harmonia dead and Lord Obscura accused of his murder, the New Order is barely holding on to power. If we're a no-show to our own People's Ball, we might as well strip to our bloomers and throw ourselves off the battlements."

"You voted for this," I said.

"And I'd vote for it again," sniffed Memoria. "This is the New Order's last stand. If we fall now, we will not recover."

"They should cancel it," said my mother, standing at the

window. "There are people rioting out there, carriages on fire... It's not safe."

"If we cancel it, it will look like we're running scared of our own people. If the trade agreement falters, the food shortages will continue. The people will have our heads, like they did with the Florentine royals who suggested serving cake to peasants during the famine."

"Lady Memoria is right," I said, in a flat voice. "We have to show our faces. Everything is resting on this night."

"Forget the politics for a second, OK, and just think of yourself," said my mother, the twang in her voice growing stronger as she became more and more agitated. "The killer's still not been caught. No one's figured out who's ruling the Sixth House yet. You're not responsible for this mess. You're out of your depth. It's just not safe."

"When is it ever?"

"What kind of mother lets her daughter go dance with assassins?"

"But surely you can see that I can't just hide away? Someone has been conspiring to frame Oliver. He suspects Ambrose Fairchild. I need to go tonight and find out what that man's up to. I need to be there to protect people."

"Do you really think Oliver was framed?" my mother asked.

"I'm sure he was," I said. Yet ... I couldn't shake off the vision of that grotesque monster he had become. What was he truly capable of? Did any of us know?

I stood in front of the mirror, adjusting my red phoenix

dress. I was so damn sick of red. I wanted to wear green or purple or white again. But Cordata was all about the optics. House colours. Keeping up appearances. At least it made me feel like my grandmother was still with me.

"We should go," said Lady Memoria, snorting another generous pinch of snuff. "Time is wasting, and more quickly than usual."

At the bottom of the red-carpeted stairs, to my great surprise I found Octavia and Rani waiting, both dressed in formal wear: a scarlet suit for Rani with a black tie and pocket square, and a red and silver dress for Octavia, with a black feathery fascinator.

"What's going on?" I said, cracking a smile.

"We're coming with you, obviously," said Octavia. "To protect you from the possible deadly assassin. Also, for the dancing."

"Seriously, we're not going to let anything happen to you. If it turns out that Oliver was right, we'll be ready to fight on your side," confirmed Rani.

"Me too," said Gus, stepping forward, wearing a red waistcoat with gold embroidery. He scuffed the toe of one shoe. "Sorry I haven't been around much. This latest heartbreak is kicking me hard in the guts."

"Did you hear from your mystery man?" I asked.

"Nothing. I thought he'd just ghosted me, but apparently he joined that cult."

"Wait, who are we talking about?"

"He, uh … well, time to confess, I guess. His name is

Blade. Don't even know his last name. He's the leader of the Shades. Or at least, he was." Gus held up his hands, anticipating a lecture. "He came on strong, then he went quiet, then you told Octavia that you saw him at that gathering and uh, she told me."

"Sorry," said Octavia, but she wasn't all that sorry.

"Blade? Blade of the Shades?" I repeated, dumbly. "The guy we've been looking for all this time? Your new boyfriend … is a gang leader?"

"I should have told you. I know he hates Oliver and wants to dismantle the New Order, but … he's also extremely cool? And attractive? And smart, and caring and … he's had a rough life and … He made me feel something; something of my own, something that belonged to me. I'm always feeling other people's feelings but this was mine. I – I'm sorry."

If I was supposed to be angry, I didn't feel it. I'd seen Blade at that meeting and he hadn't been the leader of the Sixth, I was sure of it. Although, from his eyes, he hadn't seemed to have been brainwashed either.

"Hey, there's nothing like a forbidden romance, right? I understand that better than most. Been there, done that."

"You're not mad at me for fraternizing with the enemy?" he asked.

"I think I'm too tired to be mad."

"I hear that," said Octavia, agreeably.

"Or maybe things aren't as black and white as they seemed. Good, bad and shades between. The New Order was never going to work," I admitted. "Not like this, with all the familiar faces. We should have made sure the gangs were at the table too. We should have insisted, before we signed the Accord. If we can dismantle the Sixth, maybe we can sit down with Blade and have a conversation, like we should've had before. Maybe we can even reunite with Ash and Perpetua. We could come together again."

We all nodded solemnly, in remembrance of our friendship.

"You're all… You're all the best," I said, my eyes filling. "I wouldn't blame you if you'd jumped on a ship south, but you're still here."

"Don't cry!" shrilled Octavia. "You'll ruin your make-up."

"I love this dress, by the way," said Rani. "The phoenix really sums up your indefatigable spirit."

"I thought we'd never have this again. I thought I'd lost you, and him. It means a lot, that you're here. Thanks … all of you."

"Group hug?" suggested Gus.

We all pressed in, smiling, eyes closed, but when we drew apart, the sadness of the past settled on us again. So much was wrong. Oliver was in chains in the Reformatory. Ash and Perpetua had been converted. The Sixth House was ready to strike. If I attended the ball, I might be walking in to my death – but, if I didn't, I risked losing everything and everyone. If the leader of the Sixth planned to use the event to reveal themselves, I had to be there to see their true face. One might say it was hopeless, that all was lost. But I knew better.

So yes, I was going to that damn ball. I was going to clear Oliver's name, thwart the assassin, unmask the villain, and bring peace to Providence. I didn't know how exactly, but I *was* going to do it, one way or another. Tonight, I would kick some asses, maybe even break some skulls.

Someone rapped on the front door.

"Oh, good grief, what now?" said Lady Memoria.

It was a messenger in a golden tunic.

"An urgent message from Premier Cordata," she said.

"Maybe it's a notice of cancellation," said Mum, hopefully.

I snatched it out of her hand, scrambling to open it.

"No such luck," I said, reading ahead. "It's a message, from the Premier. The ceiling has collapsed at the Basilica. It's not fit for purpose after the fire. He's determined the ball will not be cancelled. Says it's moving to the top floor of the Observatory instead."

Something hummed in my mind. Oliver's vision had always featured me dying in the Basilica. Maybe this was a positive sign.

"Goodness me! Can anything else go wrong tonight?" wailed Lady Memoria.

"No, that's good, right?" said Rani. "The visions Oliver kept seeing had you dying in the Basilica. This must mean his visions are no longer applicable, if they were ever real at all."

"You think?" I wanted to believe her, but something still wasn't sitting right.

Outside, Gabriel was waiting for us, dressed in the black

tunic that marked him as a servant of House Obscura, despite his master being in prison at present.

"Good evening," he said, bowing slightly.

"Gabriel? What are you doing here?" asked my mother. She flushed up to the roots of her hair, laughing nervously.

"It's always delightful to see you, Mara," he said, eyes twinkling. "On this occasion, Lord Obscura has requested that I accompany you both to the People's Ball. Before his unfortunate detainment, he asked me to protect Ruby if ever he were not around. I'm here to fulfil that promise."

"You don't need to do that, honestly," I said, chest paining. "I'm perfectly capable of escorting myself."

"He thought you might say that," replied Gabriel, "but he was quite insistent that I should go with you."

"Then the more the merrier, I guess," I said.

Gabriel shadowed us down the drive, stepping round me to open the door of our Renato carriage. He ushered me inside, his eyes sharp to our surroundings, watching for potential threats. Lady Memoria stepped in after me, and my mother followed, thanking him demurely. Their eyes met as he closed the carriage door and lingered there a moment longer than necessary.

At least some people might get a happy ending from all this, I thought.

Amid a stream of red Renato and black Obscura carriages, we made our way through the dark city. We drove past groups of rioters throwing burning bottles, past the skeleton of a ravaged carriage, even past a large gathering of several hundred people all wearing masks and crowded around a single speaker.

The closer we got to the city centre, the pavements filled out, creating a vast mass of bodies. It was just like on the morning of the Accord, but this time they weren't cheering or waving banners proclaiming me. They were spitting and snarling, hoisting placards full of hate.

"Try not to pay them any attention, Lady Renato," advised Lady Memoria as she busied herself with another pinch of snuff.

As our carriage slowed, I glimpsed their eyes with those thin crescent pupils, but before I could focus on any of the faces we pulled away again, joining the queue of traffic headed towards the First Borough.

Mum squeezed my gloved hand.

"Soon we'll take a little holiday, hey? How does that sound?" she said through gritted teeth, her eyes slightly too wide. "Just me and you."

I knew she was trying to distract me from the chaos outside.

"We can sun our freckly selves on the beach and watch gulls fly away with our ice creams. We can go to one of those fairgrounds at the end of a pier, and ride rollercoasters until we're dizzy and throw up. What do you say?"

It was the kind of dream you wanted to hold on to tight, in the darkest, most hopeless moments of your life.

I nodded, smiling, but fairgrounds made me think of Oliver. The sea made me think of Oliver. Birds made me think of Oliver. I recalled sitting in Oliver's lap, and our illusionary tour of the world. His arms around my waist. Him kissing my face a hundred times.

"Sounds good," I lied, even though I felt as if there was nothing good in the world, and what was left, I still had to fight for with my life.

The latticed glass eye of the Observatory formed a squat oval dome, the shape of a squashed grape, pinned between the sandy-coloured towers that overlooked the river. The dome had pupils and irises on all sides, depicted in panels of stained glass to symbolize the fact that the Order was always watching.

"I'll leave you here," said Gabriel. "I'll be patrolling the perimeter."

"See you later, perhaps?" said Mum.

His gaze, which had been scanning the surrounding area, returned to her and melted.

"I do hope so," he said, kissing her hand before turning to me. "Lady Renato, I know Lord Obscura isn't always easy to understand. I haven't understood him too well myself these past few weeks. But I do know that he would die for you, gladly." He nodded. "You are always on his mind, and always will be. Until we meet again, it's been a real honour, Lady Renato."

Something prickled the back of my neck again, but I couldn't put my finger on what was bothering me.

Something about the Observatory.

As we approached the entrance, I plastered on the serene

smile I'd been practising as a pack of journalists called out their questions:

"Lady Renato, what do you know about Oliver Obscura's crimes?"

"Lady Renato, were you involved in the conspiracy?"

"Lady Renato, how do you feel knowing your lover is a killer?"

This time, I ignored them.

We climbed up to the top, via a thousand spiralling steps. The past was suffocating, as I recalled the night Evander Mountebank and I had broken in here to retrieve part of my soul. This was where I'd learned his true identity, where Evander became Oliver Obscura.

"They could've warned us that the elevators were broken," gasped Lady Memoria, collapsing into the nearest seat.

Once, rows of Observers had been installed here, watching the thoughts and dreams of the public through glass orbs, but the space had been hastily transformed into a party venue by members of staff from Cordata House. Extravagant lengths of gold streamers were wrapped around pillars. A champagne fountain wobbled precariously on a broken table. A single flag had been draped from a mounted eagle on the wall. Long gold tables bore an array of lukewarm foods, while a group of amateur musicians played an anxious, slightly subdued version of the national anthem of Constitution.

Removed from the Basilica, it wasn't quite the spectacular

event that Premier Cordata had envisioned, but it was still impressive, under the circumstances. The views from the glass eye entertained guests when the music did not, and there was plenty of wine and ambrosia going round.

Huddled in the centre of the room, Premier Cordata and his wife sat in conversation with the Countess Cavendish. They stared nervously at the crowd of commoners who'd been invited along and who all seemed to be hanging back, clinging to the walls, lurking in shadows. They knew they were being observed by soldiers: some in the tan fatigues of Constitution, others in the metal armour of the five Houses.

When he saw us, Premier Cordata bounded over, arms open.

"I have never been more delighted to look upon your faces," he said. "Everything is going beautifully."

"Famous last words," I said.

Rani watched the doors, as each arriving guest was scanned with a soul lantern. Octavia kept an ear to the ground. Gus sent out waves of peace that tasted like melted chocolate and cotton candy. But whether we were truly safe, I couldn't say. At least we were not in the Basilica. All the visions Oliver had had of my death had taken place in the Basilica.

Despite this, a strange feeling persisted in my gut, a floaty kind of déjà vu: the sense that I'd somehow walked this path before.

"The Governor is on his way," said Premier Cordata, rubbing his hands together. He was back to his old debonair self for the evening, stylishly dressed in a gold suit with a ruffled shirt underneath. "Hopefully his journey here won't be interrupted by the ruckus."

"We can but hope he makes it here alive," said Lady Memoria.

"And tonight we will cement the alliance."

"What if Oliver was right about the Governor after all?" I asked, keeping my voice low. "What if he really is manoeuvring to take power?"

"Not you too, Lady Renato," groaned Lady Memoria.

"Think about it for a minute," I persisted. "Providence is already weakened, with the New Order fighting for control – and then what if the Sixth House destroys what little support we had? The Governor swoops in and saves us, conveniently occupying our country at the same time. I mean, look at all these soldiers." I nodded around the room. "A coup at our own peace party. Wouldn't that be a stroke of evil genius?"

"The Governor is our best assurance for the future," Cordata said firmly.

"But Oliver said that—"

"I'm not listening to Oliver's wild theories. We saw only evidence of his instability, Ruby. The only killer here is your beau, and he's in leagues with the Empress. Put him out of your mind, for once, I beg of you."

But how could I? I still loved Oliver. I still believed in him. His absence made me feel hollow again.

The eye of the Observatory was filling with people.

There must've been more than two hundred guests, causing condensation to form on the glass. More commoners arrived, dressed in their finest clothes – some of the outfits faded or frayed or patched. They had been hand-selected by the Houses, all being people believed to be trustworthy, in step with the state. They were hard-working members of society, but that didn't mean they weren't working against us, or that the Sixth House couldn't possess them.

The terrible feeling inside me expanded threefold. I needed to concentrate…

"Tonight, we must forget our troubles, while also achieving diplomatic unity," Cordata was saying. "In the name of peace, prosperity and progress. So put on your best party faces and let's all have a jolly good time, don't you say?"

"Hear, hear," said Lady Memoria, but with little enthusiasm.

A server offered us sparkling glasses of ambrosia, just in time for the Governor's entrance. He was accompanied by a stream of security, including two muscular men in shaded glasses talking into their cuffs and collars. They embarked on a security check, moving in opposite directions as they searched the room in an efficient, military fashion.

"Clear," they kept saying to a person unknown. "All clear."

"Well, it's good to see you all again," said the Governor, coming over. "I didn't think we'd make it here tonight to be honest with you, not the way things have been going. It's feral out there, and your people are dropping like flies. But I felt it was important, to stand by your side in this time of crisis. That's what allies do."

But what would Constitution ask of us, when the time came?

His men watched the room. They could easily subdue us, I thought. They would try and use the element of surprise to their advantage, and they were heavily armed. They must've had ten times as many soldiers.

Cordata was shaking the Governor's hand. "A new government must always undergo a period of ... volatility. But Order *will* be restored. Thank you for your patience." He glanced at the clock. "Ah, time for my speech. If you would just excuse—"

"Actually, *I'd* like to make a speech too, if you'd be so kind?" the Governor asked. "Perhaps I might even go first, if you don't mind?"

Cordata blinked at him, surprised, but he did not have room to care. "Oh, well ... of course. Do go ahead, please."

"Thank you kindly, good sir."

To a round of applause, Ambrose Fairchild took centre stage. He stared out at an endless sea of heads, stretching all the way back to the glass walls of the Observatory.

"If I could borrow your ears, folks, just for a moment?" His voice was quiet but had authority; everyone fell silent at once. "It isn't often that I am lucky enough to have such a distinguished and ... captive audience."

For the first time I caught the note of steel in his otherwise gentle voice.

"I know times have been hard here in Providence but I'm here to reassure you that the dark days will soon be over. With a little help from your friends in Constitution, your struggles will soon be a thing of the past. We are sowing seeds that will provide the harvest of our future." He smiled slowly. "We need to lean on each other. Right now, it seems, you need us a great deal."

I clenched my fists, palms burning, ready for what would come next.

"Our two countries have not always been friends. I have to admit, we in Constitution were wary about the New Order at first. We feared it might not be so different to the old one – and we don't hold with dictatorships or with spying on the souls of innocents. But I'm convinced you mean to change things. We shall lift the embargo. Prosperity will return to Providence. With our support, of course."

"Let us toast to that!" said Premier Cordata.

"To my good friends in Providence," said the Governor. His smile remained fixed. "Why don't you come and stand up close here with me?"

Lady Memoria and Premier Cordata shuffled closer to him.

"You too, Lady Renato. Come on."

I followed, the dread in my stomach solidifying. We'd make for easier targets, standing beside him, exposed on stage.

"To good friends," said the Governor. His eyes met mine. We stiffly clinked our glasses, their contents sloshing.

"To good friends," I murmured.

"Thank you for a very ... *eventful* visit. And now, let the real fun begin," he said, smiling his most charming smile. "Play us out, band!"

I stared at him, confused. Was that it? No announcement of an imminent coup, no villain speech? Bewildered, I looked around. The anthem of Constitution was played briefly, before the band segued into a brassy number. The Governor stepped down, flanked by his guards, and the other leaders followed.

As we departed the stage, the Governor took my elbow. "May I have a word with you in private, Lady Renato?"

All my bravado slid back down into my boots.

"What about?" I asked. *Here we go...*

"Don't be nervous, my child," said Ambrose Fairchild. "I mean you no harm. In fact, I'm here to offer my assistance."

"What kind of assistance?" I asked, narrowing my eyes.

"I believe I can help you clear Lord Obscura's name."

"What?" It was the last thing I expected him to say.

"I have long believed that Constitution needs to be at the cutting edge of psychometry," he said. "We have been running trials for years. My scientists have recently found a way to retrieve memories from recently deceased victims: an autopsy of the soul, so to speak. I found myself ... interested in the murder of Chancellor Obscura. Oliver's downfall seemed a little too neat and convenient to me, so I took the liberty of running my own investigation. Two of my people gained access to the morgue and examined the Chancellor's body. They managed to extract the last image Tristan Obscura saw before he died." His expression was grim. "Lady Renato, it was not the same as the memory you were shown."

"It wasn't Oliver?" I whispered.

"The culprit was disguised as the assassin you're looking for, but with a little help from my security agents here, we were able to see the real man behind it. I recognize him, though I can't say from where, exactly. Perhaps he is more familiar to you?"

He handed me an eye-shaped pendant on a chain, slightly spattered with dark blood.

The Chancellor's pendant.

It was cold, giving me shooting pains in my hand that moved through my body, pulling me violently into the near-past. I watched a blurred face emerging through the gloom of a prison cell, its door hanging open. As the Chancellor squinted at them, their features sharpened and cleared, like a photograph coming into focus.

"Handsome fella, huh?"

A silver fox with a quiet but assured self-confidence, holding a black-handed gun with five chambers.

It was … Gabriel.

Gabriel?

"Until we meet again, it's been a real honour, Lady Renato."

I looked up at the Governor in shock.

"You know this guy?" he said.

"He's Oliver's trusted servant," I said. "His guardian. He's known Oliver all his life. He's – he's courting my mother. He's…"

A sudden movement caught my eye, just a blur.

A figure with their arm raised – a weapon—

I shrank back, but it was too late for me to defend myself with fire.

It all happened with a terrifying quickness.

This was the moment Oliver had been warning me about, the moment he had sacrificed everything to protect me from—

BANG!

I gasped, clutched my chest, staggered three steps backwards.

I waited for the pain, but I felt nothing. I pulled away my hands and they were clean. I wasn't bleeding.

Looking up, I saw the Governor's face slacken, become loose. His eyes showed the whites, his jaw hanging open. A hole opened up inside his chest, blood blooming around it in the shape of a heart. A chorus of screams rang out through the stunned silence as I backed away, watching the light of his soul sucked into the glass vial of a weapon held by the killer behind him.

When the Governor toppled clumsily to the ground at my feet, his assassin became fully visible, stepping into the spotlight.

The figure holding the gun was not the tear-tattooed man of Oliver's visions.

Nor was it Gabriel.

It was Lady Memoria. Lady Memoria, her pupils slimmed to crescents.

She'd been converted, right under our noses.

Constitution soldiers raised their golden muskets. I ran forward, screaming, "No, don't! She's not herself! She's been taken over."

"You won't take me alive," said the One, in Lady Memoria's voice.

"Please, don't shoot—"

It was too late. A bullet struck her in the head, her blood forming a slow, shimmering puddle on the stage that reflected the lights on the ceiling. I stared into it. The dull sound of shrieking got louder and louder, until it surrounded me, smothering everything. I stared at Lady Memoria's body on the ground, her eyes unseeing, turning white for the last time.

"Grandma!" cried Henry Memoria, breaking through the crowd to kneel beside her. "Grandmother, wake up!"

Poor Henry. Her poor cats – I imagined them waiting for her return, their cries growing louder as they came to fear she'd abandoned them.

She was wearing begonias today. Their meaning was *Beware!* Had she known that her life was in danger? Hadn't we all?

A horrible silence resounded.

I turned and saw Premier Cordata, his jaw set as he beheld the scene of chaos spreading uncontrollably before him.

"The game's up," he said, over the screams of his people. He let out a small, shrill laugh. "The Governor assassinated in our land, on our watch… Constitution will go to war with us over this. We're truly done for." Grabbing a cut-glass decanter from the banqueting table, he poured himself a measure and lifted it in a bitter gesture of salutation.

"But, Premier—"

"I fear I will be dead by morning," he said. "Who knows, maybe you will be left in charge of this mess. I do hope they'll have *something* positive to say about me, when they write about this in the history books." He drained his glass. "Farewell, Lady Renato."

"You're … leaving?" I said, flabbergasted.

He grabbed his wife's hand. "I wish you the very best of luck with it." Then they fled into the panicked crowd.

I stared after them. Our heroic leader had ditched us. Oliver was imprisoned. Harmonia and Memoria were dead at the hands of the Sixth House. The Governor had been murdered.

I was all that was left of the New Order now.

One shot to freedom.

"Good evening, Providence," came a disembodied voice, high and cloying, with a distinct, familiar accent.

The Empress.

The remaining guests hushed, frightened. I looked around hastily, unsure where the sound was coming from.

"I hate to interrupt your little party, but I thought it only polite to announce my *imminent* arrival."

The sound echoed unnaturally; it was being broadcast for miles around. The Empress was hijacking the same network once used by Birdie, the Voice of the Order. This had all been planned, I realized with dread – a trap that we had knowingly walked into. She was the puppet master all along: a villain so great and so obvious that I'd actually overlooked the danger she posed.

Hadn't Perpetua told me she could take Providence in a heartbeat if she wanted it?

Frantic, I ran through the room, searching for my mother. When I found her, her back was to me. "Mum, we need to get out of here, now," I said.

I caught her arm, spinning her round.

Her pupils were scythes.

Crescents.

"No!"

I dropped her hand.

One by one, I witnessed every pair of pupils in the ballroom turn to crescents. Octavia and Rani, converted synchronously. Gus. Countess Cavendish…

This can't be real…

"I'm delighted to inform you that as of today, Providence is under new management," came the voice. "Please do come quietly … or not at all."

The armoured guards and the gun-toting soldiers were converted too, drawn to the windows in reverence of the woman whose spectral image now appeared in the sky, huge and menacing.

"Let the big band play in the big bang!" crowed the Empress.

I pushed my way to the doors just in time to see a line of Shadow-matter soldiers materialize from nothing, their arms linked to form a great chain penning us into the ballroom.

Crescent-eyed rebels emerged from the crowd, all dressed in their finest suits and gowns and holding weapons of Shadow.

Here were Perpetua and Ash.

They're OK! They're alive, I thought, with great joy and relief, until I realized they were here to kill us.

As the mind-controlled orchestra began to play a rousing death march, something much more terrifying drew my attention. Through the glass panels of the giant eye, I saw airships drifting into view, dozens of dark balloons, as a roaring sound filled the reddening sky.

Each of the ships had glittering, feathery wings made up of sparkling, vibrating dust. Some were black and sinuous like the Shadow. Some were sleek and silver like the Song. Some were white and cloudy like the Spirit, while others were red and fiery like the Spark.

The largest, grandest of the ships had shiny, rippling golden wings, pulsing like the soul's Heart.

In my mind's eye, a vision appeared. A single, clear vision.

It was like looking through a round window.

18.

OLIVER

I don't know how long I lay in that dark cell. At some point, I heard the lightest of footsteps approaching, too soft for one of those brute guards. Heaving myself upright, I squinted through the darkness as my father had in that false memory.

A pale face shone through the gloom of my despair, followed by the jangling sound of keys in the lock. I watched in shock and awe as the cell door swung open.

"Who the hell is this?" said Blade. "Wait, I've seen you before."

Blinking, I made out the face of my unexpected saviour.

"Amelia Millefleur?" I said, hardly able to believe it. Why would she come to my aid?

She was wearing a white scarf that obscured her nose and mouth. Blade whistled, looking back and forth between us.

"Didn't you two used to…"

"Not helpful, right now … thanks, Blade."

"I heard you were being held here so I came to 'visit my mother'," Amelia said, making the speech marks with her fingers. "It's so obvious you've been set up. I just knew something wasn't right about all this. So I used a sleep canister I found to put the guard out and stole his keys."

"Wow … that's…"

"I know. I'm kind of wildly reckless when I'm not trying so hard to win my mother's love, as it turns out? Who knew? You can thank me later – but right now we've got to go."

"I like you," said Blade, pointing at her.

I staggered to my feet, looking back a final time at the sinister stain that was once my father before I exited the cell.

"What's happening out there?" I said, fighting down panic.

"Everyone has been taken over, their eyes are … strange, like half-moons," said Amelia, freeing Blade in turn. "But it's not working on me – or either of you, apparently."

"The sixth sense?" I said. "If you're immune, you must have it too."

"Ever die? Or almost die?" asked Blade.

"Measles, as a baby," she said, surprised. "How did you—"

"Join the club."

"It's … complicated," I added.

"OK, well, never mind that. We're being invaded," Amelia explained, as we retraced her steps back to the entrance of the Reformatory.

"Invaded?"

"There was an assassination at the ball—"

"Ruby," I whispered, skidding to a halt.

The ball had gone ahead, as the Empress had told me it would.

"I have to go!" I said, already running.

"Another time, brother," said Blade.

Amelia called after me, but I didn't wait to hear her.

I ran east, towards the Fifth Borough, while Providence burned around me, penning me into a ring of fire. The future was here and it was every bit as terrible as I ever predicted it would be, if not worse. Chaos reigned, even more so than I'd become accustomed to.

The skies were a rusty, bloody red.

I had failed. Everything I'd striven to prevent had happened anyway. Yes, I had failed spectacularly, and the world would pay the price.

People with crescents for eyes gathered more and more souls into the enemy's web of control. Entire crowds were being converted en masse. They flocked to the plaza in the city centre, where a large demonstration was already under way, all of them swaying as one body.

When the Basilica of All Souls loomed on the horizon, a blackened skeleton that was somehow still standing, I began to run, jumping over obstacles and pushing through groups of crescent-eyed people. Everywhere the streets were crowded with them, these hijacked souls with the empty, staring eyes, their banners emblazoned with messages of welcome and victory for the enemy.

My Shadow's strength was starting to return, pouring out in short, unpredictable bursts, but I still couldn't form a portal. I jumped over the barricade that cordoned off the Basilica, taking out the five Shadow-matter guards who were stationed in front of it, exploding them into plumes of glittering smoke.

Climbing through a pane of broken glass, I entered the blackened foyer, which was still decorated for the People's Ball, burned banners hanging from the walls, ravaged blue bunting strung along the ceiling. The stage had been set up ready for the band but now a pile of dusty rubble had collapsed in on it. A dripping, sparking hole had formed overhead, trailing wires from its void.

I pushed on, up the soot-dirty marble staircase and along the corridor to the right, just in time to see a familiar girlish silhouette pass in front of the round window, oblivious to my presence.

"Ruby!"

I burst inside, as she vanished into the shadows.

"Lily?" I said again, my voice catching.

There was no one there. Her shadow wasn't her, wasn't real. Through the window, I looked out on to the city as the crescent moon hung above, like the blade of the reaper himself.

This was the moment I'd seen so many times in my mind, so where was she?

What was I missing?

As I looked around, I realized something didn't fit. This wasn't the location I'd been seeing after all. The band had never played here. The ball had never happened in this place. Ruby didn't die here.

Because I had burned down the Basilica…

"*They moved it. Cordata's idea, or so he thinks.*"

The Empress's voice.

I turned sharply, but I could see only darkness.

"*The ball was moved to the Observatory at the last minute, which is exactly what I wanted. Surprise! It's me. It was me all along.*"

She manifested in front of me, wearing an extravagant ceremonial cloak and carrying a giant black scythe. Her Shadow soldiers materialized behind her out of nothing, and seized me between them as I struggled.

"I always knew how it was going to end, but I'm still entertained. Let's watch your lover die in a fireball, shall we?" she said, turning to the window.

We stared out at the Observatory. Through the glass panels of the eye, I could see that it was filled with people, all of them trapped. The ships had cannons that pointed towards them. I had enabled the dark future I'd dreaded so much. I had been its vessel, its weapon.

"No … Lily—"

"It's a shame, but I warned you," she said. "Don't say I didn't."

My father had warned me too. Sometimes the worst person you know makes a good point, I guess.

"I told you your actions would have unforeseen consequences. Unforeseen for you, that is. But there was nothing you could've done to stop it. Honestly, don't beat yourself up over it." She batted one hand, casually. "I just needed you distracted so you wouldn't get in the way."

Because I'd burned down the Basilica, hundreds of people were now gathered in the tower's bullseye, like bait.

"Are you sad? Are you going to cry?" She tilted her head back and forth, watching my reaction as she attempted to mimic my horrified expression. "You thought she was here, didn't you? What a terrible shock this must be."

Her dark eyes shone, all pupil.

"But ... but I saw," I spluttered, in shock.

"She was never here," she continued. "She was always going to die at the Observatory. It was the only possible future. I made sure of that. The sixth sense showed me everything. The sixth sense will ensure my victory, finally."

More and more airships filled the skies, the drone of their propellers loud enough to rattle the panes. I could do nothing as a slim dark missile fell from one of the ships, plunging into the glass eye of the Observatory on the horizon.

BOOM!

I cried out, losing gravity as the Empress stood firm, unmoved.

A peal of high-pitched laughter cut through me like a hot blade. She held up the scythe, which transformed into the dark-matter weapon I'd seen in my dreams.

"A grand finale. Don't you agree?"

"Not really," I said, shaking uncontrollably. "I think it's shit."

All those visions, and everything I'd sacrificed: it had all been entirely meaningless. The revelation stung bitterly.

"I told you how easy you were to fool, Oliver," she said. "It was all right there for you to figure out. You should've paid more attention to me. Too late now."

I waited for a sign, a feeling of absence or loss to signal that Ruby's soul had passed. Her psyche was so intertwined with mine, I wanted to think it would cause me physical pain or that her last screams would echo through my mind.

I couldn't feel her, but I couldn't feel her absence either.

"None of it was real?" I said, unable to accept it.

"The sixth sense is real and you truly do possess it. That was the problem," she said. "I needed to stop you from interfering. But a mind like yours will never learn to master the sixth sense as I have. You have, as we say, a haunted heart. Haunted by the ghosts of your past. It makes you vulnerable. We have a lot in common like that, though I have defeated my demons. Your father made me what I am today too. He destroyed my family and left me behind. He saw only a girl, weak and eager to please. He underestimated me. But when he cut me down, I grew back stronger."

She rounded on me.

"When I started having visions, I learned about the sixth sense. I studied it and practised it, just as you did. I began to sacrifice memories for premonitions to stay alive. I used it to rule my people. Some of them were generous enough to donate their memories to me, even their whole souls. Isn't that kind?"

I shook my head, disgusted and confused.

"You said it had to be *my own* memories I sacrificed."

"Well, I wasn't going to tell you the truth, was I? Keep up, Oliver." She tapped my shoulder playfully. "I needed you to question your sanity. You were easier to manipulate that way. It's not personal."

"But why?"

"I foresaw an alliance between the New Order of Providence and the government of Constitution. I wanted to change that. But the one future in which the alliance failed rested on three key events." She counted them off on her fingers. "One: the Governor and the Premier would not fulfil their trade agreement. Two: Ruby would die. And three: you would be imprisoned, your reputation shattered. I made that happen. Me. I watched you through what was left of the Eye network you destroyed. I established the Sixth House and influenced the new presses. SIX SHOTS TO FREEDOM! – snappy li'l catchphrase, wasn't it? I made sure Providence was on its knees, primed for my takeover."

"Big villain speech, blah blah blah," I said, still scanning my psyche for Ruby and still finding nothing. "Skip to the end."

She growled at me, her teeth vampiric.

"The future was set. Everything was in place. There was just one small, *extremely annoying* problem."

"Me?"

"Yes, *you*. Another with the sixth sense, who could disrupt my plans. I saw more and more futures in which you thwarted me. I died so many times because of you. I wasn't going to let that happen, so I made sure you were distracted, chasing the assassin all over town, preventing the death of your beloved, even plotting to kill the Governor... All this was my doing. I knew I had to destroy you from within. I have to say, I'm quite proud of myself." She patted herself on the back. "And now here we are, at the epilogue."

"That seems like a lot of effort to go to, when you probably could've just turned up with your airships," I said.

"Do you know how boring it is, being so much smarter and more powerful than everyone else in existence?" she said. "Do you know how lonely it is, being so many moves ahead? I like to have a little fun every now and then. To play with my food, so to speak."

"This isn't a game. This is people's lives."

"Oh, Oliver. Everything is a game, if you know how to win." She raised the gun, her fingers caressing the trigger. "Besides, I already told you: there was only one future in which I won. I had to follow the visions, to do as I was shown. There was only one victory for me, and I did everything in my power to ensure it came to pass."

"Where is he? Where's your assassin?" I asked desperately. "Did he shoot Ruby? What have you done to her?"

The Empress laughed again, covering her mouth with her free hand.

"That's the best part," she said. "The *pièce de résistance*.

355

You see, the face you saw, the face you've been hunting for all over the city? That was the face of a dead man. Your assassin doesn't even exist. Aren't you embarrassed? Don't you feel such a fool?"

"Wh-what?"

"My dear brother Anton was sent to Providence to spy on your father's regime. He died in the Reformatory five years ago, buried in an unmarked grave. I used Anton's memory. I took his face and cast an illusionary mask. I used him to haunt you. You were chasing a ghost, in the most literal sense. Anton would have liked that. He was a Spirit soul, you see."

"But I saw him kill Lord Harmonia."

"You saw only what I wanted you to see. An illusion. My accomplice killed Harmonia, while wearing Anton's face as a disguise. I fed you clues – the playing card was a false memory I gave to Ruby through her Countess friend. If this had been a game of chess, I was the grandmaster. That was another clue just for you, Oliver, the chess piece. I knew Ruby was the jealous type so I used illusion to push her buttons. It was fun, like playing with dolls."

"You set me up. From the start."

"At first I was scared you'd see the truth and wanted to discredit you. Then I realized how gullible you were. Why not aim big? You might even kill the Governor for me. I knew he had to die somehow. The visions showed me. But you lost your nerve. It's lucky I had an understudy waiting in the wings in the form of Lady Memoria. She was a last resort but she served me well tonight. One last accomplishment before she popped her clogs."

"Wait. So the Governor was attacked, not Ruby?" I said.

She rolled her eyes. "Don't get your hopes up now. I don't think she'll have survived."

"How can it all be false? The vision I saw came true," I said, rubbing my forehead. "I saw the ice sculpture fall and then it really did…"

"Oh, that was especially clever of me, if I say so myself. I needed to convince you that you were truly seeing the future through the sixth sense, so I planted the vision, then on the night I briefly inhabited the people around you to make it look real. I took over Lord Harmonia to topple the ice sculpture, and the Premier so that he argued with his wife. I set you up so you'd attack the messenger. It made you seem unstable. Eventually you were locked up for your father's murder." She narrowed her eyes. "Also thanks to me. But I didn't expect you to escape. That means I'm unsure which future we're currently in, and that … that is a problem."

"You used me."

The ricochet of explosions sounded beyond the Basilica.

"The Governor is dead. Your Premier has fled. Everyone else has been blown to smithereens. The New Order is over. It's too late. You are all that stands between me and the future."

"I thought you were the most powerful Shadow soul in the world," I said. "Surely you're not afraid of me?"

"I didn't say I was scared of you," she spat. "You're an irritation."

Footsteps on the stairs. A silhouette at the door. A shadow the Empress didn't see. A figure, holding a finger to his lips. Gabriel.

My knees quaked in relief at the sight of him. His eyes met mine through the gloom. I looked pointedly to the Empress with her gun. He gave a tiny nod. I readied myself to fight, drawing my Shadow as a blade, hidden deep inside me…

Gabriel took a step closer. He wasn't wearing his House uniform, but a grey coat with a high collar and black leather gloves, like the person in the playing-card memory, the one trading souls at the pleasure house…

He bowed, deeply. "My Empress."

The Empress said something to him in return in her own tongue, gazing at him lustfully as he lifted her hand to kiss the back of it.

"Gabriel?" I managed to croak.

"My name is Bastien," he said, turning to stare at me with those cold eyes.

A traitor, in my own house! I had suspected it, filled the halls with eyes. I thought it was Blade I had to worry about but, no – I had been looking in the wrong direction, just like the Governor had told me I was.

"You've been spying on me, all this time? Giving me fatherly advice? Romancing Ruby's mother? No wonder it was so easy for the enemy to follow my movements," I said.

"I was not your servant. I serve only the Empress."

"Who *are* you?" I demanded.

"I told you, I am Bastien. Your father had me imprisoned

as a spy. I swore revenge – he made me what I am, just like he made the Empress who she is."

"I liked you," I whispered. "I trusted you."

He shrugged. "Of course you did. I'm very likeable, but you're not going to like what happens next."

"Fine, go ahead and kill me," I said, still held in place by the dark-matter soldiers. "Get it over with. You already took everything from me anyway."

"Not quite everything," said the Empress. "I still need your soul. Wait till you find out what for. Another surprise! You're going to love it."

"Am I? Really?"

"No, but at least this way, your life won't be a total waste," she said. She raised a hand, finger on the trigger.

BANG!

19.

RUBY

Of all the strange visions I'd seen in Oliver's mind, one had burned deeper into my psyche than the others, so horrific and searing that I saw it in the darkness between blinks. It waited behind my eyes to frighten me at the precise second when I dared to relax. A truly apocalyptic image.

Those cloudy scarlet skies.

That razor-sharp moon.

The fiery mushroom plume that arose as the glass eye shattered.

I had seen it.

As I watched the dark airships gathering outside, and every hijacked soul inside flocked to the windows in frozen-faced, crescent-eyed awe, I knew one thing. I knew it almost as surely as I knew myself. The Empress would attack the Observatory.

I had to get everyone out.

"*Fire!*" I tried. "FIRE!"

That didn't even attract a glance.

I tried pushing, shoving, screaming, crying: none of

these seemed to work, but, as a Spark soul, I still had one last-chance tactic at my disposal. I whipped up a ring of fire, forcing back the advancing rebels. I let it mutate into a vast dragon of flames, as all of those little pieces fell into place, like a shattered soul coming back together.

I saw it all, as Oliver's mind connected to mine once more, allowing me to dive into his psyche for answers.

The sixth sense *was* real, but the Empress had been manipulating him, using false visions and memories to drive him to self-destruction. She had pushed us apart so I would not discern the truth and so he would be consumed. She had led him to the Basilica so he would not prevent the catastrophe that was about to turn Providence to dust.

But she hadn't counted on me.

The fire dragon roared as the rebels dived out of its way. It reared up to ram the doors and ripped through the Shadow soldiers, blowing a hole for an exit.

That was the easy part. The difficult bit would be directing several hundred people who weren't in charge of their own minds to escape down a thousand stairs.

Well, here I go.

I grabbed my mother's hand and also Octavia's hand, sending the fire in my veins through theirs, forcing them to take the hands of the people on either side of them in turn, so now Gus and Rani were linked with us, too.

This time I was careful not to overpower them, maintaining a balance with just the right amount of fire to form a chain of souls that I could direct.

Now I was the puppeteer.

Sweating with the effort, forcing their feet to keep moving, preventing them from tripping and causing a crush, fighting against them like competitors in a tug of war, I led them down the stairs. Every second felt like an hour, as the droning of the ships became so loud that I couldn't hear myself think. The possessed chanting continued but started to fade in ferocity and volume, as if the Empress's attention was waning. By the time we reached the bottom of the stairs, the crowd was silent and I was completely drained.

Somehow, we'd made it.

Small stones chittered on the ground. Birds flocked overheard, screeching in panic. I took a deep, expectant breath. Hot and sick, I felt my legs give out beneath me just as a deep, ground-shaking noise rang out.

BOOM!

Looking up, I saw the glass eye blown into a spectacular fireball.

"Run!" I screamed, as glass rained down, pulling the chain along. The explosion seemed to wake people from the Empress's remote hold, their pupils filling in.

"What's going on?" yelled Gus.

But Rani and Octavia remained hypnotized. So did my mother. To free them, I needed to destroy the Empress.

I shepherded everyone towards the city centre where I thought they'd be safe. They stumbled forward in confusion, not really being directed any more but moving in response to their own will. Then I ran in the opposite direction.

On the corner, I bumped into two familiar faces: a tall blonde girl holding a baton, and a man with dreads wearing a leather jacket.

Amelia Millefleur ... and Blade? The leader of the Shades and Gus's secret anarchist boyfriend? "What in the name of—"

"Ruby! Oliver is free," gasped Amelia, "I broke him out of the Reformatory, he went to the Basilica ... to find you."

No time to ask more.

"Thank you!" I yelled, fleeing.

If I was going to get to the Basilica in time, I'd need to take a short cut. I climbed into the driving seat of the Governor's abandoned carriage, its team of horses ready to ride. I took the reins, trying to remember how to drive. We clattered away, cab shaking, racing past a group of rebels with flaming torches, a trio of Inspectors, a troop of Constitutional soldiers and a posse of crescent-eyed nobles.

A high-pitched whine heralded a falling missile. It plunged into the Auditorium in the distance, as the anthem of Arctica played through the listening posts, its brassy regimented sound singing out loud and proud.

"My apologies for the inconvenience," came the voice of the Empress. "Order will be resumed in Providence shortly. Thank you for your patience."

I cut across the roundabout that connected five exits, speeding away on the wrong side of the road as an angry cacophony of horns erupted. Then through an underpass, where I drifted on to the pavement, forcing people to dive out of the way on either side like lines of synchronized swimmers. Cutting through a cobbled pedestrian square I lost a wheel as the carriage's front left side dropped with a violent judder. The metal part of the chassis ground against the road, spraying sparks. The horses were whinnying, fighting against the reins as the vehicle veered dangerously out of control, smashing into a low brick wall.

Jumping from the cab, I belly-flopped on to one of the horses' backs, cutting him and the animals free from their leather harnesses and breaking away, just as the carriage crashed into a wall. The other horses scattered at the blast of another missile strike.

Leaning forward, I squeezed my thighs against the horse's flanks to gain speed, guiding us through narrow lanes towards the Basilica. It was lucky my grandmother Rubella had taught me to ride when I joined her House, or I'd have been thrown off. I barely waited for my horse to come to a standstill before dismounting, lunging sideways on to the ground on my hands and knees, then scrambling up, patting the mare thankfully before running into the fire-blackened building as it creaked and groaned beneath my feet, burst pipes spraying arcs over my head.

Gathering my skirts, I sprinted up the damaged steps, looking left and right at the top.

To the left, I saw Oliver from behind, standing in front of the round window beneath the crescent moon, held in place by two soldiers made of Shadow matter. I saw the Empress facing him, holding a strange gun.

In the split-second it took for her to nurse the trigger, I'd sent out a long plume of soul fire, disintegrating the bullet before it could strike.

BANG!

The Empress fired again but I ducked, missing it. The bullet struck the wall instead. A small hole appeared. It swirled, forming a larger, much more menacing black hole that began sucking all matter into it, including the fire-damaged furnishings.

"*Lily*," said Oliver. "You can't be here. You're—"

Grabbing his hand, we fled through the void the Shadow-weapon had created, following the path of the bullet into the room beyond.

The Empress fired again, trailing after us. I manifested a shield of fire that deflected it, shattering a window.

"You're supposed to be dead," she said.

Gabriel emerged from the shadows at the end of the hall, flames dancing around his fists. I saw the hard, twisted expression on his face.

"Ha! I should've known," I cried, as he sent a fireball my way. "My mother always had the most *horrible* taste in men."

The fireballs he'd manifested chained together, stretching to form a rope, which he used to lasso me, drawing me towards him. Oliver lunged, using his Shadow to manifest a blade that sliced the fire, allowing us to break free again. We backed up, racing away in the opposite direction.

"The Governor is dead," I panted. "Memoria killed him.

Cordata has fled. The people – I got them out, but we have to incapacitate the Empress to free them—"

We dived into the next portal, and the next, rings of Shadow creating a tunnel. The Empress fired again as we disappeared into nothing, striking the statue behind us. Every missed bullet was creating a black hole, unstable portals that acted as whirlpools.

"How did you escape the Observatory blast?" he asked.

"I saw it," I said. "I saw in my mind, like an *actual* prophecy. I had just enough time to drag everyone out of there, literally. You're not the only one with a sixth sense, Oliver."

"But how—"

"When my soul was shattered, I must've died for a moment."

"She wanted my soul," said Oliver. "She wanted my soul for something."

"Like what?"

"'A little surprise', she said."

I didn't like the sound of that.

Dropped out into the streets of the Fourth Borough, we watched as the largest, gold-winged airship descended into the park beyond. The horizon was burning as another boom resounded. We turned to each other, actually looking at each other for the first time since we'd been reunited, our bodies pressing together. He cupped my face, kissing my cheeks as his eyes filled.

"Lily," he said. Just that one word.

In this together, like always.

A crackling noise filled the sky as the enormous projection of the Empress appeared above the rooftops.

"I see you," she said, giving us a regal little wave. The smile slipped from her face as her eyes turned black. "I see *EVERYTHING.*"

The lamp post nearby illuminated on cue, its cracked, eye-shaped glass globe revolving. One by one, every closed, broken eye in the network we'd destroyed blinked awake, watching us once again as the Empress reactivated it … and she was using Lady Memoria's soul to do it.

Twenty eyes turned to look at us, currently hidden in position.

"You can't hide from the monster with a thousand faces."

When her spectral avatar pointed in our area, distant figures began to advance on us: crescent-eyed converts drawn from nearby. They strode towards us, unnervingly briskly, their faces eerily blank.

"I have something here that might interest you," she said.

The Empress whistled. A moment later, two Shadow guards appeared in the peephole in the sky, revealing the prisoners held between them: Octavia, Rani, Gus, my mother.

No longer possessed by the Empress's Shadow, they now looked abjectly terrified.

"Hand yourselves in and I'll spare their souls," said the Empress. "Come to the ship that has landed in the Fourth Borough park. You know what they say … 'Two souls are better than one'." And, with that, she vanished from the sky.

"This would be a great time for me to have a prophecy," said Oliver.

I turned to him hopefully. "Anything?"

"Not a damn thing," he said. "Typical."

"If we don't hand ourselves in, she'll kill them."

"She'll kill them anyway. And us too."

"We have to try. How can we not?"

"We need that gun," he said. "If we could shoot her with it, we could try and trap her own soul inside it."

"What if you entered her mind?" I asked. "Do you think you could defeat her from within somehow?"

"She's the most powerful Shadow soul in the world."

"So she *says*," I said. "She's a megalomaniac. She could be bluffing."

He fell quiet, his eyes turning black.

"We need Gabriel out of the way first," he said, after a moment. "There's a chance, a miniscule chance. There are probably a thousand futures in which we fail, though."

"Not in this one," I said. "Not if I have anything to do with it."

He held my gaze. "Are we OK?" he asked, touching my cheek again. "You and me I mean, after everything? I'm so sorry for … everything."

"There's no one I'd rather die beside," I said, leaning my head into his hand, only half joking. "Me and you, until the end."

He kissed me and we fell into each other, spiralling through the clouds of Shadow before landing back on earth.

"Until the end," he said, taking a deep breath.

If this was a game, we were ready to play.

Hand in hand, we began walking towards the airship, down the aisle of bodies formed by the crescent-eyed park-goers. The ship's giant shadow loomed ahead. It was the same squashed-grape shape as the eye of the Observatory, with those glittering golden wings stretched out on either side, each one as big as an omnibus.

Gabriel – no, Bastien – was waiting there for us, standing at the top of a small ramp, his face free of any of the warmth or charm he'd once pretended to possess.

"Move, both of you," he said, pointing the dark weapon at us, forcing us forward.

Mounting the ramp, we disappeared into the gondola suspended beneath the envelope of the ship. The doors closed behind us with a metallic groan, shutting out the rest of the world.

"What about the prisoners? Our friends?"

"There are no prisoners, other than you," he said.

"What?"

"The Empress is very good at impressions. Impersonations, made by psyche. Your friends were never here. They could be dead for all I know and care."

We'd given ourselves up for nothing.

Well, not nothing… We could still save the world. Maybe. But, for now, we were entombed, trapped inside with the enemy.

Bastien marched us at gunpoint through the rear loading bay, which was filled with dark vibrating crates, and past a large glass chamber connected to many silver wires. It housed a glowing, throbbing silver light that made me shiver. It pulsed like a heartbeat, casting waves of sound.

It was … screaming.

A disembodied human soul.

The Empress's airships were all powered by souls, I realized.

We passed into a compartment with a blinking control panel and windows all round, offering panoramic views to the passengers. It was a compact space, decorated entirely in black. A large jet-drop chandelier swung overhead, tinkling gently.

The Empress was waiting here for us, sitting at a table laid for a lavish meal; a large domed silver serving dish was set before her.

"Please, take a seat," she said.

When we didn't move, her Shadow shot out in two long arms, pushing us into the two chairs that were waiting for us.

"Don't be so rude!" she scolded.

Her dark-matter attendants − three-dimensional silhouettes without faces − set a plate before each of us.

"Hungry?" she said brightly.

"Not really," said Oliver, slightly grey.

I shrugged, baring my palms. "I could eat."

"Did you know that the gods are said to have eaten the souls of mortals to gain their powers?" she said. "Some even claimed it made them immortal."

She removed the silver dome, revealing a smaller glass bell jar with a cork-stopped spout. Inside, a burning soul floated mid-air, its five colours blurring together.

The fire of the Spark. The dark of the Shadow. The pale steam of the Spirit. The golden mass of the Heart. The vibrations of the Song.

"Is that…?" I began, pointing in revulsion.

"Don't say it," Oliver said, one hand over his mouth.

"… the Governor's soul?" I said anyway.

It smelled like an orchard, sounded like the anthem of Constitution. It felt like dog fur and the warm hug of three daughters.

"Isn't it spectacular?" she said. "Each soul is different, but this one has a particularly powerful Heart. All the more delicious to eat."

The Empress removed the cork, calmly inhaling the vapours that came down the spout, her eyes flickering white.

"You're *consuming* his soul?" I said, my face twisting.

"Why, yes. A soul can have many purposes," she said. "To power a ship, such as the one we're in, for example. You have Lady Harmonia to thank for that. To catalyse a reaction, such as in the weapons I'm carrying onboard – that is what the Chancellor was for. And Lady Memoria's soul was powerful enough to fully reanimate the Eye network. But the most efficient way to use a soul's power is to consume it directly, until it becomes a part of you. With every soul I consume, I become stronger, wiser, my visions of the future gaining clarity. One day I will become truly omnipotent. I will control all people at all times. I will become a living god."

"You're not a god, you're just … a psychopath," I spat.

"Same thing. Don't be such a sore loser, Ruby Renato. Just because I'm going to kill you, it doesn't mean we can't have a nice time," she replied. "In another world, we could've been friends, you and I."

"Not possible."

"I have seen. Many incredible things are possible, in the realm of all possibility. You should not discount the improbable."

As she breathed in the vapours, her eyes turned black.

"How interesting," she said. "I can see a new future now, one in which you sign a decree and acquiesce without incident, handing over your lands to me."

"Nice try. I'd rather burn in hell."

"Oliver?" she tried, holding out the stem. "Care to partake with me?"

"Not in a billion lifetimes," he said.

"Your loss, and I assure you, it *will* be a loss."

She stared at us, her face free of feeling.

"Which one of you wants to die first and which one of you wants to watch?"

Oliver and I looked at each other, trying to communicate without words. For a second, something flashed through the space between us, a prophecy that throbbed in both our minds. In it, Oliver challenged the Empress to fight him soul to soul. They battled and the ship turned upside down. The weapon slid into my hand. I fired, driving a hole in her chest. We fell, flames blooming around us. But we lived. We lived.

There was still a tiny chance of a happy ending and, by the smug look on her face, the Empress was not yet aware of it.

"How about neither?" I said.

"Never mind, I've already made my choice. Ruby, you will fuel my ship when Lady Harmonia's soul runs out, and Oliver, you will be *dessert*." She licked her black lips. "I just know you're going to taste so … umami."

"How about we play one last game first?" said Oliver.

"Ooh, I do love games," said the Empress. "What sort of game?"

"Psychic combat. One-on-one, Shadow-to-Shadow."

"And what do I win?" she said, her hands forming excited little fists.

"The glory of knowing you truly are the best."

"That is *not* in question."

"Really? Because I think that I can beat you," said Oliver. "In fact, I *know* I can. I've seen the future too, remember?"

"You dare to challenge me?" she said, laughing forcibly. "*I* have seen a vision of me victorious. I win. It is already written."

"Prove it," I said.

"Then we shall play one last time," she said, rising to her feet.

20.

OLIVER

Before I could count to three, the Empress was inside my head.

A battle ensued: two souls in one body.

She did not come softly or gently but like a mace with sharp spikes, scraping me all the way down. I felt her penetrating through the layers of Shadowy protection I wrapped my psyche in, tearing through them like tissue.

I watched her manifest behind my eyes, her Shadow cast enormous. If mine was a monster, hers was the devil himself.

We girded ourselves, facing off against each other as our dark sides flexed and stretched, ready to fight.

Before I knew it, her Shadow form had slammed into me, knocking me backwards as dark smoke poured down my nose and throat. I watched the lights from my eyes growing distant as I was pushed backwards, hurtling through the void, even deeper and deeper inside myself.

When I tumbled to a stop, I was in that strange infinite dark place. On the horizon, I saw only the silhouette of the Empress, waving daintily.

Grunting, I sent a dark wave of Shadow her way. It rolled through the vast space between us, tossing her up like a buoy on the surface of my mind.

"Is that it?" she said, giggling.

"I'm just getting started," I said.

By materializing an anchor, she sank back down towards me, through layers of memory and fantasy like descending through the storeys in a building – fairy-tale woods and horror carnivals, snowy lakes and burning castles – plunging into the deepest waters towards the sea-bottom of my psyche. She embedded into the fabric of my subconscious, using her Shadow like a grappling hook.

I sent another wave to try to throw her off but she held firm, laughing hysterically now, though her face was an emotionless mask.

God, she was creepy.

I rammed into her like a cannonball, propelling her away from me. Her fingers slipped from the grappling hook and she was sucked backwards and out of my body. The smoke receded like a memory played in reverse, pulling us both into an episode from her childhood...

I am small and dressed in many layers of lace and velvet, sitting in a lonely room full of dolls: an army of porcelain dolls, with marble eyes and vacant expressions. Each one is dressed for a special occasion, its hair curled. I am the princess and I live in the castle, locked away where our enemies can't hurt me.

"You will be my friends forever," I say, pointing a baton at them threateningly as I march up and down the line of dolls. "You

will love me always and never leave. Not like stupid Mama and Papa and Anton. Good riddance! I didn't want them to stick around anyway."

"No!"

Screaming, she pushed me out of her mind. But it was too late. I'd already glimpsed her humanity, just like I had with the manager of the pleasure house.

Maybe we weren't so different. We were both the privileged children of villains, desperate for love but unlovable, savage in our weakness. Maybe if I reached out to her, made her feel seen, she might change course. She was not responsible for her trauma, just as I was not responsible for mine, but we were both responsible for the trauma we inflicted upon the world.

"It doesn't have to be this way," I said, back in the dark place. "You don't have to be this person. You can still choose to do the right thing,"

Matrina gazed at me with huge doe eyes, shiny as if with tears, her expression both adorable and pitiful. She looked younger, smaller.

"You think so?"

"I do."

"You think I can still be saved?"

"I—"

I had been fooled again. Laughing, she made herself enormous. Her gigantic boot came down, trying to squash me like a bug as I skittered back and forth, tiny compared to her.

"If you wanted to save me, you're too late!" she sneered. "Whatever goodness ever existed in me, it died out long ago."

"Are you sure?" I yelled up at her. "Are you sure you're just not a sad and lonely person in need of a friend? Dolls don't really count."

She screamed at me, stamping her giant feet. "I'll kill you!" she boomed.

Our Shadows took over. In this moment, we were like quarrelling siblings, monsters born from the same dark breed. Two beasts battled, one horned and demonic, the other winged and fanged. We wrestled back and forth before she assumed control, dragging me into her own mind, sinking us into her murky depths. She had not defeated her demons. She had become them.

Darkness consumed me.

My mother manifested first, causing me to fall back.

"*I miss you, Oliver,*" she said. "*Come here – let me hold you.*"

"*Come with us, darling boy,*" said Aurora, appearing beside her. "*We will protect you.*"

My heart ached, pulling me towards them. What I wouldn't have given, to hold my mother close again…

Part of me believed it, or wanted to. But her voice was too flat. Her expression blank. In life, her voice had been warm, laughing. Her face had been welcoming and familiar.

It wasn't really her.

The Empress's face bled through my mother's, laughing her high-pitched laugh. It wasn't real. Her, any of this.

My mother and grandmother vanished, but my father appeared in their place.

My true weakness.

"*Now, Oliver,*" my father said. "*Do as I say. You belong with me.*"

He was dead yet his ghost still haunted me. I backed away.

"No. I belong with Ruby. With my friends."

"*You are destined to die, destined to fail,*" said the ghost of my father.

"You're wrong."

"*You have no future, Oliver—*"

I manifested a black, eye-topped staff, the same kind my father had used to shatter Lily, and fired it in his direction.

"SHUT! UP!"

It struck him violently in the chest, allowing the Empress's face to shine through briefly before he morphed into Mr Sharma.

"*You could never disappoint me, my boy. I'm so proud of you, even in your darkest moments.*" His eyes turned black. "*I'm so lonely. Come, Oliver. My son. We should be together.*"

For a moment, I was drawn to him, pulled towards his light.

But Mr Sharma would never ask me to die just to comfort him. He wasn't real either.

I flung out another wave of darkness. I watched the five colours of his fake soul glow and burn out, my whole body shaking.

He's not real, I reminded myself. *Not real, not real, not real.*

Smoke, thick and choking, surrounded us again.

When I could open my eyes, I looked out on a cavernous,

dark-skied landscape with rivers of lava, like a primordial Earth. Dark jets spouted, sending up plumes of black smoke, as the ground rumbled and cracked.

This was what the Empress looked like inside, in the innermost part of her psyche: an inhospitable, vulcanoid wasteland.

It grew bigger and bigger, as I became lost inside her darkness.

A dark monster loomed, its slippery tentacle rising like a tree trunk from the lava. It hurtled towards me, slapping down on the rocky ground and splitting it open, causing more flaming rivulets to branch out. The ground was breaking up beneath my feet. I scrambled back as more giant limbs shot up, all of them oily and slimy, covered in gaping suckers, each one an eye.

I shuddered. "Gross."

This was the monster that lived inside the Empress, and it was much more horrifying and fearsome than the one inside me. One of the tentacles struck me, knocking me on to my back and winding me. I felt myself hoisted into the air, dangled like one of her dolls over the pit of fire that spilled out of a crater.

No. *No.* I wasn't dying today.

I wanted to hold Lily's warm hand again. I wanted to smell her vanilla-scented hair. I wanted to hear her laughing, teasing voice. I wanted to dance again, make love again, get married, grow old, die happy.

I wanted all of that.

I wasn't done here.

We weren't done.

"Any last words?" came the monster's voice.

"Yes, actually," I said. "Can you maybe … go fuck yourself?"

Manifesting a crescent-shaped scythe, I slashed it up into the dark flesh of the beast, causing it to drop me. I sprouted wings of Shadowy feathers to prevent me from plummeting into the boiling hot swamp and flew back towards the light on the surface. There, my psyche blended with hers, as if we were two dark seas meeting at the horizon with a cold sun between.

She struck out again, sending a snaking spear that attempted to pierce my heart. I felt her darkness consuming me, dragging me under, until I was lost inside the infinity of darkness inside her. I staggered back and forth through the pitch black, becoming increasingly hysterical as the nothingness consumed me, bit by bit.

I was so tired. Tired of fighting. I just wanted to lay down and die. If she was lost, then so was I. If she was a monster, then I was one too.

I had sacrificed myself. There was nothing left of me to save now.

But faint music drew me back from the edge of her despair. At first, I couldn't make it out, but by following the sound, it became clearer.

The Haunted Heart.

It was mine and Ruby's song – so powerful it could be heard even from the darkest and most hopeless places.

What was it my grandmother had said? Listen for the sound of the soul that loves you?

It was her. Lily. She still loved me. She hadn't given up on me, even after everything. That was worth fighting for, wasn't it?

I let the music guide me back to the surface, where Matrina was waiting for me.

Hovering mid-air, surrounded by dark clouds, we regarded each other coldly before launching into battle, manifesting matching weapons.

"You won't win," I said. "I saw it."

"You have already lost," she hissed, sending a cloud of daggers hurtling towards me. "You already know what you will become, Oliver. You know what your future will hold. You were born a monster. You will always be a monster."

"I'm not a monster. I'm not damned. *I'm not him!*"

I lunged forward and drove the Shadow scythe into her chest.

"Here, take a look," I said. "Watch how you lose."

I forced her into the vision I'd seen, the one in which she died. It was a risk, but she had told me herself: it was dangerous to know your own end.

"See? You're going to lose, Empress."

I felt her stumble, faltering as she doubted herself. We tumbled out of ourselves, back into the airship. I saw the Empress sprawled awkwardly on the floor, blood running from her lips. She wiped it away with her sleeve, eyes widening in horror.

"This doesn't mean you've won," she said.

"Oh, I think it does," I said.

Then, suddenly, Ruby was there. Taking her off-guard, she swooped in with a roar. I saw the flare of fire and heard the sounds of a struggle, blinking rapidly to see them fighting over the weapon. As they fell against the control panel, the airship began to veer to the right, with the gondola tilting as everything flew up into the air.

With a nightmarish groan, the airship fell into a spiral, just as I'd predicted, turning us upside down as it hurtled at a sickening angle towards the ground. We were spun and swung about, but a particularly powerful jolt landed us upright again, and Ruby, seizing her chance with the forward momentum, used it to crush the Empress up against the wall, electrifying her by touch. The dark weapon toppled out of her grip, sliding along the floor and coming to a stop by Bastien's feet.

No. Shit. That wasn't right.

That wasn't supposed to happen.

"Kill them!" the Empress screamed.

Bastien raised the gun as we began to spin again, the droning sound increasing as we began to plummet from the sky again. He aimed at Ruby but, as he fired, the vessel flipped, sending the projectile into the glass tank that powered the ship.

BOOM! Lady Harmonia's stolen soul flared hot and white like flashlight powder as fire spread quickly across the floor. I could still hear her wailing, the sound turning to raw fury.

The ship lurched with the sound of grinding, spitting metal, causing us all to scream along with her. I watched as Bastien slid into the flames with one last roar.

That left only us and the Empress.

"I will haunt your soul for the rest of your days," she snarled.

"Get in line," I said.

"Oliver! It's going to blow!" Ruby yelled.

I kicked the ship's door open, letting air forcefully gust in as we spun wildly. As the gun slid back towards her, Ruby snatched it up. She pointed it at the Empress and managed to fire before we toppled backwards out of the open door.

With one last scream, a hole opened up in Matrina's chest. Her soul was violently sucked out, into the chamber of the gun, flittering against the glass like a captured insect as a tiny, barely perceptible voice cried: "No! No! No!"

I watched the hole growing as we plummeted down, spiralling. By the time the impact came and the explosion happened, we were already falling through the smothering dark of the Shadow passage I'd manifested. It deposited us on to the concrete road below, from where we watched as the ship above burst into a spray of bright fireworks overhead.

All the soul-powered weapons on board the ship exploded too, striking other ships in a chain reaction, casting psychic shapes and patterns through the night sky, messages to the loved ones they'd left behind. A heart.

A flower. A musical note – this was their last act as their consciousness died, or perhaps before they went to the Beyond, the place with good weather where my mother and grandmother waited for me.

In Ruby's hand, the soul of the Empress buzzed and pulsed, its five colours churning angrily. It looked like an oil spill and tasted like poison. It sounded like a broken accordion and felt like tacks in the soles of your feet. But it smelled sweet and creamy, like the head of a newborn baby, suggesting there was still something human left in her after all.

Maybe redemption was always possible.

Citizens crowded around to watch the aerial show, the crescents in their eyes giving way now to the full moon of their pupils.

"I can't believe that worked," said Ruby.

"Just like in the vision."

As the burning wreckage tumbled to earth, I sent out my Shadow to meet it, smothering it like a fire blanket.

The airships retreated. Providence was battle-scarred and broken up, but it was still standing, just about, along with at least two members of the government. Possibly three, if Lord Cordata was still in the country, though I doubted he'd dare return to show his face.

I felt all of those alternate futures crumbling, disintegrating. I watched those dark scenarios fade away in my mind, until there was only one world.

One future.

Only one.

This one.

As a torrent of dust and ash rained down, Ruby turned to me, her amber eyes searching mine.

"You still here?" she said tentatively.

I clasped her hands. "I'm still here," I said. "I think. Never entirely sure, to be honest. But how can any of us be certain we really exist? How can—"

"Oliver?"

"Yes?"

"Shut up and kiss me."

"Oh, right."

Laughing, I kissed her face, tasting the salt of her tears. We fell into each other, my hands in her hair, her hands on my neck.

Ruby was in my arms, thriving and strong. She didn't need me to protect her. She just needed me to love her.

Perhaps I had misunderstood the prophecies.

Perhaps it had been me I was meant to save all along.

EPILOGUE

RUBY

There is no Order any more, old or new.

There are no Houses – not in the aristocratic sense, anyway. A peace treaty has been signed, forged between the new rulers of the free republics. There will be trade and diplomacy but no oppression or subjugation. There will be trials and reparations, but also, a clean page.

A fresh start.

Things aren't perfect, but I think they're better now.

The disembodied soul of the Empress is kept in a high-security vault at what was once the Memoriam. Still horribly conscious, her imprisoned soul can do nothing but watch the world she's no longer a part of. Perhaps one day she will truly know peace.

Arctica has a new ruler and Constitution a new Governor, both of them working towards the signing of a pax.

The colonies are becoming independent, one by one.

Fellow fire souls, Ash and I run the Reformatory, where those who commit crimes are treated with counselling. My mother, Amelia and Perpetua, all Spirit sisters, protect the

Memoriam, where historical memories are accessible to all in a museum of remembrance. Octavia and a team of Song souls operate the listening posts, which broadcast music (including her own original songs) and useful information for both tourists and civilians. Gus welcomes the homeless into soup kitchens and sometimes takes food to Oliver, Rani and his lover Blade at their workplace, as they watch over the Eye network together, using the lenses not for intimidation but protection. Animated billboards advertise the candidates in the upcoming electoral race. Change has come, and is coming still, but we won't be part of it any more. It's someone else's turn now.

I'm at Renato House with my mother, playing board games and listening to Octavia's latest record, when a knock sounds at the door. I go to open it. Oliver stands there on the doorstep with a bouquet of lilies, wearing not the House Obscura tunic but plain clothes: a light coat for a warm summer night, a pressed shirt and shiny shoes. The white in his hair is just a thin streak.

"I thought I'd try my luck and invite you out on a date," he says. "I had a prophecy, you see, that you would say yes."

"That's very presumptuous of you," I say, burying my nose in the sweet-smelling petals.

"Well, if my Lady has unforeseen plans, I'll be on my way." He moves as if to leave, his expression playful, but I catch the back of his coat and pull him back in for a kiss.

"Go on then," I say.

We don't look to the future any more. We don't try to

cheat destiny. We live in the here and now, treating each moment as if it's our last. We talk to each other, to our friends and to our House counsellors. We heal. We live.

We climb into the black carriage that awaits us outside, nestling together in the darkness. Oliver pulls the door shut.

At once, the interior of the cab transforms into a portal. The dark hole drags us and the carriage in entirely, into another place and time, and we reappear on the flowery streets of a cosmopolitan continental city. A huddle of ancient pillars and arches loom in the near distance, with ring roads and boulevards of boutiques with awnings arranged around them.

"Is this … Florentine?" I gasp. "The *real* Florentine?"

I look out at the ornate Metro signs, the paintings lined up along the bridge, the wine bars full of noise and light.

"You said you wanted to go on a date. To the opera, I believe. There's no better place to see the opera than Florentine."

"Oliver! This is too much," I say.

"You don't like it?"

"No. I love it … and you." I place my palm flat on his chest, in the place where his heart is. I can feel it pounding in time with mine. "How about we just stay here in the cab a little while?"

"Why would you want to—"

I let my psyche run through him. A warm, vibrating wave of energy that makes my skin buzz. My emotions bleed into his, showing him how I feel, what I want, what I need…

"Oh," he breathes, melting a little. "I see."

He leans in to kiss me, deeply but tenderly, our lips warm, skin flushed, flattening against the window. We press together, swaying, dancing to the silent song of our souls.

His pupils dilate, and I fall into him again.

ACKNOWLEDGEMENTS

In the immortal words of Miley Cyrus: "I had all the perfect things to say but none of them could come out." The bigger the feel, the harder it is for me to put into words. I try to express gratitude as much as possible in my daily life, in the hope that one day it will feel like enough, but it never really does. It's a bit like saying, "I love you." The words seem too small. How do I properly acknowledge the work of everyone who makes a book happen, and how fortunate I am to be doing this for a second time?

A sophomore novel is a famously difficult task at the best of times – everyone warned me that it would be – but it was still much harder than I'd anticipated. Debuting is very exposing (your first book baby, yeeted out into the world all alone!), but writing in and of itself will forever be a bit terrifying. People underestimate how soul-baring it is to put your heart on paper. Writing a sequel is especially daunting. It was so difficult at times I didn't think I'd ever be writing this, but I'm very glad that I am.

I thought this book would beat me, but I caught it and caged it, tamed it like a feral cat. I grew to love it. Reading it back now, I want to kiss its little head and smooch it for working so hard. I owe that to the people who supported me through the tough times. Like my agent, Hannah Sheppard, who has fought for me from day one. Hannah is always in my corner, doing the absolute best for me, even when I tell her she should put that story I sent her in the bin. Also Yasmin Morrissey, whose unwavering belief in me is the reason I keep going. My end goal is always to be the writer she saw in me back when my only readers were my cats. Thank you to Lauren Fortune and the entire team at Scholastic, who gave me the space and time I needed. Thanks to Genevieve Herr, who has the incredible gift of being able to see a story's hidden potential and bring it out. I also want to thank Sarah Hall: when I read your first comment, I knew I was in the presence of a real wizard. To Jamie Gregory, whose cover art is perhaps the best thing about my books. To Wendy Shakespeare, Olivia Towers, Hannah Love, Sarah Dutton, Harriet Dunlea, Sophie Cashell, Ellen Thomson and Hannah Griffiths, for everything you do and have done and will yet do. To Garzanti and La Martinière and Roca Editorial, for translating my book into a multitude of languages. To all the people whose names I've forgotten or never knew in the first place, who nonetheless championed my book as if it was their very own baby. A thousand thank yous.

To every reader, to every bookseller, to everyone in the rights team, to the people I knew from school who hadn't spoken to me for a decade but bought my book anyway, to the reviewers and all the people who reached out to DM me to tell me how much they loved *The Girl With No Soul*: I'm so grateful for you. You entirely made this experience for me. To my family and friends: sometimes home is a person and you are the only place in the world where I belong. To the Animal Crossers and Simmers who create just for the sake of creating: you are the real artists of the world. To the other 2022 debuts who inspired me with their resilience, good advice, good humour and great talent: we will always be strapped in together, Patricia. May the bonk dog protect you from checking Goodreads on your delicate days. Sometimes the people you meet are even better than the experience of being published.

It's easy to take things for granted. Anxiety can make even the best experiences of your life stressful. I spent so much time worrying about the future that I let the present pass me by at times. That's kind of what this book is about, actually. Don't let your fear destroy you. Don't let loss make you lose yourself. You don't have to wake up terrified of what the day will bring. I poured a lot of my suffering and dysfunction into this sequel, so I really hope you enjoy it as much as I ultimately enjoyed writing it. Finishing felt like a triumph at the time, but right now it feels like a loss. To Oliver and Ruby (or should I say Lily?), Octavia, Rani, Gus, Perpetua, Ash and all the other characters I loved too much to kill: thanks for making this all possible.